# Flashes of light blinked downslope.

His subconscious pinged. He twirled to shove Liz to the ground, shielding her with his body as the shrub they'd been standing in front of exploded.

"What was that?" Liz's scream blistered his ear. Riggen rolled Liz, body over body, until they were sheltered behind a jagged outcropping of granite. He whistled for Yakub. The dog belly-crawled to them.

"Stay down and be quiet."

She nodded.

He army-crawled to the edge of the outcropping and peered around the corner. Twigs broke as something crashed away from them and rushed down the path.

"He's on the run."

He wiggled back to Liz and settled in next to her. His eyes followed her shaking hand as she stroked Yakub's coat in the silence. The engagement ring he once gave her was missing. Of course it was. Why keep the reminder?

Shoving the fresh wave of guilt and regret inside his strongbox, he leaned close, and her hands stilled in Yakub's fur. "Don't worry. You're safe."

*ae*

# DEADLY MOUNTAIN TARGET

## STEPHANIE M. GAMMON

### &

*USA TODAY* Bestselling Author

## LAURA SCOTT

**2 Thrilling Stories**

*Treacherous Mountain Investigation*
and *Wyoming Mountain Escape*

### LOVE INSPIRED
INSPIRATIONAL ROMANCE

# LOVE INSPIRED®

## INSPIRATIONAL ROMANCE

ISBN-13: 978-1-335-46368-5

Deadly Mountain Target

Treacherous Mountain Investigation
First published in 2020. This edition published in 2022.

Wyoming Mountain Escape
First published in 2021. This edition published in 2022.

For questions and comments about the quality of this book, please contact us at CustomerService@Harlequin.com.

Love Inspired
22 Adelaide St. West, 41st Floor
Toronto, Ontario M5H 4E3, Canada
www.LoveInspired.com

Recycling programs for this product may not exist in your area.

**Printed in U.S.A.**

# CONTENTS

**Stephanie M. Gammon** fell in love with romantic suspense as a Sherlock-obsessed girl with bookshelves full of Grace Livingston Hill novels. She's been writing ever since and placed third in the 2019 Daphne du Maurier contest for Excellence in Mystery/Suspense. Living in Cincinnati with her police lieutenant husband, four kids, two dogs and one sassy parakeet, she owns a business-writing company and spends free time blogging about faith.

### Books by Stephanie M. Gammon

#### Love Inspired Suspense

*Treacherous Mountain Investigation*

Visit the Author Profile page at LoveInspired.com.

# TREACHEROUS MOUNTAIN INVESTIGATION

Stephanie M. Gammon

Be strong and of a good courage, fear not, nor be afraid of them: for the Lord thy God, he it is that doth go with thee; he will not fail thee, nor forsake thee.

—*Deuteronomy* 31:6

For Grammy and Poppy,
who gave me my first typewriter,
my first suspense book and my first great adventure.

## Acknowledgments

Thank you to my husband, who, like every true hero, loved me when I didn't deserve it.

Thank you to Kim, whose friendship, guidance and knowledge paved the path to my becoming an author.

Thank you to my babies for supporting me, even when I forgot to make dinner.

Thank you to my mom for teaching me Jesus is most important, and to my dad for teaching me hard work is as important as talent.

Thank you to Janine, Jerusha, Kris and Laura for encouragement and inspiration.

Thank you to my amazing agent, Cynthia Ruchti, for every prayer and piece of advice.

And thank you to my editor, Dina Davis, who saw this story's potential and refined it to be the story it is today.

# ONE

Alone on the summit of Manitou Springs Incline, Elizabeth Hart focused her camera phone down the slope on the town that had started her career. She clicked one perfect shot. When this project was complete, she'd sever the weight that had hung from her like a bag of rocks for five long years.

Shudders quaked her. Manitou Springs, Colorado, was trouble. She had planned to never step foot in it again. Gravel crunched under her feet as she jumped onto the closest boulder and pulled out a worn piece of paper.

With a shake of her head, her topknot fell to blanket her chilled shoulders. The sweat she'd worked up on the mile hike was plummeting her core temp and this cotton tank was no match for the cool July morning.

She'd forgotten this climb had always fallen closer to intense than fun on the adventure spectrum—even when she hadn't been so alone.

Fisting the faded letter in her hand, she kneaded her knuckles deep into her pectoral. Visiting Manitou Springs on the tail end of her Colorado project should have been easy. Why couldn't she let go? "I'm not alone anymore," she whispered. "God will never leave me or forsake me."

If only her recent trust in God's love would stop the shivers from winding down her spine. Just being in this town brought life and color back to moments best unremembered. That was exactly why she'd almost given a solid pass when *American Travel* magazine had sought her out to create content for a Rocky Mountain regional showcase.

She shoved the wadded paper back into her pocket. If she aced this project, she'd have her foot firmly in the door for the magazine's full-time travel editor position—and the chance for a steady paycheck. Lucas deserved that security.

She rolled back her shoulders at the thought of her son. It was simple enough. For Lucas, she'd relive every Manitou memory.

Shielding her eyes, she surveyed the valley. This view from Pikes Peak was worth every muscle-quivering, solitary tread. She'd post a social media shout-out to her hotel's concierge for suggesting the early hike because these views would go a long way toward solidifying her chances with *American Travel*. Manitou Springs, Colorado Springs, and the Garden of the Gods glimmered like gold.

She looked up at the sky. "And thank You, too." She might still be new to her relationship with God, but she knew where to give her appreciation.

A group of hikers ascended from the false summit a few hundred steps below. The trail was beginning to buzz with activity and she closed her eyes to savor her last drop of solitude.

Her phone vibrated. She opened her eyes. A picture of her four-year-old son lit the home screen. She pushed away the memories, shrugged back into her mommy armor and swiped the Answer button.

"Mommy!"

Liz grinned at the precious pixelated face and held her phone at arm's length so Lucas could see the mountain behind her. "Good morning, handsome. Guess what I just did." She caught her forced smile in the corner thumbnail. She was an expert at the having-it-all-together act.

That's all it was. An act. Someday, Lucas would see right through it. But for now, he just rubbed chubby, dimpled fists over his eyes and grinned. "Adventuring?" his small voice asked.

"You bet." She stood and turned to show him the two-thousand-foot descent into the valley. She'd teach Lucas to seize every day—even if it scared her to death. "I climbed a mountain."

"Wow." His tiny head bobbed in excitement.

Nostalgia and disillusionment wrapped twin vises around her middle. He looked just like his father. The note burned like an iron in her pocket. When she was finished with this hike she'd leave it in a trash bin and finally put Riggen Price behind her. Forgetting that man was the best thing she could do for her son.

The screen pixelated again, sliding Lucas's lazy smile and dark hair with a white patch on his cowlick into a crazy kaleidoscope of color. Pieces of her heart seemed to slide around in the same disjointed disarray.

She kissed the screen to the sound of garbled giggles and shoved all thoughts but those of her son away. "Mommy loves you, kiddo. I've got to get back to work. Tell Aunt Kat I'll be home tonight." Kat would be listening in the background. Liz pitched her voice higher. "Tell her I'll pack everything up in time."

The picture cleared as Lucas fish-kissed the screen. Kat passed into view behind him and disapproval flitted across her sister's face.

What had she done to deserve that look now? Shouts below her dragged her attention from asking. Like human stairs, hikers stood on separate railroad ties and gestured her way. She kissed the screen and ended the call before waving back at her fellow hikers. No doubt Kat would regale her with a complete list of her failings soon enough.

The hikers' shouts didn't stop. They rose up the slope with avalanche force. A man jabbed the air in front of him with his trekking pole. The others pointed. Their words flew away on mountain wind. She tilted her head, trying to pluck their muffled message from the air.

Then scrapes sounded behind her and rocks cascaded around her feet. Before she could turn, callused palms scraped down her biceps. Hot fingers dug into her bare skin.

Terror leached down her spine. She tried to heave her body forward but all she felt was the scrape of her thighs against jagged stone as she was wrenched back and over a boulder.

She threw her head back as an arm wrapped around her skull. Her heart jolted to a stop. Another arm squeezed her waist with python strength and moist breath flooded her ear canal as she was pressed back into a hard embrace.

She flailed her arms. Fear pulverized her gut. *Help!* She squeezed her phone, fumbling with the emergency sequence on her power button. But pain slashed through her wrist and her grip opened.

Echoing thuds rose to her ears. Her phone and canteen hitting the ground? The stranglehold loosened as fingers moved down and clamped a choke hold around her neck.

*God, help.*

An intense crushing force snaked through every muscle, rendering them useless. She tried to fight, to cry out, but her head was too heavy. Her tongue wouldn't move.

Then, only darkness.

Twenty minutes. A Manitou record. He was going to crush it. Riggen Price lunged to the left of his 1987 Ford Bronco for one last glute-warming stretch and gazed up the almost three thousand steps of Manitou Springs Incline.

It was good to be back. The Incline's siren song called with a promise to wash away the fog of the last few days. He'd hit his limit of slow vacationer pace during the two-day hike he'd led for Price Adventure Excursions, the business he ran with his brother.

Tightening his climbing backpack, he dragged in a deep breath. His legs itched to let loose, to pound out his frustration on the mountain. He'd finish this run and head back to the job that actually paid the bills—serving his hometown as an officer with Manitou Springs Police Department.

Maybe it was weird—he was ready to own it—but conquering the Incline kept the nightmares and memories at bay. He shook his head to dispel the images that fought to creep in. Tonight he planned to sleep like a baby.

Yakub nosed his hand and Riggen scratched the mutt's favorite spot right behind his ears. "Sorry, pal.

Not today." Opening the back door to his Bronco, Riggen let the dog, who had been his constant companion since Iraq, jump into the back seat.

Though he'd love to take the animal with him, dogs were prohibited on the Incline hike. He cranked down the window partway to allow Yakub plenty of fresh air.

Taking one last swig from his water bottle, he emptied the rest into Yakub's bowl and placed it on the floorboard. Yakub slurped the water, droplets hanging from his whiskers and falling to the ratty carpet. Riggen chuckled and patted the dog before tilting his wrist to check his smartwatch.

Even after he'd climbed out of bed an hour early to help his brother clean and store the hiking gear, his morning routine was still on time.

He secured the door and shook off the guilt that tickled his conscience. He should have let Trevor take a morning off. There was no need for them both to lose sleep. It wasn't as if he slept well as it was.

Zeroing in on the trail, Riggen broke into a jog. He needed to concentrate so he could be up the Incline and down Barr Trail with enough time to snag a cup of coffee before his shift started.

His watch vibrated and he skidded to a stop. Lieutenant Carr's number scrolled across the screen.

He jabbed his finger on the smooth watch face. "What's up?"

"We've got a situation on the Incline." His boss's voice boomed through the minuscule speaker. "Woman. Caucasian. Attacked by male in a black hoodie, black pants. Hiker called it in two minutes ago."

He retraced his steps. "Backup?"

"On the way. Knew you'd be there already. Search and Rescue has been alerted."

Riggen grunted. "It'll take Search and Rescue at least an hour. Do we know the woman? Local?" He pulled his key from his cargo pants and jammed it into the Bronco's lock.

"No. Caller recognized her from his hotel. Says she's some big-time travel blogger over from Colorado Springs for the Juniper's grand opening."

Riggen's stomach clenched. He yanked the door open and slid across his cracked leather seat. *God, no.* Where did that come from? He'd never tried the God thing before, and he was pretty certain he'd only find God's silent back if he tried now. Of all things he'd stuffed into his emotional do-not-touch strongbox, well-known travel bloggers topped the list. "Elizabeth Hart?"

"Yeah?" The speaker distorted as Carr barked orders to someone.

Riggen pulled his Glock from the glove compartment and secured it in his holster before slipping his neck-chained police badge over his head. Yakub slipped across the center console and into his lap. The dog's hackles raised in a ridge down his spine.

Carr was back, all gruff annoyance. "Sorry, Price. That's the tall and short of it. Backup's on the way. Don't go up alo—"

Riggen pushed End Call, cutting off the lieutenant's words, and climbed from the truck. Yakub's paws hit the ground next to him and dust puffs exploded around their feet. Carr would be spitting fire, but he'd deal with that later.

He had bigger problems now. He had known his mistakes would find him, but he'd pushed Liz far away from his mess. What was she doing here?

He broke into a jog and shook his head clear. This was coincidence. God wouldn't punish Liz for mistakes she'd had nothing to do with. His teeth ached. He loosened his jaw. *Right?*

No voice answered as he approached the looming mountain. All two thousand, seven hundred and forty-four abandoned railroad ties mocked him. He'd run the trail hundreds of times, but never had it mattered like today.

Early morning hikers meandered up the stairs in front of him, each one blinking in his consciousness like coordinates on a map. If he wanted to save Liz, he couldn't jeopardize the crowd's safety to do it.

Yakub brushed his side. Riggen groaned low in his throat. No time to secure the dog in the truck. Together, they zigzagged up the ever-steepening grade.

Railroad ties blurred as their feet devoured the distance. Riggen hit the first hand-railed section in record time. Blood pulsated in his ears, a steady drumbeat of dread. He didn't break pace when his wrist vibrated with another call. He'd check for updates when he hit the top.

When it would be too late to stand down.

"On your left!" He slipped past a young couple and surged onto a broken section of the track. Not much farther now.

Soon the tracks were narrowing. Too narrow. He leaned forward and used his hands to steady himself. *Your fault*, the wind whistled in his ears. Yakub jumped off the broken ties and ran up the dirt that sided the trail.

They hit the false summit and Riggen gulped the

thinning air. Jelly replaced his thigh muscles and his body threatened to collapse. But he couldn't fail now. Not again. His toe caught on a railway spike and sweat poured into his eyes as he caught himself with a knee in sharp gravel. The trail blurred. Dragging his forearm across his face, he cleared his vision and pushed himself upright.

Three hundred more stairs. He pummeled the ties under his feet. A crowd of hikers had gathered around something at the summit. They were antsy. Agitated. Riggen tugged his badge from under his shirt and held it high.

They parted, letting him through. Riggen doubled over and dragged oxygen from the air. When he caught his breath, he straightened and nodded at them. "The woman?"

A gnarled hiker pointed his trekking pole at a smartphone lying in the dust. The man's face was a mixture of fear and concern. His eyes clouded under bushy white brows before darting in the direction of Barr Trail.

"That way?" Riggen picked up the phone and waited for the old man's answer. He turned it over. The screen was shattered.

"Half an hour ago," the hiker answered. "'Fraid to go down there myself.'"

The man's voice faded away as Riggen depressed the power button. His own mirror-image miniature grinned back at him through splintered glass.

Bile soured her mouth as her stomach heaved. Liz rolled to her side and vomited. Her churning stomach competed with the searing pain in her head. Each heartbeat was a hammer blow.

She wiggled her hands, but they were weighted to her chest, strapped by an unseen force. Terror drifted over her like mountain mist. She'd been attacked. Where was she?

She peeked one eye open then the other. Sunlight filtered through an evergreen canopy and danced on her face. Tree limbs swayed above her as a tiny rosy finch perched on a branch and chirped. It was peaceful, like the falsely serene opening of a horror movie. She twisted against her restraints and the bird flew away.

Her hands were duct-taped over her chest in a funerary position. Sobs burst from her chest as her grip tightened on the curious bouquet taped within her clasped fingers. She kicked her feet. They were taped, as well.

Swerving her head back and forth only skyrocketed the pinball circus in her brain. It was worth it to find herself alone. Her attacker was gone. Or at least out of sight. As far as she could tell, she was wedged between two massive boulders with the packed dirt of Barr Trail to her right.

*Be strong…* She willed her pulse from its frenetic gallop, but the spicy scent of sagebrush wafted into her nostrils with every breath. *And courageous…* The bouquet had been artfully positioned in her empty canteen. Her heart slammed against her rib cage.

Sagebrush. This wasn't a coincidence. Why had she ever come back? Closure wasn't worth this. A steady job wasn't worth this.

*Lucas.* What would he do if she didn't make it back? His sweet smile flashed through her mind and dove down to spear her heart. Would he miss her, or would Kat slide in to take her place, giving him the life he should have?

Liz closed her eyes and bit her lower lip. *Control yourself.* No more tears. She wouldn't give whoever this was the satisfaction. Instead, she cried out to the only One who could help her.

*Do not be afraid*— Something wet and warm slid up her cheek. Her whispered prayer ratcheted into full-blown screams and echoed off the rock-edged face of Pikes Peak.

She swiveled her head to stare into two milk-chocolate irises. The tongue came at her again and a dappled mutt knocked her face with its wet, tan muzzle before sitting by her head, its floppy brown ears on guard.

Panic crashed into giddy relief and tears pushed against her floodgates. If there was a dog, there would be an owner. Twisting to look behind her, she fought the pounding in her head and ran her tongue over her cracked lips, summoning every last ounce of energy. "Help!"

Footsteps pounded down the trail and a figure appeared. He was hidden in shadowy bristlecone pine, but the dog perked and stood. His tan tail wagged. Gratitude washed through her veins like summer rain. Her guardian approved. "Thank You, Jesus."

The masculine figure stepped closer. Knelt beside her. Moved from shadow to light. "Jesus? You're talking to Jesus now?"

Liz pressed her heels into the hardened earth under her, certain the entirety of Pikes Peak had shifted. Shock clamped its hands over her mouth to silence her as Riggen Price leaned close. Had he been conjured by her silent cries?

He pulled a pocketknife from his pants' pocket and, with a flick of his wrist, had it open and slicing through her restraints. He shifted, moving to free her wrists. His skin, rough and real, brushed against her arm.

It couldn't be. This had to be an illusion induced by trauma. Like an oasis in a desert or some other cliché mind trick. She clamped her eyes shut. She must still be unconscious and dreaming. How else could the man she had spent five years trying to forget be peeling duct tape from her hands?

The illusion's movements stopped. And the only sounds were warbling birds and rustling trees. She forced one eye open. He was still there and her heart flip-flopped. Still Riggen. He hadn't evaporated into the low-hanging clouds.

Confusion and lingering fear swirled in her stomach until they hardened into hot anger. *Anybody else, Lord. Anybody but Riggen Price.*

His gray eyes evaluated her, stormy and turbulent. Then he shoved his hand through his hair, mussing the hereditary white patch cowlick that swirled through his dark waves, and leaned forward. "I need to check you for injuries."

She swallowed a mouthful of sandpaper, unable to spit out the million questions bombarding her. *Why did he disappear? Where had he been? What right did he have to look at her with concern flooding his eyes?*

Instead she nodded, letting the breeze fill the silence between them.

Tension radiated from Riggen's body as he pulled a Kleenex package from his pocket and snapped a tissue open. He used it to remove the canteen bouquet from her chest. He studied it, storm turning to steel, wrapped another tissue around it and shoved it in his backpack. "Evidence," he murmured.

Before Liz could move, his hands were back, gliding with expert precision over her head, neck and shoulders. He probed her arms and legs with gentle fingers and her skin pebbled under his touch. When he was finished, he held out his hand in the electrified space between them. She watched as her own hand rebelled to bridge the gap.

He helped her up. "Are you okay?"

"As okay as I can be." Her words nudged past the lump in her throat.

He nodded. "Let's get you to the station. Take your statement." The muscles in his jaw tightened. "Whoever did this will pay."

The mutt pushed between them and broke their handclasp, nudging into Riggen's thigh. Riggen stepped back and a sigh surged from him as if from a closed-off cauldron of boiling chaos. He dug in his pocket and pulled something out. Her phone.

Glacial ice seeped through each limb and Liz prepared her shredded heart for another slice of betrayal. He clicked the power button. Lucas's dimpled face flashed on the broken screen.

"When we're done at the station, we need to talk about this."

# TWO

The sight of her phone sent Liz swaying toward him like sagebrush in the breeze. She reached for it, her cold fingers scraped against the tender skin of his palm. Riggen released her phone, the image already seared into his soul.

He rubbed the back of his neck. A knot of stress was building by the nanosecond. That phone created questions he never knew needed asking. The how and what and why nearly smothered him, but now wasn't the time.

He stepped away, snapping himself back to reality as his heel hit Barr Trail. Liz shoved her phone into her black cargo shorts and brushed the dirt from her legs. When she looked up, he motioned for her to stay still. He'd seen no sign of her attacker, but they weren't in the clear. He surveyed the path in both directions.

It was quiet, but that only meant their enemy was patient. Squirrels darted down the trunk of a spruce and bounded across the split-rail fence before leaping into their path. Riggen caressed the reassuring weight of his Glock where it was situated snugly below his right arm. Out in the open, they'd be vulnerable. But if they stayed here, her attacker would know exactly where to return.

He lowered his palm and turned his hand over, beckoning her forward. They were safer on the move.

She froze. *Why should I trust you?* Her unspoken question couldn't have been more blatant if she'd rented a skywriter and emblazoned it over Pikes Peak.

He let his hand fall. Her earlier acquiescence must have just been a reaction to shock because now an almost visible shell of self-protection enshrouded her. He got the message. She'd let him through once. She wasn't about to let it happen again. He jerked his head down Barr. "We need to move."

The only indication she'd heard him was the tightening of her jaw. She looked down the switchbacked trail. Masses of golden-brown waves spilled over her shoulders as she shook her head, then flinched. The action must have been torturous after an attack like that.

His fingers itched at the sight of her. Distressed. Disheveled. Disheartened. He wanted to pull her close. He took a step farther away and shoved his hands into the fur on Yakub's back. "I get it. You don't trust me."

She made a sound that landed somewhere between a sob and a snort. Yakub left Riggen's side and trotted to Liz, nuzzling his snout into her hand. Her stance softened as Yakub flopped his head and threw her hand upward.

Reluctant acceptance showed in the purse of her lips and the way she scratched Yakub's head. She turned her face to him, eyes dull. "I suppose I don't have a choice."

Riggen puffed out his chest and wiggled an eyebrow at the mountain face behind her. "You could say you're between a rock and a hard place."

Her snort was unmistakable that time.

Smiling, he tried again. This time Liz placed her

hand in his. He wasn't prepared for how the touch of her hand sucked the breath from his body. "Help's on the Incline and coming up Barr." He eyed the trees and ground cover around them. "We'll catch this guy. But I'll breathe easier when we get to safety."

She nodded and intertwined her fingers with his. He pulled them into motion. Their feet thudded the earth in unison. Gravel knocked loose as they moved down the trail. Riggen scanned right to left and then right again, looking for anything out of place. Movement. Disturbed wildlife. Sunlight reflecting off a scope.

He caught the faint sound of a chopper as it cut through the air. Liz halted, pulling him back. She dug her heels into the middle of the path and shielded her eyes, searching the sky. She was a sitting duck. He tugged her to the side of the trail.

She shook him off and speared him with hazel darts. "Why are you even here?"

Shake him off or not, he wasn't letting her play the part in some sicko's target practice. Dragging his ex-fiancée behind a bush, he peered down the trail. Nothing seemed out of place. Except this conversation.

"I run the Incline every morning." He sidestepped a weathered log and extended a hand to help her over it. "Let's keep moving."

Liz studied his palm as if hoping a better answer were written there. Then she shoved his arm aside and climbed over the log. "I don't need your help." Yakub nosed his way between them and Liz followed the dog back toward the trail. "Besides, that's not what I meant."

Riggen jogged to keep up and hopped in front of her, blocking her angry barrel back into danger. Of course she didn't need his help. He'd never known any woman more independent. She collided with him and his arms surrounded her. Stilled her. Twigs stuck from her hair in every direction and her soft lips were downturned, begging to be righted.

He dragged his eyes away from her face. Dangerous attacker loose on Pikes Peak? Not the time to explore the implosion of their relationship—or wonder if those lips were still as soft as he remembered. This emotional detour had them off the trail and nestled behind bushes. Two feet more and they'd be back on track.

He scoured the trees lining their descent. The hair on his arms prickled. Something didn't feel right. Liz shifted, pulling away. Regret sliced through him, but he gulped it back. He wasn't meant to hold her safe against him. He'd do best to remember that. Shaking his head to clear the fuzz, he concentrated on the tree line.

Flashes of light blinked downslope. His subconscious pinged. He twirled to shove Liz to the ground, shielding her with his body as the shrub they'd been standing in front of exploded. Ear-shattering howls filled the air. Yakub climbed onto Riggen's back and covered them both.

The familiar mix of thrill and terror powered through his veins. As a second eruption shattered the dead log they'd stepped over moments earlier, soft pine needles under them melted into mortar-damaged sidewalks. He scrubbed images of Iraq from his eyes.

"What was that?" Liz's scream blistered his ear and jerked him back to reality. Pushing Yakub off, Riggen rolled Liz, body over body, until they were sheltered behind a jagged outcropping of granite. He clamped his hand over her mouth and whistled for Yakub. The dog belly-crawled to them.

They were stuck. The trail was too exposed. He tugged his cell from his pocket with his free hand and dialed.

Scooping Liz against the wall of granite, he held a finger to his lips. Her eyes threatened to engulf her face, her pupils dilated to the size of nickels. He whispered into her ear, "Stay down and be quiet."

She nodded before she scooted farther away from him and buried her head in Yakub's coat.

Riggen cradled the phone between his ear and shoulder so he could unsnap his holster and slide out his Glock. "We're taking fire halfway down Barr."

"Hold tight. I'm on the Incline." Carr's response filtered over the line. "Rosche and Jones are on Barr."

Static from the lieutenant's radio bounced across the line along with his directions to Detective Rosche. "Suspect headed your way."

More static. Then Rosche's voice. "Closing in."

Riggen applied pressure to Liz's shoulder. When she looked up, he motioned for her to stay put. She nodded. He army-crawled to the edge of the outcropping and peered around the corner. Nothing but pines and blue sky. Twigs broke as something crashed away from them and rushed down the path.

He zeroed in on the area. Without a visual, it was too risky to shoot, and he wasn't about to take the chance of walking Liz back into the path of danger.

Whoever it was seemed headed straight toward Rosche and Jones, and they'd be ready.

He wiggled back to Liz and settled in next to her. Adrenaline churned through his veins while Liz's frantic breaths bounced off the granite behind them. He slung an arm across her shoulder and pulled her close.

"He's on the run. We'll stay here until the all-clear."

She stroked Yakub's coat over and over in the silence, her hands shaking. Her ring finger was naked. His engagement ring was missing. Of course it was. Her fiancé had disappeared, why keep the reminder?

He gritted his teeth. He'd done the right thing. He couldn't have come home to her, not after the damage he'd caused.

Life didn't hand people like him happily-ever-afters. Now all he could do was protect Liz. And that included protecting her from him.

Shoving the fresh wave of guilt and regret inside his strongbox, he gently chucked her chin with his fist. Her hands stilled in Yakub's fur as he leaned close. "Don't worry. You're safe."

She ducked from his touch and wiped away a tear. Her eyes were full of fire. "With you is the least safe place I can think of."

Riggen's dog jumped onto the ambulance gurney and turned once before settling onto Liz's feet. Apparently near-death experiences made for fast friendships. Tucking her toes farther under his warm belly, Liz stared through the open doors as a baby-faced paramedic pushed a blood pressure sleeve onto her bruised bicep.

The paramedic was talking but his words dropped to the floor. All she could concentrate on was Riggen, who was having it out at the base of Barr Trail with the gorgeous Detective Rosche, who had just shoved their attacker into the back of a Manitou Springs Police Department SUV.

The detective didn't look happy. She also didn't look bad in the police-issued polo and form-fitting cargo pants. Liz squelched the thought. Riggen had abandoned her. It was over. Done with. Whoever this woman was to him, this sudden surge of jealousy was as misplaced as a dolphin on a mountaintop.

Even if the detective did possess ridiculous superpowers, like taking down would-be assassins without mussing a single strand of her blazing red ponytail.

Liz growled and the dog raised furry eyebrows at her. "It's okay, boy." She patted his head before pulling the tenth twig from her own tangled mane.

A crowd was gathering—reporters rubbernecking to see inside the ambulance. Liz melted back into the gurney. It wouldn't do for her potential employer to see this story on the five o'clock news. She had one chance to prove she could handle the big leagues. With just two days until the Rocky Mountain Travel and Adventure Expo, she couldn't let today derail her chance at landing the job.

The paramedic freed her arm from the sleeve. "One twenty over eighty. Pretty impressive."

She cut a glance at him, still straining to hear Riggen's conversation. "Thanks."

Snatches floated through the open doors.

"...you should've waited for backup. You probably just sacked your chance for the promotion." The red ponytail flopped as Riggen's sparring partner flung a look at the ambulance.

Riggen's answer was swallowed up as the paramedic held out his hand. "Hey, I'm Devon."

Liz exhaled through pursed lips before turning to Devon and flashing a smile. "I'm a single mom with a four-year-old son."

Color lit Devon's smooth cheeks. He pushed away

from the gurney and grabbed a small white device. "Let's get those oxygen levels checked." He stuck the monitor on her finger.

Typical. Flustered at the hint of responsibility. She'd been down that road. Throw a kid in the mix and men's interest disappeared like snow in July.

A vision of her dad's disappearing Buick as he'd left her and Kat with Child Protective Services played against the open ambulance doors. She swatted the memory away like an annoying mosquito and refocused on Riggen. Their eyes locked. Something sparked between them before his shutters were drawn.

Liz slipped her free hand into her pocket. He'd said he wanted to talk. He'd even looked like he'd meant it. But the note she'd never been able to throw away pretty much promised he'd disappear no matter how the conversation went.

The monitor beeped and Devon removed it. "Oxygen looks great."

With her focus on Rosche, Liz barely heard him, watching as the detective scribbled something in her notebook then glanced in her direction before starting toward the ambulance. Liz stiffened.

"I have questions for her." The command in the woman's voice was unmistakable.

Riggen blocked her. "It will wait until we get back to the office."

"She needs to answer while her memory is sharp." Rosche pushed forward, obviously nonplussed at the six-foot wall of muscle.

But she stopped when Riggen placed a hand on her arm. Unspoken words flew between them. The redhead nodded and backed down.

"No one questions her until I do." Rosche closed her notebook and tucked it in her pocket while sending a warning look toward the news circus. "There were shots fired on our mountain in the middle of tourist season. The mayor will want this open and closed."

Riggen gave a curt jerk of his head then turned toward the ambulance. Tension drained from Liz's body as the beautiful detective walked away. It was time to get out of here. The bright white walls of the emergency vehicle were closing in and Devon's hovering was fraying her already tortured nerves. She shrugged off her borrowed blanket.

Riggen grasped the door frame and pulled himself into the space, somehow making the small area impossibly smaller. His muscles rippled under his thin cotton sleeves as he filled every spare inch with his presence. Dirt smeared across the sharp cut of his cheekbones and flecks of dust smudged along the shadowy ridgeline of his shaved facial hair, ending just shy of his lips—the corners of which were tugging up into a ghost of the smile he once had.

Liz jerked her head at the news van to conceal that she'd been staring. Heat spread like wildfire from her neck to her face. "Any chance we can escape without media coverage?"

He threw a lazy look over his shoulder before he slid one eye down in a heart-stopping wink. "Sneak out for you?"

She pressed her lips together. His words painted the picture of a different life. One where he'd sneaked into the blacklisted Sagebrush restaurant to spend time with her. She ignored the double entendre and simply nodded.

"Cover for us, Devon." Riggen slipped past the EMT

and helped Liz up. She stumbled into his arms and was surrounded by his scent. It was so familiar that she drew a sharp breath, fight or flight pounding through her. She planted both palms on his hard chest and shoved away. It was time to get out of here. Out of this ambulance. Out of Riggen's arms. Out of danger.

They exited via the front and crept to Riggen's Bronco. When he pulled open the passenger door, his dog jumped into her seat.

"Sorry." Riggen laughed. The sound wiggled behind her armor. "Yakub likes the front." He pushed the dog's furry bottom over the armrest so she could climb in.

Why had she taken the trolley to the Incline this morning? Her own vehicle was still at the Juniper and now she was stuck riding in Riggen's emotional time machine with memories hitting her like a flood. She slammed the door, sending specks of worn blue paint into the wind.

Riggen jumped in and rummaged under his seat for a moment. When he sat up, he handed her a Colorado Rockies ball cap and scratched-up sunglasses. "Disguise?"

"Thanks."

Deafening silence settled between them as they backed out. Riggen maneuvered through the crowd and onto free road, but his frequent glances unnerved her. He had questions. He'd seen her phone.

But she had questions, too. First, why hadn't he opened the last letter she'd sent him? She tugged the hat down over her eyes and hugged her legs to herself. *Just do it. Spit them out.*

"Who do you think would do this?" Riggen snapped on the turn signal and turned onto Manitou Avenue.

Liz bit her tongue and pulled her damaged armor around her like a threadbare sweatshirt. It had been Riggen who'd told her to lay off the Sagebrush's owner. But that was before he had left for Iraq. Researching and writing the Sagebrush story had been the only thing that kept her mind from constant worry over his safety— and the only thing that distracted her from her sister's relentless nagging.

She rested her cheek against her knees. "It's your town. Who do you think would do it?"

He raised one dark brow in a way that said she wasn't pulling anything over on him. "I think it had something to do with the bouquet you were holding."

So he'd caught the message, too. Her gut tingled. She could still smell the tangy sagebrush oil on her skin. She squeezed her eyes shut and tried to push away the terror. "Feel free to say 'I told you so.'"

The warmth of Riggen's hand sliding down her arm startled her fear away. His eye twitched as he lifted and dropped his shoulder. "I was the wrong one."

He stopped for a crosswalk and covered her fingers with his own. His sculpted features softened and she let herself believe for the briefest of moments that he was talking about more than the Sagebrush.

But as the pedestrians cleared the road, she pulled her hand back and stuffed it into her lap, safely out of reach.

"I'll drive you back to your hotel when Rosche is finished questioning you." His voice was matter-of-fact. Like he took for granted that they'd talk. Pick up again.

Pick up what? He didn't want her. He'd been clear about that. Her stomach turned and her skin went clammy. She couldn't afford picking up the pieces when he disappeared again. The stakes were too high. She had Lucas to think of now.

She leaned her head against the window. "Sure."

She'd be long gone before he knew the interview was over. She wasn't about to let Lucas experience the same pain Riggen had put her through.

# THREE

Riggen pulled on a pair of blue nitrile gloves, snapping the form-fitting synthetic rubber against his wrist. Liz was finishing with Rosche and their suspect was in lockup. Hopefully they'd get an open-and-shut confession and he'd be able to take his first deep breath since breathing Liz's name that morning—and since seeing her phone.

He unzipped his backpack and pulled out the canteen bouquet that had been taped into Liz's hands. Tension vibrated his jaw as he set it down on the sterile tabletop in the MSPD's evidence room.

He had warned Liz to let her review of the Sagebrush go. When they had first met, he had been a staff sergeant at Fort Carson and the Sagebrush had occupied a definitive place on the Army's "do not go near" list. Why she had picked that restaurant to review, he couldn't understand.

It had had a bad reputation. And for good reason. He glared at the wilting plant. Liz hadn't taken his advice. She'd continued pursuing the review even after his deployment. And, when he'd been immobilized in an overseas hospital, he'd read how her journalistic travel article had blown away Manitou's worst-kept cover-up—the Sagebrush's forced labor and human trafficking ties.

Sure he'd been proud, happy that the viral exposure had launched her into the regional tourism limelight. He'd been on the verge of sending congratulations when his doctor had arrived with the news that his injury obliterated any chance of fathering children. He'd learned that day that mistakes had consequences and his consequences didn't include fairy-tale endings. The God Lizzy seemed suddenly familiar with had made it clear Riggen was not even on the waiting list for His favor.

After that realization, he hadn't felt anything anymore.

Last he checked, Sammy Malcovitch, the now-convicted owner of the Sagebrush, was lounging in state prison. But even if that man had outside reach, would he be this blatant?

The military-grade canteen goaded Riggen, reminding him of dust-filled Baghdad streets—and of the family he'd failed. Heat spread across his face like the Iraqi sun. He could still see that little boy's anguished face.

He blinked. Shook his head. The sun of his haunted memories morphed back into the evidence room fluorescents.

"Price!"

Riggen jolted. The canteen crashed onto the metal tabletop, releasing the pungent odor of sagebrush into the dry air.

Lieutenant Carr thundered into the ten-by-ten room, shaking the walls with his anger. His face was a mottled red that never boded well.

Riggen righted the canteen before picking up an evidence bag. The paper bag they used for biodegradable items crinkled in the silence that followed his boss's dramatic entrance. He'd get this canteen tagged into evidence and sent off to Metro for fingerprint analysis. He dropped the items into the bag and folded the top, sealing the evidence—and his past—inside.

He turned to Carr. No need to ask what was wrong. He had ignored a direct order. On this job, lives depended on following commands. Guilt pulverized him—in that respect, this job was just like the Army. At least *this* disregard for orders hadn't blown up in his face.

He hitched his hip on the table. "Liz was my fiancée." He grimaced. "I couldn't wait."

Anger seeped from Carr's face, replaced by disbelief. "Was?" He ran a hand back and forth through his buzz cut. "Small world."

"Tell me about it."

"Sorry, man. Thankfully, everything ended smoothly… Today, I mean." Carr reddened as he hooked his thumbs in the armholes of his bulletproof vest and rocked back on his heels. "But think about next week. You're too close to make a mistake this big."

Sweat beaded on his brow at the mention of his upcoming interview. Carr was right. Riggen shifted against the counter and sighed. "Jones will be all over this."

"Jones wants the position. Thinks he deserves it over you." Carr's eyes narrowed, his brows forming a perfect vee. "He'll make sure Chief hears about it. I'll do what damage control I can."

Riggen shrugged. "Can't change it now. But thanks for having my back."

Carr shifted from one foot to the other, looking uncomfortable with a moment that could crash too quickly into feelings territory. "It's interesting you were there the exact moment Ms. Hart needed you."

It was no secret Carr didn't believe in coincidence. The man always seemed to steer conversations to divine intervention. And though Riggen respected him, what Carr didn't realize was that Riggen had lost any goodwill he'd had with God the moment that bomb had exploded in Baghdad.

He turned his attention back to the table and used evidence tape to seal the bag. He scrawled his initials across the tape before handing it to Carr to do the same.

Time to stop Carr's providence train before it left the station. "Simple coincidence. Co-incidents that were happening at the same time. Liz happened to be on the mountain. I happened to be out for a run. Nothing magical about it."

Carr signed the bag and handed it back. "I agree. Magic had nothing to do with it."

Riggen's eye muscles twitched and an uncomfortable feeling shivered up his spine. Not going there. It *was* coincidence. Easier to believe that than think his mistakes were coming around to hit Liz in the face. Even so, he needed to get Liz out of town and far away from the cloud that hung over his life.

He headed for the door. "I'll drive Liz to her hotel."

Carr stopped him before his feet hit the threshold. "Rosche finished and cut her loose ten minutes ago." Carr held something in the space between them. A folded sheet of paper. "She did ask me to give you this."

Riggen took the wrinkled paper and opened it. His own writing. *I'm sorry, Lizzy. It's over.*

So much for easy breathing.

* * *

Liz thanked her Uber driver and slid from the back seat onto the cobbled sidewalk that fronted Manitou Springs's newest outlying hotel property—the Juniper Resort. She slammed the sedan's door and let her eyes drink in the Juniper's late nineteenth-century architecture.

With the sun high in the sky, the Victorian-esque picture windows appeared brilliantly on fire. Pikes Peak reflected in their paneled glasses. She captured the moment with her phone, hoping it would show better on her computer than it did on her shattered screen.

She climbed the broad stone steps onto the Juniper's wraparound porch and allowed herself to enjoy a single moment of fulfillment. No matter how she felt about Manitou, this morning, or the wreck that was her life, this project was wrapping up well.

When Kimberly East, the editor-in-chief of *American Travel*, saw her finished vision at the expo booth this weekend, the job would be hers. Then she and Lucas would finally be on their own, no longer dependent on her sister.

She breathed the promise of freedom and let it fill her lungs. As long as she could keep all hints of mountain attacks on the down-low and stay safe, she'd have *American Travel*'s audience hungering for a taste of fresh Rocky Mountain air and adventure.

She squared her shoulders and let the morning's terror fall away before pushing through the ornate front door.

"Good afternoon, Miss Hart." Kris Dupree beamed at Liz from behind the rosewood concierge desk that dominated the front lobby. "Did you enjoy your hike?"

"I wouldn't go straight to enjoy." Liz set down her phone and leaned her head to the side, stretching her neck. She tried to push out a smile but every muscle ached. She'd kill for a soak in her suite's elaborate claw-foot tub and a catnap before hitting the road.

It was time to put Manitou and the morning's madness in the past. "I lost my key and half my sanity this morning. So 'enjoy' wouldn't top my list of adjectives."

Concern dimmed Kris's eyes like clouds over a bright blue sky. "I can help with the key." She tapped on her keyboard, programming a secondary key. "I hope all's well now."

Liz managed a weary nod.

Kris slid the new key across the counter and flicked an invisible piece of dust from the plastic surface. Her manicured nails shimmered under the light of an elegant chandelier and her face beamed with the warm concern of womanly sisterhood.

The kind of concern Liz had always wished to see on Kat's face. But real sisters weren't that warm. At least, not in her experience.

"Oh." Kris's fire-engine-red lips rounded. "I almost forgot. A package was delivered today." The woman disappeared under the counter then popped back up with a large Bubble Wrap envelope.

When she pushed the parcel across the counter, all of Liz's fatigue melted away.

"I'll send up mineral water bottles and fresh towels. Ring the desk if you need anything else."

Liz nodded and grabbed her manila treasure, wiggling her fingers at Kris before trotting to the elevator. When the mirrored doors closed behind her, she ripped open the envelope. The elevator dinged as she studied the mock-up T-shirt her assistant on the *American Travel* project, Emily Bancroft, had sent.

It was perfection. The sketched idea she'd sent Emily had been executed with precision. Her artistic soul hummed. Liz's original drawing of Pikes Peak now had the *American Travel* logo superimposed over it with the Rocky Mountain Travel and Adventure Expo information in small neon script.

Pikes Peak. A prick of fear deflated her elation. It had been more like Perpetrator Peak this morning. She replaced the shirt in its packaging and made her way to her room. If it hadn't been for Riggen... She shook off the shivers and waved her updated keycard against the RFID reader.

The light blinked green and she entered, slamming the door behind her. But she wasn't fast enough to stop the guilt that slipped in on her heels. She should have rallied the courage to confront Riggen, but all her strength had been knocked from her.

She tossed the expo T-shirt and her keycard onto the bed and kicked off her climbing shoes. The cozy wallpaper of her hotel and its furnishings could almost convince her the twenty-first century was more than a hundred years in the future. She perched on the edge of her room's antique four-post bed and peeled off her socks.

But if Riggen wanted to talk, he could find her. Her throat tightened and she jerked his ball cap off her head. She stared at the Colorado Rockies emblem before tossing the battered cap to the floor. The man had been living less than twenty minutes from her for who knew how long. He'd had every chance to find her. If he had a good reason for ending it with no more than a note, then why hadn't he come to explain?

Facts were facts. Riggen had run from commitment like a stream down a mountain. She wasn't about to wait around to watch him run again. Depressing the power button on her phone, she stared at the screen. No missed calls.

Why did that get under her skin?

She stalked through twin bathroom doors onto cool, tiled floor. A hot bath would clear her head. As the faucet poured water into the tub, she let steam swirl around her.

Half an hour later, when the water had cooled and she'd emerged refreshed, Liz nestled into the plush depths of her hotel-provided robe. A knock sounded at her door. She squeezed the last drops of water from her hair and padded to the entry to squint through the peephole.

Room service with her promised bottles of water. The sight of the water made her mouth water. She secured the robe's belt and pulled open the door.

"Compliments of management." The employee handed her the bottles along with a small basket of toiletries. "Local amenities."

She thanked him and shut the door. Uncapping the miniature lotion bottle, she inhaled sweet lavender. Another point for the Juniper. Turning the bottle over in her hand, she studied the label. She'd be sure to include this in her article.

Her phone buzzed from the dresser, interrupting her perusal. She traded bottle for phone and slid the answer button, wincing as splintered glass pierced the pruned flesh of her fingers. "Hello?" She sucked on her finger.

Silence.

"Hello...?" She pulled back to look at the number. Local. But only breathing transmitted across the connection.

"Hello?" It was the second time she'd said it. Her tone bordered on exasperation, but a creeping misgiving about reaching out to her kept Riggen mute.

He'd served in Iraq. He'd survived a suicide bombing that had taken out three-quarters of his squad and a family of civilians. Why couldn't he make his own tongue move? Because he knew this was a bad idea. He punched his thigh and went for it anyway.

"Hey, Liz." *Don't hang up.* "I have an update on your attacker."

The clock over his desk ticked into the awkward silence.

"I'm listening." Her annoyance was tangible.

He shoved back from his desk and flattened her note against his mousepad. Liz's attacker had been transferred to the El Paso County Jail after confessing to the entire attack, but his motive seemed as thin as the paper under Riggen's hand. "Rosche isn't buying the guy's story." He paused. "Though parts of it were convincing."

"And...?"

He leaned back. Kicked his feet up on the desk. "He confessed. Says he's been following your blog for years... because you're his soul mate."

She snorted. He could picture the adorable way her nose wrinkled when she made the noise.

"You believe my soul mate wants to duct tape me and leave me on Pikes Peak?" she asked.

A smile played around the corners of his mouth. "I

can believe half your blog followers are in love with you." He set his feet back down and rested his elbows on the desk. "But this guy? No. Something's off about his whole story. First, he doesn't fit the typical stalker MO."

She murmured a throaty agreement. The sound warmed his blood. "And there's the sagebrush," she added.

He nodded. "There's that."

"Sammy Malcovitch is still locked up, right? Could he pull off something like this? And why now?"

"I don't know if he could." Riggen hit a few keys on his keyboard. "But, I agree. Why would he?" Information lit his monitor. "He's been a model prisoner for the last few years. Seems out of the blue."

"Great topics to discuss with your 'Detective Rosche.'" Dismissal crept into Liz's reply.

"I'd rather discuss them with you." He ran his finger over the written goodbye. "We didn't get to talk. Dinner?"

"I don't think that's a good idea…"

She was shutting down. He didn't blame her. But he had to do something, even if he wasn't clear on what.

He hated to admit it, but a tiny shred of hope had been dragged up by Carr's comments. And that hope was chipping away at the reality by which he had lived for five long years. *What if*…what if he'd been wrong?

He studied the ceiling. Was he talking himself in or out of this? The only thing he was certain of was that he couldn't make himself disappear again. Not now that the image from Liz's phone had been burned into his brain.

"Then just coffee." He held his breath and bore a hole into the floor below him with his foot as five silent years threatened to suffocate him. "I'd like to do the right thing by you, Lizzy." *Or at least figure out what the right thing is.*

The clock taunted him from the wall, ticking the stillness away. Five seconds. Ten. Fifteen.

"I'll give you half an hour."

"Great. I'll pick you—"

"No." Her refusal exploded in his ear before she continued, her voice layered in resignation and annoyance. "I'll meet you."

He'd take it. "Where? When?"

"At our old place. Three o'clock?"

His foot stilled as relief pulsated through his limbs. Relief from what? Confusion strangled him. "I'll see you then."

He placed the phone back in the cradle and stared at the mess of mugshots on the memo board. For the briefest of moments, he hoped Carr really did have a better understanding of divine intervention than he did.

Liz chugged her water bottle and leaned against the marble sink to swipe on one final coat of mascara. She frowned at her reflection in the gilded mirror. Why did she care what she looked like?

Anything the Manitou Springs Police Department needed to speak to her about could easily be handled through the fierce Detective Rosche. There wasn't a single, solid reason to meet with Riggen.

*Besides your conscience.*

She groaned and pulled a brush through her hair. The feel of Riggen's hands as they'd drifted over her head and neck flitted through her mind. The brush fell from her fingers and clattered against the counter. His touch had been careful. Tender. Gentlemanly.

That was probably how he treated anyone in distress. It didn't mean he still had any feelings for her, and it certainly didn't mean he knew how to handle relationships with care. If he had cared about her, he would never have abandoned her.

*Give him a chance.* The thought whispered its way through the widening chinks in her armor. She grabbed her lavender lotion and dumped a blob into her palm.

"Okay, okay. I'll give him a chance." She rubbed the soothing scent into her skin. No matter what he'd done, he had a right to know about his son. He'd returned the letter in which she had written of her pregnancy. Unopened. With that awful note attached.

Thirty minutes would be plenty of time. If he wanted any place—and she meant *any* place—in Lucas's life, he owed her an explanation.

She walked to her bed and plopped down to send a text to Emily. The T-shirt was too amazing to go unremarked. She wanted to build up her team, even if she wasn't the official editor yet.

Great job on mock-up! Looking forward to our collaboration.

The message thread blurred, running the words together. She rubbed her clammy hand over her eyes. Today's stress was too much. The sooner she got out of Manitou, the better.

Emily's reply landed in her hand and she squinted at it.

Cheers to teamwork! :)

Liz adjusted the thin, blue strap on her romper and bit her lip between her teeth. Just a few more days and the team would be hers. But tonight—she grabbed her purse from the desk as she passed—she'd finally put Riggen's betrayal behind her.

New job. New start.

Moments later, she was in the enclosed parking garage and pressing Unlock on her key fob. Her Wrangler beeped twice. Just a short drive and she'd be sitting across from Riggen at what had been their favorite restaurant, figuring out what closure looked like. It wasn't what she had planned on happening when she'd arrived in town. It was surreal.

Their relationship had halted soon after Riggen deployed, along with their plans and their dreams. She'd hung on every call and letter, but then, there was only silence. His phone had been disconnected. His social media and email accounts closed.

After she had received his note, she'd been frantic, even going as far as calling his stepbrother. She'd hit a dead end there. Trevor had refused to give any information. And she'd been hesitant to use her pregnancy as a bargaining chip.

The message was loud and clear: Riggen was finished with her.

Her stomach turned over, filling her mouth with bitterness for the second time that day. Why was she doing this to herself? Sweat trickled between her shoulder blades and she grabbed the Jeep door to steady herself. *Just get to the restaurant. Get the conversation over. Get home to Lucas.*

Peace flooded her. Lucas. His tiny arms would make everything okay. But then her peace was crushed by the thought of Lucas slipping his arms around Riggen's neck—their identical heads together. Her pulse threatened to match Pikes Peak in elevation.

She climbed into her Jeep and revved the engine. Lucas loved military men. The community lived and breathed them in Colorado Springs. She shoved the gearshift into Reverse and swung from her parking spot. What would her little boy do if his very own G.I. Joe daddy showed up?

She licked her lips as a fine sheen of perspiration broke out across her Cupid's bow. Her lungs felt like an old balloon unable to inflate. Whatever happened, she couldn't let Riggen back into her life. He could shatter Lucas's tender heart into a million pieces.

That was the last thing she'd let happen. Flicking her turn signal, she wiped her lip and turned onto Manitou Avenue. Tourists meandered down sidewalks in the afternoon sun. Two miles down the road, her phone rang, a muffled chirp from inside her purse.

She reached over the armrest, grabbing at her purse, and wrapped her tingling fingers around the strap. The air in the Jeep seemed to be thickening.

Brake lights flashed in front of her and she stomped her brake pedal. Why did her brain feel like a bowl full of dandelion fluff? She blinked hard. Was it possible the paramedics had missed a mild concussion?

She slipped her hand inside her purse and struggled to pull out the phone and hit Speaker. "Hello?"

"Finally."

*Kat.*

The band around Liz's chest tightened again but her mental fog cleared a bit. "What's wrong?"

Her sister's exaggerated sigh whooshed into the Jeep. "The landlord wants us out by Friday. Why am I the only one who can do anything?"

"I'll get the packing done." Her reply was clipped as she tried to steady her spiraling emotions, but her mind refused to focus. Her sister was right. On the list of responsibility skills, Kat had received the larger portion.

"Sorry, Kat." She lifted her fingers from the leather steering wheel, the surface wet under her death grip. "I put a deposit on an apartment yesterday. I've already got a place for Lucas and me to go. Stop worrying. I'll be home to pack after this errand."

"Home?" Kat's voice cracked. "Home is with family. You should be going with us to California. Not sticking my poor baby boy into a cramped apartment. No yard. No room to play. No family."

Her sister's words hammered Liz's shredded confidence as she slowed for a trolley that was stopping ahead. Squeezing the bridge of her nose, she stopped the fresh tears from filling her eyes.

"I appreciate the home you and John provide us, but we need to strike out on our own. You know? As in not tagging after my big sister anymore." Liz steeled herself with a breath. "Besides, he's my baby boy, not yours."

The sound of a door slamming echoed over the line. "I have to go," Kat snapped. "We'll talk tonight."

The trolley, the traffic and the congested sidewalks blurred around her again as Kat hung up. Zaps of pain prickled her fingers and her phone clattered against the steering wheel as she tried to power it off. She watched in horror as her suddenly lifeless arms fell into her lap like sinking stones.

Everything swam in muddled, panicked confusion. Why couldn't she see?

The trolley stopped in front of the mineral spring fountain a split second before Liz crashed into the camper in front of her.

# FOUR

Fifty-five. Fifty-six. Fifty-seven. Fifty-seven vehicles had passed the Stagecoach restaurant since he'd been seated. None had pulled in. Riggen tilted his wrist and his OLED screen blared the truth. Liz was standing him up.

He crumpled his empty sugar packet and tossed it on the table. His legs ached for a run and he stretched, kicking against the opposite booth. He needed to run. Run until the only thing that remained was the mountain and his own burning muscles.

Pulling his wallet out, he tossed a ten on the table. Liz wasn't coming. And he completely understood. Half of him even agreed. Scratch that. All of him thought she should run far and fast.

Today had thrown him through the ringer. Now he couldn't tell which way was up. When he had turned her shattered phone over and seen what had to be *his* little boy's face, every atom of his being had wanted to throw caution to the wind and claim his family.

But reality slugged him in the face. Every moment since Iraq had pounded painful reality into him—he was a failure. He didn't deserve a family. Real fathers protect but his decisions in Baghdad had cost an Iraqi family everything.

And they hadn't been the only ones. He'd walked his squad into an ambush that had decimated them. Good men, good fathers, who should have gone home to their own families.

So he hadn't even tried to argue or bargain with God over his injury. It was a punishment he deserved. But not what Liz deserved.

Even so, could he walk away from that phone and its revelation? What was he supposed to do? He hauled himself from the deep cushions of the booth, no closer to an answer than he was when he'd first stared down at that phone screen.

He left his attempt at reconciliation behind and pounded pavement to his SUV. The sound of his name stopped him in his tracks. He turned and searched the crowd. His stepbrother was pushing toward him, his brown eyes dancing with laughter, when a two-kid stroller rammed Trevor's heels.

Trevor hit the sidewalk and careened to a stop, waving an eight-by-eleven sheet of paper through the air. "I've been at the library for a presentation." His dark blond brows bounced. "We even had some tourists."

Riggen glanced across Manitou Avenue at the two-story historical building and then back at Trevor.

"For publicity." His brother landed an arm punch before stuffing the paper in Riggen's hand. "Can't build business without advertising."

Riggen examined the crumpled paper. "Advertising is your area of expertise." He handed the paper back. "Give me the grunt work any day."

Trevor deflected Riggen's words with a wave of his

hand. "Soon we'll see if our efforts have made a difference. I'd love to get you off the force and working full-time for the family business."

Trevor packed the flier into his shoulder bag before continuing. "It's what Dad would have wanted." He slipped his aviators down his nose. "You don't look so great. You doing okay?"

All the frustration of the day bubbled up; Riggen flexed his fingers to keep his nails from biting into his palm. Maybe it was years of frustration threatening to overflow.

Trevor stepped back. His forehead scrunched. "That bad?"

"Liz is back."

Understanding sparked in his brother's eyes. "Ah."

The radio chirped from its perch on Riggen's shoulder and he nodded down the street to where his SUV was parallel parked. "I need to get back to it."

"I'll walk with you." Trevor fell in step.

"It's more than Liz, though." Riggen swallowed as they covered the distance, weaving through the constant human flow. This morning he'd been a man walking out his sentence. Alone. Now he was the last thing he had ever expected to be—a father.

"She has a son."

Trevor stopped and placed a hand on Riggen's arm. "Your son?"

There was no doubt. "If I had known…"

Trevor's eye twitched. "She called, looking for you after your injury. I knew you had wanted to cut off contact… You know how much I disagreed with you. 'Bout killed me, but I stood by you." He wiped an errant strand of blond hair from his face. "I never mentioned it. Thought it'd be easier for you." Trevor squeezed his arm, his eyes darkening. "I had no idea she was pregnant."

Riggen shook his head and resumed walking. The entire situation was impossible.

Trevor jogged to keep up. "You'll just have to show her—" his voice cracked "—that there's nothing more important than family."

Pain ripped through Riggen's chest. It had been their father's motto. Reverend Price had been more family to Riggen than any blood relative ever could have been.

The reverend and Trevor had adopted him into their home when he'd been a scared kid watching his young mom's life slowly wilt. Their love had transformed him from neglected to accepted.

Now, their father was gone from a heart attack. Riggen's throat burned. It had happened when he was in Iraq. He hadn't even gotten to say goodbye. Now he and Trevor were all each other had. Trevor's support meant more than he could express.

"Don't worry about this week's excursion. I'll cover it." Trevor kicked out one sandaled foot. "These feet are good for more than running numbers. But we'll have to postpone any more bookings until after next week. I'm at the expo this weekend."

Riggen cracked a smile before closing the door and rolling down the window. "I appreciate it."

Dispatch broke across the line again. This time it was for him. Riggen tilted his head to listen as Trevor walked away. Traffic accident. He'd wrap this up, grab Yakub from the station, and head home for the night.

Liz had made it clear she wasn't ready to figure things out. He pulled into the flow of traffic and turned on lights and sirens. Cars filtered to the shoulder. He just needed to recoup. Run it out and puzzle out the next step.

*Pray about it.* He shook the thought from his mind. God had drawn a line in Iraqi sand. Not that Riggen had ever tried talking to Him before. That was Dad's thing. Besides, if God hadn't wanted him to have a family, He probably wouldn't approve if Riggen tried to skirt that line now.

No matter what, he had a responsibility to his son. Did that include being present in his life? That was an answer he didn't have. Whatever he decided, he had to handle it with care. That little boy was the only shot he'd ever have at being a father.

Tourists crowded the crosswalk ahead. He tooted the sirens and they cleared. Smoke billowed from the next block.

Pedestrians surrounded the scene of the accident. A barrier of human curiosity. Some had their phones out, recording. He pulled up and blared the horn. As they slithered away, he could see a Jeep smashed into the back of a camper. The driver's door hung open on the Jeep and the driver was slumped over the crooked steering wheel.

Coffee soured in his stomach when he saw the familiar, bright, caramel-blond hair that spilled onto the dashboard.

Throbbing pain accompanied any attempt at coherent thought, but Liz had to try. It was such a struggle to open her eyes. Dim fluorescents shone down on her and she squirmed, trying to remember. Soft hands feathered her forehead.

"How you feeling?" A woman's soothing voice calmed the thump of her heart.

Running her tongue over her cracked lips, Liz tested her voice. "Like I've been in the ring with a grizzly?" But, no, that couldn't be why she was there. Right?

The nurse laughed, the sound tinkling like wind chimes in the breeze, and pulled a medical chart from the bottom of the hospital bed. "No grizzly, but you did get hit with a beastly cocktail."

Liz pushed herself up onto one elbow. The pillow gave way and she crashed back into the rock-hard bed. Her nurse laid down the file and knelt beside her, pushing a series of buttons. Suddenly, Liz was sitting upright without exertion.

"The doctor ran blood tests while you were unconscious."

Liz frowned. The last thing she remembered was driving away from the hotel. Why would she need a blood test?

"I don't know what you're talking about." Pressing her fingertips into her eyes, she sighed. "It's all dark." She tried to grab hold of what came next but there was nothing other than aching ribs and sore arms.

Why was she there and not at the Stagecoach? She reached out and grasped the woman's hand. "How long have I been here?"

"Six hours. You had a nasty bump from your accident. Plus the Rohypnol in your system."

"Accident?" She probed her head with careful fingers. "Wait—Rohypnol?"

"Mmm-hmm. Date-rape drug."

There was a fly on the ceiling. She watched it fly from drop-tile to drop-tile. "Not possible."

"Blood tests don't lie, sweetheart."

She should be on the way home to Lucas. Not drugged in a hospital. The fly landed on her knee. Kat was right. She'd dropped another ball. "When can I leave? I have a son."

"We'd like to keep an eye on you a bit longer."

Liz bunched the scratchy hospital sheets into a wad. "I need my phone." Her eyes whizzed around her stark room.

"The cute cop dropped your stuff on the chair. I'll check your vitals then find your phone."

Liz shuddered as the blood pressure sleeve tightened around her arm. It wouldn't be one twenty over eighty now. "The cute cop?"

"He's down in the cafeteria. Asked me to page him when you woke up." The nurse slid the blood pressure sleeve from Liz's arm at the same time her eyelid slid closed in a wink. "You're blessed he was on duty."

Being ambushed by an attacker and blindsided by a missing fiancé wasn't the kind of blessing she was looking for.

The nurse rustled through Liz's purse and pulled out the cell, humming low in her throat. "Looks like you did a number on this little baby." She handed Liz the shattered phone.

Liz clicked the power button and stared into Lucas's sweet face. She should be home with him, packing.

Her notifications showed five missed calls from Kat. Heat filled her face while her insides twisted in knots. She slid the open button, cautiously. The bars on her phone were low. She looked up. Only flies could get through those ceilings.

Helplessness flooded her as Kat's voice mails berated her: she was late, she was unreliable, she was ir-responsible and Kat was better for Lucas.

Riggen hated hospital cafeterias. He'd spent so many hours under their bright lights, waiting to hear if Mom would improve.

As he reread the nurse's text, he choked down the last of his processed burger and fries. Liz's blood tests were back. Rohypnol. Date-rape drug?

Anger jolted through him like lightning through a wet summer night. The same drug used on his mother by her abusers. Calculating the dose and efficacy, their attacker now sitting in county jail couldn't have slipped Liz the drug.

They were dealing with a larger-scale threat.

He grabbed his tray and slammed it on the trash receptacle. He needed to be at Liz's side whether she was awake or not. And whether she welcomed his presence or not. She was alone. There was no one else to watch over her.

He strode through the corridors that buzzed with endless activity and studied each face he passed. Memorial Hospital was the busiest hospital in the state. Tonight was no exception.

He wasn't a stranger to the place, but he shouldn't be there for this. Two attacks on Elizabeth Hart in a single twenty-four-hour period? This couldn't be coincidence. He swiped open his phone and shot off a text to Rosche.

Liz in hospital. Rohypnol in her system.

Rosche's response flew back.

We need 2 question suspect again.

They sure did. His boots thundered against polished floors as he hit the emergency wing. The nurse manning the reception desk eyed him through the glass-paned doors. Her brows drew down.

He slowed and waved. Her expression lightened, recognition spreading across her face as the doors slid open. "Did you hear the news, Officer Price? Your girl is awake. She said you could go on in."

He nodded, not stopping for small talk. "Thanks."

His strides covered the distance to Liz's partition in seconds and he pushed aside the curtained divider. Metal grommets bounced along the ceiling rods in brash protest. The anxiety that had been nipping his heels calmed when he laid eyes on Liz.

She turned. Her cheeks matched the sheets she was sitting on. Her bottom lip quivered and she tugged it between her teeth.

He approached, angled sideways and held one hand toward her, as if she were a wounded animal. "What's wrong?"

She thrust her broken phone into the space between them. "She wants to take our son."

# FIVE

Quaking had started deep in Liz's core as soon as Kat's tirade spewed from her voice mail like unbridled wildfire. The words scorched her heart.

They hurt so much worse because they were true. If she were reliable and responsible—like Kat—she'd already have a steady job instead of random deposits whenever a contracting job finished. The affiliate links on her blog were barely enough to pay her car and insurance payments. How did she expect to cover monthly rent?

Yeah, the link income was climbing, but she needed money now. Kat would just get the nine-to-five job. She couldn't fathom why Liz wouldn't do the same.

*If she loved Lucas.*

Those words had seared her soul more than every other fiery dart. She cradled her head in her hands.

Kat was right. If she were more like her sister, she wouldn't be stuck in this hospital bed with danger swirling around her.

Riggen cleared his throat. "Liz?"

He was still there. She held her phone aloft, her tiny world shaking.

Riggen moved to her side. Restrained energy spiraled around him like steam off a hot spring. He rubbed his palms up and down his pant legs. "What's happened?" His voice was low. Calm. Controlled.

She hit Speaker. Kat's voice penetrated the air. With each accusation Kat lobbed at her, Riggen tensed. He looked as though he were carved of stone, as unyielding as Pikes Peak.

For a second, Liz wished back his earlier warmth. Did he agree with Kat? She shrank into the thin hospital pillow.

If she closed her eyes and prayed hard enough, would the warmth return? Because at this moment, she was scared and hurt, and the only other person who had as much of a right to speak an opinion about Lucas's life was unapproachable.

Her heart bristled. Unapproachable and untrustworthy. She pulled the thin blanket up under her chin. The days of finding comfort in Riggen's arms had vanished into their past. "I don't know what to do." The words ripped her raw.

She'd been struggling under this load—this uncertainty—for five years. More like her whole life. Kat had always been the strong one. Liz was the one who couldn't hold anything together.

She couldn't stop the weakness that pushed her to share a portion of that weight with the man standing next to her.

"My sister and brother-in-law are leaving Colorado. This week. He's got a new job in California. As you can hear, Kat thinks I'm not fit to be a mother. That my baby would be happier, better off, in a more stable environment. With them." Her mind clouded from an entire lifetime of self-doubt. "I can't provide stability. Maybe she's right."

Riggen tilted his head to the left as if working out tension. "That's not true. Look at what you've accomplished all by yourself. Just because your life doesn't look how Kat thinks it should look doesn't make you irresponsible." His brows snapped together. "And it definitely doesn't make you unfit."

"Look at me, Riggen." She tried to wave one bandaged arm in his face, but it got stuck in the blanket. She ripped the blanket off and jabbed her arm his way. "I can't even keep *myself* safe. This isn't what he deserves."

"That's Kat's voice coming out of you. She is so wrong." Riggen slowly enunciated each word as he sank down on the bed.

"What about stalkers, Riggen?" Her voice squeaked. "I wouldn't have stalkers if I had a Kat-approved job."

"I don't want to discount the danger, but at this point, the stalker story is falling flat." He pulled his phone out and tapped the screen. "The attacker knew you'd be on the mountain. Knew you'd be alone. He came prepared. So why—after all the prep—did he leave you basically unharmed?"

Liz's heart pounded in her ears. "He shot at us."

"And missed." Riggen pulled up a photo on his phone and showed her a lethal-looking rifle and scope. "M&P10. Scary accurate gun. If he wanted to hit us, we wouldn't be sitting here discussing his motives. We'd be dead."

Liz pressed the back of her hand to her mouth to keep from being sick. Dead. What would Kat say to that? She grabbed at hope. "But we're not dead. And the drugs in my system…the nurse said it wasn't a fatal dose."

"True." Riggen scratched the scruff on his chin. "So why drug you? Why are you being targeted but not taken out? And by whom? This morning's perp is still locked up." He reached over and engulfed her hand in his, catapulting her back to starry nights and safe arms.

Her heart rate steadied. Warmth surrounded her despite the danger. "This all seems to be connected to the Sagebrush, but why?"

He intertwined their fingers. "Obviously whoever is sitting in El Paso County Jail is miscast as a stalker. We need to consider the possibility that there's a bigger threat here."

His hand was so warm and she was so tired. Could she trust him? Turn to him? She closed her eyes and shook her head. Kat always said parenting wasn't a lone job. Well, Lucas had more than one parent and that other parent wasn't Kat. That parent was the man sitting right in front of her. Had God thrown him back into her life for this moment?

She pulled back her hand to wipe the tears that snuck from behind her closed lids. She was tired of shouldering the weight of her world. Tired of always being on duty. Tired of standing alone.

She studied Riggen. His eyes narrowed under her perusal and he shifted closer. The fabric of his duty shirt drew taut across shoulders that had seen war and combat and who knew what else. Maybe she couldn't trust him with her heart, but she could trust his ability to keep her and Lucas safe. At least until this threat passed.

Liz felt her emotional footing falter as she stepped out onto the slippery slope of security. If she could guard her heart, then she and Lucas could take advantage of the protection Riggen would provide.

At the end of the day, it was either her heart's safety or her son's well-being. There was only one answer.

She swallowed the sensation that told her this was a bad idea and faced the man who had haunted every lonely dream. "We need you, Riggen."

Liz's vulnerability hit Riggen with a nagging sensation. Maybe this entire circumstance was more than coincidence. Maybe he didn't understand God at all.

She couldn't sit still. Or hide the pain and fear that clashed in the brown and green depths of her eyes. He could see she was trying, but every few moments her hands would flit from her lap to her face and back again in an agitated dance. Her helplessness touched parts of his heart that he thought had died in the dust with his squad.

He shifted to the edge of the bed and caught her hand before it flitted back to her hair. *Game face, soldier.* "Where is he?" His voice cracked. "Our—"

He couldn't push it out.

Shame flooded him. Yes, he'd thought God had punished him for his failure and that the only way he could keep his mistakes from hurting Liz was to disappear. But a new picture was being painted for him in real time. When he gave up on life, he gave up on them both.

Now, sitting with the mother of his son, harsh truth blinded him. Maybe it had been him, not a divine sentencing, that had killed their dreams. He shook his head. Either way, dead was dead.

"Kat lives just southeast of Colorado Springs. She's married to a pastor." Her answer dragged him from exploring this new and excruciating truth.

He hadn't seen that one coming. The sisters had never been what he'd consider religious. "Pastor?"

"A lot can change in five years." She took back her hand and turned to look out the darkening window. "For the better."

*For the better.* Did she mean Lucas and God? Or did she mean that she'd built a life without him?

His teeth ached and he relaxed his jaw. He didn't want to know the answer.

Rising from the bed, he walked to the curtained opening and watched the endless hospital activity. "I'm sure my boss would understand if I need to take time off." He scrubbed a hand over his face. Jones would love this. He could feel the promotion slip from his fingers. "I'll stay with you until this clears up."

The chaos outside their partition subsided for a moment and Riggen locked eyes with a man who was exiting the elevator. He stared straight through Riggen.

The air between them radiated with something undefinable. Recognition? A slow smile lifted the man's lips, raising sallow cheeks. It never reached his eyes.

An ER nurse pushed her computer cart between them, cutting off Riggen's view. Had he met the man before?

"How much time can you take off?" Liz's question came from behind him.

He turned to answer. "Couple weeks at least. I was going to use it to work on Dad's ranch, but that'll wait. The excursions aren't bringing in the money they used to. I've been living at the cabin and fixing up the property as a way to bring in more clients. Overnight bookings."

He pressed fingers into his temples. He didn't want to drain the family business if it couldn't employ two people. There had to be a way to get Dad's business on solid footing again.

He'd figure it out, but now wasn't the time. He turned back to the bustling hallway and searched the faces again. The man was gone.

Crossing his arms, he pushed away the ache that surfaced when he thought of Dad. "So, why did you stay with your sister if she was this controlling?"

Liz climbed from the bed and stood. She swayed and sat back on the edge, pulling her purse strap over her shoulder. "She took me in when I couldn't take care of myself. You think I should have repaid that by abandoning her?"

He held up his hands. "Touché. I'm not trying to find fault with your parenting. I'm the last person who should question your decisions. I didn't even know I had a son when I woke up this morning."

He froze. Opened his mouth but nothing came out.

Liz rose from the bed and edged closer. What must he look like to cause the expression of alarm that swept over her face?

"I…" He swallowed regret the size of a boulder. "I don't know his name."

She was close enough to slip her hand down his arm. "Lucas James."

Her answer knocked him back. Lucas. After Dad.

Her fingers stroked up and down his bicep. She was so close, he could feel the heat of her body. "I read about his death. I'm so sorry."

His vision blurred and he stared up at the ceiling, unprepared for the emotions that washed through him. Soft fingers sneaked into his hand, pulling him back to reality.

Somehow, this woman who he didn't deserve and no longer knew, understood him better than anyone else did.

Then she stepped back, her eyes blanked as if she'd spent her emotions and had nothing left to give. "Don't think that means I got over what you did. I need—" she gripped her purse strap so tight her fingers turned white "—answers."

The emotional tidal wave that came with the revelation of his son's name crashed against the blunt edge of her words. He nodded. "Thank you. For the name, I mean. As for the answers, we'll talk when we—" His words were swallowed in the explosion that threw him across the room.

"It's safe to say that our guy in lockup didn't do this." Rosche's irony bounced off the hospital's surveillance monitor as she squinted at the frozen footage.

Riggen's ears still hadn't stopped ringing. They had started as he'd watched Liz crumple to the floor after an explosion that was too close to his past. He'd failed again. Did he really think he could ever keep them safe?

Well, there was no going back now. He squirmed in his chair and focused on Rosche. "Safe bet. And—" he moved the ice pack from his eye to get a better look "—I think it's also safe to say that this, along with the Rohypnol, proves we're not dealing with a single stalker."

Rosche hit Pause as the screen showed the man who had made eye contact with Riggen in the hospital corridor attach a detonation device on the half wall surrounding the nurses' station. He'd then blended in with a group of interns and disappeared.

Thankfully, only one employee had been within the

blast radius. Last he had heard, she had escaped with a minor concussion and a few stitches.

"We'll have to wait for Arson to tell us what type of explosive was used, but it sure didn't pack much of a punch." Rosche stepped back from the monitor, letting Colorado Springs PD resume control of the recording equipment. She cocked her head to the side. "Why such a small payoff?"

Riggen pushed his aching body from the chair and joined Rosche at the side of the monitor. Recognition still tugged at his gut. "Rewind that," he asked the Colorado Springs Police detective. "I think I know him."

The footage moved in slow motion until the moment their suspect looked up into the security camera. The man smiled, as if not caring that the world witnessed. The detective paused the tape and Riggen peered into the man's eyes. Where had he seen him before?

Rosche looked over Riggen's shoulder. "It's like he's taunting us."

He nodded and leaned closer. "Or taunting Liz." The guy had something on his neck, just visible above his collar. He pointed. "There. I remember that distinctive tattoo." He snapped his fingers. "The memo a few months back, from Vice—he's wanted on human trafficking charges."

Both Rosche and the CSPD detective nodded. The memo had circulated to both departments. "So what's he doing terrorizing a travel blogger?" Rosche asked.

Riggen shoved his hand through his hair. It was grimy from the blast. "I think it's tied to Malcovitch and the traffickers Liz exposed."

Rosche pulled out her phone. "Our other guy has a

trafficking history, too." She typed for a moment before handing it to him.

Their first suspect's computerized criminal history filled Rosche's screen and Riggen read through the file. So was their first perpetrator a simple fan? Not a chance. He looked up. "It has to be Liz's Sagebrush review—"

"The Malcovitch write-up with the viral reach." Rosche nodded.

He handed the phone back. "Yeah."

"So we think her post is coming back to bite her five years later?"

"There's a good chance. We have the sagebrush in her canteen and the trafficking ties to both suspects."

Rosche handed a flash drive to the CSPD detective. The man inserted it into the hospital's computer to save the security footage.

"I'll check into it." Rosche pocketed the flash drive. "But Malcovitch is in prison and, from all accounts, he's a model inmate. Turned his life around when his wife and kids left. Even his known associates cut ties. He doesn't have the influence he once had. It's not likely he'd be able to orchestrate this."

Riggen couldn't argue but the evidence overwhelmingly pointed back to the Sagebrush. If the former owner didn't want revenge, who was terrorizing Liz? He tossed the Ziploc of melted ice into the trash and headed for the door. "Whatever is going on, I need to get Liz somewhere better protected."

Rosche popped a piece of gum in her mouth and chomped. "What are you thinking?"

"Out of the open. Somewhere less exposed. Less public."

"Ideas?"

He shook his head. "I haven't had time to shower since this started, let alone plan." He stopped in the doorway and turned back. "My most immediate priority is getting to my son."

Rosche choked. She hammered her chest as her eyes bulged. "Son?"

Funny. He'd never heard her voice hit that octave. Questions fired from her eyes, but he turned and stepped into the hallway. He couldn't answer the questions in his own mind. And Liz's questions still hung over his head like a storm cloud waiting to let loose.

It was time to hit the road.

"Yeah." He threw the quip over his shoulder. "But you're too late for the baby shower."

# SIX

A full moon hung heavy over Colorado Springs as Memorial's doors slid open. The wheels of Liz's borrowed wheelchair hit rough cement and she felt the transition deep. Every cell in her body hurt.

Riggen pushed her down the sidewalk. He was as silent as the night that surrounded them. The last thing she wanted right now was silence. Silence let her second-guess her desperate appeal for help. Silence let her sister's accusations roar through her thoughts. Silence didn't answer her questions.

Before the roar could overwhelm her, Rosche appeared, driving Riggen's truck under the pie-shaped overhang. The engine shuddered to a stop and the redhead climbed out. Riggen's dog nosed the back window, his breaths puffing at the glass. Rosche tossed the keys through the air and Riggen caught them one-handed.

"Thanks for driving up—" he nodded at the car "—and for bringing Yakub."

Rosche winked. "No problem."

She approached and held out her hand to tug Liz from the chair. "Take care of yourself. Three incidents in one day seems a bit overboard."

Liz couldn't stop giggles from overpowering her exhausted body. "Believe me—" she gasped for air "—I'm as finished with this as you."

Rosche nodded, the overhead lights reflected in her green eyes. She pushed the wheelchair back toward the ER entrance and turned to wiggle her fingers over one shoulder. "Stay low, both of you."

Liz was watching Rosche's retreating back when warmth from Riggen's hand on her own back shot energy up her spine. She jerked, the motion slicing pain through her bruised ribs.

He didn't remove his hand, just held her gaze while emotions chased each other across his face. She caught the last one because she knew it well. Fear.

But fear of what?

"Time to go." He guided her to the passenger door, sliding his hand from her waist to her arm as he helped her climb inside. A line of fire trailed after his touch. She shook it off.

"Thanks." She refused to meet his eyes, closing the door to barricade herself from the feelings he stirred. Complicating the situation with long-dead emotions wouldn't do anybody any favors. The feelings he was raising were simply a product of their traumatic day. Nothing more.

Riggen jogged to the driver's side, his eyes constantly scanning their surroundings. The parking lot. The hospital. Even the air. As soon as his foot cleared the frame, he slammed the door and fired up the engine.

He cut a glance at her as they sped away from the building. "Does Kat know we're on the way?"

The acceleration jerked her neck muscles and pulled a groan from her throat. "She didn't even ask if I was okay. Just wanted to know if Lucas would be safe when we took him."

She looked down at her romper. The baby blue was stained an ugly brown with drops of her own blood. "I don't want to scare him. What if he's awake and sees me like this?"

The day had left its mark on Riggen, as well. She pointed at his pants. "You're a mess, too."

He nodded his head toward the back of the cab. "I always carry a change of clothes. I'll pull something else on."

Tears of frustration pricked the backs of her eyes. She pinched herself to maintain control. "Of course, *you* can." Her voice shook. She pinched harder. She wouldn't cave to the anxiety that was riding her. She knew it wouldn't release control without a fight.

Drawing her knees up, she laid her face on them. *Be strong.* Her legs grew wet as tears dripped on the ripped fabric of her romper. She had nothing left but a crying heart, so she let it cry out to God. *Be my strength.*

The Bronco rocked gently. It should be soothing. It wasn't. Only this morning, she'd been ready to take on the world, climb a mountain, face down her past, and forge a new future for herself and Lucas.

Now her past was threatening to crash her future in ways she'd never seen coming and she couldn't even pull back on her safe-mom façade. The pounding started behind her temples again. The thought of Kat's reaction to her appearance pulsed icy cold dread through her veins.

Maybe her sister was right. Maybe she wasn't enough. The thought made her want to run for the mountains. The explosion had obliterated her patchwork armor and she couldn't piece it back together.

The Bronco slowed. The click-clack of the turn signal echoed in the silent interior. She rubbed her face into her legs and wiped away any evidence that she didn't have it all together. She couldn't be vulnerable. Not now. Not before going home. And definitely not with Riggen.

Liz pushed herself up and straightened her shoulders. They were pulling into a twenty-four-hour shopping center. Bright lights flickered across the deserted parking lot and cast shadows on Riggen's face.

He pulled in as close to the retail entrance as possible then turned to her and draped his arm across the back of her seat. Yakub rested his head on Riggen's shoulder. They both stared. At her.

"Good grief." She hiccupped. "What?"

"Let's run in for clean clothes." He reached over with his free arm and traced a finger down her cheek. When he pulled back, his fingertip glistened with tears.

Then he swiveled with the grace of the mountain climber he was and grabbed a duffel from the floorboard of his back seat. He dug around for a moment. "Here." He handed her a windbreaker. "To cover some of the blood."

She stared at it a moment before shrugging into it. The scent of Riggen cocooned her. She immediately felt secure. Like a child in strong arms. She ignored her traitorous senses and risked a look into his gray eyes. "Thanks."

His expression was unreadable. "No problem."

He sank back into his own seat and scanned the lot. Checked the mirrors. "No one followed us from the hospital. But this day has me on edge." He yanked the door handle and jumped out. "Let's do this as fast as possible."

She nodded. He was at her side before both of her

feet hit the pavement. This time when he offered his hand, she almost wanted to take it.

They hadn't been followed, but he wasn't taking any chances. Riggen kept an eye on the lot while he shot off a text to a friend at CSPD. He could trust a fellow cop to watch their backs while he and Liz were in the store.

He placed a hand on Liz's back and guided her the short distance from the Bronco to the store entrance. As they hit the crosswalk, a black sedan pulled in. Every nerve in his body fired.

*Am I even capable of protecting them?*

He pushed the thought away and quickened their pace. What choice did he have but to try? He had a responsibility to Liz and their son. Just like he'd had a responsibility that day in Iraq. His heart thudded. Could this be God giving him a chance to redeem his failure?

Trevor's words played through his mind like a broken record. *There's nothing more important than family.*

He'd thought letting Liz go had been his just punishment. That if he stayed, the consequences to his mistakes would rain down on her, too.

But even if God hadn't had it out for him, that still didn't mean he deserved Liz. He glanced at her. Not now that he could see the damage he'd caused.

A heavy sigh escaped as they entered into safety through the sliding doors of the store. He'd do his duty by Liz until she found someone who deserved her. Until she was safe.

Soft rock trickled from the overhead speakers, lulling the few late-night shoppers who lazed down empty aisles. No one looked up. Good. The less attention they drew, the better.

Liz booked toward the clothing, her tangled hair swaying with each step. He followed slightly behind, analyzing every inch of the layout.

Within moments, she had a fitted long-sleeved T-shirt and a pair of sweats draped over her arm. She nodded her head at the register, still blissfully unaware of the smudges of blood and dust that caked her forehead.

He matched her pace and tapped the clothing. "Aren't you going to try them on?"

She slid a look at him. The first hint of a smile peeked through. "I'll be fine."

He shrugged and sidestepped an impulse bin in the middle of the aisle then halted, his attention captured by the contents of the display. Toy cars.

Little boys liked cars. At least he had. A dull ache started behind his eyes and he rubbed the back of his neck. Grabbing a three-pack from the bin, he sprinted to catch up to Liz, who was already setting her items on the self-checkout.

She ran her sweats over the scanner, the infrared light bouncing off the tag's bar code. He threw the Hot Wheels onto the counter and she paused, her brow arching. He just shrugged. She scanned the toy and then froze, her hand halfway from the scanner to the bag.

"What's wrong?"

She didn't move. Her face, the perfect picture of confusion. "I don't have my purse."

He removed the Hot Wheels package from her immobilized hand and dropped it in the shopping bag before grabbing a Hershey bar. "Was there anything else you needed?"

She shook her head, her hazel eyes unreadable. He grabbed his wallet and stepped closer, leaning his head close to hers. "It's okay, Lizzy. Your purse is in the back of the Bronco, in the bag from the hospital."

She sniffed as he slid his credit card through the card reader.

"Why didn't you tell me?"

He shrugged. "You didn't need it. I didn't see the point." He signed the signature pad and gathered their shopping bags.

"I needed to buy clothes."

He turned at her short tone. Better tread carefully. Shifting all the bags to one hand, he placed the other on her back and steered her toward the restrooms. "It didn't occur to me that you'd be upset."

Her back muscles tightened under his palm. "A lot of things must not occur to you. Like letting the woman you're engaged to know why you're never coming back." She ducked away from him. Her voice was low and trembling. "It wasn't your decision to make. I can take care of myself."

What decision was she talking about? The purchase or their engagement? The dull ache behind his eyes morphed into full-blown throbbing. He gave a tight smile to the concerned-looking door attendant as they exited the main entrance and approached the women's restroom.

Liz hustled toward the restroom door but he stopped her with a hand to her wrist. When she looked up, a wisp the color of butterscotch fell across her nose. He pushed it aside and tucked it behind her ear. "I've no doubt you can take care of yourself, and do an amazing job, but I wanted to take care of this for you."

She grabbed the bag from his hand. "I don't understand why. You didn't want to take care of me before." Then she was gone, leaving him wondering what to do next.

\* \* \*

Liz scowled at her grainy reflection in the stainless-steel towel dispenser. It didn't matter how heartfelt his words sounded, they couldn't be trusted. Balling up the sopping paper towel she had dried her hands and face with, she threw it into the bathroom's overflowing trash can.

The man had abandoned her to raise a son alone. No explanation. Just a single note. One note that had erased a future of promises. She scooped her hair and secured it on her head with a dingy hair tie that had somehow survived both crash and explosion.

She'd forged into the murky waters of "why" right before the explosion rocked her hospital room. But was there really any explanation that would make it all right? Her heart climbed into her throat. Did she really want to hear him explain why she hadn't been enough?

Nothing would erase the years of pain. And now she was stuck with the man who had broken her heart with no hope of shaking him loose until whoever was targeting her either lost interest or was put behind bars.

That reality alone sent any desire for reconciliation right out the window.

She pulled her ponytail tight. Heartfelt words aside, the man hadn't even said he was sorry. Her shoulders stiffened. She'd keep her distance.

Her soiled romper lay on the counter, ruined. No amount of laundering would save it. She stuffed it into a discarded grocery bag and pushed it far into the trash, feeling every inch the mess-up Kat thought she was.

With one last peek at the mirror, she turned to charge back into her new reality. After yanking open the heavy metal door, she crashed straight into Riggen's back.

What was he doing? He turned to her and nodded before pointing at the phone on his ear.

Shimmying past, she stood beside him. All the fight she had mustered slowly drained into the dirty floor at her feet.

"Unbelievable." He shook his head. "Same story?"

Liz cocked an eyebrow, but he only held up a finger. She tapped her foot on the worn rug. Whatever patience she'd had today had been lost somewhere between being tied up and drugged.

"Keep me updated," Riggen said and ended the call. He cut his hand toward the door, motioning them outside. "CSPD arrested our guy from the hospital about half an hour ago. He walked right into their main office and confessed."

She followed his lead, her heart thrumming in her ears.

"He spouted the same story as the first guy."

Her toe hit the curb and she stumbled into the crosswalk. Riggen caught her and nestled her close, under the safe weight of his arm.

"Another alleged stalker. The stories are identical. Down to the soul-mate line." Riggen guided them to the Bronco, his arm never leaving her shoulder. "You don't have some weird fan club you haven't told me about, do you?"

"Yeah. They meet quarterly and plan my demise." She elbowed his ribs. "You can sign up for the newsletter."

He stopped at the Bronco. "CSPD is going to collaborate with Rosche on the investigation. They'll get further working together."

Liz climbed in, wanting to believe that was true. But this new development was exhausting and terrifying.

Riggen dropped their bags onto the floorboard at her feet and leaned against the door frame, his biceps flexing. "I called my station while you were changing and was cleared for a leave of absence." His jawline hardened. "I want to stay close to you until this is resolved."

She wrapped her arms around Yakub, reluctantly giving mental points to Rosche for bringing the dog to the hospital. Stuck with Riggen wasn't the stuff of dreams, but she was realistic enough to begin admitting it was what she needed. *What they needed.* There had to be gratitude somewhere inside her. She dug deep and pushed it out.

"Thanks." She scratched behind Yakub's ears. "So that takes care of the police department, but what about your side gig—your business?"

He pushed off the door frame, his shirt stretching as he moved. "Trevor's got it under control. He's used to it. He handled it fine while I was gone." He pushed her door shut.

And with that, the wave of turmoil she'd ridden through the last twelve hours crashed like a tidal wave onto her weary shoulders. She didn't even know when he'd come home to Manitou Springs. How long had they lived so close but so far from each other's lives?

If nothing else had been clear today, one thing was. Riggen needed to stay at arm's length, where he belonged.

# SEVEN

It was well after midnight when Riggen pulled up to a single-level ranch on the outskirts of Colorado Springs. A green light illuminated the driveway, its emerald rays showing military support. He sent Liz a searching look.

She nodded. "Retired Army. Chaplain's assistant."

He shifted into Park. He hadn't been expecting Liz's brother-in-law to be a veteran—like him. He scratched his jawline and climbed out. The Hot Wheels hung from his grip like a ten-pound weight as he searched the street.

Were they being watched? Cold swept his body. He scanned three-hundred-and-sixty degrees, watching for signs of movement. All was quiet. Other than a stray cat, the street slept on—unaware of the danger that plagued his and Liz's steps.

A CSPD cruiser sat at the curb, keeping an eye on the home. He nodded at the officer before turning and trudging up the sidewalk. Each footfall thudded through the silent night.

Liz inserted a key into the metal door. He took in the well-manicured landscaping that fronted the cozy house and tried to gulp back the guilt that pummeled his gut.

Riggen hadn't stepped foot inside a pastor's house since his father died a little more than five years earlier. And back then, he'd only pretended interest in church out of loyalty to his father. He'd never been religious himself. Would the last few years have turned out differently if he had actually tried following the Jesus Dad had preached?

He shook his arms out as if he could shake off all what-ifs. Now wasn't the time. He had enough to think about. When he stepped foot over that threshold, his life would forever change.

He entered the still foyer behind Liz. Footfalls sounded from deep inside the home. His heart slammed around his rib cage like a wild animal trying to escape and sweat dampened the clean Henley he'd thrown on. He was more terrified at this moment than at any other of his adult life. Including on the battlefield.

He could do this. It was just one little boy.

His little boy.

The Hot Wheel package crackled under his death grip. Light flipped on at the end of the hallway, silhouetting Kat, a slight brunette with shadows under her eyes. The years had added streaks of gray through her now-short hair.

"What's going on?" Kat's words were as piercing as the daggers she shot from her eyes.

Liz slid past her sister and disappeared around the corner. "I don't see that there's more to say than we already discussed." Her retort faded as she melted into the home's interior.

Riggen followed down the dim hall, passing family pictures and discarded toys. Nodding at Kat, he blinked hard, his eyes fighting to adjust to the harsher light of the kitchen.

"They're in the den." Kat folded her arms and tilted her head.

He rolled his shoulders back, refusing to be cowed by the look. "I wish we could be meeting again under better circumstances."

She motioned for him to follow her. "We all have regrets." Stepping back, Kat held her hand out to allow Riggen first entrance into the den.

He made it about two steps before all air was knocked from his body. Liz knelt in the middle of the den, next to a man in a wheelchair. A sleeping boy lay in his arms.

His son.

"It's really remarkable." Kat shifted next to Riggen.

He looked down at her. He'd already forgotten she was there.

Her brow raised. "He looks just like you."

It was no use trying to answer. The shock had removed all normal functioning ability. From the swirling tip of his cowlick to his tiny toes, Riggen had never seen a more perfect child.

A fierce protective instinct surged through him and pushed him off balance. He gripped the railing that separated the kitchen from the den. Liz raised her head, catching his eye. She nodded as if understanding the feelings blasting through him.

Cupping Lucas's head with her hand, Liz spoke softly to her brother-in-law before scooping the boy into her arms. Then she was walking toward Riggen and everything slowed. Her mouth was moving. He knew there were words coming out and that they were meant for him, but all he could hear was the pounding of his own heart.

She stopped in front of him, his son so close that all he had to do was to reach out a finger to touch the porcelain skin of the little boy's cheek. Riggen tore his eyes from Lucas and looked at Liz.

She jerked her head in the direction of the hallway. "Let's get his things."

He looked over her head at the man he'd yet to be introduced to, and swallowed, his throat raw. "Thanks."

Liz's brother-in-law inclined his head, understanding volleying between them.

Together, Riggen and Liz walked down a cramped hallway to Liz and Lucas's room. She sank onto a twin-size bed that was covered with more cartoon blankets than he'd ever seen in his life. Her eyes drifted shut and she hummed a quiet lullaby. She was the picture of exhaustion.

He leaned against the doorway for support. The stakes had just been raised three hundred percent and Riggen hadn't been prepared for it—this feeling of complete responsibility.

His gaze ran the length of his son before settling on Liz's face. "He's beautiful."

"He is." Liz snuggled Lucas farther into her neck as the boy continued sleeping.

Riggen crossed his arms over his chest and shifted on anxious legs that were screaming for a run. He nodded his head back the way they'd come. "Your sister is…"

"Poised? Protective? Capable?"

None of those words summed up his current impression, though obviously they summed Liz's feelings of inadequacy. He pushed off the door frame and walked to the rocking chair next to the bed. "I was going to say still overbearing. When did she get married?"

Liz's soft humming stopped and she ran her fingers through Lucas's hair. "Almost five years. She and John met while I was pregnant."

He nodded.

"I was trying to find you." Her voice cracked and she shrugged. "We found John instead."

The hurt in her tone punctured his heart. He reached across the toy-strewed floor that separated them and squeezed her knee. "I'm sorry."

She shook her head. "It is what it is. Now Kat has John and Lucas has us all. One big, happy family." Irony dripped from her reply.

He pulled back. "So, what happened to him?"

"John?" she asked. "Drove over an IED. Paralyzed from the crash." Her voice lowered. "He can't father children. I think it makes Kat even more overprotective of Lucas. They've considered adopting but…well, with Lucas here, they were content."

"And he's okay with that?" Confusion bubbled from his throat. Liz's brother-in-law was a pastor. If anyone should be exempt from such a disaster, it should be him. Riggen gripped the chair's handles. But then again, Dad hadn't been exempt.

Liz's forehead scrunched. "Okay with what?"

"Okay that the God he serves let him be paralyzed."

She laid Lucas down on his pillow and pulled the covers up to his chin. "I asked him the same thing once." She raised a brow. "When my anxiety had the best of me. He said sometimes things just happen. If we try to make sense of the why, we'll go crazy." She settled back on the bed and pulled her legs up, resting her chin on her knees. "Sometimes we're harmed from the sin of others, sometimes from the result of natural processes, and sometimes from our own neglect or distraction."

He cringed. The memories he always tried to push away crowded his brain. War or disregard of a direct command? Had his disaster risen from the sin of others or his own neglect?

She raised her face and speared him with pure conviction. "The sense comes from how God shapes us as we walk through the wreckage. How do we respond? Do we pull away from His touch and let bitterness harden us or do we run full-speed into God's embrace so He can shine His light through our brokenness?"

"What can possibly shine about a loss like that?" His breath choked in his chest.

"Contentment. And peace. John has taught me to run full-speed after God." She rubbed Lucas's back.

Riggen couldn't feel more exposed if she had sliced him open and spilled his deepest struggles on the cartooned coverlet she sat on. Running full-speed toward peace? He'd been trying to do that for the last five years but inside…he was paralyzed.

"And you?" He broke the silence. "Could you see yourself like Kat? Loving a man who couldn't father children?"

A fine line formed between her brows as bewilderment swept across her face.

"Never mind." He grated the words out. What was he thinking? There was no future for them. Nothing had changed. He still didn't deserve her. He turned his attention to the stuffed animals that dotted the bed.

Liz fiddled with Lucas's blanket, confusion lingering in the brown-and-green flecks of her eyes. "What do you mean?"

Moments ticked by with only Lucas's rhythmic breathing to break the silence. Riggen felt as if opportunity was knocking on a door he couldn't open. No matter how he looked at it, he had lost.

His fingers dug into the wood of the rocking chair. If the reason he couldn't father children was God's retribution for the lives Riggen couldn't save, then who was he to grasp a forbidden life? But, if this new disquieting conviction that he had had God all wrong was right, then his own treatment of Liz had been unforgivable.

He stared deep into her eyes, the flickering moonlight glinting in their depths. Either way, he didn't deserve Elizabeth Hart and no matter how badly his arms itched to pull her close the way he once had, he needed to keep his distance.

He tried to push an answer through his dry lips but his tongue tied as her eyes flickered with more intensity.

Warning pinged in his brain. Too much intensity. That wasn't the flickering of the moon. He jumped from the chair and yanked the window wide open. Smoke stung his eyes. Flames were licking up the legs of the pergola that covered the back deck.

He pulled his phone out and dialed 9-1-1 as he squashed all of his renegade feelings back where they belonged. His emotions needed to go on the back burner before his family's safety went up in flames.

Kat paced the front lawn, an angry mamma bear waiting to pounce on someone. *Please, God, don't let it be me.* Liz buckled a still-sleeping Lucas into a car seat in the back of Riggen's Bronco.

She willed Riggen to finish his huddle with the Colorado Springs' police officers and fire captain before Kat's powerful attention turned her way. She couldn't handle another lecture. The guilt was about to eat her alive. This was all her fault.

Flames shot over the top of Kat and John's rented home. The sight crushed any remaining shreds of courage she'd been holding. Danger and destruction were following her like a mountain lion after the kill. She'd always been more trouble than she was worth.

Was that why Riggen had left?

She inched as close as she could to the car seat and nuzzled her face into Lucas's neck. Her brain was shutting down. It couldn't handle her relentless need to process the situation. Who was behind this? Why terrorize her? Why had Riggen left? Why hadn't he run again?

John pushed his wheelchair toward the open door of the Bronco, his arm muscles bulging with each rotation over the ever-dampening grass. He ramped onto the driveway, a reassuring smile on his face, and pointed at her head. "You're doing two things."

Liz sat straight and puffed her cheeks full of air before letting her sigh trickle out. He usually read what was going on under the surface and she wasn't sure she wanted to hear what he saw. "What?"

"First, you're forgetting God loves you deeply and will take care of you." He sent a covert glance at his wife before continuing. "And second, you're forgetting Kat is not in control."

She couldn't stop the snort that fell out.

"As much as she can't stand moving without you and Lucas, deep down she knows he's your child." A mask of sadness fell over John's face. "We both understand the best place for him is with you."

Liz stared past John at the flames that refused to bow to the steady attack of water. Did they understand that? She wasn't sure she did. "Even now? When I don't know what's going on or who is behind this?"

John reached out to pat her knee. "You're forgetting number one again. God will take care of you. He knows exactly who's behind this. Besides—" he thumbed at Riggen, who was breaking away from the huddle and heading their way "—looks like He's already sent you a protector."

Her heart skipped a beat as she caught Riggen's bloodshot eyes. Had God sent Riggen? Is that why he hadn't run again yet?

As he got closer, she could see his face sported a five-o'clock shadow. He rubbed the back of his neck, his mouth a grim line. "The captain expects to have this under control soon."

He turned to John and laid a hand on the man's shoulder. "Do you have somewhere to stay?"

John nodded. "We're leaving day after tomorrow. Most of our belongings are already packed up in the moving van. It won't be a problem to hole up in a motel for the night."

"That would be best. I'm sorry to say this may delay your departure."

Kat joined them and hitched a hand to her hip. "Of course it will. Perfect."

Liz retreated into the interior of the Bronco.

"Climb out of the car, Elizabeth. Lucas will need to go with us to the—"

John placed a hand on his wife's arm, halting her.

"Number two." He winked at Liz, his eyes tired but strong. "*If—*" he stressed the word "—you or Lucas need our help, you will always have a place to stay with us."

As Kat's shocked look melted into an angry barrage, John wheeled himself back and shut Liz's door.

Riggen nodded at her brother-in-law and trotted around to the driver's side, hopping in and locking the doors before Liz could process the fact that they were driving away from her sister's home toward free road.

# EIGHT

Buildings whizzed by as they left Colorado Springs behind for Interstate 24. Liz climbed over the armrest and settled into the front seat. She gripped the door handle. Nothing about tonight had been smooth riding.

Riggen flipped the turn signal and merged. It was amazing that Lucas had never woken, even during the hoopla of the fire. She turned to look at her baby, tears blurring her view.

She wiped them away. Lucas was curled up against the side of his car seat. And Yakub—a giggle blubbered past her tears—lay with his head in Lucas's lap, guarding his pack's newest addition.

She closed her eyes and thanked God that Lucas hadn't seen the flames. Or witnessed Kat's displeasure. An invisible hand squeezed her chest. All of their belongings were in that house and it was hard to leave them behind. Now it would be up to Kat to pack up whatever survived the fire—just one more ball that she'd dropped.

God willing, the fire would be contained before it destroyed a lifetime of memories. Five years of Lucas's life. Pictures. Baby books. Toys. And her own memories.

The only pictures she and Kat had of their family before Mom died, Dad disappeared, and they had landed in foster care. She stuffed her fist into her mouth to keep from crying out.

*Be strong and courageous.* As brave as she pretended to be in front of Riggen, Liz wasn't one-hundred-percent sure she was ready to be pushed onto this type of raging sea. She stared out the window. *What are You doing, God?*

But what other choice did she have? The only step she could take was the one that led her closer to God. There was no other place to go. Unfortunately, that step was taking her closer to Riggen, as well. But she had to take it, even if it meant heading into the terrifying waves of past hurts.

*I will not be afraid.* She hugged her arms around herself and pressed into the cracked leather of Riggen's Bronco, opening her heart to peace. Who was behind this? And why now? She let her head bounce against the old seat as the truck careened down the highway.

He changed lanes and passed a semi. Its beams flashed in his side mirrors and blinded her even as the lights of Colorado Springs faded behind them. But they weren't turning off toward the main drag of Manitou. Instead, Riggen accelerated down the nearly empty highway.

He raked his fingers through his hair. "I don't know much about what your normal looks like anymore, but I'm assuming this hasn't been a typical day."

She kicked her feet up on the dashboard and pointed her toes at the roof. "You'd be right about that."

"Have you had any harassment over the Sagebrush in the past?"

"Not since the original post went viral." She closed her eyes and remembered. "At first, Malcovitch was furious. But his threats—" she turned to Riggen "—which never escalated to this level, petered out after his sentencing. Then the story eventually sputtered down to nothing."

Riggen slowed to turn onto Serpentine Drive. They passed the entrance to Rainbow Falls and continued following curvy mountain roads.

"Any renewed interest lately?"

"In the Sagebrush article?" Her blog traffic had hit and remained at record levels after that post. But not solely because of it. Her brand—More Than A Destination—had been forged through hand-in-hand collaboration with regional tourism leaders. She'd worked hard to promote and display Colorado's beauty and uniqueness. Her following had grown from there.

"No. I try to steer traffic away from that post. I was still finding my niche back then. Now?" She lifted her shoulders and let them fall. "The gotcha angle doesn't fit my brand anymore."

His forehead puckered.

"It has a lot to do with Lucas." She nodded at the back seat. "When that post went viral, I was as surprised as anyone. I never expected so much exposure. But the visibility came with the Malcovitch threats.

"I had our son's safety to consider and the harassment was making me fall apart. It was never overt enough to report, but he had his goons stalking me, sending bouquets of sagebrush to my house, slashing my tires, calling and hanging up.

"It was enough to scare me to death and no one was there to help but Kat and John. The anxiety of wondering how I could keep my baby safe was too much to handle. No wonder Kat thinks I need her to run my life. I was definitely having problems handling it then." She winced at the look of pain that flashed across Riggen's face.

Well, she couldn't change the truth to make it more palatable for the man who had disappeared on her. "So I focused less on finding the most interesting angle and just went with painting a compelling picture that would lure people from behind their computer screens and into the waiting arms of nature. Anyway, it pays."

"But not enough to move away from John and Kat?"

"Ouch. Straight for the jugular. No, not always. But I have a steady job lined up with *American Travel*. It's good money. Enough money. And it's remote work."

At the mention of the premier, regional travel magazine, Riggen emitted a low whistle. "I'm proud of you, Lizzy."

Ridiculous warmth flowed from her heart down into her belly at his words. "Thanks. It's not a sure thing... yet." She massaged the sore muscles in her neck. "If I can prove that my voice meshes with their corporate vision, then I'll get the open travel editor position. Kimberly wants proof I'm a good match.

"My opportunity is Friday at the Rocky Mountain Travel and Adventure Expo. It's kind of a big deal." She stuck her hands under her legs and leaned forward. "Needless to say, I've put the Sagebrush behind me, except..."

"What?"

She chewed her bottom lip. "Except for a strange comment on the Sagebrush blog entry last week. It slipped my mind until now."

"What did it say?"

"'Your fifteen minutes has come to an end.'"

His hands gripped the steering wheel until each knuckle stood out as a white-tipped peak. "Who made the comment?"

"No clue. My filter placed it into the blocked comments. I barely paid it any attention."

A lone streetlight flashed across the granite-like set of his jaw and then they were driving away from the last cluster of homes and farther into the inky darkness of the mountainside. "I'd like to take a look at the back end of your web site. I have a friend who can track those things."

"Police?"

He gave her a bemused look. "Faster."

The higher the Bronco climbed, the lower her stomach plummeted. Her usernames, passwords and saved log-ins were on her laptop—and that was at the Juniper. She couldn't go back there tonight, and she couldn't go home. She was anchorless, at sea, and at the mercy of her ex-fiancé.

She leaned her head against the cool glass of his window. For once she wished she could sit and throw a Lucas-worthy tantrum. But there were no tears left.

She just stared into the dark night. The sky was backlit by a million flickering wishes. "Yeah," she mumbled. "Maybe."

"Make yourself at home." Riggen placed Liz's plastic bag on the Price cabin's kitchen island and leaned against the wooden surface before pulling up his phone's contact list.

He scrolled through the names to find Alex Ivie. He

and Alex had served together until the explosion. The injuries Alex sustained had retired him early. Now he was pursuing a different kind of fight—contracting to the FBI as an ethical hacker.

Just the guy they needed tonight. Riggen typed out a text, asking for help in finding the origin of Liz's blog comment.

Setting his phone down, he returned his attention to Liz and Lucas. Liz puttered around the cabin, cradling their son against her, Lucas's little-boy body almost engulfing her. Lucas still slept. Riggen grinned. Maybe the boy took after his old man in more than looks. The little guy could probably sleep through an air strike.

Walking deeper into the cabin's main area, Liz turned in a circle. Her eyes roved over every inch of the open living space as she trudged across the worn cowskin rug into the fully updated kitchen.

She was graceful even while her arms overflowed with sleeping boy. When she reached the farmhouse dining table, she sank into a cushioned chair and snuggled Lucas closer.

His son stirred and nuzzled his face into Liz's neck, mussing his cowlick against her chin. Riggen's breath caught. *His son.*

They looked lost and vulnerable. He shifted against the island. If anything could drive a man to prayer, it was this.

No matter how he wanted to spell it out, they were tied together. Family. He'd overheard John telling Liz that God had sent her a protector. That single sentence had sparked a sliver of hope that refused to be snuffed.

He ripped his eyes from Liz and Lucas to double-check that the cabin door was locked. Somewhere out there, someone wanted to harm his family. It would be nice to lean on someone stronger than himself.

Then again, Dad had relied on God. He stiffened. Look where Dad's trust had gotten him—dead from a heart attack in the prime of his life. He should be here, teaching his grandson to fish and climb and ride.

Riggen shoved his hand through his hair and pushed away from the counter. "You'll both be safe here while we figure out our next steps."

Liz startled at his voice then stared at him a moment before nodding. The lids over her hazel eyes were drooping. Was she taking in his words or just fighting to stay awake? He lumbered to the closet, each worn pine board groaning under his tread.

"No one would link this place to me," she agreed. "I never even told John and Kat about it."

He opened the closet door, pulled down a quilt and tossed the bedclothes on the couch. He'd bunk down here and let Liz and Lucas sleep in the bed that dominated the open loft above them.

He turned back to Liz and found her shoulders were drooping. He plopped on the couch arm. "Would you like to head to bed? Or I can rustle up a midnight snack if you prefer."

Lucas stirred in Liz's arms and sat upright for the first time that night. His hair stood on end and he unplugged his thumb from his mouth before fisting the sleep from his eyes. "I'm hungry."

Liz straightened and tickled his belly. "You wake up in a strange place with a strange man and the first thing you say is 'I'm hungry'?"

*Strange man?* Liz's words were like a fist in the eye. He was a stranger with no place in their lives.

Lucas lifted tiny shoulders to even tinier ears and let them fall back. His scrunched brow said he didn't appreciate being questioned. "My tummy wants food." The boy gave Liz a coy look before diving back into his tattered blanket. Watching them, Riggen could see Liz was putty in his son's hands.

Liz turned to him with a questioning look and he swept his arm at the efficiency-size kitchen behind him.

"We keep the freezer pretty well stocked." He jumped up and headed to the kitchen, ruffling Lucas's hair on the way by. "My specialty is mac and cheese."

Giggles ignited behind him. He turned and winked before pulling open the freezer door.

"Mac and cheese please," Lucas said. But it sounded more like "pwease." And just like that, Riggen felt his heart reduced to the same putty-status as Liz's.

"Coming right up, buddy." He pulled out the cardboard box. "Anything for your momma?"

"Momma wikes russel snouts." Lucas shuddemred.

Riggen caught Liz's eye just as she stuffed a hand over the lower half of her face. Her eyes twinkled above her fingers.

"That sounds awful." Riggen mimicked Lucas's shudder. "I don't have any of those." He stuck his index finger to the side of his chin in exaggerated thought. "But…what do you think about…mac and cheese?"

Lucas fist-pumped the air. "Yes!"

Liz snuggled Lucas until he sighed and pushed away to explore his new territory.

"He's not shy, is he?" Riggen pulled out three frozen meals and set them on the counter.

Liz joined him, opening drawer after drawer until she reached the flatware. "No. That's one of the things

I love most about him." Her eyes clouded. "Life is such an adventure to him. I hope he never loses that."

He took the fork she held out. "Have you lost that?"

Her face blanked and she pushed the drawer closed. "Sometimes adventure doesn't seem worth the pain." Reaching across him, she grabbed one of the boxes, ripped it open, and then stood on tiptoes to place the tray in the microwave oven.

His phone vibrated against the granite countertop and he stepped away from her to glance at the screen.

Love to help. Send the info.-Alex

Riggen wiped his hands down his pant legs and picked up the phone to respond.

Don't have passwords now. Will let you know when we get them.

His phone buzzed again before he could put it back down.

Funny you think I need them. Just send web address.

Riggen shook his head. Ethical hacker. Thankfully, Alex stayed in the realm of integrity. He set the phone down and looked at Liz. "We have help on tracking that comment."

Her eyebrows touched the wisps of bangs that refused to stay put. "Do you think it'll help?"

"He's the most effective tech resource I have. If there's anything behind that comment, he'll ferret it out."

She nodded, relief sweeping the signs of tension from her forehead.

Lucas came crashing back into the kitchen, Yakub at his heels. "Look what I found!" He grasped the Hot Wheels package to his chest.

Riggen set another freezer tray in the microwave. "They're all yours, buddy."

"Thank you, sir." Lucas plopped down in the middle of the kitchen floor and tore into the package. Soon, he was zooming cars along a tile-and-grout track.

Riggen leaned against the counter and watched. His son's manners were impressive. What was more impressive was that Liz had done this all on her own. The microwave dinged behind him and Riggen whirled to remove the steaming tray, suddenly desperate to shut the sweet display from his sight.

Liz was there because she needed him. It was simple logic. When this was over, he'd just be the strange man again. He listened to Liz and Lucas play, their giggles and chatter filling the lonely cabin space. They were complete—and better off—without him.

# NINE

Liz cuddled Lucas under Riggen's warm down comforter and listened as the man himself washed dishes in the kitchen below. He'd insisted she and Lucas go on to bed as he cleaned up alone, mumbling something about rest after trauma.

She pulled Lucas's warm body closer. But had there been more to it? Was he regretting taking on the role of protector now that he was faced with the reality of a son?

"Mama?" Lucas turned in her arms and waited, thumb in mouth, his face contorted into a concerned frown.

"Yes, sweetheart?" She rubbed the worry crease in the middle of his forehead.

"Why was that man sad?"

Her sigh whooshed the bangs away from Lucas's face. Her sweet boy was observant, but she didn't even have the beginnings of an answer. She wished she had. For him. For herself. For Riggen. The realization that she cared how Riggen felt floored her.

She stared over Lucas's head into the darkened cabin, the faint sounds of Riggen preparing for bed drifting up to the loft. "He's had a rough day."

Lucas, in typical four-year-old fashion, accepted the answer at face value and clamped back onto his thumb, his eyelids drooping slowly until they closed.

"He'll be better tomorrow. Do you want to know why?" Liz kissed the crook of Lucas's neck, tickling his warm skin with a shower of love. Giggles washed over her like rays of moonlight.

"Because we'll have an adventure?" he answered, breathless from giggling.

"You betcha." They leaned heads together and nestled back into the plush pillows. Liz prayed her words were true.

Lucas relaxed and his breathing evened into the comfortable sound of childhood trust. What would she do to have his innocence again? She turned and kissed his perfect cheek. To be able to rest in the absolute peace of knowing she was wanted and loved.

"May you never know any different." She could almost feel the vibration of Dad's old Buick under her, the scratchy seat cover on her legs. He'd promised to come back, just like Riggen had. Both men's promises had turned out false.

Moonlight poured through the two-story picture window and curtained their bed. In the morning, they'd look out on Pikes Peak, but tonight all she could see was the light of a million stars. A million reminders of how small she was. *Be strong and courageous.* She repositioned Lucas on the pillow and slipped from the bed.

Crossing to the loft railing, she leaned into it and stared through the window. Surely if God had placed every one of them in the sky, He could place her and Lucas in safety.

A scraping drew her attention to the first floor, and

she looked down to see Riggen moving from the kitchen to the couch. Was John right? Had God really sent Riggen to them?

She wrapped her arms around herself and watched as he laid out his blanket and pillow before hunching on the edge of the seat like an old man, tired and worn. He removed his boots and placed them beside the coffee table then cradled his head in his hands.

She felt pulled to him as if he was silently summoning her. She reached out and grasped the railing, gripping until her knuckles turned white. Closing her eyes, she held on tight until the temptation passed. Only danger lay that way.

Lucas whooped from his perch on Riggen's shoulders. *Ouch!* Though Lucas gripped handfuls of his hair to keep from falling, Riggen wouldn't trade this moment for anything. It would be over soon enough. Yakub bounded around their feet, the new Hot Wheels forgotten on the front seat of the Bronco as the three ran through the police station parking lot in the early morning light.

Riggen reached up and pulled a still-giggling boy over his head, swinging him in a wide circle before setting him onto the pavement. He'd already been inside to discuss the case developments with Rosche and now Liz was retrieving her belongings from evidence.

Rosche was done at the Juniper. After running tests on Liz's discarded water bottles, food containers and toiletries, they had found the evidence they needed. Rohypnol in her mineral water—compliments of management.

According to the general manager, the concierge who

had provided the bottles hadn't shown up for work. Kris Dupree was in the wind.

Lucas stumbled toward the open Bronco on unsteady feet, the parking lot rang with his laughter. Despite the danger and tension, the boy's shining happiness was weaving into the fabric of Riggen's soul in a way he'd never be able to unravel.

He'd played with Dad and Trevor in the same way once upon a time. Concerns of a less-than-ideal childhood had been blown away by the whoosh of fresh air and adventures in their mountainside playhouse.

He'd love to show Lucas his old playhouse someday. He squelched that dream before it had a chance to settle, instead helping the boy climb back into the Bronco. Lucas gripped the now-remembered toy cars in his dimpled fists the same way Riggen wanted to grip his family.

What if he did hike mountains with Lucas, roast marshmallows and count the stars? Surely God wouldn't hold it against him if he gave Lucas a glimpse into the fun he'd had as a kid.

Riggen leaned his shoulder against the truck and crossed one foot over the other. He wanted more than to just be their protector until this danger passed. He wanted a relationship with his son.

That was going to make it that much more complicated when Liz didn't need his protection anymore. He fisted the aching spot in his chest and pushed the thought away.

The station door screeched open and Liz walked out. She rolled a suitcase behind her, a laptop bag strapped across her chest. He pushed off the truck to help her.

"Get everything?"

She nodded. "My phone's dead, so I called Kat while I was inside." She hefted her bags down the stairs and into the lot. "That went well."

He raised an eyebrow as he took her suitcase and transferred it into the back of the Bronco.

"The damage to their rental was minimal." She pulled the laptop bag over her head. "They've met with their landlord and can leave Colorado tomorrow after they get the rest of our things into storage. But she doesn't think it's wise for Lucas to stay with me."

Riggen reached for the laptop. "You and Lucas are under my protection until we have a clearer picture of what's going on."

Liz froze, her grip firm on the bag. Its bulk hung between them. "So I'm doing the wrong thing if I keep him and the wrong thing if I send him away. Everyone thinks they can make this decision for me."

He let go of the bag's strap and leaned back against the Bronco, surveyed the parking lot. "I'm not trying to insinuate either decision is wrong, or that it's not your decision to make." He crossed his arms over his chest and forced himself to relax. She looked like a doe about to bolt. "You asked me to protect both of you. I intend to do that."

She shoved her computer bag against her well-worn luggage then leaned against the bumper as if the weight of the world had fallen on her shoulders. Her head drooped. "I know."

Lucas's whirring car noises floated through the interior as Yakub's back became his newest racetrack.

Riggen sidled up to Liz and bumped her hip with his. She was closed off, and it was probably best if he left her that way. But he couldn't let her fade under the weight alone.

He pulled her close. Her hair tickled his nose, the lavender sweetness of it teasing his senses and pitching his pulse. He pressed her head against his shoulder. "It's going to be okay."

She shuddered. When she tilted her head to look at him, his breath caught and his arms tightened around her, instinctively trying to steady himself.

"What if it's already over?" she whispered, her lips so close he could almost feel their movement against his jaw. "What if that's all it was?"

As much as he wanted to reassure her, he couldn't. Her worried forehead begged for comfort and he pressed a light kiss across the creases. Then he stood, desperate to distance himself from the emotions she was stirring. "You know that's not true."

"So I'm just stuck with you until this ends? I can't put my entire life on hold."

He stepped away before she could twist the knife again. "Yeah. Stuck with me."

She rubbed her temples. "I didn't mean that how it sounded."

Lucas stopped playing with his cars and two sets of eyes turned to watch them. Riggen took a deep breath and lowered his voice. "I'm not asking you to put your life on hold. I simply want to provide for your safety." He nodded in Lucas's direction. "And his."

"I only ever think about what's best for him." Liz pushed the words past gritted teeth.

"I wasn't saying you weren't." Jones picked that moment to strut from the station and head their way, a smirk on his face. He'd probably just heard the news that Riggen wouldn't be back for a while.

He shook it off and leaned down to speak in Liz's ear. "I'm going to ensure no one will threaten or hurt my family."

Her eyes widened, her pupils black pinpricks in a sea of green and brown. She stepped closer. The tips of her shoes butted against the toes of his boots and her nose was inches from his chest. She looked up at him all fire and fury. "Blood doesn't make family." And with that final twist of the knife, she climbed into the Bronco.

Riggen hadn't spoken more than was necessary since she had stomped to the car. Shame wormed through Liz over her outburst. She'd thought her days of losing control were behind her.

She could feel her hold on her emotions loosening. It was terrifying. She'd never go back to the black days she'd experienced when Riggen had abandoned her. With the help of God, she'd worked too hard to climb from that pit.

Blowing air from her cheeks, she swallowed. *Do not be afraid.* "I told Lucas we might have a bit of an adventure today. Do you think it would be safe?"

"Adventure!" Lucas chimed from the back seat.

Riggen winked at Lucas through the rearview mirror before turning to her. She cringed at the pain in his eyes. "All the other—" he glanced in the mirror again and lowered his voice "—incidents were obviously planned. Everyone knew where you were staying thanks to social media updates. It was easy to follow you. We're off-grid now. As long as we stay that way, a brief stop won't be a problem."

Relief nudged the shame aside when she heard his friendly tone. An apology for her earlier barb sat on the tip of her tongue but five years of loneliness held it in place.

"Thanks." She threaded her fingers together and placed her hands in her lap. She cut a glance at him. "Ice cream and Rainbow Falls?"

"Ice cream?" Lucas strained against his seat belt, his eyes widening.

She laughed and swiveled in her seat. "You must have bionic hearing, child."

Riggen turned right down a backroad and then turned right again at the next intersection, taking them by the police station again.

"Did you forget something?"

"Just backtracking to make sure we haven't been followed."

She studied the side mirror. The road behind them was empty save for a trolley. She shrugged. "Anyway, ice cream?"

He nodded, pressing the gas and angling off of Manitou Avenue. "Sure. I need to make a quick stop at the office and then we'll head over."

He pulled out his cell. "Do you mind if Trevor meets us? I'd love him to see Lucas."

Her earlier anxiety returned and settled in her belly. Trevor hadn't helped when she had tried to find Riggen. Did she want to wade into the mess of feelings that surrounded that? She was already further down the reconciliation road than she wanted to be.

She looked back at Lucas, playing with his toy, and then over at the man who was his mirror image. Hope flickered in Riggen's eyes—faint, as if one word from her would snuff it out.

She couldn't bring herself to hurt him again today any more than she could make herself ready to hear why he had left, to hear why Trevor had turned her away. She squeezed her hands together and took a deep breath. It was just a couple minutes and then it'd be over. "Sure."

The grin that overtook his face whisked the breath from her body.

# TEN

Liz set Lucas down in the parking area for Rainbow Falls, better known as Graffiti Falls to the locals. She scrubbed her palms up and down the sides of her cut-off shorts, her fingers gooey from Lucas's ice-cream treat.

Multicolored drips oozed down her son's chin and stained the front of his T-shirt. Yakub lapped up drips as they hit the ground. She hunched down and pressed a kiss to Lucas's sticky lips. "Silly boy."

She swabbed a wet wipe over his mouth and his face crumpled. Well, someone had to remove the sugary mess. The cleaning wasn't as horrific as Lucas made it out to be. Any onlooker would think she was torturing him. Riggen met her eyes over Lucas's head, his expression mirroring her amusement.

She tossed the dirty wipe into the Bronco. It landed on a stack of business files. After they had stopped for ice cream, Riggen had driven them to Price Adventure Excursions. Trevor had been out of the office. One small prayer answered.

"Did you find what you were looking for?" She moved the wipe off the files.

"I have some ideas for additional income. Thought

I'd look through to see if it'll work with our vendors." His lips thinned. "I don't know how long Trevor can pay us both."

"I don't need to leave for the expo until tomorrow if you need help."

At her words, Riggen stopped scanning the lot and speared her with a look she couldn't quite place. She reached down and grasped Lucas's hand. "We can start after the falls. This guy's about tuckered out."

As if to prove her point, Lucas plugged his mouth with one very sticky thumb and frowned. Then he tugged away from her, his hand slipping from her own. Closing the few feet that separated them, Lucas held his arms up to Riggen.

Riggen blinked quickly, his Adam's apple bobbing up and down as he bent to gather his son into his arms. Their identical heads leaned toward one another and Liz stumbled back.

Riggen ruffled Lucas's hair. "Do you know what's down that path?"

Lucas plopped out his thumb, the suction noise bringing a smile to his father's face. "Adventure," he whispered.

"Adventure," Riggen echoed. The man shifted Lucas's weight to one arm as if the boy weighed no more than a bag of groceries and then turned to her, his hand extended.

A barrel of bees raged in Liz's stomach. The moment reflected every errant daydream she'd had over the last five years. *Trust him.* The thought blew the bees away and knocked off the armor she had been trying so hard to hold in place.

She sidestepped Yakub and slid her hand into Riggen's calloused grip. The friction of their touch sparked a million memories. Lucas snuggled into Riggen's chest, his tiny bottom secure in her ex-fiancé's arms.

"You know they spent over a million dollars to remove the graffiti from these rocks last spring."

Liz looked at the cliff wall. They were strolling down an avenue of urban art. "Did they not get to this part?"

He chuckled and kicked a pebble along the trail. Red clouds of dirt puffed in its wake. "They cleaned it all. Within a matter of months, it was back."

She studied the kaleidoscope of color. "I guess people didn't want to lose Graffiti Falls."

"It's a local treasure."

Silence fell as they walked under the bridge that arched over the small oasis. Its aged surface was covered in messages and pictures that matched Lucas's ice-cream stains for vibrancy.

Beyond the bridge, a thin, sparkling waterfall thundered forty-five feet to a plunge pool encased by steep rock walls on three sides. A few teens were wading under its shower, their laughter echoing in the canyon.

Lucas wiggled and pushed against Riggen's chest, his excitement sparkling as bright as the water itself. Liz nodded her approval.

"Stay along the edge." She cocked an eyebrow at her son. "We don't want to take a soaking-wet boy back to the car."

Lucas bobbed his head up and down so fast she was afraid he'd give himself a headache. "Okay, okay." She laughed. "Go play."

He and Yakub ran to the edge, both skidding to a stop as their feet met the cold mountain stream. Riggen stepped back and stood next to her. She'd forgotten how he towered over her. She found herself leaning slightly closer, pulled in by his steady presence.

She slanted her head up and shielded her eyes against the sun. "Did they find Kris yet?"

He met her look and searched her eyes a moment. "The concierge? No. Rosche will update us after they pay a visit to her home."

Liz hugged herself and rubbed her hands up and down her arms. "She seemed so nice."

"I've seen nice people do awful things."

She kicked a pebble between her feet. "What about the blog comment?"

"Alex'll get back to us as soon as he finds something." Riggen cleared his throat and squeezed the back of his neck. "I don't want to step in where I've not earned the right...but maybe you should rethink the expo."

Heat radiated up her neck and her muscles tensed in a domino-like effect at his words. First Kat, now Riggen. Could neither of them leave her to make her own decisions?

She leaned down and picked up a rock, skipping it over the turbulent surface of the water before she trusted herself to answer. "I can't miss it."

"Look, Mama!" Lucas splashed a toy down into the water and gasped with surprise as he sprayed himself in the face.

A crowd of tourists ran behind them to the falls and Riggen moved closer, his arm brushing hers. "Anyone who knows anything about you knows you've been planning on attending." The gray depths of his eyes stirred with intensity. "It's crowded, chaotic. The perfect opportunity to attack."

She shook her head. "What if this is all just scare tactics? What if that's the point? Other people want this job. What if one of them thought they'd get it by scaring me off? I'm not letting them win."

"So you'd take Lucas with you?" He stuffed a hand in his hair, sticking his white cowlick straight in the air.

She sighed and turned to watch Lucas plunge his toy back into the frigid water. "I don't know what to do." Boy, did that hurt to admit. The last twenty-four hours crashed on her with a thousand gallons of worry. "I can't lose a job that will provide for him."

He grasped her hand. "We'll figure it out. But the job isn't worth—" He let go and pointed at Lucas's hand. "What's that?"

She squinted. "The toy you bought him?"

But Riggen was already charging toward the water's edge. "It's not," he called over his shoulder. "Where'd you get this, buddy?"

Liz followed him, reaching Riggen just as he hunkered down next to Lucas. A blinking red light emitted from the undercarriage of a toy bomber.

Lucas puffed out his chest. "The wady at the ice-cream store."

The color drained from Riggen's face as he shot Liz a questioning glance. She shook her head, no idea what Lucas was talking about.

Hefting Lucas into his arms, Riggen pressed his son's face into his chest before hurling the toy into the swirling stream. It crashed on an exposed stone. "Tracking device. We need to leave."

Liz's heart splattered on the graffitied ground even as a cry of angry despair burst from Lucas.

Riggen tugged her hand, pulling her back the way

they had come. Yakub bounded behind them and Lucas's cries swirled around them. "Call 9-1-1."

"My phone is dead." Her voice cracked.

He dropped her hand and passed her his cell. She dialed and relayed their location as he unsnapped his holster.

The swollen stream roared to their right and tourists congested the path to their left. She turned her head to search the faces behind her and stumbled. Riggen caught her, pulling her against him.

Lucas whimpered at their collision. They were so close to the Bronco now. Within sprinting distance.

Four other cars sat in the lot. A woman pulled a toddler from one. Teens poured from another. Every person was unaware of her terror. Yakub growled, setting every hair on her arm on end.

Riggen's grasp tightened. "Almost there."

Someone screamed. "He has a gun!"

She looked at Riggen, but his hand was still on her. His other arm surrounded Lucas. They weren't talking about him. "God, help us," she moaned.

Riggen crouched, shielding Lucas. He pulled her close and pushed them toward the Bronco. Yakub's growl intensified with every second.

Riggen yanked the door open. "Get in."

She scrambled in and pulled Lucas into his seat, grabbing at his seat belt. Yakub jumped in behind her. Her hands trembled, clattering the buckles as she struggled to lock them.

Riggen crashed into the driver's seat and slammed the truck into gear. "Hold on!" Gravel hit the undercarriage as the passenger's mirror exploded into shards of glass.

She screamed. Lucas burst into body-shaking sobs. "Get down!" Riggen reached back and pushed her head down. She threw her arms over Lucas.

Riggen steered the truck in reverse through the lot. Screams filtered through the half-open windows. Then he jerked the wheel, sending the Bronco into a turn that threw them forward. They shot from the lot onto Serpentine Drive.

Liz bolted upright and stared out the back window. A black SUV peeled out of the lot behind them.

"Phone." Riggen held out his hand. He hit Speed Dial and cut the wheel to the right, sliding the truck onto a side road. Dirt clouds surrounded them in a golden-red haze. "Shots fired. Officer in need of assistance." He handed her the phone. "Speaker."

She hit the button, letting him shout updates over Lucas's sobs as they careened down the mountain road.

A police SUV raced at them with lights flashing and sirens blaring. It passed, its tires squealing as it executed a U-turn to join the chase. They blew past another side road. She watched in the rearview mirror as their pursuer turned off behind them, the police SUV following.

Relief hit her with the shock of a frigid mountain stream. Riggen pulled to the side of the road and another police SUV stopped behind them. He turned to her and cradled the side of her face. His eyes were full of fear and yet tender at the same time.

With that look, her dams broke. She joined Lucas in all his wailing glory.

Silent darkness had long since enveloped the cabin. After heading to the station to inspect every square inch of the Bronco for additional tracking devices, he had taken them on a long and winding journey through multiple backtracks and switchbacks to get home.

It had taken Liz the better part of the evening to calm Lucas enough to sleep. Riggen wasn't sure how she'd done it when she'd looked on the brink of a full-fledged breakdown herself.

The mantel clock chimed ten o'clock and Riggen scooted to the edge of the couch, half rising from his seat to go call Yakub inside, but he stopped. The dog would serve them best outside, prowling the perimeter. He'd alert if anyone came near.

Wind whistled through the cracks of the ancient cabin walls as the ticking clock beat a steady cadence over the empty fireplace. He punched his pillow. Sleep wouldn't come. Every time he closed his eyes, he saw Liz's anguished face.

He'd seen that fear on another mother's face. Guilt swirled through his gut. He should have been here, protecting and providing for his family. But, instead, he'd been in Iraq, trying to protect another woman's child from a suicide bomber, and he'd failed all the way around.

Pulling a heavy quilt up over his shoulders, he tried to shut out the memories. Memories of failure. Of hospitals. Of finding out that being thrown in the explosion had ruined any chance he'd had of being a father.

How he wanted forgiveness. From Liz. From the family he hadn't saved. From God even. He punched the pillow again. Forgiveness was a fool's wish. The best he could hope for now was the strength to get Liz and Lucas through this threat without failing again.

The couch cushion beside him lowered. He shot forward and slid his hand across the butt of his Glock.

"Just me." Liz pulled her legs up onto the small cushioned ledge and rested her chin on her knees.

Moonbeams illuminated the sweep of her cheekbone. Five years had formed subtle changes in this woman he'd once loved. His fingers ached to trace her wounded but brave beauty. He curled his hands into fists. She wasn't his and never would be.

"Couldn't sleep?" he whispered.

"Something like that." She stared out the window.

They sat for a few silent moments and then she snaked her hand into his. Electricity shot from his palm to his heart. He paced his breathing so she wouldn't know how her touch affected him.

She turned to him and scooted closer. Her eyes shimmered. With what? He couldn't read her anymore. "Thanks."

Riggen nodded. The way she had held Lucas safe in her arms at the station had been all the thanks he needed. At least he had given her what he had failed to give the family in Iraq.

She inhaled sharply, holding her breath as though about to dive into deep water. "I've made a decision."

"About?"

"I'm sending Lucas with Kat until after the expo." She pulled her hand away to wipe the tears that streamed down her face. "I have to think about what's best for him."

"And after the expo?"

He was acutely aware of how close she was and how vulnerable she looked. She leaned back into the couch and stared up at the darkened ceiling. "If I get the job, I'll bring him home—to our new apartment." She sniffed and giggled. "Who knows, maybe someday we'll even be able to get a white-picket-fence house and a dog."

"And if you don't get the job?"

She shuddered. "I'll figure it out. Don't worry about me."

His heart climbed into his throat along with words he knew were better locked away. "But I do worry about you. I always have."

"Then why—" She choked and pulled her lips between her teeth. Her eyes rounded in a way that told him she regretted her question.

They'd danced around it long enough. It was time to push past his shame and really talk, because his heart was shattering at the sight of her turmoil. "I thought it would be the best thing."

She angled her body toward him, moonlight glinting off her tear-wet skin. Her eyes flashed. "How?" The one-word question burst from her, demanding he open up. Unlock his strongbox.

Snippets of grief from the first weeks of recovery flashed through his mind. He straightened his aching back and shook it off.

"There was a suicide bomber. A family caught in the middle." The memory he never let himself relive threatened to swallow him whole. "I ignored a direct order and pushed my unit toward the chaos to get to a family trapped in the square. Then the guy blew himself up."

He squeezed the bridge of his nose. "When I woke up in a German hospital, I found out some of my men hadn't survived… We hadn't even saved the family. When the doctor came to tell me my injuries had eliminated a future that included biological children, I guess I saw it as God's way of showing me I didn't deserve a family."

He threaded and unthreaded their fingers, unable to meet her eyes. "I wanted you to be my family, Lizzy, but I didn't want to ruin your life like I'd ruined so many others."

Liz reached out and cupped his jaw, running her fingers over his chin. Her tears fell to the couch between them. "Rig." Her whispered use of his nickname gave him strength to meet her eyes. She pulled her hand from his face. "God doesn't work that way."

Conflict raged in her eyes then she squeezed her lids shut over whatever internal battle she was fighting. "He sent His son, not to condemn you for your mistakes but to die so you could be forgiven." She leaned toward him and pressed one finger into his chest, right above his heart. "But you have to ask for it. You have to turn your life over to Him.

"I can't imagine what you've gone through or the pain it caused, but God would never tell you to right one wrong with another. You abandoned me." Her eyes shot open and she jerked her head to the loft where Lucas was sleeping. "Abandoned us."

The truth of it slugged him. "Dad was the preacher. I never professed to be an expert on how God works." He tried to organize his turbulent thoughts, to grasp what she was saying, but it was like walking upstream in thundering rapids. "I thought I was doing the right thing."

She glanced over his head at the darkened loft and lowered her voice to a tortured whisper. "By making a life-changing decision—without me—that left me alone with our son?"

"If I had known about Lucas…" He couldn't keep the pain from his reply as she lurched to her feet and paced in front of him. "If I could go back, I would do it differently."

Liz hugged herself as if trying to provide the safety and love he had taken from her. "Of course you would now that you've seen Lucas. But would you rewrite it if it was only me?"

He couldn't answer. Would he have come back, carrying all the shame and regret he'd picked up from that bomb-blistered street? God hadn't caused the pain rolling off Liz in almost tangible waves. He had.

She stopped in front of him. Instinct screamed to bridge the gap and pull her close, told him to erase the betrayal from her face. He inched closer. "Liz?"

She blinked and a mask fell. He recognized it. She was locking her own strongbox. He'd never have that key.

He took a deep breath and tried. "I want to be there for you."

In the darkened room, he could almost see a spark light between them. Then it was gone. She stepped back, the distance between them as gaping as a mountain pass. "You've said that before."

"I meant it then and I mean it now."

She turned on her heel and headed for the stairs. "You can't imagine how much I want to believe that."

She trudged up the stairs and never looked back. Falling back on the couch, he pillowed his aching head with his arms and, for the first time in his life, Riggen tried to pour out his desperation to a God whom he was beginning to suspect had never wanted to punish him at all.

# ELEVEN

He'd barely slept. The anguish he'd seen in Liz's eyes, along with the thought of Lucas leaving, had occupied his mind until the first rays of sunlight peeked over the mountain. Not long after, Lucas himself had peeked over the side of the couch.

Riggen stretched the sleep from his body and patted the couch beside him. Lucas wriggled close and Riggen covered his lips with a single finger. Lucas giggled but nodded.

From the sound of suitcases hitting the floor, Liz was just as upset as last night. Riggen rose from the couch and tiptoed toward the front door, pulling Lucas along.

He eased the heavy door open. Liz had purchased Lucas's flight ticket online last night. He'd be leaving Colorado Springs' airport in three hours and there was no way Riggen was going to allow his son to go without some sort of protection. Yakub would serve that purpose and calm his heart.

They climbed off the wraparound porch and crossed the driveway. Each breath he took increased the dull ache behind his ribs. Lucas still didn't even know who he was, but their family tie was as fragile as a cobweb in the wind. He clamped his mouth shut. It wasn't his truth to tell anyway.

He stopped and squatted next to his son. At least he had this moment. "I have a surprise for you." He looked to the left and the right and then back into Lucas's widening eyes.

"More cars?" Lucas hopped from one foot to the other.

"Nope. Something even better." Riggen straightened, his bones crackling, and grasped Lucas's hand. His breath caught as Lucas's pint-size fingers wound through his. They stood together in the morning's golden glow.

Riggen pursed his lips and let out a whistle. The sound bounced across the mountain and echoed back. He searched the ridgeline. "Yakub!"

The beat of Yakub's paws reached them before the dog crested the rise and galloped their way, a blur of brown and white fur.

Lucas bounced on the balls of his feet at the sight of Yakub. Bending to scoop his son into his arms, Riggen held his excited body close. "You and Yakub have become great friends." Lucas nodded in agreement and wound a thin arm around Riggen's neck.

Too soon for Riggen's heart, Yakub slid to a stop at their feet. A swirling dust cloud enveloped them all. When it cleared, Yakub looked up at them with soulful eyes. His brows raised and his head cocked.

"Friends take care of each other," Riggen whispered into his son's ear. "Now Yakub wants to take care of you."

Lucas pushed away from Riggen's chest, his body a bundle of barely restrained happiness. Riggen set the boy on solid ground and Lucas's sandal-clad feet immediately stepped toward the dog. Lucas pulled Yakub into a bear hug and buried his face in dappled fur.

"Yakub will keep you safe until we're together again." Riggen knelt in the dust. "Can you take care of Yakub, too?"

Lucas nodded his head faster than a bobblehead on a dashboard. The sight was enough to restore Riggen's spirits. He guided his small human and canine pack back in the direction of the cabin. "Let's find your mommy."

With Yakub watching over Lucas, at least he'd have one less thing to lose sleep over.

Warm air breezed through the open Bronco windows and whipped Liz's hair into her eyes as Riggen ramped onto I-24. She cranked the window halfway up and leaned her head against the glass, focusing on the wildflowers that littered the mountain.

It was that or she'd have to think about untangling the messy mix of feelings she had for Riggen right now. She turned and looked at Lucas's shining face as he hugged Yakub close. Good idea or not, Riggen was still oblivious to the fact that he couldn't continue to make decisions for her.

She glanced in the side mirror. A Manitou Springs Police SUV followed close behind and she appreciated the extra protection. It'd make saying goodbye to her baby easier.

Hopefully, once Lucas was safe with John and Kat, this crushing guilt would disappear. She pressed her fingertips into her eyes, trying to blot yesterday out and sort her jumbled feelings.

Her phone buzzed. She squinted at it, waiting for the blurriness to pass. A text from Kat.

Not 2 late to buy yourself a ticket. Flight not full.

She sighed and turned the phone over. So much for guilt disappearing.

"Anything wrong?" Riggen changed lanes.

She watched Officer Jones follow suit behind. "Do you want the list in alphabetical order?"

Riggen stayed silent. She appreciated it. Kat could never give her space. She gripped the phone tighter. Her sister had been mothering her their entire life—while reminding her what a burden she was.

Not that she hadn't needed it, though. When Riggen disappeared, Kat had been the only thing that had kept her from falling apart. Kat drove her to pre-natal appointments… Kat made sure she took her vitamins…

Kat was everything Liz wished she could be. She scuffed her feet along the floorboard and sighed. Just for once, though, she'd appreciate a pause in the big sister act. She needed a friend.

She slid a glance at Riggen's profile. She had no idea what to do with the emotional avalanche his confession had caused. Running her index finger over her opposite hand, she rubbed her naked ring finger.

She wasn't ready to forgive him. Maybe she never would be. But there was a small part of her that sympathized with the panic he must have felt when he'd woken up injured and found out everyone he had tried to save was dead.

She couldn't be sure she would have handled it any

better. Pain shot through her fingers as she squeezed them together. She *was* sure of one thing. She wouldn't have abandoned *him*.

The back seat had quieted down. Liz looked over her shoulder. Lucas was fast asleep, his fist grasping a tuft of Yakub's fur.

She pushed aside the betrayal that had been firmly lodged in her heart for five long years and allowed herself a giggle. She gave Riggen's bicep a punch. "I've been sitting here furious that you didn't ask me about Yakub, but thinking about how much *more* furious Kat's going to be lessens the sting."

Riggen slanted a deliciously evil look her way. "That was half the satisfaction of the gift."

The dimple in his right cheek deepened when he grinned like that. She peeled her eyes away and turned back to the window. Heat crept from her neck to her cheeks and she pressed her face even closer to the window, the wildflowers once again so incredibly interesting.

"Kat doesn't understand why I don't just give up the job at *American Travel*." She scratched at a fleck of dirt on the window. "She says I don't need a better-paying job when John's new church will pay him more than enough."

He grunted. "There's no promise the threats won't follow you to California."

"That's what I told her. Anyway, I refuse to run. I've worked too hard for this." She kicked the matted rug. "Give up the chance at standing on my own two feet? No way. Besides…"

"What?"

She flipped her phone over and over in her hands. Might as well share the plan that had kept her awake last night. "You were right about the expo. It's the most logical place for an attack. If I'm there, it will force whoever this is to make another move."

"I don't like the sound of this."

"You'll be there," she stated.

"So?"

She raised her shoulders. It was obvious, wasn't it? "You'll protect me."

"No."

"No?" Her voice rose an octave. "Are you saying you *won't* protect me?" Was she too much trouble to bother with when their son was safely out of the picture?

His eyes narrowed as he stared down the road. "No, as in I refuse to use you as bait."

She turned in her seat until her entire body was facing him. "It's not your choice. I'm going. If attending draws out whoever is targeting me then I say it's a solid win. You won't let them get me."

"I'm only one man." He stiffened. "What if there's another option?"

"*American Travel* is the culmination of five years of work." She pushed the words through her teeth. "There is no other option."

"There's—"

"Momma—"

She bounced her attention from Riggen to Lucas and back, but Riggen shook his head and clamped his mouth shut. Obviously, he was finished with whatever was on his mind.

She shifted so she could view Lucas. Yakub licked straight up the side of his face and into his hair, standing his cowlick on end. She patted the dog's rear end. "What, sweet boy?"

Lucas frowned. "Yakub needs a toofbrush."

A belly laugh burst from the man next to her and melted away the strain that hovered over the front seat like a storm cloud. "He really does."

Lucas wiped the slobber from his face. "Aunt Kat gets mad when I forget to brush." He pulled Yakub to him, tiny lines marring his smooth forehead. "Will she let me keep him?"

"Of course, sweetheart," Liz answered. "And after this weekend, I'll have a new job. Then you and Yakub will come back to me. Remember? Our big adventure."

"I get my own room."

"Your very own." *Please, God, let it be true.*

"Can Yakub sweep in my bed?"

Riggen turned into the airport entrance. "Be careful what you wish for. Yakub hogs the bed. Last week I woke up on the floor!"

Lucas's giggles soothed Liz's climbing nerves as they pulled into the parking area. She wasn't ready to hand her baby over to her sister, even if it was only for a few days. What if he never wanted to come back?

He couldn't believe he'd been about to suggest leaving Colorado Springs. Going off-grid. Starting a new life. *Being a family.* What had gotten into him? The impossibility of it made Riggen's head spin.

Thankfully, Lucas had interrupted. He could only imagine her scathing reply. He would have deserved every searing word. She had a life, one without him.

Officer Jones pulled his SUV into a parking spot across from them, and Riggen scowled. If he could have picked backup, Jones would be at the bottom of the list. Scratch that. He wouldn't even make the list.

Riggen climbed from the Bronco and nodded across the lane that divided their cars, receiving a brief nod in response. Jones looked as happy to be there as Riggen was to have him.

What Jones would be happy with was Riggen missing the interview next week because of the threats against Liz. Riggen rolled his head to the side. He'd worked hard for this promotion. He stretched his neck and looked inside the Bronco, but Liz was more important.

She was stuffing Lucas's blanket into his cartoon carry-on and Riggen took advantage of the delay to text Rosche.

How did I end up with Jones?

Within moments, her answer landed in his hand.

Couldn't come. Suspect from hospital wants to talk. Heading to jail now.

The door finally opened and Lucas and Yakub tumbled out. Riggen caught Lucas before he sprawled onto the concrete. "Careful, buddy."

Lucas wrapped his fingers around Riggen's index finger and smiled up into his eyes. "Yes, sir."

Riggen pressed Lucas safely against his leg before shooting off a final text to Rosche, asking her to keep him updated. The passenger door squeaked open and Liz climbed down, her shoulders stiff and chest out. She looked as though she were preparing for battle.

"Let's do this." She smiled at Lucas and then started toward the terminal, Lucas's miniature luggage in her hand.

Riggen wrapped Yakub's leash around one hand and caught Lucas up in his other arm. Yakub trotted proudly beside them, his bright blue emotional support vest in place.

As they entered the towering atrium, Lucas gawked at a suspended sculpture of stainless steel, copper and gold-plated brass in contemporary design. "Ooh." His whispered awe puffed into Riggen's ear.

Liz stopped ahead of them, streams of travelers flowing around her like water gurgling around a stone. She studied her phone. "Kat says they're opposite Security."

Riggen nodded as he analyzed every person who came close. Height, weight, build. Clothing. Ability to conceal a weapon. Jones shifted on Liz's other side, his eyes constantly scanning.

Then Liz resumed moving. She sidestepped fellow travelers, pulling Lucas's luggage behind her. They made their way to the checkpoint and found John and Kat right where Kat had said they'd be.

As soon as Lucas spotted his aunt and uncle, he wriggled in Riggen's arms, begging to be put down. He sprinted in his uncle's direction when his feet hit the floor. Then he was clambering into the wheelchair as if he'd been doing it his entire life.

He probably had. Jealousy slicked through Riggen.

Yakub skidded to a stop next to John and nosed his snout under the man's hand. John laughed. "Who's your new friend?"

"Yakub! He's coming wif me!" Lucas bounced in John's lap, unaware of the scowl that flitted across Kat's face.

Riggen caught it. He also caught the whispered conversation between the sisters. Kat was less than pleased with Lucas's new companion.

Lucas leaned over the arm of John's chair and scratched behind Yakub's ear. "He has siwwy hair like me."

John laughed and patted Yakub's dappled head. "Special, not silly."

Lucas's eyes drifted to Riggen. He zeroed in on his hairline. "Riggen has special hair, too."

"Of course he does," Kat blurted. "That's because he's—"

Liz's frantic gaze bounced between Riggen and Lucas before she put a hand on her sister's arm, cutting off the woman's words. "Because he's special, too."

Riggen shifted from one foot to the other, all eyes on him.

"Well…" John broke the tension that had descended like a low-flying airplane. "I think it's time we head through Security. It'll take a while for me to get situated."

And with that Liz was kneeling and holding out her arms. Lucas catapulted himself into her, knocking her backward. Riggen couldn't swallow past the sudden knot in his throat as Lucas held tight to Liz.

When he had been not much older than Lucas, he had held on to his own mother that way. She had been leaving for her last trip to the hospital. His arms had held as tightly as Lucas's were, but that hadn't made a difference. Riggen hadn't been able to do anything to save his mother. She never came home.

The memory burned Riggen's throat. He would stake his life on the fact that Liz and Lucas would be reunited. Riggen would make sure of it.

Liz's face was hidden in her son's hair, but Riggen could still hear the tears in her voice. "Be good for Aunt Kat and Uncle John. I'll see you when I'm finished with work."

Lucas nodded.

She leaned back. Her cheeks were damp, and Lucas wiped away the wetness. "Don't cry, Momma. Riggen promised to keep you safe."

She met his eyes over Lucas's head at the same time Kat mumbled under her breath, "You wouldn't have to keep her safe if she knew where her place was."

Anger rocked him like summer thunder. He clenched his fists and took a deep breath. "I'm sure your support is everything to Liz."

Kat opened her mouth then clamped it shut again, her hands tightening on the back of John's wheelchair.

"Say goodbye to Mr. Price." Liz steadied Lucas on his feet and pushed him Riggen's way.

As Lucas walked to him, Riggen's heart melted in his chest. He squatted and looked his son in the eyes, man-to-man.

"I'll take very good care of Yakub."

Riggen set Lucas on his thigh and whistled Yakub to their side. "He loves to play fetch at sunset."

Lucas shifted until he could see John. "Do we have a ball?"

"I think we can find one."

Lucas turned back to Riggen, his gray eyes serious. "I can do that."

Unable to stop himself, Riggen held his son close.

Purpose pulsed through his veins. No threat, no amount of distance and no past failures could hold him back from pursuing a relationship with his son.

The sliver of hope that had flickered and waned for the past few days started to burn with intensity. There was no way God would want him to keep his distance from his child. Liz said that's not how God worked. His sin against Liz might be irredeemable, but he no longer believed their reunion was a coincidence. God had a purpose.

And that purpose was tightening tiny arms around his neck. Riggen breathed deeply and ran full-speed into hope.

# TWELVE

"It'll take two hours to reach Denver." Liz's seat belt cut into her as she leaned out the open window, watching planes fly overhead. After a few moments, she settled back in her seat and turned to Riggen.

"I reserved an extra room at the Kimpton Hotel Monaco. They placed you across the hall from me."

He didn't respond. Just stared.

She plucked at her sleeve. "The Kimpton is unique. You should enjoy it."

He continued staring. Rocking back and forth, she stuck her hands under her thighs. "What?"

His phone buzzed in the cup holder, but he ignored it. "When will we tell Lucas who I am?"

She stared at the phone. It rattled around, knocking an old French fry to the floor. Her stomach growled. Picking up the fry, she tossed it outside. "Do you really want to discuss this now?"

Officer Jones lounged in his police SUV, waiting to leave. She'd rather not have this conversation with an audience. Then again, she'd rather not have it at all.

Swift conviction plunged between her desire to avoid any conversation that might make Riggen a real part of her life and the sight of his heart in his eyes. She sighed. "I want to trust you."

"But?"

"What happens to Lucas when you leave again?"

He winced. "Last night I told you I want to be there for you, that includes Lucas. I don't plan on disappearing again. Ever."

"You didn't plan on it when you gave me an engagement ring." She squeezed her hands together. "I want to believe you. I do." She narrowed her eyes. "I'm not over what you did. I guess I'm saying I'm not ready to tell Lucas."

Color flared up Riggen's neck to his face then vanished as swiftly as it had come. He was white as the clouds, but he simply nodded before turning to start the truck.

The buzzing in the cup holder began again. He grabbed the phone and hit Speaker, setting it back into the holder as they pulled out of the lot.

"Good news and bad news." Rosche's voice battled with the clunk of the engine.

Riggen pulled into traffic. "Let's hear the good news."

"Pikes Peak Chocolate has security cameras."

"Catch anything?"

"A woman handing Lucas the toy." Rosche's excitement danced across the connection. "Liz's back is to Lucas. You were busy ordering. The woman was in and out so fast, even the camera almost missed her."

"ID?"

"You'll never guess who it is." Rosche didn't give them the time. "Kris Dupree."

Silence followed the theatrical unveil. Riggen shot Liz a look. "Did you bring her in?"

"Can't find her." Rosche's tone was more subdued. "We're waiting for a warrant to search her place."

"Thanks for letting me know." Riggen reached toward the cup holder but Rosche's voice stilled it midair.

"No problem. But you haven't heard the bad news yet."

"That wasn't it?"

"Nope. I went to the jail. Our guy'll only talk to you."

Riggen slowed at a red light, his face a picture of confusion. "Me? I'm heading to Denver."

Liz reached over and squeezed his arm. When he focused on her, she mouthed, *We have time.*

He nodded and pressed the gas as the light turned back to green. "Let El Paso know I'm on the way. We'll see what this guy has to say."


Metal doors clanged behind Riggen as he waited for their perpetrator from the hospital. He shifted in his chair. White surfaces melded together in every direction, creating a colorless, creeping dread.

He'd been here an eternity already. He tilted his wrist and sighed. It'd only been thirty minutes. But when Liz had said they had time, he doubted she'd meant all day.

He kicked at the opposite chair. He wanted the freedom of open mountain air so bad he could almost taste it.

The click of a lock and the whoosh of the door announced his suspect. He straightened. The corrections officer walked his man in.

Same guy he'd locked eyes with in the hospital. Now

his hands and legs were shackled but, even in an orange jumpsuit, he oozed an aura of danger.

He clanked to the table and eased down. Midfifties, white hair, dead eyes.

Riggen tented his hands on the table. "You have information?"

"Make it worth my time." The man smiled. He tongued discolored teeth.

"That's wasted on me." Riggen held up a finger to signal the officer. He wasn't playing the game. "Rosche was the one to negotiate with."

"I like your hair," the guy drawled.

"I like your jumpsuit. I didn't come to trade—"

"Knew a woman with hair like that." He jerked his chin at Riggen's cowlick. "When that elevator opened and I saw you... What can I say?" He pounded his chest with a manacled hand. "Maybe there's a heart here, after all. I only planted one device."

Waves of heat and cold threatened to knock Riggen from his chair. He refused to blink. Just an everyday conversation. "I guess I should thank you?"

The man shrugged.

"There were supposed to be more explosions?"

"Oh yeah."

"That won't go well for you when your boss finds out."

The man held his cuffed hands in front of him in mock supplication. "You wouldn't want any harm to come to your momma's special friend."

Riggen surged to his feet, his chair squealing against the tiled floor. "Who ordered the hit? I'll see what we can do."

"You look just like your momma. Bet she never did

tell you who your daddy was." The man grinned like a Cheshire cat, looking for all the world as if it meant nothing to him.

Riggen fisted his hands to hide the shaking and leaned on the table, staring down this new enemy, hoping he wouldn't see anything of himself staring back. "Name."

"Kris Dupree."

"We're done." He turned on his heel and stalked from the room, the man's laughter echoing behind him.

"I've just never been so wrong about a person before." As the words were coming out of Liz's mouth, she bloomed a pretty shade of pink and looked everywhere but at him.

She had to be thinking of when she'd been wrong about him. Riggen executed the last turn toward Denver. "They'll double down on Kris's past and any possible links to you. Had you met her before you checked in at the Juniper? What possible connection do you share?"

"I've already been racking my brain, even while you were in the jail. I just keep coming up blank."

He scratched the shadow of a beard that wouldn't stop growing. He didn't have time to shave. "She could just be another player."

"In a game I wish were over." Liz sighed.

"Rosche sent a picture to Denver PD. The security teams at the Kimpton and the convention center, too. If Kris shows her face in Denver, we'll be ready."

Each rotation of the wheels carried them closer to the next possible threat. He snuck a look at Liz from the corner of his eye. She was leaning against the window, her eyes closing. She was exhausted.

He should just turn west and deposit Liz safely with John and Kat in California. He shook his head. That would only work if he could be sure the distance would guarantee safety.

Liz's head bobbed in sleep as the forested wilderness slowly evolved into suburbs. They'd hit Denver at the height of its rush-hour glory, and he eased the brake, navigating them through the stop-and-go traffic. Liz stirred as they passed Coors Field.

He reached over and squeezed her hand. "Almost there."

She rubbed sleep from her eyes and ran her fingers through her hair. "Thanks." Her voice held a rumble of sleep.

He stared at the high-rise buildings they were driving past. Fortresses of steel and concrete closed them in. Hitting Champa Street, he pulled up to the Kimpton Hotel Monaco Denver.

They were greeted by a uniformed valet before he'd even shifted into Park. Riggen chuckled as he handed over the keys to his rust bucket. He tugged his Colorado Rockies cap on and followed Liz inside.

She led him through the living-room lobby to a sleek front desk and introduced herself to the staff.

"We've readied your rooms, Ms. Hart." Their hostess slid room keys across the glossy black surface. "Let us know how we can make your stay more pleasant."

Liz thanked her before crossing in front of the room's fireplace. Riggen sidestepped a yellow armchair to follow.

She stepped into the elevator and moved aside for him. "I'll check in at the *American Travel* booth after we freshen up."

He squeezed in between a luggage cart and the wall. Another couple piled in and Liz stifled a giggle as he inched even closer with exaggerated exasperation.

He stopped a hairbreadth from her, his hand brushing against hers, and she didn't pull away. New hope breathed to life.

He leaned close. "When do you want to head over?"

She rocked back on her heels and tilted her head until they were looking eye-to-eye. "It's not cheap, you'll have to pay full admission price."

"Trevor has a booth. He'll get me in."

Her shoulders rose and fell. "It'll be long. Presentations tonight. Tomorrow, too. Not to mention, Kimberly East from *American Travel* wants someone manning the booth constantly."

They exited the elevator and their footsteps were muffled against plush carpet. Liz's steps slowed the closer they came to their rooms. When they reached her door, she slid her keycard into the reader then kicked her overnight bag inside and slouched against the door frame. He slid around her to check the bathroom and closet.

She didn't look up as he rejoined her. He nudged her foot with his own.

She pushed off the doorjamb as if pulled from a trance, her face blank. Inching closer, she reached a hand to his face. His heart thundered in his throat, but she only shoved his ball cap back. "Maybe this was a bad idea. I should've found someone else."

The change from elevator to room catapulted him into a pool of confusion. "Someone else for what?"

"For protection. I'm sure you know someone on Denver PD who'd do a good job." Her last sentence came out as more of a question than a statement.

He took a step closer and tipped her chin up with his index finger. Peering into her eyes, he tried to see past this new façade. "What's going on?"

Her eyes slid shut. "This is so much. You'll just disappear when it's too hard to handle."

This was all his fault. "I know it doesn't hold much weight at this point, but I'm not going anywhere."

"I overheard you with Rosche at the Incline."

He pulled back. "Okay…about what?"

"About the fact that you're messing up your promotion."

"I haven't messed up anything other than my relationship with you." He held his arms open, inviting. "I mean that."

She took one step forward then stopped. She opened her mouth. Shut it. Then stared over his shoulder into space.

"What is it?"

"You didn't care about our relationship until you saw Lucas's picture. Would you still want to be in my life if I didn't have him?" She ducked under his arms and slipped through her open door. "Because I don't have him now." Her door closed before he processed what was happening.

He turned to knock, but his pocket started buzzing. He pulled out his phone. Rosche. Moving to his door instead, he slid his finger along the answer button.

"We got the warrant. Dupree's place is trashed. Looks like a struggle." She was breathless. The thrill of the chase radiated from every word.

"No sign of Kris?" He slammed his door behind him.

"None." She clicked her tongue. "Unravel that mess. Prime suspect missing in what looks to be an abduction. We found a burner phone wedged under an overturned couch. It's a smartphone model." She sounded giddy. "The GPS location services were enabled. You'll never guess what I found when I checked the frequently visited places."

"What?"

"Your family's property. Coordinates are farther up the mountainside than the actual cabin, but you know how it goes. They can be off a good amount."

The room spun. He sank onto the nearest chair. "That doesn't make sense."

"This case doesn't make sense." She forged ahead. "I wanted to give you a heads-up."

He hit End Call and kicked off his boots. Why would Kris be at his property? Not to see him. That left one other person. He hit speed dial.

Trevor picked up on the second ring. "What's up?"

"Do you know a woman by the name of Kris Dupree?"

There was a pause from the other side of the line. "The Juniper's concierge?"

"Yeah."

"Sure." Trevor said. "We just started booking excursions through her. Why?"

"Any reason she'd be out at the cabin? Or anywhere on our property?" Might as well get to the heart of the matter.

"No." His brother dragged out the word into what sounded like a question. "What's going on?"

"Nothing." Riggen shrugged off his questions and stared out the window. If his brother didn't know anything, this conversation was useless. "You in Denver already?"

"Got in last night." A knock sounded across the line. "Look, I gotta go. I'm meeting up with some folks before I put the finishing touches on the Price Adventure Excursion display."

Riggen sat straight. "No problem. I'll come see your hard work. I'm here with Liz."

"Really?" Trevor's surprise jolted over the line. "Let's do lunch then."

"Sure thing. See you later." Riggen hung up and squeezed the bridge of his nose. If Trevor didn't know why Kris was on their property, what had the woman been doing?

# THIRTEEN

Liz sat cross-legged in the middle of her queen-size bed. She punched her keyboard and her laptop's monitor lit up. She wasn't ready to leave yet and time was slipping away, but she needed to clear her head.

Why hadn't Riggen had a good answer to her question? Or any answer? And why was she letting feelings for him resurface? Caring for him was like hugging a grizzly bear. Warm and fuzzy until her heart got mauled.

Words were cheap. He'd disappeared for five years and only reappeared when he had a son in the picture. It was the height of stupidity to trust him again.

She groaned and pulled the computer up onto her lap. *Distract. Abort. Replace.* The words flashed like neon in her mind. If she went 'round-and-'round about this, she'd dive through the mental door labeled Distress. That wasn't going to happen. Time for research.

If Dupree was behind these threats, then how was she connected to the Sagebrush? Liz shut her eyes, picturing the tall blonde with the piercing blue eyes.

Nothing about Kris had put her on guard. Not a single detail had seemed out of place. Pulling up the back end of her web site, Liz navigated to the spammed comment section. Alex still hadn't gotten back to them, but that didn't mean she couldn't take a look.

She clicked on the comment and read it again.

Your fifteen minutes has come to an end.

She checked the email address associated with it: pikespeakmustangs@denmail.com.

Something danced along the edge of her memory. She pressed fingers to her eyes. She couldn't grab hold of it. Shoving her laptop aside, she untangled her legs and climbed from the bed to pace the patterned floor.

Pikes Peak Mustangs. The phrase stirred something. Connections lit her brain like a Christmas tree. She plopped into a bright red armchair and stared at the paisley wallpaper that peeked from behind her tufted headboard. *Pikes Peak Mustangs.*

Was this the missing connection? Dupree plus Pikes Peak Mustangs? Her phone buzzed and she hung over the chair's arm to grab it. Text message from Riggen.

Dupree apartment searched. She's gone. Could be abduction.

She stared at the message while thoughts continued to rearrange themselves. Pictures and data points swirled together so fast she couldn't consciously follow them. Dupree plus Pikes Peak Mustangs equals what? Where had she heard the combination?

She shot from her chair to the bed like an eagle after prey, swooping down on her laptop to pull up old files.

Five-year-old files—all the research she'd done on the Sagebrush.

She had ridiculous amounts of information. These files represented her outlet. The obsessive research had been her way of fighting the terror she had felt when Riggen deployed.

She chewed on the end of the hotel pen. All the rabbit trails she had gone down were listed for her in alphabetical order. There was partially related information along with information that had nothing at all to do with Malcovitch or the Sagebrush.

Excitement swarmed her. For once, her fight against anxiety had paid off. There it was. The file labeled "Area History." Her eyes strained as they flew over the document. She couldn't wait to tell Riggen what she'd found.

Liz bounced on the gray cushions next to him as late-afternoon travelers swarmed through the Kimpton's lobby. Riggen sent off a text to Rosche and turned to face his ex-fiancée. She was so close, the tips of their noses touched. "You really did your homework on the Sagebrush."

"I needed something to distract me." She leaned away and slid a gold bangle up and down her arm, not meeting his eyes.

He took a deep breath. "But the connection between Dupree and Malcovitch is circumstantial."

Her chest heaved as she opened her mouth to reply. Then she pitched forward to pull her shoulder bag from the floor by their feet. Yanking out her laptop, she pounded a few keys and thrust the device his way.

"They didn't just attend the same high school. Look

at this." She jabbed a newspaper headline that filled the computer screen. "Circumstantial but compelling. Who knows why Malcovitch and Dupree reconnected. Maybe they never left each other's lives. But for some reason, Kris Dupree is taking up Malcovitch's cause and coming after me."

Riggen studied the computer. A teenage Malcovitch and Dupree stood arm-in-arm as Manitou Springs' homecoming king and queen. The school's mascot mustangs were painted on a full-size mural behind them. He nodded slowly. "Pikes Peak Mustangs."

"Exactly. The email address was their school mascot."

In the fifteen-year-old, black-and-white photo, Kris's hair was dark as night. No wonder Liz hadn't recognized her.

He handed the laptop back. "So, we have a link between Dupree and Malcovitch. We have the email address that could be an emotional nod to their teenage glory days. And we have the lowlife sitting in El Paso jail, pointing the finger her direction. But if Kris is the mastermind behind the whole thing, then who ransacked her place? And where is she?"

Liz wrapped a strand of hair around her finger and shrugged. "Maybe she did it herself to throw off suspicion?"

"Then why leave the phone?"

"Accident?" she asked. "There's something else bothering me."

"What?"

"I don't know." She shrugged and retrieved her laptop, sticking it in her bag. "I can't place my finger on it, but I feel as though I haven't remembered everything. Something's still out there. Tickling the back of my brain."

He cupped a hand over her knee. "It'll come to you."

She pulled away from his touch. Her eyes narrowed. "So if she faked an abduction to throw us off track, where do we look next?"

"I think the question Rosche will be following now is, has Kris been masterminding this alone or was she collaborating with Malcovitch?"

Liz nodded.

He sent off a last text to Rosche. "It's time she finds out what Sammy Malcovitch has to say."


Wrapping her arms around her waist, Liz stood back to gaze at her finished product. Six months of work had gone into the decorated fabric walls and folding tables of the *American Travel* advertising booth.

But it was so much more. It was five years of blood and sweat and grueling uphill climbs as she had built her platform. Each step had led her to this moment.

She stuck her chest out and raised her chin to the ceiling, shivering as a bolt of sheer delight tickled her spine. That was her Pikes Peak panorama underneath the *American Travel* logo. When Kimberly East arrived, the job would be in the bag.

"Where would you like these T-shirts?" Emily Bancroft broke into Liz's thoughts and hefted a box of black T-shirts with Liz's Pikes Peak design onto the front table. Emily cocked a hip on the edge and waited.

"In the corner by the freebie stylus pens."

Emily nodded. They worked well together. Liz wouldn't have a problem bringing her new team on board with her vision when the job was hers.

From what she'd seen, each person, Emily especially, was competent and talented. Liz licked suddenly dry lips and clasped her hands together to keep from clapping. In a few short days, she'd take the editorial reins.

All around her, the conference center buzzed with excitement. It almost matched hers. She bounced on the balls of her feet and pivoted, looking for Riggen in the chaos. Emily could finish the last-minute details.

If she didn't share this moment with someone, she was going to burst. She wouldn't let the fact that it had to be Riggen ruin it.

There he was, leaning against the perimeter wall, his eyes locked on her. His lips tipped up when their eyes met.

That smile sent her insides into a warning dance. Maybe she should just hold her excitement inside. Or share it with Emily. It was too late. He was striding her way, weaving through the bustle of activity without once breaking eye contact.

*Breathe.* Her internal dance exploded into a frenzy. He shouldn't be able to do this. Not with one smile. She fisted her hands at her sides and dug her knuckles into her hip bone until her heart hit normal rhythm again.

"Do you want to grab a bite before the fun starts?" His voice rumbled over the surrounding chatter.

"Sure."

He nodded toward the far corner of the convention center. "Trevor has a booth for Price Adventure Excursions. Want to walk over?"

"Sure." She pushed the word out a second time and tried to ignore the way he was looking at her.

Emily cleared her throat behind them. It was enough

to jolt her from the gray hypnosis of Riggen's eyes. Familiar heat spread from her neck into her face.

She turned to Emily. "Riggen, this is Emily Bancroft, researcher extraordinaire for the *American Travel* team." Riggen reached out his free hand. "And Emily, this is my...my..." She stuttered to a stop.

Riggen took Emily's hand. "Her old friend, Riggen Price."

*Friend?*

"Nice to meet you, Riggen Price." Emily's face split with a smile and Liz rolled her internal eyes. She'd forgotten Riggen's effect on other women.

She cupped a hand around his arm. Her fingers barely reached halfway around, but she squeezed and pulled him from the booth.

He rested his warm palm on the small of her back and pointed out several vendors that they passed. Some provided tours, some offered accommodations, and some—like *American Travel*—supplied entertainment and education.

The amusement in his voice had nothing to do with how she had pulled him away from Emily. She cringed. That's what she'd keep telling herself.

"This looks amazing." Riggen stopped, his voice now awed. They looked up at an orange inflatable river raft that was hanging from the ceiling with Price Adventure Excursions stamped across the side in bright blue lettering.

Trevor picked himself up from the floor and stretched his back. "Thanks." Tightening a figure-eight knot in the rope he was tying, he nodded at Liz. "Good to see you."

*Was it?* Liz bit back the memory of his brush-off and forced out a smile.

"We're going to lunch." Riggen tilted his watch. "There's a good forty minutes until this starts. You in?"

"Let's do it." Trevor ducked under the raft and followed them into the wide aisle that separated the vendors.

Liz gawked at Riggen. The thought of lunch with both Prices churned her empty stomach. "I'm sure Trevor has last-minute details he doesn't need distracting from." She edged away from the men toward the main entrance.

"Nah. I'm pretty much set," Trevor replied.

Riggen stood between them, a confused look on his face. How long would it take to get this through his head? She didn't need or want him making plans for her.

He bent down and whispered into her ear. "You okay?" The low vibrato added to her irritation.

Why bother explaining? He'd be gone soon and then it wouldn't matter. She flipped her hair over her shoulder. "Let's get this on the road, then. We don't have much time."

His eyebrows arched but he turned anyway to lead them from the room. Instead of heading for the main entrance, he took them through a series of doors and hallways until they finally pushed through a heavy metal door.

Liz stumbled outside and blinked at the sudden burst of sunlight. The orange brick of the Denver Fire Department towered in front of them.

Trevor emerged behind her. "Are we avoiding paparazzi?"

"Just staying safe." Riggen grabbed her hand and

started toward the street. "I hear Denver Diner has a killer open-faced roast beef sandwich."

The clink and crash of dishes crescendoed around them as they entered the busy diner. There was a single table open in the back corner and Riggen led the way.

When they'd ordered, Liz sipped her Coke and eyed Trevor, annoyed with herself. She might not like being stuck with the Prices, but she didn't have to act like a child. She pushed out a smile and knocked ice around with her straw. "You've got a stellar booth and should have customers eating out of your hand. Hopefully it'll help your slump. It just doesn't make sense to me, though. Prime tourist area like the Springs?"

Trevor leaned back as a waitress set down a foot-tall hamburger. He gripped the sandwich with both hands and shrugged. "Nature of the business, I guess. We'll figure it out."

She caught the movement of Riggen's head as he nodded agreement. Maybe Price Adventure Excursions would turn around if Trevor's booth was a success and Riggen really did have an idea sliding around the back of his Bronco with that stack of files.

Trevor wiped a spot of mayo from his mouth and tapped his phone screen. The time flashed. He stood, slurping his pop. "I do actually have a few last-minute details to finish. See you back there?"

They both nodded and Liz drew in her ketchup with a fry as she watched him leave. Riggen's hand landed on hers right before he stole her fry. He chomped on the ketchup-laden potato. "Nervous?"

She nodded, her mind back on the night ahead of her. "It's such a big deal. This job is everything I need. Remote position with minimal travel. With the salary they're offering, I'll be able to afford a sitter when needed."

"Then let's go ace it."

Pedestrians congested the crosswalk. He'd never been a city boy. He could think of a million places he'd rather be than Denver on a Friday night, but as the crowd pushed Liz closer to him, Riggen savored the moment.

His shoulder brushed hers and she looked up. Her eyes danced with excitement. Sure, it was excitement for tonight, and not for him, but his pulse still skipped. The light clicked yellow. He jerked. He had a job to do.

Vehicles sped down the highway. Multiple lanes of traffic separated them from the convention center. Wind swirled between the high-rise buildings, pushing them against the sidewalk and the crowd of pedestrians pulsated with life in the dimming evening light. As the walk light flashed, the moving mass marched as one.

Loud whining caught his attention. He scanned the road and pulled Liz against his side, squinting into the lanes of stopped traffic. He knew that sound—gears squealing through shift changes.

There it was. A motorcycle burst between two lanes of traffic and bounced into the intersection, heading straight at them.

Screams rent the air. The human mass shattered into a hundred individuals, each running a different direction. Liz's fingers crushed his and they sprinted toward the fire station, dodging the fleeing mob.

He weaved around pedestrians, pushing through the confusion. An elderly man fell to his knees to the right of them and Liz ripped her hand away, running to the man and dropping to the pavement at his side. Riggen sprinted to them both and pulled the man back to his feet.

The squeal of tires screeched behind them. It was getting closer. "Liz!" he shouted as he dropped the man's arm.

She blanched, looking over his shoulder. "He's coming!"

He turned. The bike zigzagged through downed bodies and running people, its rider concealed under a black helmet. People leaped from his path.

Liz wasn't watching where she was going. She stumbled, crashing to the pavement. Her head bounced against the curb. Riggen's stomach dropped. Blood trickled over her eye. *Get up!* She scrambled back to her feet.

Riggen vaulted onto the curb and tugged Liz behind him. The station's garage doors were open. Just a hundred more feet.

Liz hunched to the side, whimpering, her head in her hand.

"You can do it!" he shouted.

The biker jumped the curb. Grass and mud shot into the air. The engine idled for the briefest moment as its rider aimed the bike.

There was no doubt now, the biker was here for Liz.

Riggen launched at Liz, scooping her into his arms. His legs screamed as he pushed them to run faster and harder than ever before.

He heaved her the last few feet to safety, his lungs on fire. Plunging into the open garage, they rolled out of reach just as the bike rocketed past at breakneck speed.

# FOURTEEN

The ice pack was melting. Liz tossed it on the ground as rivulets of water ran down her face. At least it had calmed her insides, which had been simmering like a hot spring ready to bubble over.

She struggled to sit upright. The paisley walls of her suite twirled, churning the lunch that was already threatening to make a reappearance. She closed her eyes until the room stopped spinning.

Riggen was pacing but he paused to push a tissue into her hand. She pushed it away, every sense on overload. Her mind was too full.

The steady stream of insanity was suffocating her. The paisley walls were closing in. It was too much to process and helplessness clawed her throat, squeezing her hope until her breath came in short, gasped puffs. She clutched a velvet throw pillow to her chest and stared at Riggen, her eyes beginning to burn. "This has to end."

He lowered himself to the floor and leaned back against the couch. "Denver PD can't track down the biker. No license plate. No facial ID from surveillance cameras."

She scrunched the pillow in her fists and dropped it next to him before climbing to her feet. Ignoring the wave of weakness that turned her legs to Jell-O, she shuffled to the window and pushed the thick curtains aside.

Night was falling over Denver. Lights twinkled in multicolored profusion. "I missed the entire session."

When she turned back to the room, Riggen's eyes caressed her.

"I'll be surprised if Kimberly has any confidence in me now." Her voice broke and she threw her hands in the air. "I didn't show up for opening night."

How could such a large man move without a sound? One moment he sat watching, the next he towered over her, holding his arms open wide. She took one tentative step forward and he pulled her against his warm chest. When his arms circled her, her anxious energy dissipated.

"Shh," he whispered against her hair. "They'll understand when you explain."

The familiar smell of his skin enveloped her, and she relaxed in his strength. His heart pounded under her wet cheek, a steady boom-boom-boom of comfort.

She leaned back and wiped her tears with her sleeve. "Lucas depends on me. If I don't get this job, what am I going to do?"

He pulled another tissue from his pocket and this time she took it. "You'll figure it out."

Every muscle tensed. She pushed away. "What did you say?"

He blinked, confusion entering his eyes. "You'll figure it out?"

Their entire history avalanched in her mind. His promise to love her forever. His disappearance. Lucas's birth.

Riggen had left her to figure things out alone and she'd never been able to stop. Not even for a moment. The weight of it pressed down on her. She shoved it away. Everything was so turned around, and she couldn't think clearly. Not with him so close.

As she backed away and breathed air that wasn't scented with his cologne, the avalanche settled. Her mind rested on reality. *Lucas is depending on me...*

"You can pretend you care, but the only reason you're holding me close is to get closer to Lucas. At the end of the day, you still want to drop responsibility on my shoulders. Lucas deserves more than that. *I* deserve more than that."

"Whoa." Riggen threw now-empty arms up. "That's not what I meant. I'd love to be involved in your lives but how can I ever prove that to you when you won't give me the chance?"

She turned away, unable to bear the defeat in his eyes but equally unable to fight the terror that was slithering into her heart. If he'd wanted to be there for her, he would never have left in the first place.

She turned away, "I don't know if you can." She didn't turn back around until the room door clicked shut behind Riggen's retreating back.

Her bedsheets were a crumpled mess from tossing and turning all night. Liz pushed aside the feather comforter and heaved her aching body from her hotel bed. Morning was creeping up on the mile-high city. She might as well give up on sleep.

Her reflection flashed in the large mirror hanging opposite her bed. Sporting a huge gash over her right eye and pretty impressive bruising, she was beginning to look exactly how she felt—like someone's punching bag.

The clock on her bedside table blinked 5:00 a.m. She didn't have to be at the convention center until seven and the lack of sleep had her queasy stomach in overdrive. Right now, she was faced with one choice and it wasn't whether to go back to bed. She needed to find breakfast.

But could she stomach eating with Riggen? She wrapped her arms around herself and stared at the beat-up woman in the mirror. "You don't know that he's only sticking around for Lucas." The bruised woman shook her head. "And you don't know that he isn't."

She gulped in air and lumbered to the bathroom. There was no point standing around and debating things she could never be certain about. *Never.* She twisted the faucet and released her lungful of air in one long, steady stream.

She splashed water on her face and neck then jolted upright. What about when she'd been in his arms? He'd seemed steady. Reliable. *Caring?*

She scrubbed her face and toweled off the water. What about his eyes when he'd pulled to the side of the road after Rainbow Falls? His concern had been directed at her *and* Lucas. Could Riggen be that good of an actor? Just to be a part of his son's life?

She pulled her brush through her tangled hair before wandering back into her room. The paisley walls drew closer as she pulled on black slacks and a white cotton top. She needed fresh air.

Slipping her feet into patent-leather pumps, she grabbed her phone and texted Riggen.

Need fresh air and breakfast. You awake? Don't want to go alone.

She tossed her phone into her purse. Would she actually go alone? No. And the admission galled her. How was she supposed to climb back into her armor with Riggen watching her down coffee and biscuits? She needed to pull herself together.

Her foot tapped against the plush carpet. The thought of going without him inched her toward the closed door but she stopped. Took a step back. Sank into the red armchair. Going alone was not a good idea.

Her phone tickled her thigh, its ringtone tinkling from her closed purse. She stuffed her hand in and dug around. Her stomach growled loud enough to be heard three floors below. She pulled the phone out. It wasn't Riggen.

It was Kat. Had something happened? California should still be in the throes of sleep. She gulped in a lungful of air before swiping the Answer button.

"Hello?" She stood and walked to the room's window, peering at the lightening skyline.

"Hey." Kat whispered.

"Is everything okay?"

"Just wanted to check in," Kat answered.

She exhaled in relief. "This early in the morning?"

A muffled laugh sounded across the connection. "Lucas had a bad dream. I couldn't get back to sleep."

Liz's stomach hardened and she leaned against the windowsill for support. "Is he okay?" The hard sill bit into her hip bones, and she shifted.

"Sleeping like a baby. Just climbed in bed with us."

Kat paused, giving Liz a moment to sigh in relief. She hated being this far from him.

A knock sounded at the door as Kat started again. *Good.* Her stomach was still growling. "I want to apologize for pressuring you to come to California."

Liz tripped over her own feet as she headed to let Riggen in. Kat never apologized. She stopped at the door and leaned against the cool metal for a moment as Kat continued. "Take your time. I'll take good care of Lucas."

"Momma?" Lucas's sleepy voice drifted over the line and stopped Liz in her tracks. Kat shushed him with loving tones. "Look, Liz, I'll catch up later." With that, her sister clicked off.

Apprehension shivered up Liz's spine and wrapped cold fingers around her heart. Was this an apology or Kat's agenda to keep Lucas to herself? She closed one eye and looked through the peephole. Riggen's Colorado Rockies hat swam before eyes that were suddenly full of tears.

She hated herself for opening the door. Hated herself for needing the comfort she had shoved away only last night.

But she did it anyway and when she looked up into Riggen's face, terror pulled and twisted her like a whitewater whirlpool.

It wasn't Riggen. A man hulked over her, three-quarters of his face hidden behind a high-altitude mask. The rest was covered with the Rockies cap she had thought to be Riggen's.

She jerked away, slamming the door forward, but the stranger lunged through the closing portal and knocked her back.

She stumbled, heel over heel, before crashing against the glass of her closet door. It shattered as her skull bounced against it. The scream that pushed through her throat was muffled as her attacker smashed her onto the room's desk.

She slid across the surface and fell backward onto the armchair. Like a ragdoll thrown by an angry toddler, she landed in a heap on the seat. The exposed wood arm dug into her backbone. She clawed at the man's face.

Fear weakened her. She was trapped under the mass of man, her bones cracking under his weight. She whaled with both fists but he pinned her arms as easily as if he were fighting a newborn deer. He jammed her wrists against the wood of the chair with bone-shattering force.

She tried to scream again but he clamped his hand over her mouth. It smelled of sagebrush. Her entire body went cold. She tried to bite but he rammed his palm forward and up, locking her mouth in place. Her vision tunneled then blurred. All she could see were his glittering eyes. Were they gray or blue? The altitude mask hid his features from view.

Her mind filled with Lucas, sleeping safe in Kat's bed. Would she ever hold him again?

Her attacker dipped his head closer, the plastic breathing piece brushing her face. "Leave Colorado. Now."

Tears burned her eyes and wet his hands. She swiveled her torso and jammed her knee into his stomach. He hunched over and grunted in pain as the room's phone shrilled into the terrifying silence.

He jerked her head up until her nose pressed the

mask. Warm moisture exhaled into her face. "Leave or you'll be sorry."

The phone stopped as he pulled his hand from her mouth. She swallowed dry fear and screamed. Her voice choked as he slipped his hand around her neck and into her hair. Revulsion washed from her brow to her heels. He slammed her head against the wood of the desk behind her.

Then he was gone. Her shoulders slid against the velvety chair cushion as she crumpled to the ground. The chandelier over her bed dimmed. The renewed ringing of her phone sounded so far away.

Consciousness ebbed and flowed as her lips moved on the prayer that Riggen would read her text and come.

Riggen burst from his room into the hotel hallway and looked up and down the empty corridor. Had he heard a scream or was it his sleep-fogged imagination? He glared at the text on his phone before dialing her cell. What was Liz thinking? Had this week taught her nothing?

He pounded on her door, the sound thundering through the corridor. She couldn't go out alone. He pounded again. He'd always admired her independence. But this? This was recklessness and irresponsibility. Pure and simple.

She wasn't answering, phone or door. His stomach dropped to the floor. Turning from her closed door, he looked once more at the deserted hallway. If she'd left, she could be anywhere in the city by now. He crushed his cell phone in his hand. Alone, she was completely unprotected. Vulnerable.

He'd barely felt the weight of her body last night

when he'd heaved her into the fire station. She'd been no challenge for him to sweep up. And she'd be no challenge to an attacker, either.

He dialed her room number, his finger pounding his phone's screen. He could hear it trilling behind her closed door. No answer.

He pounded out her cell number again. Nothing. Foreboding slammed through him. If she was there, why wasn't she answering the door? Not a good sign.

He thudded his fist against the door again. This time, so hard it rattled the wall next to him. Still no answer. Stuffing his hands in his pockets, he glared at the closed door and shifted from foot to foot.

Maybe he was overreacting. He stilled and chugged a calming breath. Counted the ceiling tiles. There were six between his room and Liz's. Maybe she was blow-drying her hair? Or in the bathroom?

He punched her number and let it ring again. Each ring spiked his heart rate. With a roll of his shoulders, he tried to drop his pulse out of the danger zone but every sense was firing. His body was in fight-or-flight mode.

He'd never been a foolish man, but standing there, listening to the phone ring, reality socked him between the eyes. No matter how hard he tried or how fast he ran, he'd never be able to protect everyone he loved. He wasn't all-powerful.

He wasn't God. He jabbed End Call. Redialed.

First ring. He couldn't save Mom from a life of misery. Second ring. He couldn't get home to say goodbye to Dad. Third ring. He couldn't protect innocent people from a suicide bomber.

The call went to voice mail. He rocked forward on the balls of his feet. He hadn't been strong enough to come through for any of them. Why would Liz be any different?

He scrubbed his hand over his face. It was hopeless. He couldn't slow his heart rate and he couldn't stifle the fear that something was very wrong.

Cold dread raced through his veins, but surrender pounded on his heart's door. He clenched his hands and stared at the closed door. He looked back at the ceiling. *Help*. The silent cry hit the back of his teeth as a moan sounded from inside the room.

Years of training took over. He stepped back and braced himself. Driving his heel right above the door's lock, he let all his energy transfer to the steel. The wood splintered, separating the door from the frame.

He pushed it open. Something was piled on the floor next to the armchair. Sun rays glinted off a pat-ent-leather heel.

*Liz*. He crashed into the room and dropped to his knees. Her hair was matted with blood and her head rested awkwardly on the floor. Bruises the color of the morning sky spilled across her face in a grotesque tie-dye effect and a single trickle of blood ran down her face to pool in her ear.

He swallowed as he pressed two fingers to her neck. Relief blasted through him. She had a pulse. He checked her neck and spine with quick, practiced movements then pulled her into his arms. Staring up at the ceiling, he nodded. *Thank You*.

Liz had been right about one thing and one thing only… This had to end.

# FIFTEEN

"I just want her safe." Fear laced Riggen's words and pulled Liz from a dreamworld of white picket fences and boyish giggles. *No, not yet.* She clamped her eyes tighter and nestled into her pillows. She wasn't ready to leave.

She could still see Lucas. He was jumping from a sprawling box elder into a beautiful green yard. And he wasn't calling Kat "Momma" by mistake.

"Take her away, then." Trevor's response chased off Lucas's happy smile and tugged Liz further into reality.

"I would in a second if I thought it would make this all end."

Liz slit an eye open. Riggen was at her side, his arm resting on her bed. Why was she in bed?

"I guess you won't know unless you try. You seem to be at the end of your rope here." What was Trevor talking about?

And why couldn't she move her head without searing pain? She searched Riggen's face through her narrow view. He looked as beat-down as she felt.

He shifted and rubbed his shadowed chin. "But what about you? What about Price Adventure Excursions?"

"I can handle it," Trevor answered. "I did before. If

you make it permanent this time, I'd be happy to buy you out. A nice nest egg for you and Liz. Where'd you say her family went? California?"

Tension rippled across Riggen's shoulders, down his arm and into the hand that was now methodically flattening her bedsheet. Trevor's words were a cold splash of water on them both and she bristled for Riggen. The Prices meant everything to him. How could Trevor write his brother's future off with so little emotion?

Siblings were the worst. She pushed her eyelids up, fighting the tightness in her face, and slid her hand over to Riggen. Her messy mix of emotions slowly melted into a single, shocked realization. Somewhere deep inside she was still attached to the man at her side.

He turned and pushed a strand of hair from her face. "Hey there."

She tried to respond but her tongue stuck to the roof of her mouth like a dry lump of cotton. Riggen reached over her and grabbed a plastic pitcher of water. He poured her a cup.

Their fingers tangled with each other as she took it. He helped her sit upright. Resting her cheek against his shoulder, she waited for the nausea to pass. Something struck her. Her walls were missing paisleys. In their place was cold gray plaster. She was in a hospital again.

Churning waves sloshed the sides of her faith boat and she gripped the cup of lukewarm water, chewing on the waxy edge. "What's going on?"

Riggen shot a glance at Trevor before answering. "We were hoping you'd tell us."

She started to shake her head but the motion sent her empty stomach into doomsday mode. "I don't know," she whispered.

She set the cup down, the paper bottom clattering against the table. Pressing an index finger to the aching area over her temple, she cut a glance at each Price brother. "My head is screaming."

"You don't remember the attack?" Trevor rose from the chair he'd been sitting on. She shrank back into her pillow. He wasn't as tall as Riggen but he still made her feel so small.

"Should I?" she asked. When he and Riggen exchanged a concerned look, her fingers dug into her thin blanket.

She slammed her fist on her table, slopping water over the sides of her cup. Droplets splashed her arm and she wiped them off. "I'll tell you what's going on..."

The men waited, heads cocked to the side. Expectant.

"My world's falling apart." She froze. "Wait...what time is it?"

Trevor glanced at his watch. "Just past nine thirty."

"A.M.?" Her voice squeaked.

They both nodded.

"Good." She grabbed hold of Riggen's arm and used it as leverage to pull herself from the bed. She balanced on unsteady feet and let go. "I still have time to get to the convention center."

Trevor's brow crinkled and Riggen shot from his seat. They both stared at her as if she had grown a third head. She stood still until a new wave of nausea stopped threatening to take her out.

"You'll make it," Trevor agreed. "But do you really think it's the best idea?"

"Emily covered for me last night, but if I bail again today, I won't be able to show my face around Kimberly or anyone else from *American Travel* ever again."

She took one step toward the door. They didn't understand. How could they? Their lives weren't balancing on getting to that show. Visions of Lucas climbing into bed with Kat and thinking she was his momma spurred her on.

Then she was tipping like a felled blue spruce. She grasped for something to grab on to but caught empty air. She was going over. The floor rose to meet her in slow motion.

Then an arm slid under her stomach, catching her before she face-planted into ugly hospital tile. Riggen pulled her into his arms and turned her until she was safely cradled against his neck.

But the dizziness didn't stop. It hit her in wave after wave. She squirmed. "I think I'm going to be sick."

He nodded and grabbed the bedpan from the rolling table. When there was nothing left in her stomach, he carried her back to her bed, lowering her onto its surface. Her eyes were closed but she felt Riggen's fingers drift across her forehead.

Trevor cleared his throat. "I think I can help."

Liz groaned. She'd forgotten about Trevor.

Riggen's voice was tight as he spoke for her. "How?"

"I'm having lunch with Kim today. I could try to explain what's been happening. Smooth it out a bit."

Liz sat straight, immediately regretting the motion but needing to clarify. "You're having lunch with Kimberly East?"

Trevor shrugged. "We go way back."

"That's a great idea." Riggen pulled her hand into his own. Gray concern overflowed from his eyes. "If you can't make it two steps across the floor, you can't possibly work all day. You need to call in and let the chips fall where they will. Maybe Trevor can smooth it over."

She hated that he was right. She nodded her consent and Trevor left them alone.

All she could do was sit back and trust. She settled against the cold, hard hospital pillow. Riggen's fingers tightened around her own and she let her lids droop.

She'd trust that whatever was going on, God would work it out for her good. Because whatever chance she had with *American Travel* had just walked out the doorway and down the hall.

A nurse had been in to let them know Liz was clear to go, but the woman in question was still asleep, her fingers curled in his palm. Riggen stretched out his legs and leaned back into the uncomfortable faux-leather armchair. She'd been out for hours.

He closed his eyes and listened to her breathing. He could sit there and listen all day. The sound meant she was alive. God had answered his prayer.

Now what was he going to do? Trevor was right, he was at the end of his rope. Riggen didn't know what to do next. He'd made a promise to Lucas to take care of his mother. He slipped his hand from Liz's and crossed his arms over his chest. He couldn't figure out what to do with emotions clouding his mind.

This wave of danger seemed unending. Unending and unidentifiable. He couldn't continue watching Liz be prey.

She may not belong to him, but that didn't mean he'd stand by and watch her be hurt. Sure, he'd hurt her himself, and he'd rewind his mistake in a second if he could. But now it was someone else bent on hurting her. Some faceless enemy he'd happily decimate if he knew where to find them. He wasn't going to let them close again. Not while there was fight left in his body.

He drew his foot up and crossed it over his knee. Maybe there was something to what her brother-in-law taught. Deep down—where he couldn't lie to himself— he saw today that there was no guarantee he could keep Liz safe. No guarantee he could keep her from pain. No guarantee he could keep himself from pain.

He shoved his hands through his hair. Maybe if he ran full-throttle after today, then he could let tomorrow worry about itself. Something surfaced in his memory, dim and watery, misshapen from years of neglect. As it took form, he could hear Dad's voice. *Life is a mist. You appear, then you disappear. Live for God, it's the only thing that lasts.*

He slammed his eyes shut to catch hold of Dad's voice before it floated away. What wouldn't he give to run after life instead of living in this paralysis of fear?

It's what Dad had taught him after he'd been adopted as a Price. It's even what his mother had embraced before she'd died. He'd never bought into it, but after meeting John, he was drawn to how the man wholeheartedly lived it.

Riggen's phone buzzed in his pocket and he leaned to the side to pull it out. Soreness pulled at his strained muscles. He swiped open the screen. Incoming message from Alex. He drew a deep breath, his nostrils widening at the effort to keep silent. *Finally.*

Got address for your commenter.

The stiff plastic of the chair squeaked under him as his body tensed. He typed a reply.

Great. Send it over.

His phone lit again but it wasn't with the information he wanted. Confusion had him in a headlock.

"What is it?" Liz's voice was slow and slurred from sleep. She rolled toward him and placed a hand on his arm, grazing the phone with her ponderous movement. He lost hold and it slid across the floor.

"I'm not sure." He stood and walked to the neglected food cart, where his phone had come to a stop. "Alex just got back to me."

He hunkered down, pulled the device from under the rolling cart and studied the new text again.

Are you pulling my chain?

"That's good, isn't it?" She sat up, peering at him with tired eyes.

He walked to the door of Liz's room and held the phone in his palm, his thumbs hovering over the keypad, the wheels in his mind whirling.

What was Alex saying?

No. Why?

The answer hit his backlit screen and his entire world shook. There were multiple moments he wished he could reverse in life. Asking that question was one of them.

The comment was posted from Price Adventure Excursions.

# SIXTEEN

He was driving her away from the center of Denver, not toward it. Liz shifted in her seat so she could see Riggen without straining her neck. "Where are we going?"

Riggen wore a scowl she'd never seen before. His eyes were glued to the cars in front of them, his fingers beating against the steering wheel to a tune only he could hear.

"Riggen?" The weird silence that had started in her hospital room hung between them like a fog. She still didn't know what Alex had said. The not knowing tumbled suspicion through her head like a rockslide.

Her nurse had arrived with discharge paperwork the moment after Alex's text. The following flurry of activity had eliminated any chance to question Riggen.

She reached across the armrest and tapped his shoulder. His entire body jerked. The rockslide crashed into her stomach. What was going on?

They'd been in pretty tense situations this week, and he'd yet to lose his cool. She pinched the skin on her wrist as sweat started to trickle down her back. What had Alex said that gagged him into silence?

Pulling one leg up under her, she angled toward him. "What's going on?"

He didn't take his eyes from the winding line of cars that snaked out in front of them and her attention drifted from traffic to driver then back again. He needed to turn around. The convention center was behind them.

He signaled to merge onto the entrance ramp and jerked his head at the hazy horizon. "We need to disappear."

"Um…" Her voice wavered as she pulled her other leg up to sit cross-legged. "You're officially freaking me out."

"Denver isn't safe." He ramped onto the highway and pressed the gas. The snow-peaked Rockies met the clouds and mist with pastel watercolor beauty. Traffic cleared as they drove away from the city and hit open freeway.

Denver's high-rise buildings disappeared in the rearview mirror along with all hope. Anxiety crashed around in her stomach and climbed up her throat. "I need to get to the expo."

"It isn't safe."

"Nowhere is safe, Riggen. Take me back." She puffed her cheeks with air and blew it out again.

He just kept driving. She glared out the window at the mountains she loved. He was making another decision for her and there wasn't a thing she could do to stop him. All fight had melted from her body. Her head throbbed and she hovered on the edge of collapse.

Slumping her shoulder against the cool window, she slid her lids closed. She'd figure it out when they got… well, when they got to whatever destination Riggen had in mind.

Halfway between Denver and the Air Force Academy, Riggen's phone buzzed from the cup holder. Trevor's name rolled across the screen. Instinctively, she grabbed for it.

Had he smoothed things over with Kimberly? The woman had been less than happy when Liz had called to explain she wouldn't make another session. If Trevor's charm worked on *American Travel*'s editor-in-chief, then Liz could stop worrying that the damage done by her chaotic life was irreparable.

Riggen's hand grasped hers midair. "Don't." His voice was granite. Cold and hard.

"But—"

"Do you trust me?" He cut through her objection and caught her eyes with his, her hand still encased in his grip.

She pulled back as his question rolled over her. "Do I trust you?"

And in that moment it was as if someone had installed one of those preposterous epiphany lightbulbs above her head and given Riggen the string.

She shook her head, rebelling against the truth her heart was pounding. It was as clear as pure mountain water. Against all that made sense, she trusted him.

She must have hit her head harder than she'd thought. "Why in the world would I trust you?"

He slashed a look her way. "Right. Well, either way, I'll explain later. Right now I need to think."

Her body started to shiver and fatigue wilted her into her seat. He needed to think? She pressed her fingers into her aching temples. She needed to do the opposite. She needed to get as far from her rebellious thoughts as she could.

Maybe for this moment, she'd let him do the thinking. What else could she do? She was beat-up, nauseated, targeted. Ready to throw in the towel. She let the roar of tires on concrete lull her into the muddled bliss of dreamland.

Riggen braked the Bronco and she jolted awake. She sat up and looked around. He was pulling them into Manitou PD's station. She rubbed the sleep from her eyes.

He parked the Bronco and walked around to open her door. His muscles rippled under his thermal shirt as he hefted her duffel from the floor. He stuffed his stack of Price Adventure Excursion files into his own bag then reached in and pulled her into his arms. He kicked the door shut behind them and carried her as though she weighed no more than Lucas.

She turned her face away as he strode up to the entry door and entered a code into the mounted keypad. The heavy metal door clicked open.

She pushed against his hard chest. "Put me down."

He cocked an eyebrow but set her down on the sloped concrete of the parking lot. She stumbled back and threw her hands out, grabbing at his shoulders to keep from falling. He slipped his hands around her waist.

She might have had a concussion and felt like she'd just taken a tumble down Pikes Peak, but she wasn't about to let her ex-fiancé carry her across any thresholds. Their relationship was still as unsteady as her own footing.

His hands weren't unsteady, though. They stayed firm on her waist, guiding her through the entry and into a long corridor with doors opening on either side.

He reached around her, his arms enveloping her, to turn the knob on the closest door.

They walked inside a small galley-style kitchen and Riggen dropped his keys on the Formica countertop before guiding her through to what appeared to be the station break room. It was empty. No sign of anyone else.

She stumbled past a rickety old dining table that looked like a relic from the eighties. Her eyes zeroed in on a faded red couch situated just under a massive poster with America's top ten Most Wanted criminals. *Cozy.*

The worn cushions called to her. She sidestepped a coffee table and collapsed onto the soft surface, her eyes shutting in relief. She sat still, unable to muster the energy to ask what was coming next.

She didn't open her eyes back up until a blanket was draped over her. Riggen stepped back and pulled a brown folding chair from under the table, turned it around, and straddled it. He rested his elbows on the back while she tugged the emergency blanket he had covered her with to her chin.

She kicked off her shoes and wiggled her feet into the corner of the couch. "So what's going on?"

"Alex found out more than I expected." Anger edged his voice.

"That's great, isn't it? What are our next steps?"

A flash of pain, swift as summer lightning, lit his eyes. She would have missed it if she had blinked. He tilted his head back and stared at the ceiling. "I'll know more after I update Rosche. For now, let's finally get some rest, lay low and recover."

She fell back into the cushions. She did need rest. But she needed to get back to Denver more. Whatever this development was, she hoped Rosche would act on it fast. And by fast, she meant by the end of the nap she was about to take because the ceiling tiles over her head were flexing in an optical illusion that made her stomach heave. A nap was nonnegotiable at this point.

She squinted at Riggen. "Tomorrow is my last chance. If I don't get back to Denver and clear this mess up, I might as well say goodbye to the job."

He didn't say a thing and his silence only increased the roil of her stomach. She pulled the coarse blanket over her head and pressed it into her face. It smelled like disinfectant and car tires. She still had the Trevor card. If Trevor had put in a good word for her, it might not be so bleak.

Footsteps clunked against linoleum. She pushed the blanket aside to see Riggen's back as he disappeared through the break room door. Then again, maybe it was hopeless.

He couldn't do it. He couldn't tell Liz everything was going to be okay. Not when the sky in his own world was falling. Riggen stomped into Rosche's office across from the kitchen and closed the door.

He leaned against it and pinched the bridge of his nose. How in the world had he missed this? Trevor had been the one unchangeable in his life. How had he over-looked the fact that his beloved brother was entangled with the likes of Sammy Malcovitch?

He pushed off the door and stalked to the window. He'd been a fool to start believing God wasn't punishing him for his mistakes. What else could this be? He was a trained officer. An experienced soldier. How could he miss the signs?

Unless God had hidden them from him. Liz's voice echoed through his mind. *That's not how God works.* But the shame and rage overtaking him drowned her words out.

He'd been so young when they'd met the Prices at a soup kitchen in Colorado Springs. Too young to understand most kids didn't eat Christmas dinner at soup kitchens. Too young to understand what his mom had been caught up in.

Instead of dinner, she'd found a new life that night. And when Mr. Price had brought them home to his ranch and given Mom a job cooking for the ranch hands, Riggen had immediately latched onto the older Trevor, shadowing the teen's every move.

Trevor had been there ever since. He'd comforted Riggen when Mom died. He'd been the one to break the news of Dad's death. And after Iraq? Well, Trevor was the one who'd helped him pick up the pieces and move on.

Now nothing made sense. If Trevor was in on this, that meant he was working with Sammy Malcovitch and Kris Dupree. There had to be some feasible explanation. A detail they were overlooking or a missing piece to this messed-up puzzle. He didn't want to believe that Trevor was in on these attacks.

Sunlight poured through beat-up vinyl blinds and spilled onto the desk behind him, marking the smooth glass top with parallel lines of light. He peered through the blinds then slammed his fist into the window frame.

Pain spread like wildfire into his bicep and shoulder. It was nothing compared to the betrayal winding itself around his chest, bending and twisting until he doubled over. *Why?* He gripped the window ledge. Why would Trevor go after Liz?

Because his mistakes were coming around to slug him in the gut. There was no getting around it.

Riggen didn't know how long he huddled there before his phone started pulsating with an incoming call. He grabbed at it. It better be Rosche. And she better have answers.

He held the phone to his ear. "What do you have?"

"It's not good." Rosche clicked her tongue. "I'm pulling footage from the novelty store across the street. Their camera is pointed right at Price Adventure Excursions. It looks as though Trevor was at the office during the entire timeframe."

"Anyone else?" He walked to the desk and sat down, pushing a stack of notepaper across the smooth surface.

"Yeah," she answered. "Kris."

"Why?" The cry erupted from his gut and he swept his fist across the desktop, sending notepaper flying to the floor in a flurry of white.

"Dude," Rosche whispered, "I can't imagine."

"What's the motive?" he asked, more for himself than Rosche. He'd been around and around this merry-go-round and kept coming up empty. He needed to get it into the air.

"Maybe she posted the comment without his knowledge?" Rosche threw out. "But that doesn't factor in the smartphone we found with your family's property in the frequent locations. Trevor being involved fits."

He flicked the one remaining sheet of notepaper to the floor, Trevor's denial that Kris had ever been to the property flitting through his mind. "It does, but he's my brother. I don't want to jump to conclusions." Not that the desire was stopping him.

There was a pause before Rosche hummed agreement. "What can I do?"

"Find solid evidence." He could hear his voice hardening. Not so different from his heart. "Then we bring him in."

"You're closest to him. Any ideas what's going on or where we should start?" She cleared her throat. "Does Trevor have a history with Sammy or Kris?"

"As in trafficking history? You think I wouldn't tell you something like that?" He dropped his voice and cut a look toward the closed door.

"Not trying to imply anything." Her words rushed out. "Just looking at all the angles."

He jammed his hand through his hair. "No history. But I don't have any ideas about where to start, either."

He popped off the chair and went to a knee, gathering the mess he'd made. He gave up and sat in the middle of it. With one leg straight out, he bent the other and rested his arm against it. *Did he have ideas on where to start?* He almost laughed out loud.

He'd had ideas before this morning. Ideas about who he was, who his family was, and what he was beginning to want from life. He'd even started having ideas about running toward a relationship with God.

"You still there?" Rosche's voice was wary. Did she think he was teetering on the edge?

He'd handle this. Soldier on. "Search the office. Maybe we'll find some kind of connection. Or evidence."

Tapping floated over the connection and he could almost see Rosche rapping her ever-present pencil against the phone receiver. "We don't have a warrant."

"What do you need a warrant for?" he asked. "I'm on the lease. You have my permission."

"Copy that."

"I'm at the station. I'm setting the key on your desk. Let me know as soon as you find something. And… Rosche?"

"Yeah?"

"Thanks for prioritizing this investigation. I don't know how I can repay you."

"No problem." Her voice was soft, the superhero façade vanishing for a moment. "Just keep an eye on that girl and don't do anything foolish."

He ended the call. While he appreciated the sentiment, he had little faith he could heed the words.

That's something she'd never thought of before— brooding men were only thrilling in novels and rom-coms. Liz pulled the emergency blanket tight and sunk into the break room's couch.

She stared at Riggen. In real life, they were frustrating. He hadn't said a word since he'd returned almost half an hour ago.

She scooted to the edge of her red perch and stuck one foot across the coffee table to nudge his knee. No response. He just stared at the blank television screen in the corner with as much intensity as if he had a twenty-point elk in his sights.

She wiggled on the couch, impatience rising off her like steam from boiling water. Enough was enough. She'd given him plenty of time to explain but he'd only stomped around the room like a caged mountain lion. Much more of this and she'd hitchhike back to Denver.

She poked his knee again, this time with the sharp point of her three-inch heels. "Rig, I'm missing the job opportunity of my life and I guess we're at the station as a safety measure, but I'm tired of not knowing what's going on."

He turned. Focused. Blinked. Slow and steady. Well, that was something. At least he was still alive.

"You said to trust you." She crossed her legs over a pile of old magazines. "How can I if you won't spit out what's going on?"

He tugged at the neckline of his charcoal thermal. "Rosche turned over info that led me to believe it was beyond my ability to keep you safe in Denver."

His eyes darted away. He looked everywhere but at her. "Is this job opportunity more important than your life? You have a son."

Defeat pushed her deep into the couch. "But without a steady job, what type of life can I give him? I can't move to California to be the third wheel in his life. He deserves better."

Silence. He'd gone back to staring at the blank television set. Her nauseated stomach flipped. Maybe her problems were too much for him and now he was shutting down. Just like Dad had right before he'd left.

She pulled her knees to her chest, contracting the buzzing beehive in her abdomen. It was time to refocus her thoughts on the here and now. "Do you think Rosche'll have it figured out by tomorrow? The last session ends at 6:00 p.m."

"I don't know, Liz." He closed his eyes, frustration riding his words.

She was shut out.

Anxiety zapped through her heart and robbed her breath. Was he wondering if she was worth this? She didn't want to be at his mercy, but she also didn't want to lose his protection. There was no one else. She placed her hands on her temples and squeezed. *Be strong and courageous.*

Her heart wouldn't stop racing. *Do not be afraid.* She was too tired. Her fear shouted louder than the truths she had memorized.

Pushing herself as far into the couch's cushiony depths as she could, she huddled into the blanket. "I need more rest."

"Okay." Riggen stood and headed for the door. With a flick of his fingers, he turned off the break room lights.

That was it. One word. *Okay.* Nothing was okay but she couldn't fight the exhaustion that hounded her as Riggen's footsteps faded into deafening silence.

# SEVENTEEN

Twilight kissed Riggen's face and pulled him from the first deep sleep he'd had in days. He fought awareness. He didn't want to remember why his heart and body felt like he'd been hit by a rockslide.

Peeling his eyes open, he looked around at the tan walls and Wanted posters. He was in Rosche's office. He scrubbed a hand back and forth over his face until the desire to crash back into sleep left him. He was here because of Trevor.

A snicker sounded from the door. His gaze bounced to the hallway to see Lieutenant Carr standing in the doorway. Boots clattered on the hall floor behind Carr and Jones stuck his head around the corner.

"Good morning, sunshine." Carr's voice rippled with laughter as Jones pulled out his smartphone and clicked a picture.

Riggen glared at them both and climbed from Rosche's uncomfortable office chair. "What time is it?"

Carr hooked his thumbs in his bulletproof vest and grinned. "Second shift just clocked in. I would've let you snore longer but your lady's in the kitchen." He grimaced. "Scavenging."

"Thanks." Riggen rubbed the remaining sleep from his eyes and ignored Jones. "Did Rosche talk to you? We didn't have anywhere safe enough to crash."

Carr cut a look at Jones and gave the man a jerk of his head. Jones nodded and trotted away, leaving them alone, or as alone as they could be in a busy police station.

"Rosche is at Price Excursions now. You need to go check out what she found." Carr's brows drew together over his eyes before he jabbed a thumb over his shoulder. "And maybe get the little lady something to eat."

Riggen stiffened but Carr reached out and placed a massive paw on his shoulder. "Don't worry. We'll keep her safe."

Riggen glanced around Carr and saw Liz half in, half out of the fridge. If she was looking for something edible, she wouldn't find it in there. Last time he braved the station fridge, all he'd found was Chinese leftovers of indeterminable age.

He made a beeline for her, grabbing a doughnut when he stepped into the kitchen. He leaned against the counter. "You won't find anything worth eating in there."

She glanced over her shoulder, her hair falling in waves over her wrinkled shirt. She raised one perfect brow at the glazed dream in his hand. "So the stereotype's true."

He took another bite before he answered. "Yep. No shame. But if you'd like something else, I can pick up dinner. What sounds good?"

She straightened so fast it looked as though an invisible puppet master had pulled her strings. He finished the doughnut as she pushed the fridge shut with deliberate slowness. "Hitting the road for Denver sounds good."

"Not possible." He inched sideways toward the hallway and snagged another doughnut. "It's best you stay here. For now."

Perfect lips pulled down. "So you're locking me up?"

"This place is as safe as Fort Knox."

She snorted and crossed her arms. He jangled his keys to distract her. They'd both feel better with full stomachs. As her eyes locked on the keys, he took a step toward the exit. "No social media or blog updates. I don't want anyone to know where we are." He strode for the door. "I'll be back in a few."

Liz stalked back to the couch that had been her refuge all morning and afternoon. She sipped coffee from a foam cup, but the burnt-bean taste wrinkled her nose. She couldn't get the first drink past the dry lump in her throat.

Of course she was safe here. *Physically.* But losing the opportunity to work for *American Travel* was swiftly becoming a danger.

The back of her throat began to burn and she slammed the cup down on the coffee table in front of her. Resting her elbows on the tabletop, she held her head in her hands and listened to the muffled sounds of the police department. Would she ever be able to keep all her balls in the air at once?

Why did she have to choose between physical safety and material safety? *God, where are You?* No answer. Just the sound of police radios filtering through the silence of the break room.

She stood and glared at the cramped kitchen with its overabundance of doughnuts. Yes, Denver was dangerous until they found Kris and this game was over, but she couldn't let the *American Travel* ball drop.

She sank down onto the folding chair and pulled up her recent calls. She'd not heard from Trevor yet but she needed to clear the air with Kimberly.

Riggen pulled through the drive-thru and hung out his open window to grab their order. The smell of hamburgers and coffee hit him with a sickening one-two punch. Maybe fast food hadn't been his best idea.

He dropped the grease-stained paper bag onto his passenger seat and pulled away from the building. "Carr said you had something for me to see." Rosche's call was on Speaker.

"How soon can you meet me over here?"

He braked for the Manitou exit. "I just grabbed dinner. How about the Cliff's Notes?"

"I think you'll want to see it yourself."

"That bad?" he asked.

"Just don't want you to take my word for it."

He glanced at the dash clock. He could check this out and book it back to the station, and hopefully their food wouldn't even get cold.

"Be there in five." He hung up and took a swig of coffee. Before the burn of it cooled from his tongue, he was circling the last roundabout on Manitou Avenue and pulling into Price Adventure Excursions.

The gravel lot was empty except for Rosche's SUV. The Closed sign swung precariously from the front door.

He shoved the Bronco into Park and hopped out, stalking to the front door and rapping on the glass pane with his keys. Rosche's blazing red hair bobbed down the hallway toward him.

She shoved a thick stack of manila folders under her arm and unlocked the door. Smirking, she pointed at dark drips of coffee that added a blob of brown to his shirt.

He wiped a hand down his chest while kicking the door shut.

"Get anything inside?" she asked.

He clicked the lock in place. "What do you have?"

Trotting down the hall toward Trevor's office like a dog on the hunt, she didn't even stop to reply. Her voice drifted over her retreating back. "I pulled the surveillance footage."

"We already covered that." He shouted down the hallway as he grabbed a tissue from the front desk and dabbed his shirt.

When he got to Trevor's office, Rosche was already seated in the oversize office chair. She swiveled until she faced the computer monitor then tapped on a few buttons.

He slouched in the opposite seat, coffee swirling in his stomach as Rosche's fingers danced across the keyboard. Her eyes were locked on whatever sordid secrets the monitor displayed.

He looked everywhere but at her and the computer. He didn't want to know what she'd found. He studied the walls, which were filled with pictures of him, Trevor, and Dad. Excursion pictures. Childhood pictures of camping on Pikes Peak in their lean-to turned clubhouse. Army pictures.

Rosche cleared her throat. "It's not bad." Sympathy filled her voice as she swiveled the monitor toward him.

"We already knew Kris was here, but I dug deeper. I synced your footage here to the same timeframe as the gas station video."

The monitor showed the front door opening and Kris walking in. Trevor met her in the front of the building.

Riggen looked up. "There's a chime on the door. He would have left his office to greet whoever it was." He could feel heat creeping up his neck at the "duh" look Rosche leveled at him.

"Thanks for that detective work." Her eyes rolled to the ceiling. "But take a look at this. Trevor disappears into the storage room and leaves Kris alone for about five minutes." She fast-forwarded the footage. "While he's gone, Kris sneaks into his office and reemerges mere moments before he reappears." She stopped suddenly. "Does Trevor have a camera in here?"

Riggen looked around the small office and back at Rosche. Her green eyes were glittering. "No. There wasn't any reason to put one in back here."

Rosche leaned back in the chair and sent it spinning. "I think we need to revisit my original theory."

"That he didn't know what she was doing?"

"Yeah, it still doesn't address the GPS problem, but watch this." She resumed the footage and Trevor came down the hall with a box in his arms. He handed it to Kris.

Riggen pointed at the screen. "That's a box of brochures. Our area partners distribute them in their hotels or restaurants."

Rosche nodded then stopped the video and pointed at the digital time display in the corner of the screen. "Look at the timestamp. The timeframe for your blog comment is over."

Relief hit Riggen like a flash flood. He knew it had to have been some type of misunderstanding.

He stood and moved to the door, fighting to regain control of his emotions and suspicions. Turning back, he leaned against the door frame. "I guess you'll be wrapping up here."

"Soon." She nodded at the stack of files she'd set on the desk. "I need to put these back. No urgency in filtering through them now. I'll lock up when I finish, then I'm heading to El Paso to talk to Malcovitch."

He grabbed the files and stuffed them under his arm. "I'll just add these to the ones I'm working on."

She saluted then leaned forward, tenting her fingers over the desk. "So, you think Kris's got some beef with your family? Some reason to be framing Trevor and going after your baby mama? Or is this just all about Sammy Malcovitch?"

At his raised eyebrow, she just smiled and shrugged.

He shook his head. "Reason? No clue. All I know is that she's a pro at muddying the waters. First, her disappearance looks like an abduction and, second, her involvement made me doubt my own brother."

He turned to leave. It was time to get back to Liz. "All I know for sure is that she and Sammy were made for each other."

# EIGHTEEN

Kimberly's reassurance settled in Liz's heart as she hit End Call. Whatever Trevor had said to the woman, it had smoothed her ruffled feathers. If Liz could either get back to the show for the closing session or make sure Emily had all under control in her absence, she still had a chance at the job.

Liz paced the small break room and lapped the coffee table for the twentieth time. Riggen had to take her back to Denver. If she got to the show, she could still build the life Lucas deserved. She was done with other people taking over her responsibilities.

A door slammed in the distance and she jogged through the kitchen and slid into the hallway. Riggen's voice floated through the air alongside Lieutenant Carr's.

She moved toward the voices and slammed into Riggen as he rounded the corner. His arms encircled her, steadying her against him. Her breath caught at his nearness. She took a swift step back and stopped in her tracks. A change had come over him. His eyes were clearer. His energy lighter.

She reached for the bag he was holding. "You look better."

"I feel better."

"Were you hangry?" She rummaged through the fried food while clamping down her own news. Denver hovered on the tip of her tongue.

Riggen laughed and the sound echoed off the stark walls. He placed a hand on her back and led her into the kitchen. "No."

She plopped the rumpled bag on the counter and arranged the food in a row. "What then?"

"Rosche had an update. I stopped to check it out."

"Oh." She picked the French fry box from the lineup, unease and salty grease filling the air around her.

"It's good news." He nodded at the fry she was crushing between her fingers. "As soon as you're ready, we can head back to Denver."

She chomped down on the smooshed fry, her anxiety melting into the shiny grease on her fingertips. "So I still have a chance to prove I deserve this job."

He tilted his watch. "And since we didn't check out of our hotel, we can leave now with enough time to settle back in and prepare for tomorrow."

She stuffed another fry into her mouth and wiped her hands on a napkin. She'd be able to give Lucas his own home soon. "Let's get out of here."

Liz was on fire. Riggen couldn't tear his eyes from her. Adventure and excitement radiated from her, drawing people to see what *American Travel* was all about.

He couldn't be prouder of this woman he had once loved. *Once?* The rogue thought caught him off guard. Leaning against the wall, he watched the ebb and flow of people and tried to push the question away.

Liz was still under his skin and he was beginning

to suspect she always would be. He nodded at a security guard on the other side of the aisle. So far, the session had been uneventful. Good for safety. Bad for distraction.

He'd take uneventful every time. Liz's schedule was drawing to a close and he was anxious to take her somewhere more secure. Rosche was interviewing Malcovitch now and if the man cracked, maybe they could get this threat uncovered and dealt with.

Until then he had to decide what the next step was. Back to the station? His cabin? He hitched his thumbs in his belt loops. California?

Liz looked up and smiled at him. His heart skipped the next few beats. All he knew for now was that he wasn't leaving her side.

His phone rang and he pulled it from his pocket. "Price."

"You'll never believe what happened." Rosche was out of breath.

"What?"

"Sammy Malcovitch is dead."

Cold shock obliterated his hope that Malcovitch could lead them to Kris. "How?"

"Remember our guy from the hospital?"

Riggen shuddered. He remembered.

"Somehow he got to Sammy with a homemade knife. Stabbed him before the guards could intervene. Sammy bled out in the yard."

Riggen stood straighter. "What was the fight about?"

Rosche drew a breath so sharp it reverberated in his ear. "That's the strangest part. You."

Everything slowed around him. He crossed his arms and focused on the waning crowd. "Me?"

"Appears he formed some type of bond with you and appointed himself your protector."

*I knew a woman with hair like that once.* "What does he think I need protection from?"

"That's where it gets interesting. If he can be trusted, he said the word was Sammy was finished with his revenge. He was giving his girlfriend the go-ahead to off Liz—no matter who got in the way."

"Meaning me?"

"Exactly," she answered.

"And by girlfriend, we're looking for—"

"Kris."

"Do we know if Kris got the message?"

"Can't be sure," Rosche replied. "Either way, she's going to blow a gasket when she finds out he's dead."

He hadn't stopped scanning the room all night but now his senses ratcheted into DEFCON 5. Fear weaseled into his gut. "We need to find Kris. Now. But she's evaded us ever since this started." He searched every exit and entry, analyzing each face. What if she was here now?

"We got a break." Static from a police radio cut through their conversation and Rosche put him on hold. When she came back, she was rushed, ready to get off the phone. "Carr sent Jones out twenty minutes ago to check into a tip. One of Kris's neighbors thinks he saw her."

Riggen clenched his fist. This was going to end tonight. "Let me know as soon as you have her."

Someone was waving hands over the heads of the thinning crowd. Trevor. Riggen ended the call with Rosche as his brother approached, a statuesque blonde on his arm.

"Good to see you." Trevor clapped his back. "Are

you actually making it through a whole session? No unexpected emergencies?"

Riggen pulled Trevor into a hug, hoping the embrace would obliterate the guilt hovering above his head. How could he have thought his brother had anything to do with this mess?

"Liz is determined to see this through." He nodded at the *American Travel* booth and patted his concealed weapon. "I'm equally determined to prevent unforeseen emergencies."

"I hope that works out for you both." Trevor inclined his head to the woman at his side. "This is Kimberly East. She was just on her way to see Liz. Thought I'd walk over with her."

The woman who held Liz's future in her hands reached out to shake hands with him. "Good to meet you." She spoke with the confidence of a woman used to commanding the situation.

She jutted out a hip and rested her fist on it. "Your brother told me about what's been happening. I'm impressed Elizabeth has carried on so well despite the challenges."

"She'll be a formidable force for any team fortunate enough to have her." He beamed over Kimberly's shoulder at Liz, not even trying to stop the pride that colored his voice.

"I believe you're right." Kimberly nodded as she excused herself and made a decisive march in Liz's direction.

Liz bundled up the last of the merchandise into a cardboard box and handed it to Emily. "See you on the conference call Monday."

Emily took the box and grinned. "Welcome to the team."

The team. Was it possible to burst from excitement? Liz sidestepped the torn-down folding table and skipped toward Riggen. Soon she'd have Lucas back. They'd have their own home. Their own life.

She caught Riggen's twinkling eyes. Was that pride she saw? Whatever it was, it made her stand taller. Skip faster. She felt as if she could climb to the summit of Pikes Peak. Her hard work was finally paying off.

Laughter bubbled from deep inside. Riggen had even given them a dog. Now all they needed was the picket fence. *What about the husband and daddy?* She flapped her hands in front of her face as the thought spread heat across her chest and up her neck. The success of the night had addled her brain.

Stopping in front of Riggen, she laced her hands together to still them. His brows lifted as if he could read the thoughts swirling through her mind. She focused on the large clock behind him while telling herself Riggen wasn't clairvoyant. "Ready to hit the road?"

"Past ready," he drawled.

She stuffed her hands in her pockets and rocked back on her heels. "I got the job."

Before her next breath, she was caught up in his arms, held close to his chest. The convention center twirled around them. "Congratulations."

Setting her down, he held her loosely, but she twisted out of his embrace. "Kim even asked me to take point on an international expo in California next month."

Smile lines broke out in a delightful profusion across his face, stretching from the corners of his gorgeous eyes to his hairline. "I'm so proud of you, Lizzy."

"Lucas and I can start our own life."

The laugh lines smoothed as his face grew serious. "Will I have a place in that life?"

She wrung her hands together and shifted from one aching foot to the other. The vulnerability in his eyes wiggled behind her armor and jabbed at her heart.

She was fighting so hard against trust. *What if I was wrong? What if he really wasn't going anywhere?* Some of the dazzle dimmed from her day. Lucas's life would be so much fuller with a father, but she took a step back and hugged her arms around herself.

Her arms were a poor substitute for Riggen's. She hated that fact, but she couldn't yet make the jump into trust.

His jaw tightened and a mask dropped until his eyes were unreadable.

She blinked and licked her lips. Her tired brain couldn't answer but she had to try. He deserved that much.

"Rig…" She swallowed and forged ahead. "I can't—" The overhead lights flickered then went off. Hands landed on her arms and pulled at her. She screamed.

"It's me." Riggen's voice breezed into her ear as he pulled her toward the wall that had been behind them.

Emergency lights clicked on, and the ghastly glow highlighted his face. It was hard as flint. He slid his hand down her arm and twined her fingers into his own. He was leading her along the perimeter of the room toward the exit.

Murmurs of worry and confusion rose from the remaining vendors as alarms began to blare. Riggen let go of her hand to palm his concealed holster. She grabbed hold of his shirttail as vendors and employees surged around them.

Security guards helmed the exits, shouting over the commotion, but anarchy was descending with alarming force. She followed Riggen step-for-step until her toe caught on a torn piece of carpet. She fell headlong into his back. Her bruised body rebelled. Her head swirled.

He reached around and steadied her. "I don't like the feel of this," he whispered, his breath feathering wisps of her wayward hair.

"Maybe it's coincidence." She gasped as his arm covered her aching shoulders. "Maybe it has nothing to do with me." She couldn't bring herself to believe her own words and pushed closer, huddling into his protection.

He moved them through the crush toward the door, using his forearm as a shield to push people away. "I think we've hit our legitimate limit of coincidences."

Ten booths from the exit, sprinklers blasted on. Screams echoed off the walls. The level of fear in the room became tangible. Not even Riggen's strength could keep the frantic crowd from jostling and hitting her on every side.

Her head crashed into his shoulder as someone shoved past her to the bottlenecked exit.

Riggen stopped, turned them back and retraced their steps through the melee. "This way." He separated them from the surging herd as water poured from her drenched hair into her eyes. She squinted into the darkened space.

He was leading them to the exit they'd used the day they'd lunched with Trevor. Pushing open a side door, he pulled them into a long hallway. Exit signs flashed at the end and they fell in step, jogging through the raining mess to safety.

A door opened behind them and banged against the wall. She turned but couldn't discern anything. Only shadows.

Something flew through the air. She screamed and Riggen spun her around, shielding her with his body. A canister clattered to the floor, crashing into the wall beside them.

Smoke seeped from it, weaving into dry air pockets around them. She coughed and gripped Riggen's waist, pressing her face into his back. He slung his arm over her shoulder and pushed her toward the exit.

"Keep going," he rasped.

She willed one foot in front of the other, barreling toward the saving light at the end of the corridor. Sunlight bathed her wet face as they emerged from the conference center.

Footsteps pounded down the hallway but Riggen slammed the door shut and wedged a rock under the corner. Neither one of them waited to see who would burst through the door behind them.

Sprinting her to the busy road, Riggen waved his arms wildly over his head. A cab squealed to a stop at the curb and he yanked the door open and shoved her inside.

"Hotel Kimpton," he shouted.

She fell against Riggen's chest, shivering in his arms as the taxi sped away from the convention center.

# NINETEEN

Riggen hit End Call and tossed his phone into the Bronco's cup holder. This was the day that kept on giving. The tip Jones had gone to check out had been a fluke. No sign of Kris Dupree at her house. No sign of her anywhere.

He climbed into the seat and looked over at Liz. He was ninety-nine-percent certain there was no sign of Kris in Manitou because she was wreaking havoc in Denver.

Liz pushed her wet hair from her face. The sprinklers had washed off her makeup. Bruises shone purple against her creamy skin. His heart couldn't take much more.

He roared the engine to life and pulled them from the hotel's parking garage. "What do you think about just getting out of here?"

"The expo's over. I'm done in Denver."

He turned onto the city street and sped through traffic. "I meant out of Colorado."

"Leave Colorado?" He felt her tension.

"I'm done watching Kris play cat-and-mouse. You just landed the job. You said it was remote and travel work, right?" He glanced at her and she nodded. "Then there's nothing holding you here. We can go off-grid, route our outside communications through Alex."

She picked at her sopping pants. "Do you really think leaving the state will stop these people?"

Reaching over, he captured her hand. "Not stop. But keep you safe until Rosche catches them? It could." He switched lanes. "Trevor offered to buy me out. That would tide us over for a while." He thought of Jones. Hats off to someone for profiting from this mess.

"You said they were bringing Kris in tonight."

He shook his head. "False tip."

He could see her shoulders fall from the corner of his eye. He merged onto the highway and pressed the gas.

"Kat and John put my things in storage after the fire." Resignation colored her voice.

He slid a look her way. "And?"

"I don't have much. We can grab clothes. A few things for Lucas. I'll come back for the rest when this is over." She wrapped her arms around herself and kicked her feet up on the dash. "Who knows? It could be my next big adventure."

Relief flooded him. There was a time for fight and a time for flight. Last time he'd run into the fight to save a family and it had blown up in his face. During this fight, he was flying his family as far away from danger as possible.


Riggen had driven Liz to her storage space and then they headed up Pikes Peak to his cabin. Jones's patrol car was barely visible behind them through the sheets of rain. The weather and the other officer's presence gave Liz a sense of safety.

Jones would cover the entrance to Riggen's ranch. It was the only way in and out. Once they'd grabbed his things, they'd head down the mountain and watch Manitou Springs disappear into their rearview mirror.

Thunder rocked the Bronco as they pulled up to the cabin and lightning flashed across the mountain. Riggen picked up his phone, pressed a few buttons, then held it to his ear.

Liz listened to the one-sided conversation as Riggen tried to explain what was going on and offer his resignation. She twisted in her seat to peer down the long driveway to where Jones's car had stopped.

Whomever Riggen was talking to wasn't happy. The voice blistered across the phone line, competing with the summer storm outside. She doubted the man at the bottom of the driveway was quite as upset at the thought of Riggen leaving.

Riggen's jawline radiated purpose and he held a finger up to her while climbing from the Bronco to take a few steps away and continuing the heated conversation on the porch of the Price cabin. He paced back and forth, the stony set of his face unyielding.

When he finally stuffed his phone back in his pocket, she rolled down her window and leaned out. "Boss not happy?"

He dashed through the rain and leaned in the open window. Droplets fell from his white cowlick onto her lap. He rubbed the back of his neck. "In a word? No. Good thing it's not his decision."

She bit her lip, trying to brush aside the bees that buzzed through her stomach. This wasn't right. He wasn't her fiancé anymore. He shouldn't be uprooting his life to take care of her.

Clasping her hands together, she glanced at the shadowy tree line over his shoulder. Reality seemed to shift. Riggen Price had abandoned her five years ago. She squinted at him, watching rain rivulets run down his face. Now, no matter what happened, he was sticking to her closer than a cactus bur. *He's changed.*

"Hey—" he traced a wet finger down her cheek "—no worries."

How could she explain that her worry had just shifted from wondering how long he'd stick around to realizing she was in real danger of falling for him again?

She rubbed a wet spot on the door's vinyl and tried to wrap her head around the fact that he was staying for good this time. But was it for her or for Lucas? Pain ripped through her heart. The distinction was an important one.

He grasped her chin between his thumb and forefinger and forced her to look at him. When she did, his eyes were full of understanding. She was emotionally naked under his gaze.

"The only thing—" he leaned farther through the window, refusing to let her look away "—and I mean *only* thing I'm worried about, is what would happen to you if we stay in Manitou."

Her heart took a step closer to belief but skidded to a halt before it arrived. She just wasn't ready, so she nodded instead.

"Now, I'll run in and rustle up my stuff. Sit tight."

She rolled her window back up and told herself to relax. Rain pelted the roof. Soon they'd be on the road with her problems behind them and a blank future ahead. She tapped her fingers on the door.

Riggen had done nothing but serve and protect her

since he'd stood over her taped-up body on Pikes Peak. Why couldn't she take that last step into trust?

Another flash of lightning streaked across the sky, glinting off the second-story window of the cabin. Even his annoying habit of making decisions for her had only stemmed from a desire to protect.

But could she ever get over the worst of those decisions? The one that had devastated her? Was it possible to move out of the past and live in the present?

Her gaze darted around the Bronco's interior. There had to be something to take her mind off the problem of Riggen. She stopped when her eyes landed on his duffel sitting on the back seat.

If Riggen's boss had been upset at the thought of him leaving, how would Trevor react? Would he really be okay with Riggen moving away? He'd offered to buy Riggen out, but what would happen to Price Excursions without Riggen's help?

She unclicked her seat belt and wriggled into the back to heave Riggen's duffel over the armrest. She couldn't silence the roar of conflicting emotions crashing through her, but if doing something to help Trevor's business could distract her from the terrifying thought of a future with Riggen, then the work was worth it.

Opening the files, she crossed her legs underneath her and searched through the vendor names. She knew them all. Most of them had contracted her to write travel and product reviews. She knew what they liked and how to get their attention. Making small, quick marks in the margins of Trevor's files, she noted the ideas swirling through her mind.

She flipped through more files and wrote down a few business-building ideas. She wouldn't have time to go through them all but, if nothing else, Trevor could experiment with these suggestions. Or not. It was up to him, but she'd make sure Riggen left the files in the cabin before they drove away. Satisfaction wound through her and quieted some of her inner turmoil.

She pulled a thin hard-back ledger from the bulging bottom file and ran her index finger over the book's spine. The dates listed were old, too old to care about. Opening Riggen's duffel, she stuffed it back inside, but her fingernail snagged a sheet of paper, tearing the corner free. She hissed under her breath. Hopefully it was nothing important.

She tried to tug the rest of the paper from its home in the ledger, but couldn't. She opened the book and found a packet taped inside the back cover. She peeled away the tape and reunited the torn pieces. It was a thin collection of photocopied documents. Glancing through the pages, surprise hardened her stomach to granite.

She darted a look at the door of the cabin. Riggen couldn't possibly know about this packet. She gawked at the information in her hands, devouring the words that were never meant for her. She didn't come up for air until her car door opened.

Turning to Riggen, she brandished the torn packet like a battle cry. This betrayal put her confused feelings on the back burner. The pages fluttered in her hand like a butterfly about to take flight. She thrust it at him. "Your brother's been lying to you."

Her heart stopped. The man who took the packet from her shaking hand wasn't Riggen. Raindrops plopped great big water spots on the paper in his hands as Trevor's brows snapped together.

"What are you doing?" she screeched as she jerked

her head to look down the driveway. She couldn't see Jones's lights.

His eyes shifted from her face to the cabin and back. "Why couldn't you leave well enough alone?"

She shrank away, fear melting her insides. Where was Riggen? She inched closer to the steering wheel. "Leave what alone, Trevor?" The horn was so close.

His hand closed around her wrist like an iron cuff and he yanked her across the seat toward him. "Don't play stupid and don't even think about trying to get his attention."

He pushed aside his damp flannel shirt to expose the dull black butt of a gun. "Get out of the truck."

It was as if she were moving in Hi-Def. She could feel the grain of the torn paper in her hand, hear the beat of water against the metal truck roof, see the conflict in Trevor's gaze.

She crumpled the fragment with its terrible secret into her fist and climbed from the Bronco, her foot slipping in a puddle. Trevor kept one eye on her face while he flipped through the intact pages.

The pages that contained a will, which she suspected Riggen had never seen, and a letter from Mr. Price to the family lawyer.

"What are you going to do?" she whimpered even as her fingers played around the crumpled edges of the torn fragment. She dropped the wad to the rain-sodden ground, praying Trevor didn't see, and then booted gravel over it.

Whatever Trevor read in the packet flushed his face like a strawberry in summer. He stuffed the papers in his waistband before pulling his gun from his holster.

He cocked his head in the direction of the tree line. "Walk. If you make a noise, I'll shoot him."

Her face went cold as every last drop of blood drained from it. "You won't get away with whatever it is you're planning. Riggen'll figure it out."

His nostrils flared. "Walk," he growled before jamming the gun into her side.

Her unsteady legs undermined any effort to obey, but he dug his fingers into her bruised biceps and pushed her across the muddy gravel drive. She winced, stumbling toward the tree line.

When they hit the dark opening, he muscled her onto a barely visible path. The overgrown trail ascended the mountain in front of them and she gasped for breath. Rain streamed into her eyes and her side cramped.

They climbed in tense silence for what seemed to be half a mile, then she heard the sound of a slamming door. She stopped, hunched over and braced herself with her hands on her knees.

Her head was pounding with the effort of breathing. She couldn't drag enough of the thin air into her beaten lungs. The anguished sound of Riggen shouting her name bounced through the mountain pines behind them and reverberated in her skull. That was the tormented sound of a man who cared. Really cared. *For her.*

Tears blinded her and she staggered into a boulder that dominated the path. The hard point of Trevor's gun prodded her back, exploding a rash of shivers up and down her spine.

He shoved her around the rock. "Don't stop."

Riggen's cries faded into the distance as Trevor led her farther into the dark and wet wilderness of Pikes Peak.

\* \* \*

Riggen stood next to the open door of the Bronco, his phone in one hand and a random file from Price Adventure Excursions in the other. Papers, bills, ledgers. Everything he and Rosche had taken from the office was now strewed across his front seat in a confusing array, but Liz was nowhere to be found.

He threw another sopping stack of papers onto the seat and dialed the PD before sprinting down the driveway to Jones's car. He shouted into the deserted landscape as he pounded the gravel. His cries were muffled in the sheets of pouring rain.

"Warn a man if you're going to holler in his ear." Carr had picked up. And he didn't sound any happier than he had earlier.

Riggen exhaled. If Liz had wandered off, she'd respond. But if Kris had somehow known they were here and gotten hold of her… He couldn't bring himself to finish the thought.

"Liz is missing." He careened to a stop next to Jones's patrol car. The door was hanging open. Taking a deep breath, he looked inside.

"From where? When?" Carr shouted in his ear, but Riggen's attention zoomed in on Jones, who was slouched over the patrol car's armrest.

"My cabin and I'm not sure. Jones is down." He threw himself into the car and felt for the man's pulse. It was faint and thready, but it was there. He turned his attention back to Carr. Liz hadn't just wandered off. "She was taken anytime from ten minutes ago to now."

"We're on the way."

Riggen hung up and analyzed the scene, taking in the bloody mess that was Jones's head. He ran his hands over the man's head and shoulders. It looked to be a simple head wound, but it was gushing.

Pulling Jones toward him, he looped the man's arm across his own shoulder. If he had to drag the man to safety, he would. Jones groaned and then his eyes fluttered open.

"Who did this?" Riggen pulled the man toward the cabin.

Jones's faltering feet were steady but slow. "Didn't see." He groaned as his foot collided with a tree root and he stumbled. "Saw lights through the rain. Opened the window to check it out. That's all I remember."

Riggen nodded and helped the man climb into the front seat of the Bronco.

Liz's phone lay discarded in the gravel next to the truck's door. He pushed Jones's foot inside and bent to pick up the device. As he did, a wad of paper caught his eye, wedged just under the tire and protected from the rain by the undercarriage of the truck.

He stooped to pick it up then flattened it out. There was handwriting on it. Faint, as though someone had copied it on a copy machine, but he recognized it. His hands trembled as he read the message from Dad.

Disbelief hammered him with whitewater force. Update for last will and testament? It had a date on it, scribbled underneath the script. The night Dad died. Riggen straightened and looked more at the other files.

Within minutes he had flipped through them. He recognized most of them and shoved them to the floor in frustration. Jones dodged the avalanche of files with a moan. They were nothing more than bills and invoices. Nothing here resembled a will. As far as he knew, Dad hadn't changed the will that had made him and Trevor fifty-fifty partners in the business and equal inheritors of the estate.

He glared at the open files. This was a waste of time. What he needed to be doing was finding Liz, and that wouldn't be done by looking through old paperwork.

But then a name flashed at him from the havoc on the floor. Pikes Peak Mustangs.

Trevor nudged Liz aside. Flashes of lightning filtered through the thick forest canopy to illuminate a small lean-to nestled off what once must have been a well-worn trail. He unlocked the door and stood back.

She glared and dug her heels into the soft pine-needled carpeting. She wasn't moving another step. He pointed his gun at the doorway. "Inside."

They'd been climbing so long. She wrestled each new breath into her raw throat. Battering pain in her skull blinded her. She was experienced enough to know altitude sickness was taking hold.

"No way." She shook her head, wincing at each excruciating throb. The doorway loomed dark in front of them. Whatever he had planned for her, he could just do it out here. She scrambled backward but crashed into his chest.

He seized her shoulders and catapulted her across the threshold. She fell headlong into the darkness, sprawling onto a grimy wood-slat floor.

Dust filled her mouth, sparking a fit of uncontrollable coughing. She'd had no water since before the expo other than the rain that had drizzled into her mouth. There wasn't enough oxygen in the air. She clawed at her throat.

Trevor shoved a water bottle into her hand before

striking a match. She chugged it as a clouded gas lantern bloomed to life. He kicked the door shut and sank into the only chair in the ramshackle space. Tucking his gun in his holster, he propped his feet on a mattress that had seen better days. Mud dripped from his boots to the floor.

He didn't talk until she had stopped coughing. "I didn't want it to come to this, Liz. Why didn't you listen and leave Colorado?"

She hugged the water bottle to herself and edged away until her back hit the wall. Cold fear drenched her.

"I tried to warn you." He hefted himself from the chair and it creaked in the silence between them. He leaned over her, pulling a rope from the wall above her head. Then with one smooth motion, he hoisted her from the floor and into the seat he had just vacated.

After tying her hands and feet to the chair, he stalked to the door. "Wouldn't recommend screaming. No one can hear you and you can't afford the breath."

She didn't know what was more terrifying: that he might leave her in this forsaken place or that he might stay. Thunder rocked the shack and his feet were on the threshold before her mind thawed. *Get him talking.* Distract him. Befriend him. Remind him she was human.

She wiggled her hands behind her back, trying to loosen the ropes. "You warned me and I did listen. We were leaving today. You can still let us go."

He let out a mirthless laugh. "Let Elizabeth Hart go? The woman who took down Sammy Malcovitch and the Sagebrush? Do you really think I'm stupid enough to believe you'd keep your mouth shut about this?" He waved the packet in her face then walked away, pushing the door open. Damp air rushed into the shack and flickered the light of the lantern.

She pulled against her restraints. The rope cut and burned her wrists. "Wait!"

He stopped, his back to her.

"Where are you going?" Her voice broke on the question.

"To tie up loose ends."

# TWENTY

Frustration turned to frantic fear as night fell on Pikes Peak. He had no idea where Liz was. Riggen turned her phone over and over in his hands as he paced the gravel driveway. Numbness gave way to the heart-crushing realization that he had failed again.

Blue strobe lights pulsed in the darkness and the cacophony of police radios broke what should have been a peaceful silence. At least the storm had let up. Once morning set in, Search and Rescue could start scouring the mountain.

Rosche jogged up to him, holding the file he'd found on the floor of his Bronco. She waved it in the air in front of him like a flag.

When he finally focused on her, she wasted no time. "These invoices show Price Adventure Excursions has been paying Pikes Peak Mustang Corporation a healthy chunk of money every month for the last five years."

He stopped moving and looked at the file. "How healthy?"

She flipped through the invoices and pointed to the figure. Searing betrayal gripped him. He crushed the phone in his hand. Now wasn't the time to think about how Trevor was playing him for the fool or how hard he had worked while his brother had leaked their money back out to Sammy Malcovitch and company.

*Concentrate on action, soldier.* He shifted from one foot to the other. "And we know that Pikes Peak Mustangs leads back to Kris Dupree."

"Not only that." Rosche nodded to an SUV parked a few feet away. He followed her to the front of the vehicle. Her laptop was open on the hood.

She shoved the file under her computer and banged on the keyboard. Tax records popped up on the screen. "Pikes Peak Mustang Corporation owns the Juniper."

"Where Kris was employed, and the entire reason Liz came back to Manitou in the first place."

She nodded.

He massaged the back of his neck. "But how and why is Trevor connected to this mess?"

"That, I don't know," she answered. "But there's more."

How much more could he take? He flipped the phone over again and depressed the power button. Lucas's face smiled up at him and he rolled his neck to the side. He'd handle whatever betrayal he had to, to get Liz back to their little boy. "Okay. What else?"

"I went back through old title records on a hunch and—get ready for this brain twister—Pikes Peak Mustang Corporation owns the company that acquired the corporation that ran the—"

"Sagebrush," he interrupted.

"You guessed it."

"Every string of the web ties Malcovitch and Dupree to Trevor." He scrubbed his face. "Do we have a location on either Trevor or Dupree?"

She shook her head. "Nothing. We've tried to ping Trevor's cell, but he must have it powered down."

"And Jones didn't find anything when he investigated the Dupree sighting?"

"Nada."

Cool mountain air blew across them. The storm had plummeted the temperature, but all he could feel was the heat of his every nightmare. He had tried to protect Liz and now she was gone. Another mistake that harmed the woman he loved.

He watched Rosche slam her computer shut and lean against the SUV as the reality that he loved Liz flooded his entire being. He loved her regardless of whether he deserved her or not.

He barely heard Rosche's voice as she continued. "The question we're looking at now is who has her? Trevor or Kris?"

The hair on his arms raised. "Or both?"

Her eyes gleamed in the flashing lights and she pointed an index finger straight at him. "Kris has been one step ahead of us this entire time. Could it be because Trevor has been feeding her information?"

He shook his head. There was too much to process— the connection to Dupree and Malcovitch, the ambiguous note about Dad's will. And always Liz. He needed to compartmentalize but he couldn't. His past sins were ruining everything, and he wasn't big enough to fix the mess.

*God doesn't work that way.* Liz's voice drifted through his heart like a calming balm. He rubbed his temples. If God didn't work that way, then how *did* He work? Riggen closed his eyes and pushed himself to remember. Searched his memories for Dad's voice.

*Life is a mist. Live for God. It's the only thing that lasts.* But the memory didn't stop there. Dad's words circled him, joining Liz's to fill him. *Put God first and everything else will be taken care of.*

Put God first? He shook his head. He'd only ever put himself first. He'd put his desire to be a hero first. He'd put his fear first. He'd put his wrong ideas about God first. He'd put his need to protect his family first. But put God first? A harsh laugh fell from his lips. Never.

He placed a hand on each side of his head and squeezed until his racing thoughts slowed. He had always thought he knew best. He had run headlong into making decisions that hadn't been his to make. For what? He slumped back against the SUV, seeing his heart for the first time. *A God like that would never tell you to right a wrong with another wrong...*

Liz was right. A God like that would never make a self-centered move. No. A God like that did the opposite. He took the punishment for Riggen's mistakes on His own back and then left the decision of whether or not to accept that gift in Riggen's court.

*Forgive me, God. I've been such an idiot. You first. It starts now.* Peace flowed over his body like a warm shower as he submitted the control he'd never actually held to the God who held it all.

When he reopened his eyes, Rosche was peering into the darkness of Pikes Peak. "If Kris and Trevor are working together, maybe we should start looking at this from your brother's point of view. If I were Trevor, where would I feel safe? Where would I hide?"

A flash of inspiration fired into the new quietness of his mind. He shoved Liz's phone into his pocket and barreled across the driveway. He knew exactly where

Liz would be and, with God's help, nothing would stop him from saving the woman he loved. "Follow me."

*Be strong and courageous.* Liz cringed as rope fibers bit into her bleeding flesh with knifelike precision. She twisted her wrist. Tugged. Her wet hand slipped free and she bit back a scream, her brutalized emotions boiling too close to the surface.

Her other hand was still securely tied to the back of the chair. She contorted her torso, trying to untie the remaining knot.

Something crunched in the groundcover outside the thin walls of her prison. Her hand trembled in the tangle of rope. She couldn't get the knot to loosen. "Do not be afraid because of them," she whispered into the flickering light of the oil lantern.

Her nail broke against the frayed rope edge. Sharp nylon spliced into her nail bed. She cried out, the pain pushing her tears over the edge and down her cheeks.

The doorknob turned, stopping her heartbeat and strangling her breath. She twisted back into place and slipped both hands behind her as Trevor pushed the door open and entered. Kris Dupree sauntered in behind him.

Kris's previously warm blue eyes had turned wintry cold and her red lips drew back in a snarl when they landed on Liz. "Tied up like a present." She inclined her head at Trevor.

The ice in Kris's voice froze any hope Liz had of escaping. She darted a look at the open door. Even if she could get her other hand untied to free her legs, she'd never find her way down the dangerous mountainside. Not after that storm.

Soft laughter bubbled like a mountain brook from

Kris. She strutted to stand over Liz and ran one rounded fingernail down Liz's cheek. Shivers danced through Liz's body, but she refused to react.

Kris knelt in front of her until they were eye-to-eye. "I've been looking forward to this."

*Fear not, nor be afraid of them: for the Lord thy God… He will not fail thee, nor forsake thee.* "Why?"

Kris leaned forward and rested her hands on Liz's knees. She smiled into Liz's face, their noses mere inches apart. Liz could see the shiny wetness of her eyeballs.

"When Trevor told me *American Travel* had interviewed you for a position…well, I couldn't let the woman who had ruined Sammy's life climb that ladder of success with no repercussions. Could I?"

Liz shot a glance at Trevor. He smirked at her before Kris started talking again.

"It was just for fun at the beginning. Just trying to put a smile on Sammy's face. There was so little to entertain him, stuck in that prison." She squeezed Liz's kneecap. "You understand? A girl wants her man to be happy. And, boy, did he hate you. You ruined everything for him. His business. His life. But what could he do about it from prison?"

Kris stood. "I knew he'd enjoy seeing me play with you a bit. And he did. We laughed so hard at the thought of you hog-tied on Pikes Peak. He liked it so much, he wanted me to go all the way."

Liz tried to swallow the lump of fear that was growing in her throat. She squeezed her hands together behind her. If only she could see Lucas and Riggen one more time.

*Riggen?* Tears filled her eyes. Yes, Riggen. She

wanted to wrap her arms around him. Tell him she forgave him. She wanted to see the love in his eyes one more time. She'd been so blind.

Kris turned, those blue eyes full of hate. "I would have made it tolerable for you. But then you—" Her voice clogged and she fanned her face with her hand until she had control again. "You had him killed."

"I did not have him...wait!" Liz's attention bounced back to Trevor as Kris's words fell into place in her mind. "How did you know I had been interviewed by *American Travel*?"

He plopped down on the ratty mattress. "Kim let it slip one night at dinner, along with the fact that you were a single mom. I put two and two together and figured it was Riggen's kid."

Kris's laughter echoed into the small building. She turned to Trevor. "A fact that you conveniently exploited."

He lifted his shoulders in a half shrug.

Liz didn't know who to watch, her eyes darting back and forth between the duo. Their calculation sent ice through her every cell. "What does that mean? 'Conveniently exploited'?"

Kris hitched a thumb at Trevor. "He's been looking to get good old Riggen out of the way for years. And what's the one thing baby brother desires more than anything else?" She smirked. "Family. It's simple logic. Threaten family and you have brother in your hands."

There was nothing simple about it. Liz's brain was bursting and she lashed out at Trevor with all the anger and desperation that had been building inside. "How could you? All this for what? For the business? For your father's estate?"

Trevor pounced to his feet, a vein popping out in his neck. "How could I? All I want is what rightfully belongs to me. Riggen isn't even a real Price. He's a stray we brought in off the street." He jabbed his thumb into his chest. "I've got Price blood, but Riggen's supposed to inherit all of Dad's estate? The business I've sweated over and loved my entire life?"

He shook his head, but something flashed in his eyes. Was it pain? Guilt? He swaggered over to her chair. "None of that means I wanted to hurt him, though." His voice cracked. "I love him."

Bending until his face was level with hers, he sneered. "The better question is, how could you? If it wasn't for your irresponsibility, Riggen would have already taken you and left the state. But you pushed and pushed like a spoiled brat until you got your way. No wonder he ran from you five years ago. You're exhausting."

His words pierced her soul like flaming darts. She hunched forward in pain.

He held his hands wide. "So, congratulations, you've arrived at your final adventure and it's more than a destination."

Kris chuckled as she leaned against the door frame, her back to the night. "I like what you did there."

"Thanks." Trevor slithered away from Liz until he and Kris stood shoulder-to-shoulder, staring at her.

"So, what?" Liz scowled at them. "You're going to kill me? Riggen is the smartest man I know. He'll figure out you two are working together, with or without my help."

Trevor sighed and rubbed the back of his neck, his eyes tired and—she blinked in surprise—sad. "You're right...he will."

She gawked at his response. Kris turned to stare at him as if he'd just gone off the deep end.

Neither one of them was prepared when he pulled his gun from his holster. Every bedtime kiss with Lucas, every squeeze of his tiny arms flashed through her mind. *Be strong and courageous, sweet boy.*

Then Trevor turned and pointed the gun at Kris and pulled the trigger. The woman's bright blue eyes widened in shock as she crumpled to the floor.

He kicked Kris's body against the wall and watched the color drain from her face. When the woman's eyes fluttered shut, he turned back. "And that is exactly why I needed to tie up loose ends."

"Why did you do that?" Liz choked on a sob.

She turned her face away and stared out the door. She couldn't look at Kris. Couldn't accept that Trevor had just ended one life and hers would be next. A shadow moved across the sliver of light that spilled from the open doorway to illuminate the overgrown path outside.

Her breath hitched. She recognized the familiar flash of white cowlick. Terror slicked through her. If he came in here, Trevor would shoot him.

She wanted to be with Riggen. She loved him. There was no point in denying it any longer. But she wanted his safety more. Her heart screamed at Riggen, willing the silent words through the air and into his heart. *Run, my love. Run.*

# TWENTY-ONE

When the shot thundered across the mountainside, he and Rosche ran the last twenty feet to the old lean-to. Rosche sunk to a knee across from him and pulled her weapon. Riggen tapped his fingers on the rigid body of his Glock where it rested against his rib cage. He braced himself as the ghostly echoes of enemy fire blasted in his brain.

This was Manitou, not Baghdad. His head spun and he pressed his back against the damp clapboard siding of their decaying playhouse. And this was his brother, not the enemy.

His brother who had just shot someone. He shifted, a lifetime of memories squashing in the mud under him. His brother who most likely would not survive the night. Rosche knelt on the opposite side of the doorway, her finger pointing down the barrel of her duty weapon. She was ready and primed.

Riggen's gaze ricocheted from the lit doorway to Rosche's face to the starlit sky above them. *Be with me.* He clenched his jaw, fighting off the fear that threatened to paralyze him. It still wasn't easy admitting he didn't have control of the situation. It still wasn't easy to trust.

"Why did you do that?" Liz's voice wavered and broke. From the sound of it, she was on the other side of the wall from him. He hunkered forward and rolled across the path until he was next to Rosche. From this position, he could clearly see Liz tied to the old wood chair.

Trevor walked in front of the lantern, casting his shadow across the path before disappearing behind the wall again.

"Should we take him down now?" Rosche whispered in Riggen's ear.

He shook his head. It wasn't clear enough yet.

"I've been trying to get rid of her for longer than I've been trying to get rid of Riggen." Trevor's words tore a family-sized hole into Riggen's soul.

Liz's head swiveled between Trevor and Kris, who now lay crumpled like a discarded doll in the corner. She locked onto his brother, her eyes flashing. "But why?"

"She knew what you know."

"Not to book adventure excursions with monsters?"

"Nice one." His laugh filtered out into the night. "A little insulting, though. I'm no monster. I'm a realist. Kris knew about the will. She's been blackmailing me for the last five years. So when Kim let it slip that you had a son, it was like the skies had opened up and dropped the perfect opportunity in my lap. My chance to knock out Riggen and Kris with the same stone—you.

"With a few choice reminders to her about how you ruined Sammy's life, I had Kris off to the races. And put Elizabeth Hart in trouble? Well, that got Riggen back in the game."

Anger simmered inside Riggen like a geyser threatening to erupt. His brother had played him like a banjo. He tensed and rocked forward onto the balls of his feet. Rosche's hand gripped his arm. He cut a glance at her. She sliced her hand across her throat. She was right. Calm. Steady.

He turned back. Liz was wriggling in her seat, pain shooting across her face, but still she stared down his brother. "Why would Kris blackmail you over a will that never made it to the lawyer? It has no power."

"You're right about that."

Riggen crept closer to the door, readying himself for whatever would come.

Liz scrunched her face and jerked her head at the corner. "I'm sure I'll join Kris tonight, so you might as well give me a good-night story."

Trevor's laugh bounced off the wood floor. "Story? How's this synopsis for you?" He paused. Riggen could see his shadow moving on the wall behind Liz, hands raising in the air as if framing invisible words. "Do-gooding preacher crusades to end local forced labor until son joins enemy for profit."

Chills washed over Riggen even as Liz shuddered, but she nodded. "Go ahead."

"Do you think Riggen and his mom were my dad's first project?" Trevor's words jeered. "No. They were just the only successful one. Dad was always trying to save people."

"Okay…" Liz cocked an eyebrow.

"So who do you think Malcovitch came after when he wanted to stop Dad from putting a dent in his trafficking business?" Trevor's voice screeched through the door and into the night like an angry owl. "Me."

"Tell me about it," Liz prompted soothingly.

"Bad company corrupts good character. It was either join Malcovitch or...well, you know what? Malcovitch didn't give me a second option. So I let him run workers right under Dad's nose, storing them here on our own property before carting them off to their next position."

"You could have gone to the authorities." Liz shifted in her chair, the muscles in her arms moving and flexing.

"It was either the laborers suffer or I suffer. Malcovitch would have paid me back if I went to the law. So I let him run business through here instead, for a cut of the profits, of course."

Revulsion flickered across Liz's face. Riggen's stomach turned. How had he not known the struggles hidden within his own family?

"Anyway, when Dad found out, he said I had to turn myself in or he would. He wrote me out of the will. Gave it all to Riggen. The stray!" Trevor stepped into view. He pulled a packet of papers from his shirt and threw them at Liz. "Look how much Dad distrusted me." His voice dropped to a menacing level. "I thought I had destroyed every copy."

"He's escalating." Rosche's lips were close to Riggen's ear. She was right. They needed to intervene.

But Liz spoke, stopping him. "How does Kris figure into all of this?"

Trevor stomped muddy boots across the papers before kicking them at Kris. The woman's foot twitched. Was she still alive?

Trevor laughed. "Kris was one of them. One of the people Dad tried to save. But even back then, she was Sammy's girl. How she laughed behind Dad's back while she robbed him blind. She was at the ranch that night to study—" he air-quoted "—the Bible. More like she was there to pinch Dad's wallet when he wasn't looking."

"That night?" Liz asked.

"The night Dad wrote me out of the will." Trevor bent and picked up the muddy, torn papers. "He and I fought. He was so upset. So disappointed. That's when it happened."

"What?"

"The heart attack. I just stood there. Watched him struggle for each breath. I was so angry. Too angry to call 9-1-1. When it was over, I destroyed the new will and the letter he had written his lawyer, but apparently he made a copy. Kris and I left, and I came back later to discover him."

He shrugged. "See? Loose ends. At the end of the day, I'll walk down this mountain a hero. Oh, I wasn't in time to keep Kris from killing you, but I was able to get off the shot that killed her and brought justice. Anyway, that's the story Riggen will believe. All that's left for me is to find a new way to get Riggen's hands off my property. You're useless to me now."

Searing rage blinded Riggen, propelling him to his feet. He burst into the shack and pummeled his fist through the back of his brother's shoulder.

"Nothing more important than family?" he shouted as Trevor spun around. "You're no brother to me."

Trevor clenched and unclenched his hands, but Riggen was ready. Every ounce of anguish rose to the surface as he barreled headfirst into Trevor's chest and crashed him into the wall.

Trevor grabbed him around the torso like he had

when they wrestled as kids. They fell together onto the hard floor. Riggen's breath whooshed from his body as his shoulder cracked against the uneven wood boards. They rolled together toward the door.

When they collided into the door frame, he brought his knee up into his brother's gut and slipped from Trevor's hold. Pulling himself to one knee and then both feet, he glared down at the man he had always looked up to.

From the corner of his eye, he saw all the blood blanch from Liz's face. She sucked in a breath and yanked one hand from behind her, pointing across the shack.

Riggen jerked his head to see what caused her terror. Kris, raised on one elbow, was holding a shaking gun at Liz. Everything stopped. He saw the room as if it were one enormous map. He wasn't too far off course to save the woman he loved.

Before the next breath could be drawn, he threw himself at Liz, taking her and the chair to the ground. Gunshots thundered off the walls of the shack, followed by Trevor's scream.

Another pop-pop-pop blasted the air, then only silence. Riggen rolled over. Rosche stood in the doorway, her gun trained on Kris's now-lifeless body.

But Trevor was hunched over, holding his abdomen. He staggered to the middle of the room and fell to his knees, his eyes boring into Riggen. Riggen ignored him, turned away and untied Liz's binds. He pulled her into his arms, pressing her against his chest. "Thank You, Jesus." His ragged prayer was muffled against her hair.

Liz's hands slid up his chest and rested on his shoulders. His vision tunneled. All he could see was her. But she was looking past him. At Trevor. She tilted forward until her cheek was pressed against his and whispered, "Go to him, my love."

The shack spun around him and his heart beat so loud, he couldn't trust his ears. "What did you say?" He choked out the question.

She pushed him away but this time it wasn't in anger. "Go to him," she whispered, her eyes filled with the love he had never expected to see again.

He nodded and steadied her before turning. The blood seeping from between Trevor's fingers set his feet into motion. He rushed to his brother's side. The wound in Trevor's stomach gurgled past his futile attempt to staunch it.

He grabbed Trevor's arm and placed his other hand on his brother's back before guiding him down to the bloodstained floor. Trevor coughed. The sound sputtered in a way Riggen had heard too many times on the battlefield.

He knelt close to Trevor's face, grasping his brother's hand while his heart shattered in revelation. "You took that bullet for me."

Tears slid down Trevor's cheek to disappear into his blond hair. His eyes fluttered shut. "There's nothing more important than family."

Riggen choked back his own tears and placed two fingers to Trevor's neck. Nothing. His brother was gone.

Riggen stood and backed away. Wiping the wetness from his cheeks, he turned to walk into Liz's waiting embrace.

Liz squinted against the glare of strobing police lights and huddled deep into the warm emergency blanket Devon had draped over her shoulders. The paramedic wrapped a bandage around her throbbing arm and then dug into his medic bag, pulling out ibuprofen and a bottle of water.

"Drink up."

"Thanks." She downed the medicine and watched the action play out on the gravel driveway of the Prices' property. Riggen and Detective Rosche stood in a huddle with Lieutenant Carr. Every few moments, one of them would look her way. She was about to climb down from the ambulance gurney and limp over to them when Carr clasped Riggen's shoulder and nodded him toward her.

"That's my cue to leave." Devon slipped away a moment before Riggen popped his head inside.

The man she loved with all her heart grasped the frame and hovered on the edge of entry. "Can I join you?" His gaze never strayed from her face. They both knew her answer would give him entry to more than just the vehicle.

Warmth filled her at the look in his eyes and she wiggled one finger to beckon him inside. Smiling, he pulled himself into the small space and closed the door.

She scooted over on the gurney to make room for him before patting the wrinkled vinyl. Every sense went on high alert when he lowered himself beside her. Her heartbeat quickened. She angled her head to see his face, ignoring the pain that sparked down her back. "I'm sorry about Trevor."

Riggen's face clouded and his hand searched hers out. When he had twined their fingers together, he spoke. "It'll be a long time before I can process everything. Trevor was the only family I had." He choked on the words and stared at the ceiling, blinking rapidly.

"That's not true," she whispered. She squeezed his hand. "You have Lucas." She stopped. *Be strong and courageous.* "And me."

He turned to her and ran his free hand across her new bandage. "What you said back at the shed…"

She nodded. "I meant it then and I mean it now. I love you."

He opened his mouth and closed it. Swallowed. Opened it again. "I've sorted things out with God, Lizzy. I have His forgiveness, but I don't want to move on without yours." He raised her bruised hand to his mouth and dropped gentle kisses across each knuckle.

Shivers chased themselves up her arm and through her body.

Leaning even closer, he pushed a strand of her hair behind her ear. "Before Iraq, I didn't understand love. I put my fear before your needs." He shook his head. "Now I know that real love runs full-throttle toward sacrifice, in service to others. Can you forgive me?" He stopped. Swallowed again. "And will you allow me to love you and Lucas with that type of love?"

A sense of belonging washed over Liz with Riggen's questions. She leaned her head against the shoulder that felt like home and breathed a deep breath of possibility. "I can't think of a more exciting adventure."

# EPILOGUE

*One month later...*

Liz stood back and watched Emily put the finishing touches on the *American Travel* booth. The International Travel and Trade Convention was about to kick off and her team had just pulled off the perfect opening-day launch.

Closing her eyes, she centered her thoughts on the One who had made it all possible. *For the Lord thy God... He will not fail thee, nor forsake thee.* How faithful He had proved Himself to be.

Arms circled her waist from behind. "Have I told you today how much I love you?"

A squeal of joy burst from her before she could stop it and she swiveled in Riggen's arms. "What are you doing here?"

"I didn't want to miss your first official team project." The stubble on his chin scraped across her cheek. She stood on tiptoes to kiss the defined line of his jaw. His arms tightened around her at the touch of her lips to his skin and he dipped his head to catch her mouth with his own.

When they finally came back up for air, he whispered in her ear, "I brought you a surprise."

"Better than this?" She rested in his arms, eyes closed, heart happy.

Something tugged at the hem of her pencil skirt. She looked down. "Baby boy!"

Lucas leaned into her legs and wrapped his tiny arms around her. She grinned at Riggen. "This is a surprise. He should be at preschool."

At the mention of school, both Prices tilted their heads, their cowlicks flopping to the side. Her heart melted.

"We played hooky." Riggen winked at Lucas and the boy giggled.

"Wooky." Lucas tried to mimic his hero. He'd been staying with Riggen in Manitou Springs while Liz spent a week in California, prepping for the convention. From all accounts, her men were enjoying every moment of getting to know each other.

She had a sneaking suspicion Lucas might be a tad bit disappointed when she came home to Colorado a day early. But she wasn't going to miss Riggen's promotion ceremony at the Manitou Springs PD for anything.

The man was made for serving and protecting, so she had used her industry connections to find and hire a team who could take over the day-to-day of Price Excursions. Riggen could keep the business he loved while still working the job he loved.

"That's not all, though." Riggen nodded over her shoulder.

She turned. Kat and John approached. At the look on Kat's face, Liz's heart warmed. What was that softening her sister's eyes? Approval? Love?

John wheeled to a stop next to her and nodded at the booth. "Looks great."

"Sure does." Kat offered a tentative smile and took a step toward Liz. Liz closed the gap before her sister could take a second and encased the older woman in a hug.

Then her phone beeped, reminding her the show would start in five minutes. She waved her hands at her family, shooing them off. "I've got to get my team situated. Give me half an hour and I'll come find you."

"Dad's gonna show me the camel." Lucas was breathless with excitement as he bounced on the balls of his feet, trying to see into the animal enclosure that dominated the Middle East section of the conference layout.

At her raised brow, Riggen winked and nodded. "Thought I'd show him what the Middle East looks like, give him a glimpse of where his old man used to live."

"Have fun," she laughed. Stooping next to Lucas, she tickled his belly and whispered in his ear, "Be careful, sweet boy. Camels spit."

His giggles followed her all the way back to her booth.

Within minutes of the show opening, the *American Travel* booth was a hive of buzzing activity, thanks to the vision she had set and executed. She was sending Kimberly a video of the client participation when Emily rushed to her side.

Liz stuffed her phone into her skirt's pocket, concern chilling her at Emily's breathless state. She reached out and touched Emily's arm. "What is it?"

Emily pointed to the Middle East section of the convention center. "You've got to see this."

Liz jogged to the area, visions of an injured Lucas

giving her feet wings. But when she rounded the corner of the aisle, she stopped short. In front of her was Lucas's camel, with Lucas and Riggen on its back.

The ungainly animal swayed forward, moving from one side to the other in a dance. The crowd parted, watching with fascination as Riggen and Lucas approached her. The camel stopped a few feet from where she stood.

"You once told me that blood doesn't make family." Riggen's voice was clear, his eyes locked on hers. He stopped the camel mere feet from her and wrapped an arm around Lucas. "I agree."

Slowly the camel bent one leg until it was down on one knee. Gasps sounded from the stunned crowd and she bit her lip between her teeth, not even trying to stop the tears pooling in her eyes.

Lucas, beaming from his perch in his father's arms, pulled a small, square box from his pocket and handed it to his father. Riggen kissed his son's head before flipping the box open. A solitaire diamond twinkled under the convention center's chandeliers, each facet shining with a lifetime of promise.

Riggen pulled the ring from the box and held it toward her. "Love makes family. You, Elizabeth Hart, are my love, my life, and my family. Would you make us the happiest men on earth by also becoming my wife?"

She closed the remaining distance to them, the camel nosing her wet face as she slipped past its head. Holding her shaking hand toward Riggen, she opened her mouth. Her yes bubbled from deep inside and spilled out in an answering affirmation of love.

Riggen slipped the ring onto her finger and a roar

of approval rose around them. He grasped Lucas in his arms and slid down from the camel's back.

They stopped in front of her and she wrapped her arms around both of her men as the animal lumbered away.

Nuzzling her face into the soft hollow below Riggen's ear, she whispered for him alone, "I love you, Rig." She leaned back and cradled his face between her hands. "There's nothing more important than family."

\* \* \* \* \*

**Laura Scott** has always loved romance and read faith-based books by Grace Livingston Hill in her teenage years. She's thrilled to have been given the opportunity to retire from thirty-eight years of nursing to become a full-time author. Laura has published over thirty books for Love Inspired Suspense. She has two adult children and lives in Milwaukee, Wisconsin, with her husband of thirty-five years. Please visit Laura at laurascottbooks.com, as she loves to hear from her readers.

### Books by Laura Scott

### Love Inspired Suspense

### *Justice Seekers*

*Soldier's Christmas Secrets*
*Guarded by the Soldier*
*Wyoming Mountain Escape*
*Hiding His Holiday Witness*
*Rocky Mountain Standoff*

### *Callahan Confidential*

*Shielding His Christmas Witness*
*The Only Witness*
*Christmas Amnesia*
*Shattered Lullaby*
*Primary Suspect*
*Protecting His Secret Son*

Visit the Author Profile page
at LoveInspired.com for more titles.

# WYOMING MOUNTAIN ESCAPE

Laura Scott

Now the God of hope fill you with all joy and peace
in believing, that ye may abound in hope,
through the power of the Holy Ghost.
—*Romans* 15:13

This book is dedicated to Kyle and Daniele Doberstein.

Congratulations on starting your new life together.
I wish you both peace, love and happiness.

# ONE

Chelsey Robards walked out of the Teton Valley Hotel and approached the grassy knoll where her wedding guests waited. She paused at the front of the aisle, her stomach knotted with tension. Wearing a white gown, her veil trailing from a ring of flowers pinned in her curly golden-blond hair, she looked apprehensively at Brett Thompson, her long-time friend and soon-to-be-husband. Brett smiled encouragingly from his position near the right side of an arched lattice decorated with Wyoming wildflowers—the place they'd chosen to exchange their vows. Snow-covered Tetons, a section of the majestic Rocky Mountains, loomed behind Brett, creating a picture-perfect scene. Bars from "The Wedding March" began to play, but her feet refused to move.

*This is a terrible mistake.*

Chelsey had ignored the lingering doubts she'd experienced over the past week. The doubts had grown more pronounced when Duncan O'Hare, her and Brett's childhood friend, had arrived to fulfill his role as best man. Chelsey's friend and assistant manager, Trish Novak, was standing in as her maid of honor. Seeing Brett and Duncan together reinforced Chelsey's doubts.

She couldn't do this. Marrying Brett was a mistake. How had she let it go this far? She'd known Brett and Duncan from childhood, until her parents had moved to Wyoming the summer after her freshman year of high school. She loved Brett, but she understood now that she loved him as a friend.

Not a husband.

The song continued, her guests waiting expectantly. What should she do? She couldn't embarrass Brett by refusing to marry him in front of their friends and relatives.

Duncan's intense dark gaze caught her eye, his expression full of concern as if he sensed her inner turmoil. Drawing strength from Duncan, she forced herself to take the first step. And another.

The closer she came to the arched lattice where Brett waited, the more her stomach twisted painfully. She swallowed against the urge to throw up. Despite the sunlight overhead, she felt cold to the bone.

As she approached her husband-to-be, she abruptly stopped, unable to take that final step toward Brett. Every eye from those seated in the grassy knoll was glued to her and it was all she could do not to turn and run away as fast as her white ballet slippers would take her.

Brett's smile never faltered. He waited patiently, having no idea how she felt. In contrast, Duncan's dark brown gaze was serious, and she knew she wasn't fooling him.

Not the way she'd fooled everyone else.

The song was winding down and she couldn't postpone the inevitable any longer. She had to do this, even if it meant telling Brett afterward that she wanted an annulment. They could return the gifts and walk away as if this never happened.

Couldn't they?

A sharp crack ripped through the air. It took a minute for her to notice the red spot blooming on Brett's white shirt as he staggered backward.

"Get down!" Duncan lurched forward, grabbed her arm and dragged her away from Brett who'd crumpled to the ground.

*He'd been shot!*

Screams and bedlam broke out around them, the wedding guests scattering like mice, but Duncan didn't let go of her hand. He dragged her away from the area, down the hill toward the wooded mountainside.

It was difficult to comprehend what had just happened. "Wait! We need to go back to Brett! He's been shot!"

"He's gone, Chelsey, but the shooter is still out there, somewhere. We need to keep moving."

*No! This couldn't be happening! Brett!* There wasn't time to think, to truly comprehend. She followed in Duncan's wake. Her bridal gown was long, and she kept tripping over the hem, the train picking up leaves and sticks as they raced for cover.

"But—I don't understand." Her mind was a chaotic, emotional mess. She didn't want to marry Brett, but she didn't want him *dead.* She loved him. He was a good friend. *Dear Lord in heaven, what is going on?* This didn't make any sense. Who would shoot him? On their wedding day?

And why?

"Come on." Duncan tugged on her hand, steering her toward a cluster of trees. It was mid-June and her white gown would be glaringly obvious against the green foliage.

"But—" Another loud crack echoed around them and Duncan yanked her down and behind the base of a large tree.

"We need someplace to hide." Duncan's voice was calm, as if running from gunfire was an everyday occurrence.

"My gown..." Her teeth began to chatter as if she were freezing cold. "W-we'll be t-too noticeable."

"It's okay, I'll protect you." Duncan's deep voice was ridiculously reassuring, even though she had no idea who he was protecting her from. He swept his gaze around the area, then gestured to the left. "This way."

She wasn't in a position to argue. He stood and helped her up, steering her toward another large tree. The air had fallen silent, and she hoped, prayed the shooter had cut and run.

They continued their zigzag pattern using the various trees and rocks for cover, moving from one place to the next. At some level she realized Duncan was taking them deeper into the woods and up the mountain. Her ballet slippers weren't designed for this kind of rugged terrain, and she could feel every rock and stick poking at the soles of her feet.

Duncan didn't let up his aggressive pace, moving swiftly and silently through the woods. She risked a glance over her shoulder. They'd gone so far that she could barely see the grassy knoll or the lattice arch. Only a hint of the log cabin frame of the Teton Valley Hotel was visible through the trees.

It was as if all evidence of her wedding had vanished.

A searing guilt stabbed deep. Was this somehow her

fault? That her deep desire to avoid marrying Brett had caused this to happen? No, that didn't make any sense, but she still couldn't shake the shroud of guilt.

Poor Brett. No one deserved to die. To be shot in the chest at his own wedding. He'd always been nice and kind to her, especially when they reunited just a few months ago at her mother's funeral.

Maybe it was the shock of losing her mother that had caused her to turn to Brett for comfort. That made her accept his surprising proposal. At first she'd felt complete, as if this was what God wanted—for her to move on with her own life.

Until the doubts began to creep in. Growing worse as the big day approached.

Her veil caught on a low-hanging tree branch. Tears sprang to her eyes as the flowered headpiece was yanked from her hair.

"Are you okay?" Duncan's keen gaze didn't miss a thing.

She nodded, even though she was far from okay.

She'd never be okay again.

They continued their mountain trek until she could barely move. Finally, Duncan stopped behind an outcropping of boulders.

"We'll rest here for a bit."

She dropped to the ground where she stood, pulling up the ragged, dirty hem of her gown to peer at her feet. The white ballet slippers were brown and already beginning to split at the seams. Full of despair, she kept remembering the bloodstain growing in the center of Brett's white shirt directly over his heart. Yet the horrific memory didn't bring her to tears. Her dear friend, the man she'd promised to marry, was dead. Brutally shot at their wedding.

Why wasn't she sobbing buckets of tears?

"Chelsey, look at me." Duncan's voice penetrated her internal thoughts. She lifted her head to look up at him. "I need to find fresh water for us to drink, or we'll become severely dehydrated out here. Will you wait here? Water is trickling nearby, but I'm not sure exactly where it is."

Dehydration? Was that why she couldn't cry? At least that made sense, a bit of logic in a world that had suddenly turned upside down. "I'll wait." The words came out as a hoarse croak.

Duncan's hand gently squeezed her shoulder. "I'll be back very soon."

She nodded again, because frankly she didn't have a choice. Now that she was sitting on the ground, she didn't have the strength to go on. Not that sitting on the mountain all night held any appeal.

Duncan still wore his light gray tux and white shirt. His dark blue boutonniere had been lost along the way. Other than his chocolate-brown hair being damp with sweat, he didn't show any sign of exertion. And when he moved out of her line of vision, her chest tightened with panic.

"Duncan, wait!" Her earlier exhaustion vanished. She struggled to her feet, unwilling to be left alone.

He quickly returned his dark gaze full of concern. "Easy, Chelsey, you're going to be fine. We're safe."

"How do you know? What if the gunman followed us?"

"Based on the trajectory of the bullet, I believe he

was on the roof of the hotel when he shot Brett. There's no way he could have followed us through the woods." Duncan sat beside her wrapping his arm around her shoulders. "We're going to be fine, Chelsey. We'll get through this."

She leaned against him, burrowing her face in the hollow of his shoulder. Maybe it was wrong to seek comfort in Duncan's arms so soon after losing Brett, but she couldn't seem to help herself.

If anyone could get her out of this mess alive and in one piece, it was Duncan O'Hare.

Duncan cradled Chelsey close, inwardly reeling from the brutal slaying of Brett Thompson.

What in the world had his old buddy gotten involved in?

The hit had been done by a professional, there was no doubt about that. Chilling to realize just how close he'd come to losing Chelsey, too.

The second shot had been meant for her. It was the only explanation. Otherwise, why hadn't the shooter taken off, disappearing amid the chaos?

Duncan had been in Jackson, Wyoming, for only five days, but from the moment he'd arrived, he'd sensed there was something going on with Brett.

The guy had been skittish, constantly looking over his shoulder, as if expecting someone to come up and grab him from behind. When Duncan had pressed him for information, Brett had shrugged off his concerns, focusing instead on how fortunate he was to have Chelsey as his fiancée. That he couldn't wait to marry her.

Now Brett was dead. Shot at his own wedding. Duncan's heart ached for what Chelsey had lost today. Not just a friend but her soon-to-be husband. He didn't blame her for falling apart.

Chelsey stirred in his embrace and he reluctantly loosened his grip. "Better?"

She nodded and pushed a strand of her wavy golden-blond hair from her cheek. "I'm sorry to break down like that."

"Hey, you're entitled after everything you've been through. I'm so sorry about Brett. I know the reality probably hasn't hit you yet, but I'm here for you, when it does."

She stared down at the ground for a long moment. "Thanks."

He glanced around. "I really need to find us water and shelter."

"My shoes are about to fall apart." She gestured to her mud-stained slipper-like shoes. "I'm not sure they'll hold up to more hiking."

The thought of her being barefoot concerned him. He lightly touched her bedraggled wedding gown. She'd looked so amazingly beautiful as she'd come toward Brett, but the poor dress had taken a beating during their mad dash through the woods. "I have a pocket-knife. I think we should rip strips off your gown and wrap them around your feet."

"That might work." She didn't look upset at the thought of destroying her gown. Not that it was sal-vageable at this point anyway.

"Here." He dug the penknife out of his pocket and handed it to her. "Work on that while I'm gone."

She took the knife and picked up her voluminous

skirt. Without hesitation, she sliced through the fabric and began sawing back and forth, creating the strips he'd suggested.

He eased to his feet and hurried off toward the sound of trickling water. The Tetons had snowcapped peaks even in June and he knew much of the water was melted snow. Pure enough, he hoped, that they wouldn't get sick.

Once he'd secured a water source, he could focus on a shelter and building a fire. Thankfully, his time in the army and being deployed overseas to serve in Afghanistan had provided the survival skills he needed to keep them safe.

The water wasn't far, a couple of yards and he stretched out on the ground, lowering his mouth to the stream to take a drink. They hadn't climbed up as much as they'd headed west, but it wouldn't take long for them to feel the change in altitude. Keeping well hydrated was critical.

Now all he needed was a way to carry the water back to Chelsey. Too bad they hadn't gone on the run with a water bottle. He stripped off the jacket of his tux and examined the pockets. They were a blend of polyester and cotton—not waterproof by any means, but it was possible they'd hold enough water for her to take a few sips.

After filling the pocket with water, he quickly carried it back to where Chelsey waited. The water seeped from the seams but remained halfway full by the time he offered it to her.

She eagerly drank, looking disappointed when it was gone.

"I'll get more," he promised. "But it would be easier if you could walk over there. It's not far."

"I only have two strips cut so far." She held up her work.

"Here, let me wrap these around your feet—that should hold for now. We can cut more later."

The strips helped to hold the flimsy shoes in place. He helped her stand and showed her the way to the brook. Once she'd taken her fill of water, she sat back with a sigh. "I didn't realize how thirsty I was."

He nodded, glancing around the area. "I need to find us shelter for the night."

"For the night?" Her voice rose in alarm. "We're staying out here all night?"

"Chelsey, we don't have another option. It's already eighteen hundred hours. I mean, six o'clock in the evening. Even with daylight savings time, the sun will be hidden behind the mountains soon. It will be dark here in the forest—we can't risk hiking at night."

"Why can't we go back to the hotel? I'm sure it's safe, the gunman is probably already under arrest."

He wasn't at all convinced. "Remember the second gunshot we heard?" When she nodded, he said gently, "Who do you think they were shooting at, considering Brett was already dead from being shot in the heart?"

She opened her mouth, then closed it again. After a long moment her voice came out in a squeaky tone. "Me? You think he was shooting at me?"

He hated upsetting her, but she needed to understand the scope of what they were dealing with. He glanced around again and gestured to the right. "I think that might be a small cave in the side of the mountain. I'm going to take a quick look."

This time, she didn't protest, clearly reeling from the idea that someone had just tried to kill her.

The cave was more of a shallow curvature in the rock. It wasn't much. In fact, he didn't think both of them would fit sitting together within the indentation. But Chelsey was slim and petite. She could use it and he would sit outside the opening, keeping the fire going.

He returned to get Chelsey, who took another long drink of water before following him to the shelter. She didn't look impressed but sank down and leaned against the rocky wall anyway.

Scouting the area for firewood didn't take long, and soon he had a nice pile of logs and kindling. He didn't have a lighter so he used a flint rock and dried sticks, a trick the army had taught him, to create a spark. A bit of fabric from Chelsey's dress helped.

The spark turned into a flame. Lightly blowing on the small flame, he added one twig, then another, nurturing the flame into a full-blown fire. When he was satisfied it was large enough, he added a log and scooted back to sit close to Chelsey.

"Are you hungry?" He glanced at her.

She shivered. "No. I can't eat."

He understood she felt that way now, but they'd be hungry by morning. The body had a way of overriding grief to sustain basic needs. What was left of the sunlight was already fading and hunting in the dark wouldn't work, even if he had something to hunt with other than his penknife, which he didn't.

There was no point in thinking about food now. Tomorrow he'd need to come up with another plan.

What that would entail, he had no clue.

"Take my jacket." He tucked the edges of his tux

around her shoulders. "The rock will be cold. Better that you stretch out on the ground instead."

"Okay." She did as he suggested, looking like a waif in her dirty and ripped wedding gown, wrapped in his tux. There was a long silence as they watched the fire. The flickering flames were mesmerizing, but now that he'd secured the basics of their survival needs, he wanted to understand exactly what had gone down earlier that evening.

"What was Brett involved in?"

She turned to stare up at him blankly. "What do you mean?"

"Brett must have been involved in something dangerous. Do you know anything about this new job he was all excited about? Something about working protection detail for a wealthy rancher who lived near the hotel?"

Her beautiful blue eyes crinkled with confusion. "What wealthy rancher? Brett worked as a project manager for Coyote Creek Construction. They construct businesses and residential homes. I don't know anything about Brett's alleged job of protecting a wealthy rancher."

He wrinkled his brow in confusion. "How long has he been working for Coyote Creek Construction?"

"I'm not sure, maybe a couple of years? Why would he tell you some weird story about a new job working for a rancher? Especially a wealthy one? The only rancher we know is Elroy Lansing, and he certainly doesn't need protection from what I know. Frankly, his ranch has been going downhill the past few years— rumor has it he's selling land to anyone offering a cash deal."

No wealthy rancher needing protection? It didn't

make any sense. Brett had obviously lied about his job, either to him or to Chelsey. And the more important question was, why? There was no reason, especially if he had a job working as a project manager for a construction company.

What secret was Brett covering up?

Whatever it was, it had likely gotten him killed.

And worse, put Chelsey in harm's way.

# TWO

Lying on the ground wrapped in Duncan's jacket and watching the flickering flames dancing amid the kindling was surreal. The peace and tranquility were at direct odds with the horrifying way her wedding had ended, even before it had begun.

Chelsey had lived in Wyoming for twelve years, so it wasn't as if she'd never camped outside. She had, but never in a wedding dress. And never with Duncan determined to look after her.

It seemed wrong to be resting here, somewhat relaxed, when Brett was dead. Maybe it was a sign that her body couldn't tolerate any more stress.

The week leading up to the wedding had been bad enough, wrestling with her doubts. Now all she felt was a blunt dullness. A resignation that she couldn't go back and change the past.

Brett was gone. It was difficult to wrap her mind around it. Duncan was right to explain how the reality of losing him hadn't hit her yet.

If only she'd explained to Brett how she was feeling before today. Maybe if she'd asked him to call off the ceremony, he'd still be alive. Mad and upset with her, yes, but alive.

Duncan's questions about Brett's job disturbed her. Why would Brett make up a story about protecting a wealthy rancher? Did he feel the need to be viewed by Duncan as more important than he really was? She remembered how Brett had planned to follow in Duncan's footsteps in joining the army, but his asthma diagnosis had made him ineligible to serve.

Was that what his bizarre story was about? Feeling better about himself?

They'd never know. Her chest tightened painfully. It was inconceivable that Brett was involved in something that had gotten him killed. Maybe this was nothing more than a case of mistaken identity.

But if so, why shoot at her?

The temperature dropped, making her shiver. Duncan must have noticed because he scooted closer. "Keeping close will help us both retain body heat."

She moved until her body was partially wrapped around his. Duncan's warmth was a balm to her fear and worry.

Trust in God. Wasn't that what her church pastor had taught them? She shied away from the thought. Concern over breaking her commitment to Brett had been something she'd wrestled with. She couldn't imagine what Pastor Rick would have said if she'd told him she needed to break off her engagement and cancel the wedding.

Had the local police been called? Were there men and women out there right now searching for the gunman? As well as for her and Duncan? It would make sense that they would be, especially as they were both witnesses.

Unless there was something she was missing.

It hit her suddenly, with the force of a brick to her abdomen, that she might be a suspect in Brett's murder. There was no motive, unless someone with Duncan's intuition had figured out that she had changed her mind about marrying him.

Not that it was really a motive. Killing him was a drastic measure when they could just as easily get an annulment. Yet who else would want him dead?

She had no idea. The thought of being a suspect in murdering Brett in cold blood was sickening.

"Relax, Chelsey. I can feel waves of tension radiating off you. Try to get some sleep."

It was quiet, other than the usual night sounds of the forest, but it wasn't that comfortable that she would be able to sleep. Drawing in a deep breath she tried to relax. To let go of the tension.

"You knew I was having doubts about getting married, didn't you?" The stark question popped out of her mouth before she could think about it.

Duncan didn't respond for several seconds. "You didn't look like a happy bride coming down the aisle. In fact, I was afraid you were going to be ill."

His intuition had been right on and explained the concerned way he'd been looking at her.

"Did Brett do something to upset you?" he asked.

"No." Honestly, it would have been easier if he had. But Brett was a nice and decent guy. She was the one with the issues, not him.

"Then what was bothering you?" Duncan's deep, husky voice made her shiver. It was crazy to be this aware of him. "Why were you having second thoughts?"

She couldn't tell him that seeing Duncan again had rekindled feelings she'd thought were long gone. How in that moment, she'd understood that she loved Brett as a friend and not as a husband.

"My mother died three months ago."

Duncan shifted ever so slightly, looking down at her. "I'm sorry to hear that. Your mom was a wonderful lady."

"After my father passed away two years ago, my mom and I became very close. Her death made me feel as if I was lost at sea without a boat or even a life preserver. When Brett came to the funeral, it was as if I'd been given a piece of my childhood back. One I didn't want to let go."

"I can see that."

Duncan's acceptance of her failures made her want to scream in frustration. Instead, she took a breath and continued to explain. "We began dating. It was so wonderful to have him here. His job was primarily based in Cheyenne and required him to travel a lot, so we made the most of the time we had together. When he proposed..." her voice trailed off. The memory was not a happy one. "I wasn't expecting it. I said yes, because he was beaming with excitement. And it wasn't that I didn't love and care about him."

"Marriage is a big step. It's understandable that you would have second thoughts."

"Stop making excuses for me." Her tone was sharp and she pushed herself upright into a sitting position. "I should have figured out that my caring about him was different from being in love with him. And now he's dead! Gone forever. And it's all my fault."

Tears pricked her eyes, but they came from a deep well of guilt.

"That's not true, Chelsey. His death isn't your fault."

"It is!" Why was Duncan being so stubborn? "If I'd called off the wedding ahead of time, the way I should have, none of this would have happened."

"Not in the same way it did, no. But if Brett was involved in something he shouldn't be, there would have been an attempt to get him another time. And don't forget, you were a target, too. If you hadn't walked down the aisle today, you may have been killed along with him in another location. I'm glad your life was spared."

She peered at him, trying to make out the expression on his face in the firelight. "You really believe that."

"Yeah, I do. That second shot wasn't an accident or a mistake. We were running away from the scene, which must have caught the shooter off guard. He probably expected you to go to Brett, giving him the perfect second shot. Instead, we took off, causing him to recalibrate his aim for the distance and our movements."

He spoke as if he knew exactly what the shooter had been thinking. "You're scaring me."

"I'm sorry." He didn't sound sorry. "But you need to understand why we need to keep moving. Why we can't simply go back to the hotel. There's no way for us to know friend from foe."

His tone was so rational and reasonable in the face of this insanity.

If Duncan was right, and she was in danger, then he was the only thing standing between her and the shooter.

She owed Duncan her life and trusted him to keep her safe.

* * *

Duncan was grateful when Chelsey finally stretched back out on the ground beside him. He waited for her muscles to relax enough that she might be able to get some sleep.

Her statements about how she'd become engaged to Brett had surprised him. It made sense given the fact that things had happened so quickly after her mother had died.

Seeing Chelsey again after all these years had reminded him of how much he'd liked her. They were only young teenagers back then, so there was nothing serious that had ever transpired between them, but he'd always admired her. She'd been smart, beautiful and funny. He'd been upset that her parents had moved from Wisconsin to Wyoming to take over her grandparents' hotel. It felt as if she lived on the other end of the planet—that's how far apart those miles had seemed.

He and Brett had gone out to visit her one summer after graduating from high school. They'd had fun, but it wasn't as if there were dozens of job opportunities out there. Duncan had plans to join the army, while Brett had wanted to go to college in Chicago. They'd left Chelsey behind, promising to visit again, but they hadn't followed through.

Or at least, he hadn't followed through with visiting her. Obviously, Brett had come to Wyoming and had taken a job with the Coyote Creek Construction company.

Had his old friend done that as a way to be close to Chelsey? Probably.

When Duncan had come out for the wedding, he'd learned that Chelsey's parents had inherited the Teton

Valley Hotel which had been in the family for several generations. The hotel likely belonged to Chelsey now, after the death of her mother. According to Brett, Chelsey loved playing the hostess to her guests and the hotel business was going well.

Then privately, Brett had claimed to have a new job that would enable him to live here in the valley with Chelsey. It had struck him as odd to hear that Chelsey hadn't known anything about it.

Too many things that didn't add up. As a former soldier and current cop with the Milwaukee Police Department, Duncan trusted his ability to keep Chelsey safe, but he also had a driving need to solve the puzzle of Brett's murder—and to uncover the reason Chelsey was in danger. Because he firmly believed the shooter wasn't finished with his plan. No doubt, the shooter would consider Chelsey a loose end.

Duncan added another log to the fire, then took a few minutes to rub dirt over his white shirt and light gray slacks. When he'd camouflaged himself as much as possible, he stretched out alongside Chelsey. He wanted to pull her into his arms but knew it was inappropriate. Instead, he edged as close as he dared to share his body heat.

As a former special ops soldier, Duncan knew how to rest while keeping his sixth sense on alert for a sign of the enemy. After his deployment, he'd had trouble sleeping and working as a police officer didn't help. Milwaukee had a high crime rate—not nearly as bad as Los Angeles or Chicago, but bad enough that he remained on high alert at all times.

Being in the mountains of Wyoming actually felt a little safer to him. It offered more hiding places than the urban environment of Milwaukee ever could. And was not nearly as dangerous as being in the mountains of Afghanistan.

He thought about his dad, Ian O'Hare, and his sister, Shayla Callahan, who had married her high school sweetheart, Mike Callahan. It would be nice to have the Callahans with him now, covering his back, but they were far away. As were Hawk and Ryker, his special ops army buddies.

Never in a million years did he expect to run into trouble in Jackson, Wyoming, of all places. That standing up for Brett and Chelsey's wedding would end up in a shooting that would send him and Chelsey running from gunfire.

If he'd known, he would have brought Ryker, Hawk or any of the Callahans along with him. The idea of calling his friends made him realize he had his cell phone in his pocket. Without disturbing Chelsey, he shifted enough to pull out his phone.

The bright light of the screen hurt his eyes, and he had to look away, giving his eyes time to adjust. But his hope deflated when he saw the tiny words along the top of the phone.

*No service.*

It figured. The Teton mountains were beautiful, but they didn't make for good cell reception. He shut down the phone to preserve the battery, since there was only thirty percent of a charge remaining, and slid the device back in his pocket.

A satellite phone would be handy right about now. Along with a hunting rifle. A bigger knife. And a few water bottles.

While he was at it, why didn't he ask for world peace

and the solution to world hunger? The items he longed for were just as far out of reach.

He shook off the despair and focused on next steps. If he was alone, he wouldn't be so concerned. He'd survived and thrived under worse conditions.

Having Chelsey along increased the risk. Not just because she was wearing a wedding dress that stood out like a sore thumb, but because she wasn't used to roughing it in the woods.

They needed to rest until daylight, drink more water and find some sort of food source, not to mention going on the move to find another shelter.

Was he wrong to avoid returning to the hotel? It might be safe if there were enough cops hanging around. Chelsey had a point about the shooter being long gone.

Yet his gut screamed at him to keep Chelsey hidden. At least for a couple of days. Although how he'd manage to find out who the shooter was while stealthily moving along the mountainside was a good question.

He must have dozed because a strange rustling off in the distance jarred him awake. Easing away from Chelsey, he sat up, peering through the darkness. Wild animals were not uncommon, especially deer, elk, moose and bears.

Straining to listen, he tried to distinguish between the normal sounds of the night. The fire was nice and warm, but it was also a beacon to anyone who might be out there searching for them.

The embers glowed red hot, but instead of adding wood, he kicked dirt over the fire, putting it out.

In minutes they were surrounded in darkness, only slivers of light from the moon shining through the trees offering relief.

The silence stretched in a way that was abnormal. The tiny hairs on the back of his neck lifted in warning. He desperately wished he had a decent weapon on hand but hadn't anticipated needing one at a wedding.

Since the penknife was all he had, he opened the blade and clutched it lightly in his right hand, keeping himself positioned in front of Chelsey. He wanted to go on the move, to get as far away from here as possible, but knew her dress would hinder their ability to make a clean getaway.

Better to stand his ground, taking out the enemy if that was the source of the rustling. He'd prefer any other animal to the shooter, except maybe a bear.

"Duncan? I'm cold."

Chelsey's plaintive tone sounded as loud as a scream ripping through the night. "Shh," he whispered, without taking his gaze from the wooded area surrounding them.

He was close enough to feel her go tense. "What's out there?"

"Don't talk." He bent down to put his mouth near her ear, in an effort to keep his voice as quiet as possible. "Scoot back into the crevasse as far as you can."

There was a slight rustling from her dress as she did as he'd asked.

He thought about his phone, and quickly pulled it out of his pocket. He didn't turn it on—the light would betray their location—but pressed the device into her hands. He didn't say anything but didn't need to. Chelsey was smart and would know without being told to use the phone as a way to get out of here if something happened to him.

Of course, she'd have to hike to a location where there was cell reception first.

Duncan straightened and widened his stance. He held the penknife in a loose grip, keeping the blade hidden at his side.

There was no doubt that he'd give his life to protect Chelsey's. Whoever was out there would have to kill him in order to get to her.

A familiar calm came over him, reminding him of his days in Afghanistan. He couldn't go into battle distracted, so he cleared his mind, focusing on the sounds and scents around him.

He heard the rustling sound again and he pinpointed it as coming from his left. He debated switching the blade to his left hand. He'd been taught to fight with either hand, even though his right was his dominant one. Since he hadn't been practicing the way he should have, he decided to keep the knife in his right hand, hoping the intruder wouldn't expect him to have a weapon and that he could use the element of surprise to his advantage.

Minutes passed with agonizing slowness, but the longer Duncan stood there, the more convinced he was that someone was out there. Animals didn't move with the pattern he was hearing. First rustling, then silence. Rustling, then more silence.

When he caught a glimpse of movement, he knew the intruder was close. He hoped and prayed that the dirt he'd smeared over his light clothes was enough to hide him. When a burst of movement came directly toward him, he was ready.

The man didn't appear to have a gun which gave Duncan a bit of hope. He waited until the guy was close before using the knife.

A burst of light came from behind him, blinding the assailant. The man lifted his arm in an attempt to block the light, giving Duncan the precious seconds he needed to take him down. They hit the solid earth with a thud. They rolled for a couple of feet, each vying for the upper hand.

But the guy wasn't about to give up so easily. It didn't take long for Duncan to realize he was in a brutal fight for his life.

One he didn't dare lose.

# THREE

Chelsey watched in horror as Duncan and a man wearing black wrestled on the ground. The light of Duncan's cell phone glinted off something shiny and her heart squeezed as she realized it was a knife.

Duncan's knife? It looked bigger than she remembered and realized with a sick sense of dread the man in black must have one, too.

Their grunts and groans as they struggled were difficult to watch. Yet despite how much she wanted to, she couldn't tear her gaze away. The more they struggled, the more she realized they were evenly matched. She couldn't just stand here, she needed to help. To do something.

Her gaze landed on the pile of logs Duncan had gathered for their fire. Reaching for the biggest and heaviest one, she picked it up and took a step toward the fighting men.

Using Duncan's phone as a flashlight, she waited until the man in black was on top of Duncan before making her move. She had to be careful not to blind Duncan as the men fought to have the upper hand. She held her breath and brought the log down on the side of his head with all her strength. A loud whack echoed through the night.

The man groaned and must have loosened his grip, because Duncan flipped him over and quickly disarmed him. Looming over him, Duncan held the man's larger knife at his throat.

"Who are you?"

The man's eyes were closed, his entire body limp as if he were unconscious.

Her stomach lurched. She put a hand to her mouth. Oh no! Had she killed him?

"Chelsey? Get me a couple of those strips we cut from your dress."

Duncan's hoarse voice spurred her into action. She tossed the log back on the pile with distaste and went over to where they'd cut several strips off her dress to use as extra protection for her feet.

She brought them to Duncan and watched as he quickly bound the man's wrists and ankles.

"He's not dead?" Her voice came out in a hoarse whisper.

"No, just out cold." Duncan was breathing heavily as he glanced up at her. "Thanks."

She gave a shaky nod, relieved that she'd been able to help. "Now what?"

Duncan let out a sigh. He patted the man down. Lifting the man's slacks, she could see a gun strapped to his ankle. Duncan took the weapon along with the ankle holster and picked up the man's larger knife, with a grim satisfaction. "We need to move."

"Move where?" She didn't understand what he was saying. "I thought hiking at night was too dangerous?"

"It is." Duncan rose to his feet, grimacing a bit as

if he were in pain. "But we don't have a choice. This guy is a professional. No ID, nothing to indicate who he's working for. We can't assume that he's alone, there could be others out there."

"Others?" She didn't like the sound of that and moved closer to Duncan while throwing a furtive glance over her shoulder. There was nothing to see in the inky darkness, yet she could easily imagine someone hiding out there. "Wouldn't anyone working with him have rushed forward to help once you began to struggle?"

"Maybe. Or maybe they've spread out to cover more ground, no way to know for sure."

She felt as if she'd been dropped in an alternate universe. She managed a family hotel, a place were nice people came to celebrate a birthday or their anniversary—not a place where men dressed in black came out of the darkness, searching for her with the intent to kill.

Was Duncan right? Had Brett somehow gotten involved in something sinister? As much as it was difficult to imagine, it was also the only thing that made sense.

And she couldn't help thinking about the crazy story he'd told Duncan about being hired as protection duty for a nearby rancher.

Was Elroy Lansing a part of this? As the only rancher in the immediate area, he must have been the one Brett was talking about.

"Let's go." Duncan took her arm. "We need to move."

"But—are we going to leave him here?" She glanced doubtfully at the unconscious man. "What if wild animals find him?"

"I'm sorry, but we have to. I told you, I don't think he's on the mountain alone. His team will find him before the wild animals get to him. Trust me, we need to be long gone when they do."

She couldn't argue his logic. "All right."

"First we'll wrap your feet." Duncan gestured for her to sit, and took several moments wrapping her feet in the remaining strips. Then he handed her the last one. "I need you to wrap this around my arm."

"Your arm?" She frowned, taking in his mud-stained shirt. "You're hurt?"

"It's a minor cut. But I don't want to leave a blood trail for anyone to follow." As he spoke, he stripped off his filthy shirt and turned so that she could see his arm. There was a three-inch cut on his bicep, oozing blood.

"It's going to get infected." First the dirty shirt, and now a strip from her gown.

"It will be fine for now." Duncan's tone was calm. "Just do your best."

Swallowing hard, she took the last strip from her dress and wrapped it around the wound, tucking the end over into itself to help keep it in place. His skin was warm to the touch, making her shiver with awareness.

*Stop it.* She gave herself a mental shake. What kind of woman lost her groom-to-be in a horrific murder and then noticed another man? A terrible woman. It was wrong on so many levels. She must be losing her grip on reality. This must be a weird reaction to the violence around her.

Duncan was an old childhood friend, like Brett. Nothing more.

"Okay, let's go." Duncan shrugged back into his shirt, helped her put his jacket back on, then took her hand.

"Where?" She tripped over a rock and might have fallen if he hadn't held her up.

For several long moments he didn't respond. He led the way without the aid of his phone flashlight app. She understood he was trying to preserve the phone battery, but that wouldn't matter much if they fell on their faces and ended up rolling like fallen logs down the mountain.

When they were far enough away from their makeshift camp, he lowered his voice and spoke in a whisper as if worried the man they'd left unconscious and bound might be able to hear. "Up the mountain."

Up? Was he joking? She couldn't climb a mountain in the darkness.

*In a wedding dress.*

Yet that's exactly what she did. It was slow going, especially because of her lack of decent footwear. Duncan took his time, choosing their path carefully. She followed on his heels, doing her best to step where he did, wincing when sharp rocks and sticks poked at her feet. He shortened his stride because of her, and she was grateful. Despite how painstakingly slow they were moving, she felt herself growing breathless with exertion.

She was clearly out of shape, because Duncan acted like this was a stroll in the park. She tried to control her breathing so she didn't sound like a wounded grizzly. Between her aching feet and her shortness of breath, she was slowing them down. What she wouldn't give for a four-wheeler. A minibike. Even a horse. She'd learned to ride when her family had moved to Wyoming, but the hotel kept her too busy to have horses of her own.

She took a step. And another. Winced when she stepped on a rock, then took another.

Chelsey had no idea what time it was. Or how long they'd been climbing. But when Duncan came to an abrupt halt, she plowed into him from behind.

"Oomph." Her face smooshed into his back.

"You okay?" His low voice was barely audible.

"Yes." In contrast to his ability to be quiet, her whisper sounded like a shout.

Duncan turned and gently tugged her down to the ground. She wanted to collapse against him but forced herself to be strong.

"Wait here." He moved away without making a sound. How did he do that?

Suddenly it occurred to her that she was holding him back. That if not for his willingness to protect her, he'd be long gone and safe.

Instead he'd fought an assailant for her. Led her through the darkness and put her needs before his. Caring for her in a way no one ever had.

In the months since her mother's death, she hadn't felt very close to God. Hadn't been able to feel His presence, even at church. Brett hadn't been much of a churchgoer, and she'd skipped several Sunday sermons doing things with him.

But now, she knew God was still watching over her, despite how she'd strayed.

Humbled, she closed her eyes and thanked God for bringing Duncan to Jackson, Wyoming, and for providing him the strength and courage he needed to keep her safe.

He stared out into the darkness, surveying the area. Nope. He didn't like it.

The water source was fine, but they weren't far enough from their previous campsite. In fact, he'd been pretty much following the stream they'd discovered earlier. They needed to keep moving, but he could tell

Chelsey was losing strength. Her ragged breathing concerned him. The altitude was getting to her, and they weren't even that far up the slope.

He bent down to drink some water, then realized she was still wearing his jacket so he wasn't able to bring water back to Chelsey using his pockets the way he had before.

Sitting back on his heels, he tried to think of what their best decision would be.

Keep going? Or stay here?

Neither option was very appealing.

He estimated the hour to be roughly two in the morning. It would be reasonable to stay here and rest a bit until dawn. It wasn't as if they could move quickly anyway. In fact, he'd worried that her white dress would be a beacon to any of the other men who may be crawling the mountain looking for them.

Okay, they'd stay. For now. He stood and quickly made his way back to where Chelsey waited.

But he didn't see her. His heart squeezed and he raked his gaze over the area, peering through the darkness. The moonlight offered just enough light that he could see the trees and rocks around him.

"Chelsey." He tried not to let his internal panic show in his voice.

There was nothing but silence for a long moment.

"Here." He caught a glimpse of white as she lifted her arm to wave.

His shoulders slumped in relief. In his absence, she'd covered her white gown in dirt and leaves, doing a good job of blending in with the foliage. She'd obviously learned from him and he had to smile at her ingenuity.

Thankfully she was okay.

He crossed over to take her hand in his, drawing her upright. It took every ounce of willpower he possessed not to pull her into his arms and hold her close.

No need to let her know how scared he'd been.

"This way." He took her hand and led her over several large rocks to the stream. When she saw the water, she dropped down and leaned over to drink.

"Thank you." Her gratitude made him uncomfortable. So far he hadn't done the best job of protecting her. They should have continued hiking while they'd had light or found a better place to hide for the night. He should have doused the fire.

Maybe if he'd done a better job, the bad guys wouldn't have found them.

"We'll stay here," he said, gesturing to the trio of trees, "until dawn."

"Can you make another fire?" She gamely followed him to the meager shelter.

"No. That's how they found us the first time."

"Okay." She shivered, and even in the darkness he could tell she was apprehensive.

"It will be okay. You're going to rest against me, and I'll keep you warm." He sat with his back up against two of the three tree trunks, and gently pulled her down beside him. She stretched out so that she was lying against his chest, his tux jacket pulled up over her back like a blanket. He wrapped his arms around her and hoped she wouldn't become too chilled.

The last thing he needed was for her to get sick.

She relaxed against him, clearly exhausted from their brief hike. He kept his arms around her, hoping she'd absorb some of his warmth.

Sharing their body heat was essential for staying

alive, but he couldn't deny that holding Chelsey was nice. He closed his eyes, reminding himself that not only had Chelsey just lost her fiancé, but he wasn't in the market for a relationship. Losing the woman he'd loved several years ago to a violent crime was bad enough. Amanda had been brutally attacked and robbed on her way home from work late one night and died from bleeding into her brain. Sitting at her bedside for almost a full week, he couldn't believe it when she was gone. No way was he opening his heart to that kind of pain again.

Besides, his life was back in Milwaukee, Wisconsin, not here in Jackson, Wyoming. Sure, the Grand Teton mountains were incredibly beautiful, but his dad, his sister, his nephew, his niece and friends were all back home.

Everyone important in his life.

Although, that wasn't exactly true any longer. Seeing Chelsey again made him realize how much he cared about her.

But only as a friend. He couldn't afford to lose another piece of himself the way he had after Amanda had died.

# FOUR

Chelsey huddled against Duncan, his tux tucked over her shoulder, reveling in his warmth and strength despite the eerie darkness surrounding them.

How was it possible that she felt so safe in his arms?

She closed her eyes and tried to sleep, knowing rest would be critical to her ability to hike out of there in the morning. But the rush of adrenaline, the aftermath of their close call, raced through her veins. Her mind kept going back to those terrifying moments when she thought they both might die at the hands of the assailant.

"Chelsey, please try to relax." His deep voice rumbled in his chest beneath her ear. "Morning will be here soon and we'll need to be ready to move."

"Okay. Are you going to try to sleep, too?" she whispered.

"Yes." His simple answer surprised her. "But not until you do, because your tenseness is keeping me awake."

A reluctant smile tugged at the corner of her mouth. It never failed to amaze her how in tune he was to her emotions. Or maybe it was just being in danger that was bringing them so close together. She drew a deep breath in, then let it out, trying to relax the tension from her muscles.

"Much better," he murmured. "Sleep now, Chelsey. You're safe with me."

"I know." She took another deep breath and felt a strange calmness settle over her. Maybe because she knew she was safe with Duncan.

And more so because she was certain God was watching over them.

She must have dozed at some point, because she awoke with a start.

"Shh," Duncan whispered.

She froze, her heart thumping wildly against her chest. The sounds of the forest should have been reassuring, but she couldn't be certain what had awoken her.

"A buck, see?" Duncan lifted his hand, pointing in the direction off to their right.

At first she didn't see anything, then heard the sharp snap of a twig. She realized it was the same sound that had brought her awake.

A dark shadow moved and the light of the moon fell across the deer's golden coat. He was an impressive animal with a large rack of antlers stretching up to the sky over his head. The animal sniffed the air for a moment, and she wondered if he'd smelled them because he abruptly turned and headed down the mountain.

"Beautiful," she whispered.

She felt him give a soft kiss to the top of her head. "Yes," Duncan agreed.

A blush crept up her cheeks and she was glad it was still dark. She shifted slightly, hoping she wasn't squashing him too badly. "What time is it?"

"About four thirty in the morning," Duncan said

softly. She really needed to figure out how he spoke so quietly. "In another hour, we'll need to move."

An hour. She closed her eyes and tried to fall back asleep. It was no use.

Fifteen minutes later, Duncan led her back to the stream so they could drink again. It may have been her imagination, but she thought the area looked a little brighter. Dawn rose early, because the mountains didn't block the sunrise from the east.

"Let me check your feet," Duncan said when she finished drinking from the stream.

She pulled up the edge of her wedding dress, revealing her tattered ballet slippers barely held together by the strips they'd wrapped around them.

Duncan frowned with concern. "We need more strips from your gown."

"Hiking boots would work, too," she quipped trying to lighten things up.

He didn't smile. "Maybe I should try to have you hide somewhere until I can get help."

She reached out and grabbed his hand, her chest squeezing with fear. "Please don't leave me, Duncan. I'll be fine."

Duncan didn't look convinced. He pulled out the larger knife he'd taken from the assailant and went to work cutting away more of her gown. When he was finished, he wrapped the strips around her feet and up her calves, then back down again in a way that reminded her of the old gladiators. It seemed to work—the fabric added good support.

"Thank you."

Duncan rocked back on his heels for a moment, regarding her thoughtfully. He looked as if he wanted to say something, but then slowly stood and offered his hand. She took it, allowing him to help her to her feet.

Once again, he led the way through the forest, taking some sort of route that only a mouse would call a trail. She pushed the bobby pins back in her hair to keep the curls from falling into her eyes and concentrated on keeping pace with him, stepping where he did to avoid rocks and sticks.

Moving quietly seemed an impossible task and she had no idea how Duncan was managing it. Even when she followed in his exact footsteps, she made more noise than he did.

Was he right about other assailants being out there? Were they combing the side of the mountain, looking for them?

*Lord, please keep us safe in Your care, amen.*

The sun rose as they walked, brightening the area around them. Time had no meaning—without a watch or a phone she didn't have a good way to know how long they'd been on the move.

But it felt like forever.

Duncan slowed and lifted a hand in warning. She froze, straining to listen. After a moment he turned toward her. "Need a break?"

"Yes."

He nodded and gestured to the left. "There's an outcropping of rock that way. Follow me."

She nodded. After all, she'd been following him since this mess started, which seemed like a long time ago, but was really just over fourteen hours.

A lifetime.

They reached the rock slab five minutes later. She

leaned against it for a moment, trailing her gaze over the area. It almost looked like a spot where someone would hike to in order to get a nice view. Even though they were tucked beneath the overhang, she could tell the rock was high enough that one might be able to see the entire valley below.

"We've come farther than I thought," she said in amazement.

Duncan nodded. He pulled out his cell phone and lifted it up. "I've got one bar, but my battery is less than fifteen percent."

She tried not to show her disappointment. "Probably because I used the flashlight app."

"You saved our lives, no need to apologize for that." Duncan punched in a number on the phone and listened. After a long moment, he grimaced. "Nothing. Even with one bar, I can't get through."

She shivered, realizing they were really on their own. She looked out over the landscape again, her gaze stumbling over what appeared to be a square corner.

A structure? She stared hard, trying to make it out. As dawn brightened, the corner became clearer and more evident. "Duncan, is that a cabin?"

His gaze sharpened. "Where?"

She lifted her hand, pointing toward the bit of brown that could be seen through the trees. "See the two pine trees that are taller than the others?"

"Yes." He narrowed his gaze. "I see it now. You're right, I think it's a cabin. The square angle isn't natural, but appears man-made."

"I say we head in that direction." Chelsey couldn't

hide her excitement. "Maybe there will be something in there we can use, or food to eat."

"Maybe." Duncan's voice held a note of caution. "It's a good idea to check it out."

"Lead the way," she said, feeling giddy with relief. A cabin meant a roof over their heads if nothing else.

Unless it was occupied.

No, she refused to go there. The cabin would be empty and provide them something to eat.

She refused to consider any other options.

Duncan had to give Chelsey credit for finding the cabin. Her eagle eye had caught something he'd missed. At the same time, he hoped she didn't have high expectations of what they might find inside.

The place could be something that had been abandoned years ago, falling apart without anything useful left behind. Food and clothing would be great, but he was prepared for the worst. He was hungry, his stomach rumbling loud enough to be heard by the bad guys following them, and he knew Chelsey was hungry, too.

The cabin or whatever structure they found would be better than nothing, at least providing enough protection that they could start a small fire without being noticed. Food would come next. With the gun and knife he'd taken from the assailant, he had a decent chance of successfully hunting something for them to eat.

He headed out through the dense foliage, keeping his pace slow enough for Chelsey to follow him. The best thing about the cabin was that she might be able to remain safe there for a while. He was very concerned about her feet—any cut she sustained might become infected and that would hamper their ability to keep moving out of harm's way.

He'd carry her if needed; it wouldn't be the first time as he'd carried fellow soldiers far heavier than Chelsey out of Afghanistan. Yet moving quietly through the brush with her over his shoulders would be extremely difficult.

Duncan told himself not to borrow trouble, they were doing okay so far. The cabin looked to be roughly a hundred yards away drawing a straight line, which wasn't at all how they'd be traveling.

Chelsey sucked in a harsh breath. He turned to look at her. "You okay?"

She grimaced and nodded. "Found another rock, that's all."

He hesitated, wondering if he should carry her now before she seriously injured herself. He judged the condition of the path between them and the cabin and decided they could keep walking.

Ducking beneath a low hanging branch, he heard another muffled groan at the exact same time a shot rang out. He twisted and threw himself over Chelsey.

"Are you hurt?" he asked anxiously. In his mind the gunfire had come after her groan, but he couldn't be certain.

"Other than you being on top of me?" she whispered. "I'm fine."

He eased his weight to the side so he wasn't squashing her. Relief that she hadn't been hit by a bullet made him a little light-headed, but he shook it off. "Come on, we need more cover."

"Okay."

He moved backward along the ground with agonizing slowness, hoping and praying Chelsey would be able to follow without giving away their location.

The bullet had come from a distance, likely the shooter using a rifle with a scope. Any rustling of leaves could potentially draw another shot.

They weren't far from the base of a tree. With infinite sloth-like movements, he made his way to the tree, using the trunk as meager cover.

Chelsey joined him a minute later, and he was impressed by how well she'd been able to follow his example, slithering along the ground.

When he had her tucked behind his body, he found a rock, lifted it up and tossed it off in the direction from where they had been, watching as it ruffled the leaves on the trees before hitting the ground with a thud.

Instantly the crack of a rifle echoed around them.

Duncan blew out a breath. Okay, then. There was obviously a sniper out there, watching the area for any sign of them.

"What are we going to do?" Chelsey asked in a hoarse whisper.

It was a very good question, and he desperately needed to formulate a plan. The gun he'd taken off the assailant was of little use against a sniper sitting off in the distance using a high-powered rifle.

He stretched out his arm, snagged another rock and tossed it off in the opposite direction from where he'd thrown the first one. Again, another gunshot rang out.

Leaning over, he pressed his mouth near Chelsey's ear. "I'm going to continue drawing their fire while you make your way to the cabin."

"Me?" Her voice was laced with panic. "Alone?"

"Yes." He glanced around their hiding area, wondering how many more rocks and pinecones he'd need to use so that she could get safely to the cabin.

To what he hoped and prayed was a cabin. And not a figment of their imagination.

"I can't leave you here alone. I think we need to stick together."

Normally he'd agree with her, but not under these circumstances. "Chelsey, you can't stay here. Eventually they'll figure out where we're located." He paused long enough to toss a pinecone. The resulting crack of the rifle came like clockwork, as if the sniper had every intention of sitting there and firing no matter how much ammunition he used.

Which meant the shooter had a significant amount on his person.

No rationing needed.

Chelsey picked up a rock and threw it, but it didn't go very far. Another gunshot rang out, and Duncan put a hand on her head, keeping her down.

"The best way you can help me is to get to the cabin." He couldn't hide the pleading in his tone. "For me, Chelsey. You have to do this for me."

"I'm scared," she whispered.

"I know, but I'll keep diverting their attention until you're safe."

"And then you'll meet me there?"

"Yes." He met her gaze with his. "I need you to trust me on this. Once you're at the cabin, I can move quicker without worrying about your ability to follow me."

A long minute passed before she reluctantly nodded. "Okay, I'll do it."

"Thank you." He couldn't hide his relief. "Here's how we're going to do this. The second I throw the rock, you're going to move, but stay on your belly, crawling like we did in order to get here, okay?"

She drew in a deep breath and nodded. "Yes."

"Each time I throw something, they're going to shoot. That's your cue to keep moving."

"Got it."

He hesitated, then added, "I want you to take my phone."

Her gaze clouded with worry. "Why?"

"Just in case." He didn't want to worry her, but there was the slim possibility that they might eventually start shooting within the diameter of the moving trees.

It was what he'd do, if he was the one sitting in a tree with a rifle and a scope.

"In case what?" Her blue eyes were wide with apprehension.

He smiled reassuringly. "In case there's better reception up there. You might be able to call the police to help get us out of this mess."

"Oh, okay." She relaxed. "That's a good idea."

He didn't really think the police would be able to help them, but he would do anything to get Chelsey out of harm's way. "Ready?"

She nodded and pushed up off the ground to her hands and knees.

When he lifted his arm to throw a rock, she began to crawl away in the general direction of the cabin. The rock landed and the gunshot immediately followed.

He glanced back in time to see Chelsey disappear beneath the brush.

Good. He let out a long breath and began reaching for more rocks and pinecones.

It wouldn't be easy for Chelsey to cover a hundred yards crawling on her hands and knees. But he was determined to give her every opportunity to get to safety.

Even if that meant sacrificing himself.

# FIVE

Chelsey flinched at every gunshot but didn't let fear stop her. She continued to make progress. If she thought walking in makeshift shoes was difficult, crawling along the ground with her dress hiked up over her knees was far worse.

She ignored the pain in her hands, elbows and knees fully aware that Duncan was doing this for her. He'd given her his phone and was doing everything possible to protect her. It was only right that she did her fair share.

Crawl, pause, crawl, pause, crawl. In her mind, she found herself praying with each stretch of crawling.

*Keep us safe, Lord*, she chanted over and over again, seeking solace.

Glancing behind her, she tried to gauge how far she'd gone. There was no sign of Duncan, but that didn't mean much. He was no doubt hiding in the brush.

She continued making her way in the general direction of the cabin, hoping and praying the place would offer better shelter.

Her dress snagged on just about everything around her. Bugs flew into her mouth, making her grimace, but she kept on moving. The dress and the bugs didn't matter, survival did. And she told herself it could be worse. Rain or snow would make it impossible to crawl to safety.

The minutes stretched into ten, then twenty. She found herself wondering if she'd gotten off course. When she came upon a large tree, she slowly stood leaning on the tree and hiding herself as much as possible to check her progress.

She had veered a little off course, but not bad. The corner of the cabin was easier to see now. It was a brown wooden building with a black shingled roof. The structure looked to be in decent shape and a surge of excitement hit hard.

It was so close!

Staying upright, she made her way toward the cabin using trees and shrubs as cover. It was amazing how much faster she could go now that she was walking. Duncan's phone was tucked into the bodice of her gown and she couldn't wait to reach the cabin to see if she could pick up a signal.

As she reached the cabin, she slowed and strained to listen. She didn't want to barge in on someone. Easing closer, she edged up to a window. A thick layer of dust made it difficult to see through, but the lower portion of the window was broken, so she peered inside.

The place appeared deserted. There were a few bare bones items of furniture, a rough table in the kitchen and a moldy-looking sofa. There may have been something in the bedroom, but she couldn't tell from this angle.

Moving away from the window, she moved around to the front door. It hung off-kilter from disuse. As she stood there uncertainly, it occurred to her that she hadn't heard a gunshot recently. Because Duncan was on his way? She hoped and prayed that was the case. After shooting a fugitive glance over her shoulder, she pushed at the door.

It didn't budge.

No! She tried again, using all of her strength against the warped door.

It opened, not a lot, but about a foot. Enough of an opening for her to slip through.

The interior was darker than she'd have liked thanks to the thick layer of dust covering the windows. The place smelled musty, and up close she could see that the sofa had been ravaged by mice and other small animals.

She moved gingerly through the small space. There was a kitchen and living area, with a single bedroom and what was once a bathroom. Her initial excitement at having an actual bathroom evaporated when she saw there was no water in the black toilet.

Yuck. She returned to the kitchen area, opening cupboards to see if there was anything to eat.

Her heart thumped wildly when she found a couple of cans of soup and beef stew. Gingerly picking up the cans, she looked for an expiration date.

They were good for another month. Next she searched for pots and pans, but found only a rusty frying pan.

Her hope deflated. Cans without something to cook the contents weren't very helpful.

Moving toward the broken window, she looked outside. Still no gunfire. Was that good or bad? They hadn't found Duncan and hurt him, had they?

She pulled his phone out and held it up, squinting in

the dim light to see how many bars he had. Only one. She dialed 911 and listened.

Nothing. No ringing, no one answering on the other end.

Drawing a deep breath, she lowered the phone. Turning away from the window, she swept her gaze over the cabin. How long had it been abandoned? No way was anyone living here under these conditions.

The doorway to the bedroom hung ajar. The interior was darker than the rest of the cabin and she wondered why. As she moved toward it, she heard the sound of a twig snapping.

She froze, then hurried inside the bedroom. Something dark covered the windows, and the musty smell was even stronger in here. She wrinkled her nose, fighting the urge to sneeze.

"Chelsey?"

Duncan's voice nearly had her weeping in relief. "In here!" She rushed out of the bedroom and threw herself into his arms.

He clutched her close, wrapping his strong arms around her as if sensing her fear. "Shh, it's okay. We're safe."

"I'm so glad you're here." Her voice was muffled against his shirt.

"You did great, Chelsey. But we can't stay long," he warned. "Did you find anything useful?"

She lifted her head and forced herself to step out of his arms. She gathered herself and nodded. "Two cans of soup and two cans of beef stew but nothing to cook them in. Oh, and no cell phone service here, either. I tried." She offered him the phone back.

"Clothes?" he asked, setting the phone aside.

She glanced back at the bedroom. "I'll look, but it smells really musty in there."

"Better musty than visible from a hundred yards away." Duncan smiled and slipped past her. She followed, wondering if they'd find anything useful.

Duncan ripped aside the brown drapes over the window so they could see better. There was a quilt on the bed that may have been a bit moth-eaten, but he tugged it off the bed and handed it to her. "Be careful, but I need you to go outside and shake this out. We can use it for warmth."

"Okay." Beggars couldn't be choosers, right? She eased out the door, staying well hidden behind the tress, and shook the quilt trying not to imagine bed bugs or other creepy crawlies falling to the ground.

When she was satisfied, she crept back inside to find Duncan standing near the kitchen table. "Look what I found." He held up an army-green boxy thing.

"What is it?"

"A canteen. We'll be able to carry water with us as we hike."

It didn't look like a canteen, not that she was an expert on camping equipment.

"I also found a couple of T-shirts, jeans, socks and one pair of hiking shoes." He displayed them proudly as if they were better than gold, which was true. "The shoes are for you. I know they'll be too big, but probably safer than the ballet slippers that are falling apart."

She eyed them warily. "The clothes will be too big, too."

"We'll make a belt from what's left of your dress." He gestured at her filthy, torn and tattered gown that she still wore.

"Okay, I'll see what I can do." She swept the shoes, socks, shirt and jeans into her arms and returned to the bedroom.

She had to admit that getting out of the dress made her feel light and free. It had been weighing her down more than she'd realized. Not just the fabric itself, but the entire incident.

The wedding that shouldn't have happened. The groom that should have been safe but was now dead.

Tossing the dress aside, she thought of Brett. Her good friend who had supported her in the aftermath of losing her mother. He'd been so sweet and so kind.

And all she'd done was gotten him killed.

Well, not her personally, but the situation.

She closed her eyes for a moment and sent up a silent apology to him.

*I'm so sorry, Brett. Please forgive me.*

The tightness eased and she picked up the T-shirt and slipped it over her head. It was large, hanging down to midthigh, but not bad. She removed the ballet slippers, the fabric falling away as the seams finally gave up the fight. Resigned, she pulled the socks on next, which were also large, and then the jeans.

The denim was stiff and scratchy, and the waistband gaped at her waist by a good couple of inches. She took a moment to search the room for a belt, but didn't find one. Sitting on the edge of the bed, she pulled on the hiking boots, which were also too big.

Glancing at the remains of the ballet slippers, she decided that hiking boots that were too big had to be better than nothing which was her only alternative at the moment.

"You decent?" Duncan asked from the main room.

"Yes." She stood and held the jeans in place with one hand. "I'll need you to help me make a belt."

"Happy to do that." He entered the bedroom, wearing borrowed clothes as well that fit him far better than hers. The only difference was that he still wore his rented dress shoes so that she could have the hiking boots. He grinned. "You look great."

"Wow, thanks." She shook her head wryly. "Who would have thought wearing borrowed and wrong-sized clothing would feel so good?"

"We'll be able to move through the woods easier now, which is exactly what we need." After making her a belt from her wedding dress, he then balled up some extra fabric and knelt at her feet. He unlaced the hiking boot, then stuffed the fabric into the wide toe area. He glanced up at her. "Place your foot in and see what you think. Hopefully this will prevent your feet from sliding around too much."

"It feels much better than what I had before," she admitted.

He repeated the process with the other boot, then rose to his feet and offered his hand. "Ready?"

She placed her hand in his, took a deep breath and nodded. "Ready."

He gently squeezed her fingers and drew her from the bedroom. On the table he had the canteen and the canned goods, along with a sack fashioned out of his filthy dress shirt.

Duncan slung the makeshift pack over his shoulder then tucked the moth-eaten quilt under his arm, before heading to the door, clearly expecting her to follow.

She hesitated, glancing once more around the cabin.

Leaving the shelter they'd found was more difficult than she'd imagined.

But she forced herself to move, putting her faith and trust in Duncan.

And in God.

Duncan hesitated in the narrow opening of the doorway, searching for any sign of danger. He had no idea if the gunman had gotten a glimpse of Chelsey as she'd made her way toward the cabin or not.

The last two rocks he'd thrown had not drawn gunfire. The lack of response confirmed his fear that the shooter was onto him. He'd moved swiftly after that, blending into the foliage with skills he'd learned in Afghanistan eating up the distance to the cabin in order to catch up with Chelsey.

As much as he'd hoped to stay at the cabin, starting a fire and maybe spending the night, there was no way to do that now. Not when he knew full well danger was lurking out there, waiting for them.

Seeing nothing out of place, he eased outside. Chelsey was behind him, and he reached out to take her hand in his.

They could move easier now, and he wanted to get as far from the cabin as possible. If the shooter had a scope and managed to see the cabin, he'd know to head over and look for them there.

Duncan wanted to be long gone before anyone arrived.

"Where are we going?" Chelsey asked, as he melted into the forest.

"Mostly due east." He kept his voice low. "I think there's a small town at the base of the mountain in that direction. If we can find the trail it should take us directly there. Brett mentioned hiking it once."

She nodded. "The town of Moose is at the base of Moose Mountain. But it's very small, not a lot of people."

He shrugged and kept moving. "I don't need a lot of people, just a way to reach the authorities."

"Sounds good." Chelsey fell silent, although he was glad she was able to keep up with him as they made their way through the woods. He wanted time to stop and eat, but needed to be sure they were safe first.

They hiked for nearly an hour before Duncan gave her the sign to stop. He'd filled the canteen at a nearby spring, offering it to Chelsey first.

She took a swig, then tried to hand it back. He gestured for her to drink more. "We have to keep hydrated, remember? And there are many streams around here."

After a moment's hesitation, she took another, longer drink. He took the canteen and helped himself, then glanced around.

"I think we should take a quick break and eat the beef stew."

Hope flared in her eyes. "Are you sure?"

"Yes." His military training had taught him to survive on less, but it had been several years since he'd gone without rations for twenty-four hours. He could push on, but that wasn't fair to Chelsey.

She needed to keep her strength up. And food was critical to that goal.

He knelt on the ground and opened the makeshift pack. The cans of soup would be good, too, but salty without the ability to water them down a bit.

"Are we eating it cold?" Chelsey asked, sitting on the ground next to him.

"Yes." Using the knife he'd taken from the assailant, he opened the cans of beef stew and offered one to Chelsey. They didn't have utensils, so he handed her his penknife, choosing to use the large sharp knife for himself.

Even cold, the beef stew tasted good, satisfying the rumbling in his stomach. Glancing at Chelsey, he took note of how she'd eaten hers with gusto, too.

"Never thought a can of cold beef stew could be so delicious," she said with a wry smile.

He let out a low chuckle. "Agreed."

"Now what?"

"I'm sorry, but we have to keep moving." He placed the empty cans and the canteen back in the makeshift pack. "It's best if we make the most of the daylight."

"It seems like we've been walking for hours, but I understand. We should wash the wound on your arm first, though, while we have fresh water." She pushed to her feet with a determined look on her face.

He reluctantly nodded. "Okay."

Her gaze was earnest as she washed the nearly three-inch laceration on his arm. "I wish we had bandages," she muttered.

"Soon," he promised.

"Okay." She stepped back and pushed her hair out of her eyes. "Let's do this."

He estimated the time was just after nine in the morning, so she was right about how it felt as if they'd been walking for hours.

They had been. But they were making good time now which gave him hope. As much as he didn't want to use the normal trails, he felt they needed to get back to civilization as soon as possible.

The bad guys were still out there, and he wasn't sure how many of them there were. The guy who'd attacked him, and the sniper for sure.

How many others? He had no idea.

As he picked up the pace he wondered whether or not the local authorities were out searching for him and Chelsey yet. After all, they'd taken off from the scene of a crime. His first instinct had been to keep Chelsey out of harm's way, but now they needed help from the local police, or park rangers.

Any law enforcement agency would do.

He pulled his cell phone out and held it up again. The screen was completely blank. He pressed the power button to be sure, but still nothing.

Dead as a doorknob.

He tucked it away and continued searching for the trail he desperately hoped wasn't too far off. Although what he knew about the Grand Tetons would fill a postcard.

A rustling noise made him stop dead, holding up a hand to warn Chelsey not to say anything. A tall man wearing a cowboy hat, of all things, emerged from the brush to his right, as if he'd come up alongside them.

Duncan reached for the gun, but the man held up his weapon and pointed at the star pinned to his shirt. "Don't. I'm Slade Brooks from the US Marshals Service."

With one hand, Duncan tried to tuck Chelsey behind him as he eyed the stranger. The silver star on his chest looked real, but that didn't necessarily mean he was one of the good guys.

"How did you find us?" Duncan asked, trying to

come up with an escape plan. This guy stumbling across them was too much of a coincidence.

"I've been looking for you both since you took off after Brett Thompson was shot and killed." The marshal didn't move. "I picked up your trail early this morning, following bits of fabric from Ms. Robards's wedding dress."

Duncan narrowed his gaze. "If that's true, why wait until now to come out of hiding?"

"I wasn't exactly right behind you," Brooks said. "Tracking is one of my areas of expertise, but when I heard the gunshots, I was forced to hunker down and stay low. Fortunately, I managed to find the cabin, saw the discarded wedding dress and realized you were there. Now I finally caught up to you."

Duncan hesitated, unsure if he should buy this guy's story. "Why are the marshals involved?"

Brooks glanced at Chelsey. "Because we know Ms. Robards is in danger. I'm Brett Thompson's handler—he was joining the witness protection program as soon as the wedding was over."

"Witness protection?" Chelsey echoed, pulling away from him so that she could face the marshal. "Why would Brett do that?"

"Because he was going to testify against the owner of the Coyote Creek Construction company." Slade Brooks frowned. "We had a job lined up for him as a security guard in Florida, along with new names and identities for the two of you. You're saying you didn't know anything about it?"

"No!" All the color faded from Chelsey's cheeks to the point Duncan feared she'd pass out. He reached out and placed a reassuring hand on her arm.

Brett's strange story about a new job made sense in a way, but still, Duncan couldn't believe his old friend had planned to do all of this without telling Chelsey. Or him.

Obviously, Brett's delay in going into WITSEC had resulted in his murder.

# SIX

*Witness protection.*

The phrase echoed over and over in Chelsey's mind, yet she was still having trouble comprehending what she'd been told by the US marshal.

Brett had witnessed a crime? And had been about to go into witness protection, taking her with him? Without saying a word ahead of time? Marrying her without indicating they'd be forced to move, to relocate to Florida of all places under a different name and identity?

A flash of anger hit hard. How dare he? How could Brett even consider doing something like that? Marry her, then turn her entire world upside down? As if the danger alone wasn't bad enough, she didn't like Florida. It was far too hot in the summer.

Her knees felt weak and she did her best to lock them in place, remaining upright with an effort. Wordlessly, Duncan slid his arm around her waist and drew her close, offering his support.

Gratefully, she leaned against him, her mind still reeling. As upset as she was with Brett, she was forced to accept that in reality, this was more her fault than his.

Because she'd agreed to marry him, despite not being

in love with him. Why hadn't she called off the wedding before it came to this?

If she'd looked deep into her heart earlier, maybe she'd have understood her feelings weren't love as much as friendship. Needing someone, anyone to be with after losing her mother.

There was no denying that if she'd handled this differently, Brett would still be alive.

And she wouldn't be in danger.

"We need to go." The marshal's low drawl interrupted her thoughts. "Ms. Robards's safety is our main concern."

"I…just can't believe this." She drew in a deep breath, then sternly told herself to get over it. There was no way to go back and change the past. Besides, the US marshal was right—they couldn't stand here on the mountain sheltered by the trees indefinitely.

They had to get to civilization, the sooner the better. "Okay, I'm ready."

Duncan gently hugged her, then loosened his grip. "We need to keep Chelsey between us since she's the one in danger."

"Agreed," the marshal said.

"I was planning to head into Moose," Duncan said to the marshal. "But if you have a better idea, Marshal Brooks, I'm willing to adapt."

"Moose works, and you may as well call me Slade," he said and she heard a hint of Texas in his voice. "Easier all around."

Duncan nodded. "I'm Duncan O'Hare, a cop with the Milwaukee Police Department."

"I know," Slade responded. "We dug into your background when you arrived to stand up as Brett's best man." He turned toward Chelsey. "Stay behind me, Ms. Robards."

"Chelsey," she corrected, falling in step as directed. Duncan covered her back and as they continued on their way, she hoped and prayed he wouldn't get hurt.

Brett had done a disservice to Duncan, too. Inviting him to come to Wyoming to stand up in the wedding, knowing he was in danger.

Not that there was anything she could do about that now. If not for Duncan, she'd be dead.

The tip of her oversize hiking boot caught a tree root, sending her stumbling into Slade. "Sorry," she muttered.

"It's no problem," he drawled. "I'm glad you found something to wear other than the dress."

"Me, too." She wasn't going to point out that her feet were still moving around inside the hiking boots, causing blisters to form. There wasn't anything the US marshal or Duncan could do to change it.

All she could do was to pray they'd reach the town of Moose soon.

"Chelsey, let us know when you need a break," Duncan said. "We can rest as needed."

"Okay." Truthfully she preferred to keep going, mostly because there was no way of knowing if the gunman was following them the way Slade had.

It had never occurred to her that bits of fabric from her dress may have left a trail. Slade had said that tracking was his area of expertise, but what if the gunman or the assailant had the same sort of skill?

She glanced fearfully over her shoulder. Duncan lifted a brow. "You okay?"

"Yes." She continued walking, choosing the placement of her feet very carefully, doing her best to mimic what Slade was doing.

Being sandwiched between the two men was reassuring. She knew in her heart they would both protect her—in a way Brett had not.

She gave herself a mental shake. Brett was gone, and blaming him, sullying his memory wasn't the answer.

But as they continued moving through the forest, she found herself wondering what would happen when they reached Moose.

She wanted nothing more than for her life to get back to normal. To return to the Teton Valley Hotel she owned and managed. Who was taking care of things in her absence? Hopefully Trish was handling everything okay.

Yet somehow, she didn't think that was going to happen. In fact, she had a very sick feeling that her life wouldn't be going back to normal anytime soon.

Maybe never.

Duncan's emotions swung between relief and suspicion related to the timing of Slade's finding them on the mountain. Granted, the guy seemed to be legit, and he could see how they may have left enough of a trail to follow considering the condition of Chelsey's wedding dress. But he also knew getting a marshal badge wasn't impossible and a variety of scenarios filtered through his mind.

Slade could be taking them straight into the hands of the men who'd murdered Brett, turning him and Chelsey over for a wad of cash. Or Slade could be taking them on a route leading them deeper into the woods, rather than heading to Moose, Wyoming.

He mentally kicked himself for offering Moose as an option. Too late now, but he wished he'd have made Slade come up with the plan.

The marshal had allowed him to keep his weapon, which was a point in his favor. But Duncan wasn't about to relax his guard around the so-called marshal. If his sister, Shayla, was here, she'd tell him to place his fears and worries in God's hands.

Too bad he wasn't sure how to do that. And even if he could learn to pray, better that his focus be centered on protecting Chelsey.

Slade paused, glancing down at what appeared to be a compass in his hand. At least the guy had come prepared. Duncan turned and swept his gaze over the wooded area, checking for anything amiss.

A flock of birds abruptly shot out of a tree as if startled by something. "Get down," he hissed, tugging on Chelsey's bulky jeans. She dropped beside him. Slade went down, too, but pulled his weapon, holding it at the ready.

For long moments there was nothing but silence.

"What happened?" Slade asked in a low voice.

"Something startled those birds from the tree located to the left of center behind us. Could be our sniper is setting up another spot from which to shoot."

"This way," Slade urged, gesturing toward a dense bush near the base of a large oak.

Chelsey's blue eyes were wide with fear as Duncan gestured for her to follow Slade. When he was certain they were both well hidden, he crawled after them, using all the skills he'd learned in Afghanistan to cover his tracks.

Chelsey reached out to grasp his arm when he crept up to her. "Duncan, how long do we have to stay here?"

He glanced over her shoulder at Slade, who looked grim. If the guy was working with the assailants, he deserved an award for his acting skills. Some of the tension in his chest eased with the thought that two people protecting Chelsey was far better than one. "I don't know. If I had proper camouflage clothing, I could double back, find him and take him out of the picture once and for all."

Chelsey's grip tightened. "No! I don't want you to leave."

Her concern for his well-being was touching, and he felt there was an excess of admiration in her eyes, probably because of the way they'd been forced to rely on each other to get through this. He wanted to reassure her but didn't have the words.

And he didn't want to lie, either. Even if Slade was legit, they were far from getting out of this mess.

"I have to agree. I'd rather you stick here with us," Slade whispered. "I can call for reinforcements from the Marshals Service, but that will take time we don't currently have."

"Does your phone work up here?" Duncan asked. "Mine is dead, but even before the battery gave out, I had no service."

Slade pulled out his phone, stared at the screen then frowned. "Nope. But maybe service will pick up once we get closer to Moose."

"Maybe." Duncan wasn't convinced. He glanced around, trying to come up with a plan. They were hidden from the area where the birds had flown out of the tree, but still in the open more than he'd have liked.

Reaching for his knife, he began to cut parts of brush from their hiding place. As if understanding his plan, Slade joined him.

"What are you doing?" Confusion colored Chelsey's gaze. "Starting a fire?"

"No, we're going to use this to help hide us from view." Duncan took a clump of brush and stuck it down the back of her T-shirt. "Like this, see?"

"What good will this do?"

Chelsey's whisper held a note of disbelief.

"It will help us blend into the foliage, so that we are less of a target," Slade explained.

Duncan nodded, eyeing the marshal with reluctant approval. "Yes."

The process took longer than he'd have liked but soon the three of them were covered in leaves and twigs to the best of their ability. Chelsey had even woven them into her hair, securing them in place with pins without complaint.

They continued on their path toward Moose, Wyoming. Slade remained in front, Chelsey in the middle and Duncan covering her six. They went much slower now, moving from one tree to the next without making too many jarring moves.

The woods behind them remained eerily silent. Duncan briefly considered that the birds leaving the tree so abruptly was a fluke, scared off by an animal instead of a human, but he wasn't willing to take the chance.

Not with Chelsey's life.

He hadn't been with Amanda when she'd needed him. Thankfully, he was able to be here for Chelsey now. After an hour, Slade lifted his hand, indicating it was time to take a break. They sat beneath the base of a tree.

"I have protein bars for you." Slade pulled them from a small pack.

"We have water." Duncan offered the canteen.

"And two cans of soup," Chelsey chimed in. "Nothing to use as a pan, or a fire to use as a heat source."

"We'll save the soup in case we need to shelter in the woods overnight," Slade said, handing out the protein bars.

"Overnight?" Chelsey looked horrified, the protein bar in her hand temporarily forgotten. "Won't we reach Moose by nightfall?"

Slade looked to Duncan for help.

"May I borrow your compass?" Duncan asked him.

"Sure." The marshal handed it over.

He held up the compass, verifying their course. He pictured the map in his head, the one he and Brett had reviewed as they were discussing hiking trails. From what he could tell, they were headed in the correct direction, but how far had they come?

He had no idea.

"We'll do our best, Chelsey," he whispered. "But you need to know there is a possibility we won't make it to Moose before dark."

She lowered her chin, staring down at the ground for several seconds before nodding. "Okay."

He longed to pull her into his arms, to tell her everything would be all right and he'd always keep her safe. But it wasn't his nature to make promises he couldn't keep.

Especially to Chelsey, who deserved so much better.

* * *

The leaves pinned in her hair itched, the branches stuck into her T-shirt scraped against her skin. She hadn't thought things could get worse, but at the moment it was all Chelsey could do not to break down and cry.

Stupid problems, really, compared to being safe. But she felt as if bugs and spiders were crawling around on her skin beneath her clothes and she absolutely hated creepy crawlies.

It was all so overwhelming. They went from being in danger to being safe, then more danger, until she began to wonder if she'd ever, in this lifetime, feel safe again.

She took a bite of the protein bar, reveling in the taste. The cold beef stew they'd eaten was hours ago, and her stomach had been rumbling for the past ninety minutes. Likely loud enough for Slade to hear, which is why he'd taken a break.

She hated feeling as if she was slowing them down. Her feet were beginning to burn with blisters, and she couldn't wait to get someplace to shower, change and tend to her aches and pains.

Which reminded her of Duncan's injury. She turned toward him. "How's your arm?"

"Fine." He didn't even look down at it.

Slade frowned. "I have a first aid kit."

Duncan shrugged. "No point in fixing it up now, while we're still hiking through the woods. I'll clean it up again when we reach Moose."

When we reach Moose. Not if. Chelsey held on to that thought as they once again trekked down the mountain.

Their progress was slow. Slade abruptly stopped, lifting his hand, cautioning them to be silent. She held her breath, but then he turned to look at her and Duncan.

"We're close," he said. His green eyes were bright with excitement. "I think Moose is only about a mile from here."

"How do you know?" Chelsey whispered. She could see only trees. Endless trees.

"Listen," Slade urged.

She listened, but still didn't hear anything. But then she heard it, the faint echo of music. Country and western music.

"I'm glad Moose isn't far, but we still need to be careful in case the sniper is tracking us," Duncan cautioned.

"Yep." Slade grinned. "At least we won't have to spend the night on the mountain."

"Roger that," Duncan muttered.

Chelsey wholeheartedly agreed. To know the end of this unnerving hike was so close filled her with eager anticipation. This time, when Slade gave the signal to continue moving down the trail, she found it easy to ignore the blisters on her feet, to forget about the leaves and twigs sticking all over her body, itching like mad.

Even a town as small as Moose must have a motel room with a bed, right? And real food? They wouldn't need to eat cold soup out of cans or more protein bars.

What she wouldn't give for a thick, juicy steak.

She concentrated on the soft echo of music, using it as a beacon calling them to safety. The music grew slightly louder, and she found herself silently singing along with the old country and western song.

Slade must have felt they were out of danger, because he picked up the pace. It wasn't easy for her to follow, the overly large hiking boots clumsy and awkward.

"Easy, Slade," Duncan called. "We can't run down the mountain."

The marshal shot a guilty look over his shoulder. "Sorry. I just want to get Chelsey to safety."

"We both do," Duncan said.

"All of us need to be safe," she corrected. "I'm sure by now Duncan is a target, too. Especially after the way he took care of the assailant."

"What assailant?" Slade asked with a scowl. "You didn't mention that earlier."

"I'll explain later," Duncan advised.

The woods around them thinned as they grew closer to the base of the mountain. Chelsey felt almost light-headed with relief.

They were going to make it.

Without warning, the crack of a gunshot rang out, followed by a second one. Chelsey froze, but Duncan yanked her down to the ground beside him.

Slade had whirled around and dropped to his knees while drawing his weapon, his gaze raking the area.

"I knew there was a sniper back there," Duncan whispered harshly.

"Anyone hurt?" Slade asked.

Chelsey looked down at herself, taking in the baggy jeans cinched around her waist and the long T-shirt. No blood, thankfully. "I'm okay," she managed.

"Me, too." Duncan's expression was grim. "Lead the way to shelter, Slade."

"But aren't we heading down toward Moose? It's not that far," Chelsey protested.

"Not yet," Duncan said. "Not while this guy has a scope trained on us."

She stared at him in horror. "You mean we have to wait him out?"

Duncan grimaced. "I'm afraid so. We should be able to move once it's dark."

Dark? She swallowed a cry and turned to look in the direction the music was coming from. From here, she could just make out a scattering of buildings, still too far to see details, but enough to know they'd be safe.

A wave of despair hit hard. Moose, Wyoming, was so close, yet so far away.

# SEVEN

Duncan had suspected the shooter, if there was one, would wait until they had cleared the forest to take his shot.

He hated being proven right.

Fear and disappointment radiated off Chelsey in waves. He glanced at Slade, who wore a grim expression.

"Darkness is still at least three hours away." Slade pulled out his phone and held it up. "I have two bars and can call for reinforcements."

"Like who?" Duncan asked. "Does Moose have any sort of law enforcement?"

"Many park services employees live there," Slade responded. "For all we know they're heading this way now after hearing the gunfire. June is not exactly hunting season."

Chelsey perked up at that comment. "We'll be rescued soon?"

"If I can get through to the park services." Slade lifted his phone and pulled up the number for park services. When he dialed the number, a smile creased his features when the call went through.

"This is US Marshal Slade Brooks requesting backup,"

he said. "The gunfire you heard was intended for a woman I'm trying to protect."

It went against Duncan's instincts to bring more people into this, but they obviously didn't have a choice.

"We are only about a half mile from the outskirts of Moose, hiding in a thicket of trees. We'd appreciate your assistance." Slade listened, then added, "That would be great, thanks."

"They're coming to get us?" Chelsey asked hopefully.

Slade grinned. "With a four-wheeler."

Duncan nodded his approval. "That's good. Hopefully the shooter will realize that making another attempt at Chelsey with park rangers surrounding her is a bad idea."

"Hasn't stopped them from trying while you and Slade are beside me," she pointed out dryly.

"True, but the shooter doesn't know I'm a cop, and maybe doesn't understand that Slade is a US marshal," he pointed out. In his experience most bad guys didn't make the decision to take out a law enforcement officer lightly.

Yet for all they knew, these guys who'd come for Chelsey couldn't care less as long as they successfully executed their mission. Guns for hire? Maybe.

"I don't hear the music anymore," Chelsey whispered.

"Listen for the sound of a four-wheeler," he suggested.

A hint of a smile tugged at the corner of her mouth. Her face was streaked with dirt, twigs and leaves in her hair, and her clothes, but to his eye, she was still the most beautiful woman in the world.

Strong, too, considering how well she was holding it together despite her entire world being turned upside down.

No point in blaming Brett since their childhood friend had paid for his mistake with his life. All Duncan could do was focus on saving Chelsey.

He wondered if she realized that she would need to go into witness protection to keep safe. He wasn't sure she'd thought that far into the future, but he had.

The thought of never seeing Chelsey again made his chest tight. While it was the right thing to do to keep her safe, he didn't like it.

Not one bit.

Although he wasn't interested in a relationship, he was still her friend.

They sat in silence for several long moments before the sound of a rumbling engine reached their ears. Still, they remained hidden in the brush, waiting for the four-wheeler carrying two park rangers to arrive.

Slade emerged from the brush first. He flashed his credentials. "I'm US Marshal Slade Brooks." He gestured to Duncan and Chelsey. "And this is Chelsey Robards and Duncan O'Hare. Duncan is a police officer with the Milwaukee PD."

"Milwaukee?" One of the park rangers lifted a brow. "You're a long way from Wisconsin."

"Tell me about it," Duncan muttered. He helped Chelsey to her feet. "We appreciate your assistance. I'd like to make sure Chelsey arrives in Moose without being injured."

The park ranger riding shotgun jumped down and crossed over to them. "I'm Ranger Paul Davidson, and the driver is Eric Connolly. We plan to get all of you safely into town."

Duncan, Slade and Paul hovered around Chelsey as they escorted her to the four-wheeler. Duncan helped her inside, then took a seat beside her.

"Keep your head down, Chelsey," he advised. "Bend over, so that you're as small a target as possible."

She did as he requested as Slade climbed in on the other side of her. Paul returned to the front seat of the four-wheeler. The back was crowded, but Duncan didn't care. Between his broad shoulders and Slade's, the shooter wouldn't get a clear shot at Chelsey.

Duncan swept his gaze over the forest as the rangers drove them toward Moose. No gunfire rang out, no sudden rush of wildlife indicating an intruder.

The sniper was either hunkering down until nightfall or was already gone.

Over the roar of the engine, he could hear the sounds of country and western music starting up again. Must be some sort of live band that had just returned from taking a break.

When they'd gotten into the very small, unincorporated town of Moose, Wyoming, Duncan lightly stroked Chelsey's back. "You can sit up now."

She slowly unfurled herself, looking around at the various small cabins with a look of unfettered relief. "We made it."

"Yeah." Duncan longed to pull her into his arms. "Paul, do you have a motel nearby?"

"Yes, we're taking you there now." The ranger glanced at them over his shoulder. "Looks like you all could use food and clothing, too."

"A shower, clothes including soft shoes that fit and food…in that order," Chelsey said with a sigh.

"Soon," Duncan promised.

The park rangers pulled up to a small, ten-unit motel. Duncan glanced at Slade. "I have cash. It wouldn't be smart to leave a paper trail."

"Agreed, I have cash too, and can get more if needed." Slade waved a hand. "Stay here, I'll get the rooms."

Fifteen minutes later, they were settled in two rooms located right next to each other. Duncan would have preferred connecting rooms, but Moose was too small to offer those accommodations.

"They have a two-bedroom cabin that will be available starting tomorrow," Slade said as he unlocked the door to Chelsey's room. "I've asked them to hold it for us."

"Great." Duncan followed Chelsey into her motel room as Slade moved on to open the next door. It looked like every other hotel room across the country, except maybe for the view of the Grand Tetons. "I'll pick up what you need, just give me a list."

Chelsey blushed and shook her head. "If it's all the same to you, I'd like to pick out what I need."

He hesitated, wishing he could wrap her in bullet-proof clothing and keep her hidden from view. But she likely needed personal items, so he gave in. "Okay."

Thankfully, there was a general shop located directly across from the motel. He picked out a few things for himself, then waited for Chelsey to finish before paying for everything in cash.

"I have money at home," Chelsey told him. She clutched

the bag of clothing and personal items to her chest as if it were filled with gold.

"Don't worry about it." He didn't have the heart to tell her she wasn't going to be returning home anytime soon.

If ever.

"Do you smell that?" She sniffed the air appreciatively. "Smells like roasted corn and barbequed ribs."

That made him smile. "We'll eat as soon as we clean up." He kept his gaze out for anything suspicious as they crossed the street to the motel.

"I'll be ready in twenty minutes," Chelsey promised as she unlocked her door. "I'm too hungry to wait any longer."

"Sounds good."

He waited until Chelsey closed and locked her door, before entering his own room. Slade glanced up at him. "Reinforcements should be on their way soon."

"More US marshals?" He dropped his bag of clothes and shoes on the bed closest to the bathroom.

Slade nodded. "A couple of guys I trust with my life, Colt Nelson and Tanner Wilcox."

He forced a nod, inwardly wincing at the idea of more people being brought into this. If he had his way, he'd contact his brother-in-law, Mike Callahan, and the soldiers he'd fought alongside in Afghanistan, Hawk Jacobson and Ryker Tillman, for help. Those were the men he trusted with his life.

And Chelsey's.

But very soon, he wouldn't be in the picture at all. This was a case involving the US marshals and evidence Brett had uncovered while working at Coyote Creek Construction. It was only a matter of time before the

US marshals whisked Chelsey away and stashed her someplace safe.

Leaving him behind.

A hot shower with soap and shampoo had never felt so good.

Dressing in plain clothes that actually fit was wonderful. Chelsey never wanted to wear another wedding dress ever again. She placed various Band-Aids on her open blisters, then gingerly drew on cotton socks and slipped her feet into the running shoes she'd gotten from the store. Brushing her damp, curly shoulder-length hair, she used a couple of bobby pins to keep it out of her face, then let it air dry.

Exactly twenty minutes later, there was a light rap on her door. Smoothing the cotton top over the waistband of her jeans, she crossed over and opened it. Duncan, showered and shaved, looked handsome dressed in black jeans and a black T-shirt.

Her heart gave a betraying thump in her chest. She tried to ignore it. This attraction she felt toward Duncan had to stop. She'd mistaken her feelings toward Brett for something more than friendship. No way was she going to make the same mistake again.

"Ready to go?" Duncan held out his hand.

She didn't hesitate to place her palm in his. "Yes." Belatedly she noticed Slade standing behind him. "I'm famished, those protein bars disappeared a long time ago."

Slade smiled wryly. "I'm sure they did."

She clutched Duncan's hand tightly as they walked to the restaurant attached to the motel. Tantalizing scents wafted toward her, making her mouth water. For one brief moment it was as if all the madness of the past forty-eight hours hadn't happened. This could be a nice dinner out with a friend.

Slade's phone rang as they were escorted to a table in the corner of the restaurant. "Colt? What's your ETA?"

Chelsey glanced at Duncan with confusion. He avoided her gaze and pulled out a chair for her, taking a seat beside her.

"What's going on?" she asked in a low voice. "Who's Colt?"

"Another US marshal." Duncan's serious expression gave her a twinge of concern.

Slade disconnected from the call and slid the phone in his pocket beneath the five-point silver star on his chest. "Colt will be here by tomorrow afternoon. Tanner has a conflict. We'll make a game plan once Colt arrives."

"What kind of game plan?" Chelsey glanced between the two men. "Are both Colt and Tanner US marshals?"

"Yes, they are."

She wrinkled her brow. "I still don't understand."

"Can I get you all something to drink?" Their female server was dressed in skintight denim jeans, cowboy boots and a short-sleeved Western-style shirt.

"Actually, I'm ready to order my meal," Chelsey said, glancing at the men. "Just water to drink, and I'd love some barbecued ribs and grilled corn, with a side salad, please."

"I'll have the same," Duncan chimed in.

"Make that three," Slade said. "Thanks."

"I'll be back shortly with your water."

"Let's eat first," Duncan said with a pointed look at Slade. "We can talk freely back at the motel."

"Good idea," Slade agreed.

Chelsey felt as if there was something she was missing. When their server returned with a tall glass of water for each of them, she took a long, grateful drink.

Never again would she take food, water and shelter for granted.

"I need a phone so I can call my assistant manager at the hotel," she said to Duncan. "I'm sure Trish is frantic by now."

"Trish—your maid of honor, right?" Duncan asked.

She nodded. "I need to let her know I'm okay, and that I'll be back soon."

There was a long silence as the two men studiously avoided looking at her. A chill rippled down her back. "What? Are you saying I won't be back soon?"

"Chelsey, we need to keep you safe." Duncan's tone was gentle. "Let's just take things one step at a time, okay?"

She didn't like the sound of that.

"Chelsey, I want you to think about what Brett said to you over the past couple of weeks." Slade gazed at her over the rim of his glass. "We can't discuss it here, but think about it. Even the slightest detail might help."

Help what? She wasn't sure.

Their meals arrived a few minutes later, and Chelsey made time to offer a quick prayer to God before diving in. The tangy barbecue sauce was incredible, and she savored every bite.

They finished eating thirty minutes later. Chelsey had saved half her food and insisted on a to-go bag. The men walked on either side of her as they returned to the motel.

After putting her leftovers in the mini fridge in her

room, she joined the guys next door. "I'm sorry, but I don't remember Brett talking about anything recently except for the wedding."

Slade pinned her with a narrow look. "Nothing about his work with Coyote Creek Construction?"

She frowned. "The company headquarters are in Cheyenne, but they also have a small branch in Jackson. We planned on adding a wing at the Teton Valley Hotel, using Coyote Creek Construction, but nothing else."

"Nothing about the man he worked for? Anthony Nettles?"

Chelsey slowly shook her head. "Never heard of him. Brett mentioned Kenny Martin—I thought he was the boss."

"He's the general manager working under Anthony Nettles," Slade said. "Have you met Kenny Martin?"

She frowned. "I went to the Jackson office to meet Brett once. He was talking to some guy, and when I asked who he was, Brett said he was Kenny Martin. He was a slender guy, about the same height as Brett, but with thinning dirty blond hair."

Slade let out a heavy sigh. "Brett never mentioned Anthony Nettles, or anything about being in witness protection?"

"Not a word." She pushed aside the useless anger. "Is that why you have more marshals coming? To find out who Brett spoke to? He obviously can't be a witness for you anymore."

There was a long pause.

"Tell her," Duncan said in a curt tone.

"We lost a witness in Brett, that's true. But the problem is that the men who silenced your fiancé are now after you. There's no easy way to say this, Chelsey, but you'll be placed in witness protection as soon as possible. For your own safety."

"I'm—what?" She glanced at Duncan, then back at Slade. "No, that's not happening."

"Chelsey, please..." Duncan began, but she shot out of her chair.

"No. I can't leave my life behind to become someone else!" She yanked the motel door open and headed to her room. Duncan was hot on her heels, and she abruptly swung around to face him.

"Leave me alone. I can't talk to you right now."

"Chelsey, please. I understand you're upset..."

"Upset?" A harsh laugh erupted from her throat. "You have no idea."

Hot tears sprang to her eyes and she swiped at them impatiently. She should have known this was coming. Should have realized that the gunmen wouldn't rest until she was dead.

Literally or figuratively.

Duncan's arms came around her, pulling her into his warm embrace. She wanted to rant and scream and kick, but found herself melting against him. She took several deep breaths, trying to pull herself together.

"I'm sorry," Duncan whispered.

She shook her head. "It's not your fault."

He continued to hold her, smoothing a hand down her back as if she were a child needing comfort. After what seemed like forever, she lifted her head and looked up at him.

Their gazes locked—the world around them grinding to an abrupt halt.

He gently lowered his head to press a chaste kiss on her cheek. But that wasn't what she wanted. When he lifted his head, she went up on her tiptoes to capture his mouth in a sweet kiss.

This. This was what she'd wanted from the moment Duncan had arrived in Wyoming.

Not to kiss Brett, but Duncan.

# EIGHT

Chelsey's kiss caught Duncan off guard, but that didn't stop him from deepening the kiss. A tiny voice in the back of his mind warned him that this wasn't real, that Chelsey's kiss was a reaction to everything she was dealing with, but another part of him didn't care.

He'd liked and admired Chelsey when they were younger, but had kept his feelings firmly in the friendship bucket. Then Brett had announced their engagement, which made her off-limits.

Brett was gone, but Chelsey wasn't ready for this.

And neither was he, although at the moment Amanda's memory was fading fast.

She broke off from their kiss, her breathing just as erratic as his. He tucked her head beneath his chin and simply held her, without saying anything. His heart ached for what she was facing, through no fault of her own.

After several long moments, he asked, "Are you okay?"

She drew in a deep, ragged breath and nodded. She lifted her head to look up at him. "I have to be."

"You have every right to fall apart, Chelsey. We can't be strong all the time."

Her smile was sad. "God will get me through this. I just have to place my faith in Him. And in the US Marshals Service. It's just…" her voice trailed off.

"I know." He understood that giving up the life she'd built wasn't easy. In fact, he thought this would be the most difficult thing she'd face.

Well, other than running away from bad guys with guns.

"Would you like me to stay with you for a while?" He felt helpless, unable to do anything that might ease her distress over giving up everything to enter WITSEC.

"No, I'll be okay." She offered a weary smile. "After all the hiking and lack of sleep over the past few days, I'm looking forward to being in a real bed again."

He forced himself to loosen his grip and step back. "All right, but if anything changes I'm right next door. Don't hesitate to come get me."

"I won't." She watched as he turned toward the door.

He glanced over his shoulder. "Lock up."

She nodded and he stood outside her door, satisfied to hear the click as she shot the dead bolt home.

For a moment he pressed his palm against her door, then chided himself for being foolish. When he entered the room he shared with Slade, he found the guy on the phone again.

"I need a computer, any chance you can get one?"

Duncan listened to the one-sided conversation as a way to distance himself from how he'd been rocked by Chelsey's kiss. Slade's frustration was apparent as he scowled.

"Okay, fine. Tomorrow will have to do." Slade disconnected from the call and scrubbed his hands over his face. "There's a lot to be done, but I don't have the tools I need."

Duncan dropped onto the edge of the bed. "Like what?"

"We had an identity picked out for Brett and Chelsey, but now she needs something entirely new. I can't trust that Brett didn't blab to someone about what was going on."

Duncan nodded slowly, his pulse kicking up at the possibility of having Chelsey nearby for a while longer. "What about the guy Brett was planning to testify against? Shouldn't we continue that investigation as well?"

Slade shot him a glare. "We? There is no we here, Duncan. I appreciate everything you've done, but this is a US Marshals case. A cop from Milwaukee doesn't have any jurisdiction here."

Duncan frowned. "I'm aware of that, but you should use my expertise to your advantage. Brett told me a wild story about being hired on to provide security for a wealthy rancher."

Slade looked interested. "Did he say who?"

"No, and when I mentioned this to Chelsey, she said the only rancher nearby was a guy by the name of Elroy Lansing. Only he's not wealthy at all, has been apparently selling off parcels of land to stay afloat."

"Elroy Lansing," Slade repeated. "That sounds familiar."

"His property is apparently right next to the land owned by Chelsey's hotel."

"But if Lansing doesn't have any money, how could that have anything to do with Brett Thompson?" Slade argued.

"I'm not sure," he admitted. "But Chelsey mentioned Coyote Creek Construction was being hired by the hotel to expand, and their property line meets up with Lansing's." He shrugged. "Maybe it's time to follow the money, see who purchased parcels of land from Lansing in the past year or so. See if there are any ties to Coyote Creek Construction."

"Not a bad idea," Slade said grudgingly. "Once I get my hands on a computer, I'll get on that."

"I can help," Duncan said quietly. He'd borrowed Slade's phone cord to recharge his battery. The two men had exchanged numbers, too. "No reason we can't investigate this thing while we're waiting for everything to be put in place for Chelsey."

Slade didn't comment for a long moment. "You're right. I appreciate having you here, Duncan. I feel better knowing there are two of us keeping her safe."

The tension in Duncan's shoulders eased. "Good." He yawned, exhaustion catching up to him. "Let's discuss strategy in the morning."

Slade nodded and shut off the lights, plunging the room into darkness. Duncan stretched out on the bed fully clothed and closed his eyes.

His last conscious thought was that if they could find the evidence needed to bring the bad guys to justice, it was entirely possible Chelsey wouldn't have to give up her life to enter witness protection.

And he secretly promised to do whatever was necessary to make that happen.

Chelsey awoke at dawn, feeling well rested for the first time in what seemed like forever. At least, until she began to think about the ramifications of giving up her life.

Panic clawed its way up into her throat, robbing her of the ability to breathe. A passage of scripture flashed into her mind from the book of Psalms. *"He shall call upon me, and I will answer him: I will be with him in trouble; I will deliver him, and honour him. With long life will I satisfy him, and shew him my salvation."*

Her emotional turmoil eased and she immediately felt reassured and calm. Leaving Wyoming wouldn't be the worst thing that could happen to her. She would miss her friends; the hotel her parents, grandparents and great-grandparents had worked so hard for; the guests who came to stay on a regular basis.

But she had her faith and her life. Being on the run with Duncan made her realize how grateful she was to be alive.

After a quick shower, she eased open her motel room door, glancing around before heading over to tentatively wake Duncan. He immediately answered her knock, opening the door and gently pulling her inside.

"You look well rested." Duncan's dark gaze didn't miss a thing. "Have a seat. We're ordering breakfast to the room."

"Why?" She took a seat in the only chair.

Duncan shrugged and glanced at Slade. "Just being cautious."

"Okay. I'm just thankful we'll have food to eat," she admitted. "I planned to warm up my leftovers from last night."

"No need for that yet." Duncan squeezed past, the room seemingly small with the two men taking up space. "What would you like?"

"Anything," she said with a smile.

Five minutes later, they'd placed their to-go order. Slade offered to pick it up from the restaurant as the motel was too small to offer room service.

"Check on when we'll have access to the cabin," Duncan suggested.

"Will do." Slade headed for the door. "I'm also going to find out what computer access they might have available. I'll call when I'm on my way back with the food."

The room was silent after Slade left. Chelsey blushed, remembering the moment she'd kissed Duncan.

And he'd kissed her back.

She cleared her throat. "When are you planning to head back to Wisconsin?"

He looked startled by her question. "Not anytime soon." He paused, then added, "It's possible that if we can find out who killed Brett and arrest the men in charge, you might not need to hide out in witness protection."

A flicker of hope flared in her heart. "Really?"

"I can't say for certain," Duncan hedged. "But it's a possibility. One I can't ignore. I'm hopeful that when Slade gets a computer, we can really dig into the backgrounds of the men involved with Coyote Creek Construction. It's not unheard of for construction companies to have ties to organized crime."

"Organized crime?" Her voice rose with agitation. "I can't believe Brett stumbled across something that caused all of this. And why on earth didn't he confide in me?"

Duncan eyed her steadily for a long moment. "Would you have agreed to marry him if he had?"

"No." The word popped out of her mouth before she

could stop it. She grimaced and looked away. "You know I was having doubts anyway. If he had told me anything about witnessing a crime, or entering witness protection I would have ended things long ago."

"We don't know for sure when Brett stumbled across the criminal activity," Duncan said reasonably. "Could be it all happened fast, in the last couple of weeks."

"Maybe. Looking back, it seems like Brett changed about three weeks ago. He became, I don't know, edgy. Impatient but then overly apologetic." She shrugged. "At the time I chalked it all up to prewedding jitters, but now it seems as if that must have been the time this all started."

Three weeks. She couldn't believe Brett had kept all of this a secret for nearly a month.

"We can verify with Slade when he returns with our breakfast." Duncan looked thoughtful. "But one thing that doesn't make a lot of sense to me is why the US Marshals didn't approach you sooner."

A chill snaked down her spine. "You—don't think Slade is faking being a US marshal, do you?"

Duncan blew out a breath. "No, I don't. After all, he helped us escape the mountain by calling the park services. But we need information. He hasn't told us everything he knows. I was so exhausted yesterday, I hadn't really considered the timeline until now."

She sat quietly for a few minutes, trying to think back to those days she'd spent with Brett prior to the wedding. He'd been spending less time in Cheyenne—because he was avoiding the men who he'd witnessed commit a crime? And what exactly had Brett seen?

Duncan was right. They needed answers.

A phone rang. Chelsey instinctively patted her pockets, even though she knew she didn't have a phone. Brides generally didn't have a secret pocket in their wedding dress for a phone.

Although now she wished she'd thought of such a thing.

"Okay, thanks." Duncan disconnected from the call. "Slade is on his way with our food, and we'll be able to move into the cabin rental by ten."

"Is it far from here?" She wasn't sure it was necessary to move into a cabin. The motel rooms worked fine, unless maybe it was cheaper.

"Just a mile or so, and more isolated from the rest of town which is probably a good thing." Duncan rose to his feet and went over to the window overlooking the parking lot. "This feels too close for comfort."

She didn't answer, because she liked being around people. It wouldn't be long before she'd be starting over with a new name and new identity. It wouldn't be the first time she'd had to start over: the move from Milwaukee, Wisconsin, to Jackson, Wyoming, twelve years ago had been a culture shock. The wide-open spaces with the Rocky Mountains in the distance very different than living in the suburbs of Milwaukee.

Where would she end up this time? Hopefully not Florida, she thought with a grimace. California had decent weather, but there were earthquakes to contend with. Maybe back to the Midwest area, Kansas or Nebraska.

None of the options filled her with enthusiasm.

Duncan opened the door for Slade who came in carrying several cardboard containers of food. He handed one to her, then set the others on the desk.

She bowed her head and silently thanked God for

providing her food, a bed and support from Duncan and Slade. When she lifted her head, she saw that both Duncan and Slade were waiting for her before eating their meals.

"It's a blessing to be here with you both," she murmured. "I want you to know how grateful I am for everything you've done for me."

Duncan glanced at Slade who looked just as uncomfortable with her expression of gratitude.

"It's my job to keep you safe, Chelsey," Slade said gruffly.

"I feel the same way, Chelsey. You're my friend and I'll do whatever is necessary to keep you from harm," Duncan added.

"Okay, then. Let's eat."

They all dug into their eggs, toast and bacon. Chelsey thought the food tasted amazing—maybe because she now realized the can of cold beef stew had been awful in comparison.

"Did you find a computer?" Duncan asked, glancing at Slade.

The marshal nodded. "I began a quick search on the rancher's property, was able to identify the buyer as a corporation, not a person."

Duncan frowned. "What sort of corporation?"

"Not Coyote Creek Construction," Slade replied dryly. "Something called Elkhorn Estates."

"Elkhorn Estates?" Chelsey looked askance. "Is that some kind of joke?"

"No, that's the listing," Slade replied. "But I have to admit it sounds fake. I didn't have time to dig into it to find the principal owners."

Elkhorn Estates. There were plenty of elk living in

the mountains and elk hunting was a big deal in Wyoming. People came from all over the United States to hunt here starting mid-September and going well into November.

But she'd never heard of anything called Elkhorn Estates. "Maybe the plan was to build a subdivision on the land."

"Anything is possible," Slade agreed. "How would that have impacted your hotel business?"

She winced. "Not in a good way, that's for sure. People come to vacation in Jackson, Wyoming, because of the rural setting and the mountains. These are generally people who like to camp, hunt and fish." She waved her plastic fork. "Besides, there aren't enough year-round residents in Jackson to justify a brand new subdivision."

"Unless there was some sort of new business coming into the area to support something like that," Duncan countered. "If a new company opened up shop here, then there would be more employees—some with families, right?"

She nodded slowly. "Yes, but enough to build a subdivision of homes? That seems like a stretch."

"Do you know how many acres of land Elroy Lansing owned?" Duncan asked.

"At least five hundred, maybe more."

Slade whistled. "That's a lot."

She nodded. "I know it sounds that way, but his father and grandfather before him originally purchased the land for their cattle ranch. From the way Elroy spoke about it, they had well over a thousand head of cattle in their thriving ranch."

"What happened?" Duncan's gaze was curious.

"I wasn't here back then, but according to the rumor

mill, Elroy Lansing's father went through a messy divorce, which cost him a lot of cash. He wanted to keep the ranch, so he had to pay his wife for her portion. Then a bunch of the cattle got sick and died."

"Lansing never married?" Slade asked.

"No. Apparently he was in love with a woman who hated the isolation of the ranch. She took off and he decided it was better to remain alone." She finished her breakfast and set the empty cardboard container aside. "What does any of this have to do with Coyote Creek Construction and whatever crime Brett uncovered while working for them?"

"It may not be connected at all," Slade admitted. "I just thought the animal theme was an interesting coincidence."

"This is the Wild West," she pointed out.

"Don't forget Brett told me that he was planning to work security for a wealthy rancher nearby," Duncan said. "It's possible Brett was giving me some sort of clue about what he was involved in. And we don't know how rich or poor Elroy Lansing is. Maybe Elkhorn Estates paid him a pretty penny for his land."

She didn't like hearing the stories Brett had told everyone except her. She turned toward Slade. "What crime exactly did Brett witness anyway? Stolen goods? Drugs?"

The marshal didn't answer for a long moment.

"It has to be something major, or they wouldn't kill him," Duncan added. "And I think Chelsey has a right to know."

Slade slowly nodded. "Okay. Brett witnessed a murder."

Her jaw dropped in shock. "M-murder? Are you sure?"

Slade's expression was grim. "Yes, absolutely. Brett claimed he had proof of the crime and needed a day or two to get it, but we never received anything. We were called in by the local police chief because of the suspected ties to organized crime. They'd had some concerns about Coyote Creek Construction for a while now, and Brett's allegation only added to their belief."

Chelsey felt numb from shock. Murder and organized crime. No wonder Brett had seemed on edge. It hadn't been about prewedding jitters at all.

How horrible to have witnessed a murder.

Yet as bad as she felt for him, the news only proved their relationship wasn't built on trust and love the way she'd thought.

But on secrets and lies.

Depressing, really, to realize she didn't really know anything at all about the man she'd been about to marry. Tears pricked at her eyes at how foolish she'd been.

Tears welled in her eyes. She needed to learn to listen to her gut instincts, which had told her she was making a mistake.

One that had almost gotten her killed.

# NINE

"I—I don't understand why Brett wouldn't tell me," Chelsey whispered, swiping at the tears. "He said he loved me. Why would he lie to me if he loved me?"

Duncan had no answer for that. "I'm sorry."

There was a long moment as Slade shifted awkwardly in his seat. "I'm sorry, too. I feel partly responsible for this."

He glanced at Slade. "Yeah, about that. Why didn't you talk to Chelsey about the program?"

Slade winced. "That's a fair question. In my defense, things happened pretty fast. The murder took place just over a week ago, and we were brought in about three days later. I discussed the option of testifying and going into WITSEC with Brett and he agreed to get me the proof he had of the crime, and mentioned the wedding claiming he'd told Chelsey everything. He said he'd promised to give her the wedding she wanted before heading out of town. I had no reason not to believe him."

"But you knew he was in danger," Duncan argued.

"He was off work for the wedding, and to my knowledge no one but those in the Jackson Police Department knew about Brett witnessing a murder and the proof he had of what happened." Slade scowled. "We believed him, but after everything that transpired since, I'm convinced there's a leak within the department."

The spurt of anger faded and Duncan knew this wasn't the time to assign blame. He owned a piece of this mess, himself for not pushing Brett more once he'd realized something was going on. And Brett should have clued in Chelsey, the woman he'd been about to marry.

Now their old childhood friend was dead and there was nothing they could do other than move forward from here. Too bad they didn't have whatever proof Brett thought he could obtain.

"W-who was murdered?" Chelsey asked.

Slade hesitated, shooting a glance at Duncan as if asking for help on how much to say. He nodded, indicating she had a right to know. After all, the shooter already believed she knew. Her trying to play dumb wasn't going to work.

Not at this point. Not when these men had already gone so far as to kill Brett and attempt to kill him and Chelsey, more than once.

"A guy by the name of Roland Perry," Slade said. "He was apparently arguing with his boss. Brett heard the raised voices, and crept closer to see what was going on. According to Brett, his boss, Anthony Nettles, pulled a gun and shot Perry. Brett ducked down, and remained hidden all night, until long after everyone had left. When he came out, he called the police who in turn called us."

A shiver rippled through Chelsey, and he gently squeezed her shoulder reassuringly. "I...see."

"We haven't found the body yet," Slade went on. "And we were waiting for Brett to get us the evidence he'd promised. We did find out that no one has seen or heard from Perry since this took place. Local law enforcement is doing their best to find evidence. Unfortunately, Wyoming has plenty of places to stash a body where the wild animals will find it long before we do."

Chelsey swallowed hard and put a hand over her stomach as if she felt ill. He couldn't blame her. Hearing this made him feel lousy, too.

"It seems as if going back to the local law enforcement isn't an option," Duncan said slowly. "Not if there's a leak."

"Agree." Slade sighed. "I'll feel better once Colt shows up. For now, our main priority is to keep Chelsey safe."

Duncan nodded, although he wanted to find a way to bring Anthony Nettles to justice so that Chelsey wouldn't have to live out the rest of her life in witness protection.

Maybe Brett had gotten a photo of the argument, or audio taped the shooting. There had to be something that would put Nettles behind bars.

He released Chelsey, and then gathered their garbage together. "Getting her settled in the cabin is a good start."

Slade rose to his feet. "I plan to head over there first, check things out. I can buy supplies, too."

Duncan shot the marshal a glance. "How long do you plan to keep her there?"

"Hopefully not more than twenty-four to forty-eight hours," Slade said. "I'm putting a rush on the new ID and paperwork, but these things take time."

Just two days left to spend with her. His gut clenched with fear. It wasn't that he didn't trust Slade. The guy's actions so far proved he was legit. But he didn't like the idea of Chelsey going off without him.

After disposing of their garbage, another thought occurred to him. "What about the park rangers?"

Slade lifted a brow. "What about them?"

"Can we trust they won't go to the local law enforcement about the gunfire? And about taking us off the mountain?"

"I made sure they understood this was a federal US Marshals matter, and not one for the locals to get involved in," Slade replied. "They didn't argue and didn't seem concerned about letting me handle things."

Duncan wished he felt reassured. He didn't.

Slade left the motel room, leaving him and Chelsey alone. She stood and reached for the door.

"Wait, where are you going?" He quickly moved beside her.

"My room." She glanced at him. "I don't have much to pack, but would like to take the few things I bought yesterday with me to the cabin."

"That's fine. I'll walk you over." He swept up the key card, and then eased her aside to open the door. Using his body as a shield, he took her arm and escorted her the few steps to her room.

"Thanks." Chelsey's smile didn't reach her eyes. She slipped inside the room and shut the door behind her.

Duncan stood there for a moment, wishing there was something he could do or say to make her feel better.

But there wasn't.

After he returned to his room, he used his phone to call his brother-in-law, Mike Callahan. "Hey, how are Shayla and the kids?"

"Great," Mike replied. "Brodie is being an awesome big brother to his little sister, Breena."

The image of his sister, Mike and their two kids made him smile. Then his smile faded as he realized he couldn't bring them into this.

He never should have called him.

"Great, glad to hear it." He thought fast. "Listen, I'll be here in Wyoming for a few more days. I'll let our sarge know, but he may need help covering my shifts."

"Yeah, sure. Breena is sleeping like a champ these days, so shouldn't be a problem." Mike paused. "Something wrong?"

"No," he hastened to reassure him. "The Grand Tetons are beautiful. I'm planning to do some hiking while I'm here and wouldn't mind a few days to wind down."

"Alone? Or did you meet up with some pretty cowgirl?" Mike teased. Since all six Callahans were married with kids, they had begun to make it their mission to see him settled as well.

"No cowgirl," he said, despite how the image of Chelsey walking down the aisle in her wedding dress flashed in his mind. "Just want a few extra days, is all. Thanks Mike, take care of your family."

"Will do. Oh, and by the way, you should be prepared to hear big news from your dad and my mom."

Duncan winced. His dad, Ian O'Hare, was a widower just like Mike's mom, Maggie Callahan. Their respective parents had been spending time together as friends over the past couple of years. Maybe more than friends. As much as he wanted them to be happy, Duncan didn't really want to think too closely about them dating.

Some things were better left unimagined.

"Dunc? Are you there?"

"Yeah." He cleared his throat. "Let me guess, they're getting married."

"I'm getting that vibe, yeah. Just thought you might want to be prepared."

"Thanks for the heads-up, Mike. Listen, I have to call Sarge. See you in a few days." He disconnected from the line before his brother-in-law could say anything more.

His friends, not just the Callahans but Hawk Jacobson and Ryker Tillman were all family men now. They had wives and children of their own. He couldn't bring himself to drag any of them into this.

But he wasn't about to leave Chelsey high and dry, either. He was determined to stay and help protect her.

No matter what.

Hiding in her room was childish, but she needed a few minutes to come to grips with the idea that Brett had witnessed a murder and now those responsible were coming after her.

To kill her.

Retreating to the bathroom, she gathered the few personal items she'd purchased yesterday and placed them in a paper bag provided by the motel for laundry. Just like her hotel did.

She collapsed on the edge of the bed, feeling numb at the idea of never seeing her family's hotel again. It was only a building, but also a place full of memories.

And all she had left of her parents.

She wondered if Slade and Duncan might be able to get in to get some photographs for her. Tears pricked her eyes again and she swiped at them with annoyance.

She wasn't normally a crier, but someone who liked to get things done.

Time to get a grip. There were worse things in the world than not having material items. Or the place your parents lived.

Her life was more important than any of that. She closed her eyes and lifted her heart to God.

*Help me, Lord, to understand and accept this new path You've provided for me, amen.*

She wasn't sure how long she sat there, but a knock at her door had her rising to her feet. Using the peephole, she saw Slade standing there. "Hi. The cabin must be ready, huh?"

He nodded. "Yes, it's clean and stocked with food. Stay here, I'll get Duncan."

She stepped back and grabbed her bag. When the men returned, they once again sandwiched her between them as they made their way outside and along the parking lot, keeping parallel to the building.

It felt foolish, and she wondered what the people who lived in Moose, Wyoming, thought about them as they headed toward the rear portion of the motel. In the distance, she could see a cabin, tucked off to the side, isolated from other structures.

Slade held the key in his hand, and Duncan stood guard as the marshal unlocked the door and pushed it open. She crossed the threshold, glancing around curiously. It was nicer than she'd expected, rustic but with a great view of the mountains from the back porch.

"Home, sweet home," she murmured, dropping her bag of personal items on the glossy oak kitchen table.

"For a couple of days," Slade agreed. He glanced at his watch. "I'm heading back to the motel office to borrow their computer again. Duncan, I'm sure you won't mind staying here to watch over Chelsey."

"I don't mind at all, but I'd like to dig into the Coyote Creek Construction company. Could your marshal friend bring a spare computer? Two brains working on this are better than one."

Slade nodded. "I need to check in with Colt anyway, so I'll see if that's possible."

"What can I do to help?" Chelsey wasn't the type to sit around doing nothing. Managing the hotel had kept her busy, which is what she preferred.

"Honestly, the best thing you can do is try to remember anything Brett may have mentioned about this job at the construction company, the people he worked with, anything at all." Slade smiled. "It's often the littlest things that can break open a case."

"Okay." Slade left and Duncan poked his head into the fridge and the cupboards, scoping out the lunch possibilities even though they'd just finished breakfast.

Taking a seat at the table, she sighed. She didn't hold out much hope of remembering anything helpful. Those past few weeks before the wedding, she'd been dealing with last-minute preparations while studiously ignoring the lingering doubts about her upcoming marriage. Not to mention getting everything in the hotel running smoothly while she was gone on her honeymoon.

She abruptly straightened. Wait a minute, their honeymoon. Brett had done the planning for their trip—all she'd asked for was to be able to swim in the ocean, something she'd never done, and to find a place that wasn't too hot. He'd teased her that he had all her preferences on file, and in fact had carried a file folder with the details.

She remembered he had suggested Florida. Had he settled on it? Maybe the northern part of the state? Was that why Slade had mentioned relocating them there?

"Did you remember something?" Duncan's keen gaze apparently didn't miss a thing.

"Nothing to help with the case, but I just realized Brett did all the planning for our honeymoon, someplace near the ocean because I've never seen it." She stared at him. "Do you think he was waiting until the honeymoon to tell me about being in witness protection? That the place near the ocean was going to be our new home?"

"Maybe." Duncan sat across from her. "Did he say anything else about the trip? Did you have airline tickets or anything?"

"No, although he did have a folder with details that he carried around. What was strange is that he wanted to drive to Florida, so we could see the scenery." She thought back to the snippets of conversation. "He seemed surprised when I mentioned not liking Florida. Do you think he planned to go somewhere else? Like maybe without the help of the US Marshals Service?"

"I hate to say this, but nothing at this point would surprise me. Brett apparently wanted to have a new life with you, no matter what he'd witnessed. Maybe he thought that simply moving away would be enough." Duncan's gaze hardened and she realized he was seriously angry with their friend.

"It's so hard to believe that he would think I would just give up the hotel my family owned to live with him in another state. Doing what? I mean, what was he thinking?" She dropped her gaze to the glossy table. "I don't know what I'm going to do now, when I'm forced to take on a new identity."

He reached out and took her hand. "I know nothing about this is easy, Chelsey, but you're smart and talented. You can do whatever you'd like."

She shook her head. "Not true. I wanted to run the hotel my parents left to me, but that's not possible."

"Try thinking of what you might have done if the hotel had gone under for some reason," he suggested.

"I guess you have a point," she admitted. What would she like to do? She couldn't cook so running a restaurant was out.

But at one time she'd considered becoming a teacher. She had a fine arts degree. Could she put that to use in some way?

Maybe.

And what about the so-called proof Brett said he'd get? Duncan's phone rang. He pulled away and stood. "I have to take this, it's my boss."

She listened as Duncan told his boss he needed more time off work. When she realized she was shamelessly eavesdropping, she picked up her bag of personal items and did a quick search of the cabin.

The two bedrooms were on the right side of the house, with a small bathroom between them. She chose the smaller of the two, then set her items in the bathroom. She readjusted the bobby pins in her hair, then moved on.

Catching a glimpse of the Teton mountains out the back window, she moved that way, drawn to the majestic view. That Brett would just relocate her from the mountains because she'd mentioned wanting to swim in the ocean was unfathomable.

A wave of shame hit hard. Living near mountains or the ocean shouldn't be more important than their love for each other. Which was the crux of the matter.

She hadn't loved Brett enough to move anywhere in the world for him.

Which only reminded her of the intensity of Duncan's kiss. Of how much she enjoyed being cradled in his embrace. So different than the sweet fondness she'd felt for Brett.

Kissing Duncan had sparked the old attraction she once had for him. A youthful crush, something she'd grown out of.

Or so she'd thought.

But hadn't she leaned on Brett after losing her mother? Mistaking his kindness and support for something more?

She couldn't make that same mistake with Duncan. He was very attractive, and had saved her life more than once.

It wouldn't be fair to confuse feelings of gratitude toward him for love.

Anxious for some fresh air, she opened the back door and stepped outside, breathing deep. Off in the distance, she could see a bald eagle flying overhead, enjoying the wind off the mountains.

It pained her to give all of this up.

"Chelsey?"

Duncan's voice had her turning to face him. Her feet were still sore, and she missed a step and fell forward at the exact same moment the echo of a gunshot rang out.

"Down! Stay down!" Duncan shouted as he quickly closed the gap between them. In a swift move he grabbed her arm and hauled her back into the cabin, out of harm's way. When she'd cleared the threshold, he slammed the door shut, then urged her deeper inside the cabin.

"Get under the kitchen table," he said, his voice low and urgent. "Are you okay? Were you hit?"

"I—I don't think so." Her teeth began to chatter. "A-are you sure that was m-meant for me?"

"I'm sure." Duncan's tone was grim. He pulled out his phone. "Slade?" He scowled when he realized he was talking to voice mail. "I need you back here, pronto. Someone just took a shot at Chelsey."

She huddled under the table, realizing at that moment that giving up the mountains would be easy enough as long as it meant staying alive.

# TEN

Duncan eased the gun he'd taken off the assailant from his ankle holster and held it ready, sweeping his gaze over the interior of the cabin.

The shot at Chelsey had come from the north, where there was nothing but mountains behind the cabin. The front or south side of the cabin faced the street. It was also the direction they'd come in, less than an hour ago.

How had the sniper known about their relocation?

From the park rangers? Honestly it didn't seem likely. Maybe there was a team of men watching from all sides. The more he thought about that possibility, the more he thought it correct. One shooter couldn't be following them this well. And if they were, why not take a shot while they were outside the motel? Maybe there wasn't a good enough angle from where the sniper was waiting.

Which brought him back to the idea there had to be at least two men involved. And considering the possibility of this being linked to organized crime? Maybe more.

He didn't like it. He lifted his phone to call Slade for the second time, but the marshal's number was already flashing on his screen.

"What happened?" Slade demanded.

"Chelsey stepped out the back door and someone took a shot at her." Duncan kept his voice low, just in case someone was outside close enough to overhear. "Thankfully, they missed, but it's clear they have eyes on the cabin. You need to be careful."

"On my way." Slade disconnected from the call.

Duncan hoped Slade's position as a US marshal would keep him from becoming a target. He glanced over at Chelsey. "You're sure you're not hurt?"

She nodded and offered a wan smile. "Guess it's a good thing I'm clumsy and tripped over my own feet."

He frowned. "You're not clumsy, but I'm sure your feet are probably still sore from all that hiking."

"A little." She downplayed the injury he felt certain was worse than she was letting on. Despite not having any medic training, he mentally kicked himself for not insisting on checking her feet for injuries. He didn't want her to end up with a raging infection. The wound on his arm had been cleaned out, too, and so far seemed to be okay.

"Slade's on his way back." He stayed crouched beside her, knowing they needed to find a new place for Chelsey soon.

Ten minutes later, Slade rapped on the door and called, "It's me," before using his key to enter the cabin. Duncan slowly rose to his feet when Slade ducked inside, closed and locked the door behind him.

"We need a new location," Duncan said grimly.

Slade sighed. "If I had one, we'd move. There isn't another option at the moment."

"We can't keep her here," he argued. "What's to stop them from peppering the place with bullets?"

"The possibility of getting caught." Slade raked his

hand through his hair. "Look, I know staying put isn't optimal, but Moose isn't exactly a large metropolis. The motel and a couple of cabins are all they have to offer. Until we get a set of wheels and reinforcements from the US Marshals Service, we're stuck. And don't forget, there are plenty of armed park service rangers around."

"Wait, you said cabins, plural?" Duncan asked. "Can we swap with someone?"

"And put that person, or worse, an entire family, in danger?" Chelsey crawled out from beneath the table and stood beside him. "No. I'm not doing that."

Okay, she had a point. He turned and glanced around the cabin. "We can stay away from the windows, but I'd feel better if we could cover them with plywood."

Slade nodded. "That's a good idea. I'll check with the park service, see what they might be able to dig up for us. I'm sure they won't mind helping out."

It wasn't much, but he'd take it. He pulled out a kitchen chair for Chelsey. "Please sit down. We'll do our best to make this place safe."

"I guess I shouldn't have gone outside," she murmured with a sigh. "And it's better being stuck in here, then out on the side of the mountain without a place to stay."

"I'm glad you're focusing on the bright side." Duncan took a moment to prioritize which windows needed to be covered. Those in the main cabin, including the large picture window overlooking the mountains, and the ones in Chelsey's bedroom. He glanced at Slade. "We'll need to take turns keeping watch if we have to stay the night."

"Of course." Slade didn't argue. He pulled out his

phone. "Give me a minute to contact the park rangers about plywood."

Duncan sat beside Chelsey, thinking back to what she'd said about their honeymoon. "You mentioned Brett had a folder related to your honeymoon. You never saw what was inside?"

She slowly shook her head. "No, he wanted it to be a surprise." Her expression turned resigned. "Apparently a really big surprise, like hey, just so you know I witnessed a murder and we're now going into witness protection."

He felt bad, but dwelling on Brett's lies wasn't going to help. "Think for a moment, Chelsey. If he carried that folder around with him, you must have glimpsed something. Like papers with writing on them? Or maybe pictures of the place you were going to be staying? Anything at all that you can remember?"

"Pictures," she said without hesitation. "I remember they were large and glossy, but I only saw the edges, not the entire photographs."

A buzz of adrenaline shot through him. "Photographs on heavy-duty paper? Or something he printed off the internet?"

"Yes, glossy like heavy-duty paper. Why does it matter?"

Duncan hesitated, wondering if he should confide in her. She must have noticed because she bristled.

"Don't lie to me, Duncan. Not the way Brett did. Not about something as serious as this."

"Okay, I won't lie to you, Chelsey. Not now, not ever." He took a deep breath. "I'm having doubts about Brett. He lied to you, and to me, who's to say he didn't lie to the US Marshals, too? And the local law enforcement?"

She paled. "What kind of lies? You think he made up the story about witnessing a murder?"

"No—after all, he was murdered for a reason. But what about the part of his story where he claimed to need time to get the evidence? That doesn't ring true to me."

"I see what you mean," she admitted with a frown. "Yet it seems unbelievable that he would actually have evidence but not turn it over to the authorities right away."

"Yeah. Just as irrational as marrying you without saying anything about going into witness protection," he countered dryly. "It makes me wonder if Brett was trying to play this thing from both ends."

"Both ends?" Chelsey's voice was faint. "You mean, he told the bad guys he knew something about them as blackmail?"

"Hang on, Chels, I never said he was blackmailing anyone," he hastened to reassure her. "I'm sorry if I wasn't clear while I think out loud. Frankly, if Brett had done that, the bad guys would have taken him alive to find out where he hid the evidence." The more he thought it through, the more he didn't believe that Brett would be that reckless. "But I do wonder if he thought he should keep the evidence hidden from the local authorities."

She stared at him as realization dawned. "Because he didn't trust them?"

"Maybe." Or because he wanted something to hold over their heads? He wasn't sure what to think. "Any idea where Brett may have stashed the folder?"

"Most likely my office."

"Your office?" That surprised him.

"Yes, my office. That's where I kept all the other wedding plan files. It didn't matter to me. I was too busy to peek at his honeymoon arrangements," she said defensively.

"Okay, just checking." Duncan glanced up as Slade walked over to join them. "We need to get into the Teton Valley Hotel to search Chelsey's office."

"For what?" Slade frowned.

"A file folder containing photographs that Brett carried around with him. I think there's a possibility that Brett may have taken a picture of the murder."

Slade's green eyes widened. "He did mention needing time to get the evidence to us, but you think he had it all along?"

"Yeah, I do." Duncan was just as frustrated with Brett's actions as anyone. "But I'm starting to wonder if Brett knew more than he let on."

"You really think he kept the evidence at the hotel?" Slade sounded skeptical.

"If Brett didn't tell anyone about the evidence, including law enforcement and any potential leak there, then why not? Why not practically hide it in plain sight? It's possible no one would consider Brett had photographs stashed in Chelsey's office."

"Okay, maybe," Slade said, nodding slowly. "When Colt gets here, we'll discuss this more. For now, the park rangers have agreed to help us out by delivering plywood within the hour."

Duncan would be glad to have the plywood in place, but at the moment he would have rather had a set of wheels.

His instincts were screaming at him that Brett had in fact hidden evidence of the crime he'd witnessed. If not photographs, maybe something else. An audiotape would be nice. Anything pointing to Nettles being a killer.

If they could arrest the guy for murder, there was a chance that Chelsey wouldn't have to go into witness protection.

And despite his determination to keep his heart isolated from being hurt a second time, he was forced to admit he liked the idea of having Chelsey nearby.

Very much.

Chelsey put a hand up to her temple, reassured to find she wasn't bleeding. Horrified to realize the bullet had come so close she'd felt the heat of it zipping past her skin.

She took a moment to thank God for yet again keeping her safe. It seemed the Lord was working overtime with her.

And she appreciated His grace and protection.

Along with Duncan. She glanced at him, his handsome features already imprinted in her mind. He'd reacted instantly to the sound of gunfire, charging toward her, putting himself in danger once again to rescue her.

Duncan was a man of honor. A man of his word. She trusted him in a way she wasn't sure she'd ever trust another man.

She tore her gaze away and tried to focus on the present. The idea of doing something to escape this mess was appealing.

Sitting around doing nothing while waiting for the next bullet to hit its mark wasn't productive. She wanted to do her part in finding the man who'd murdered Brett.

In her mind's eye, she cast her memory back to the

last time she'd seen Brett with the honeymoon folder. It had been a yellow folder, because yellow was her favorite color. She'd been charmed by his choice at the time. Now she was just annoyed.

He'd use a yellow file folder because it was her favorite color, but not tell her he'd witnessed a murder that was likely linked to organized crime. Yeah, how was that for twisted?

She tried to shake off the bits of anger that kept floating to the surface. Brett was dead. He'd paid the ultimate price for his mistakes.

Time to get over it, already.

Chelsey closed her eyes and tried to bring the memory into focus. She'd been in her office, finishing up a call with the florist when Brett had ducked his head in, his smile dazzling. He'd had the yellow file folder in his hand, tapping it idly against the door frame as he waited for her to finish.

*"Everything okay, Chelsey?"*

*"It will be. The florist doesn't have enough yellow roses so I'll have to have white intermixed with the yellow. No big deal, though. What's up?"*

*"Just wanted to say I love you."* Brett's smile faded when his cell phone rang. *"Do you mind if I take this quick?"*

*"Sure."* He came farther into her office, slid the yellow folder on the edge of her desk beneath several other file folders as he stepped away to take the call.

*"Yeah, I know he's been AWOL for a while, but I'm sure he'll turn up, he always does."* There was a pause before Brett said, *"Of course, I can take over his projects but not until after my wedding and honeymoon. You know how it is, gotta keep the wife happy."*

"Chelsey?" Duncan's tone pulled her from her thoughts. The way he was looking at her made her realize she must have been ignoring him for a while.

"Yes?"

"You okay?" Duncan's tone was full of concern.

"Yes, why?"

"You were staring off into space, frowning." Duncan put his hand on her shoulder and she couldn't stop herself from reaching up to cover it with hers. The warmth from his palm seemed to radiate down to her bones. "Bad memory?"

It was disconcerting the way he read her so well. "Not bad, necessarily, but I just remembered a call Brett took while we were in my office. He had the honeymoon folder with him, and he tucked it beneath a bunch of my files before moving away to take the call."

"You think it's still on your desk?"

She shrugged. "I don't see why it wouldn't be. It was the day before the wedding and we were heading out soon for the rehearsal dinner? But that's not all, Brett made a comment about a guy being AWOL."

"AWOL is a military term for absent without leave," Duncan said thoughtfully.

"Yes, then he said something like, of course he'd be happy to take over the guy's projects, but not until after the wedding and honeymoon." She didn't add the part about keeping his wife happy, because really it only showed just how clueless Brett was about her feelings. How happy would she have been after the wedding? Not very. She focused on the tidbit of information she'd overheard. "Do you think the guy that went AWOL is the same man who was murdered?"

"It's possible Brett was referring to Roland Perry," Duncan admitted. "The name doesn't ring a bell?"

She slowly shook her head. "No. I remember Brett talking about Kenny Martin, and frankly I assumed that was who he spoke to that day he mentioned the guy going AWOL. But nothing about a Roland Perry."

Duncan gave her shoulder a little squeeze. "Keep up the good work, Chelsey. You've remembered the yellow folder, seeing photographs in there, and this latest conversation Brett had about someone going missing. I'm sure there are other fleeting memories that you've picked up along the way."

"Yeah. Too bad I don't have one of those eidetic memories," she said with a sigh. "That would come in handy right now."

"Good news, I just heard from my buddy Colt Nelson. He'll be here in about an hour with more supplies, like a computer and weapons, along with a nice SUV with tinted windows," Slade informed them.

"I'm glad to hear it," Duncan said, releasing her shoulder to turn toward Slade. "I'd like better odds than what we've been dealing with so far."

Chelsey frowned. "We already have the two of you against the shooter."

Duncan rubbed the back of his neck in a way that told her he had bad news. Before she could remind him of his promise not to lie to her, he said, "I think there's at least two men out there watching us, maybe three."

"Three?" Her pulse jumped and she tried to remain calm.

"Two for sure," Duncan said firmly. "The shooter was stationed to watch the back door, maybe waiting for us to let our guard down long enough to go outside. If he's up in a tree on the mountain, how did he see us come inside through the front door? There has to be someone out front and another guy out back, at a minimum."

Slade nodded, making her realize she was the last to know. She cleared her throat. "Once Colt gets here, will we head to the Teton Valley Hotel?"

The two men exchanged a look. "Maybe later," Duncan reluctantly said. "Once darkness has fallen."

"Jackson isn't that far. We could be there and back in an hour," she pointed out.

"I know," Slade said. "Don't worry, we'll keep you well guarded while we check things out."

"Well guarded?" She glanced between the two men. "I'm coming with you."

Duncan rubbed the back of his neck again. "Chelsey, I know you want to help, but…"

"No, you don't understand. It's not just getting the file folder. I'd also like at least one picture of my parents along with the birthstone pendant they gave me." When she saw the expression in Slade's eyes, she insisted, "Two small things. One picture and a pendant. That can't be too much to ask."

Neither man spoke for a long moment. Finally, Slade sighed and turned to face her.

"I'm sorry, Chelsey, we can let you come along if you insist, but the recommendation from the US marshals is that you take absolutely no personal items with you at all. Not a photograph or a pendant. Anything material that might connect you with your old life is far too much of a risk."

She felt as if she'd been sucker punched in the stomach. No picture of her parents? No birthstone pendant? She put a hand up to her neck, feeling for something that wasn't there. Why hadn't she worn the pendant with her wedding dress? Why had she decided at the last minute to take it off? Because the pendant didn't sit well with her neckline?

So stupid to care about something like that. She lowered her chin to her chest, struggling with the need to cry.

She'd known going into witness protection would be difficult, but until that moment the magnitude of what she was giving up forever hit hard.

And heaven help her, she wasn't sure she could do it.

# ELEVEN

Chelsey's grief-stricken expression tugged at his heart. Duncan wished there was something more he could do for her.

Other than finding the evidence that might just put Anthony Nettles in prison for the rest of his life.

A knock on their cabin door had him spinning around, weapon ready. Slade lifted a hand. "Probably the plywood."

Duncan nodded, but didn't necessarily lower his weapon. Survival instincts had been drilled into him during his time in Afghanistan. He wasn't going to relax his guard.

He stood in front of Chelsey as Slade went to the door. To his credit, the marshal called out first. "Who's there?"

"Ranger Eric Connolly. I have the plywood you requested."

Slade eased the door open, verifying the park ranger's identity before allowing him in. Eric entered the cabin, carrying a sheet of plywood, with a tool belt slung over his shoulder.

"I have a small circular saw, hammer and nails," Eric said. "Will two sheets of plywood be enough?"

"I think we can make it work," Slade said. "Thanks, I know this is above and beyond the scope of your duty."

"I don't mind. Want help?" Eric stood for a moment with his hands on his hips, surveying the room. "Shouldn't take long."

"That would be great." Slade and Duncan moved forward, quickly measuring and sawing wood.

The work was mindless, and Duncan couldn't help glancing at his watch, hoping Colt Nelson would get there soon. He wanted some time with the computer, to investigate just who they were dealing with, before heading out to the Teton Valley Hotel to search for Brett's honeymoon folder.

The interior of the cabin turned dark once they had successfully covered the windows. They had just enough plywood for the main living space, and since they'd be heading out that night, decided the bedrooms would remain off-limits for now.

Thirty minutes after Eric left, a black SUV with tinted windows pulled up. Duncan hung back as Slade gestured to his fellow marshal to come inside.

Colt was tall and lean. He had short blond hair beneath the rim of a cowboy hat similar to Slade's which made Duncan wonder if the hat was part of the US marshal uniform, like the five-point silver star on his chest. Colt carried a computer bag over his shoulder, but there was only one device, not two.

"Colt, this is Duncan O'Hare. He's a cop with the Milwaukee Police Department and this is Chelsey Robards," Slade said by way of introduction.

Colt nodded. "I'm Colt with the US Marshals Service. I see you have the place locked up tight."

"There was another attempt to kill Chelsey from

someone hiding in the trees behind the cabin," Duncan said.

Colt scowled. "Not good."

"We'll fill you in. Let's unpack your computer and get to work," Duncan suggested.

Slade updated Colt on the recent events as Duncan took charge of the computer. The cabin came with internet access, but it was slow. Still, he managed to come up with a picture of Anthony Nettles, turning the screen so Chelsey could see.

"Recognize him?"

She shook her head. "No, sorry."

"No need to apologize, just trying to work through the list." Duncan went back to work, finally finding a grainy picture of Kenny Martin. "How about this one?"

"Kenny Martin." There was no hesitation in her tone.

Slade leaned over his shoulder. "I remember him. He was at the wedding."

"He was?" Duncan glanced back at the photo. "I guess it's reasonable Brett would invite his boss."

"Unless he knew the guy was mixed up with organized crime," Slade pointed out dryly.

There was that. Brett had obviously not been thinking too clearly about all of this.

"He spent a lot of time talking to someone," Slade continued, staring at the picture on the screen. "An older guy, face like leather, wearing chaps which stuck out to me as it was, after all, a wedding."

"Chaps?" Chelsey echoed. "The only person that wears chaps everywhere is my neighbor Elroy Lansing."

"The rich rancher?" Duncan asked, committing the photograph of Kenny Martin to memory.

"Not rich," Chelsey reminded him. "He's been selling off his land, remember? Which is why it was always a little sad that he wore chaps, like he was living back in the days when he was herding cattle by horseback."

"Hmm." Duncan wished he'd paid more attention to the guests at Brett and Chelsey's wedding. But they were strangers to him, and he hadn't anticipated Brett being gunned down at the altar.

"Yeah, Brett mentioned Elroy Lansing," Slade said. "We need to look into who owns Elkhorn Estates, the company which bought up a big chunk of Lansing's property."

"That might be outside my area of expertise," Duncan admitted. "I'll give you the computer in a moment." He tried searching for Roland Perry, but nothing came up. After a few minutes of trying, he reluctantly turned the screen toward Slade and gave up his seat. "I give up on Roland Perry. Have at it."

Slade worked the computer like a pro, despite the frustratingly spotty Wi-Fi. "Whoever owns Elkhorn Estates has covered their tracks really well. The president is listed as Simon Graves." He glanced at Chelsey. "Does that name sound familiar?"

"No," Chelsey said.

"Did you know everyone who was on the guest list for your wedding?" Duncan asked. "Did Brett invite a lot of people?"

Chelsey frowned. "Actually, he didn't. I remember urging him to invite more friends and family, but he kept saying that his aunts, uncles and cousins were too far away and wouldn't want to make the trip to Wyoming."

"Work friends?" Duncan persisted. "He clearly had Kenny Martin on the list."

She looked thoughtful for a moment. "For sure Anthony Nettles wasn't on the list, and neither was Roland Perry. But there were a couple of others. I can't remember their names offhand."

Duncan tried not to show his disappointment. "It's okay, maybe something will come to you."

Colt prowled the interior of the cabin, seemingly antsy to be stuck inside without any natural light. Duncan could relate. After all, he was used to being active, too.

"I'll throw together something for lunch." Chelsey poked her head into the fridge then looked through the cupboards. "Looks like grilled ham and cheese sandwiches are a good choice."

"Fine with me," Slade said absently. His gaze was rooted on the computer screen. "Guys, check this out."

Duncan and Colt hovered around Slade. "Who is that next to Nettles?" Duncan asked.

"According to the local newspaper, he's multimillionaire Travis Wolfe. Almost makes you wonder if good ole Travis isn't the brains behind Elkhorn Estates."

"Chelsey?" Duncan called. When she glanced at him, he gestured for her to come over. "Do you recognize this guy?"

She came over to peer at the photograph. "Yes, I've seen him before."

"When?" Duncan asked.

"I think he and Elroy Lansing were having dinner in our restaurant recently. I remember because their tab was well over $250 for two people and our server was gushing over the generous tip."

"That gives some credence to the possibility that Wolfe is the brains behind Elkhorn Estates," Slade said.

"But how is that connected to Coyote Creek Construction?" Chelsey asked.

"Maybe Coyote Creek Construction was going to be awarded a very lucrative contract to perform all the building associated with the new homes located within Elkhorn Estates?" Duncan offered. He pinned Slade and Colt with his gaze. "Are we sure this is all related to organized crime? Could be just plain and simple greed."

Slade hesitated and shrugged. "It was the locals who insisted they were looking at a potential organized crime ring. Otherwise why bother to get the feds involved at all?"

It was a good point and one Duncan wasn't sure how to answer.

They already suspected that someone within the Jackson Police Department was leaking information, so why would they want to involve the feds?

It was a mystery for sure, and one that he was beginning to doubt they'd ever solve.

Chelsey was glad to be able to contribute something to the investigation. As she made lunch for the group, she tried to remember if she'd noticed anyone else meeting over dinner at the hotel restaurant.

The faces were all a blur.

How many other deals had been struck under her clueless nose?

"Something smells good, Chelsey," Slade said with a smile. He was a nice guy, jet black hair cut short beneath his cowboy hat, which he'd taken off while inside.

"Almost ready," she promised.

Colt's hair was as light as Slade's was dark. Colt was slender and tall while Slade was broader across the shoulders. The two men seemed intent on seeing to her safety, and as much as she appreciated their efforts, she wished she could go back to her life as she knew it.

Which was a useless thought.

When two grilled ham and cheese sandwiches were ready, she slid them onto a plate and set it in the center of the table, then prepared to make more.

By the time they'd all finished eating the hour was early afternoon. She was in the process of cleaning the kitchen when a shrieking alarm went off with enough force to pierce eardrums.

"What is that?" she asked, trying to be heard above the noise.

"Car alarm." Colt pulled his weapon and opened the front door of the cabin just enough to see outside. "It's equipped to go off when anyone touches the vehicle."

Chelsey frowned. That seemed a little overkill considering anyone could brush up against a car.

"Let's check it out," Slade said, joining Colt at the door. The two men eased outside.

Duncan locked the door behind them, then crossed over to stand beside her. They didn't try to talk—it was impossible to carry on a conversation over the screaming alarm.

The sound stopped as abruptly as it started. Chelsey let out a breath she hadn't realized she'd been holding and rubbed her ears. "That hurt."

"Yeah." Duncan's expression was serious. "But it's nice to have."

"I would think it gives off false alarms more often than helping," she argued. "I mean, come on, who's to say a dog didn't run past the vehicle and thump it with his tail?"

"And who's to say it wasn't someone with malicious intent?" Duncan retorted. "I'd rather have a half-dozen false alarms if it scares away one bad guy."

Maybe he was right. This wasn't the world she normally lived in. Worrying about bad guys and hiding from murderers had never so much as blipped on her radar screen.

Until now.

After what seemed like forever, the two US marshals came back inside the cabin, twin grim expressions marring their features.

Colt held up a small circular device. "Someone tried to put a tracker on the SUV."

A tracker? She stared at the thing in horror.

"We need to get out of here." Duncan's tone held a hint of anger.

"We agreed to wait until dark," Slade countered. "And waiting will only make it more difficult to track us by sight."

"I've reengaged the car alarm," Colt added. "They won't make the mistake of trying to put a GPS device on again."

"I don't like it, Slade. We're sitting ducks here, and they know it." Tension radiated off Duncan. She placed a reassuring hand on his arm.

"We're also in the middle of nowhere, Wyoming." Slade spread his hands. "There isn't a lot of traffic out here. We could be easily tailed back to Jackson."

"They may guess we're heading there anyway," Colt said. "I mean, there's only so many places to go on this side of the state. If we were closer to one of the bigger cites, like Laramie or Cheyenne, it would be easier to disappear."

Duncan straightened beside her. "Can we swing by Jackson, then hit the highway toward one of those larger cities?"

She tightened her grasp on his arm. "Duncan, both Laramie and Cheyenne are on the opposite side of the state without a lot of ways to get there. Wyoming is all about wide-open spaces."

He grimaced. "Okay, so what is the alternative? Fly out of Jackson?"

The two US marshals exchanged a look. "We might be able to make that an option," Slade said slowly. "The airport is tiny, but we can hire a private prop plane to get us out of there before anyone is the wiser."

"Could work," Colt agreed. "I'll make those arrangements."

The tension eased out of Duncan. "Good. I like that plan."

Chelsey frowned. "We're all going to fly out together?"

Duncan looked at her in surprise. "Why wouldn't we?"

"I just meant, you're free to go home anytime, Duncan." She had to force herself to stay the words. "I know you asked your boss for extra time off work, but you have a life back in Milwaukee. A job, your family."

Duncan turned so that they were facing each other. "I'm not leaving you until I know you're safe, Chelsey."

Beyond Duncan's shoulder she could see the US marshals had moved off to the side to talk in private. No doubt, making plans about when to cut Duncan loose.

She'd always known it would happen sooner or later. Her desire to have him stay was her problem, not his. The only good thing about entering witness protection was that she wasn't leaving her parents behind. She didn't have siblings, and no extended family, either.

"I don't want to leave you," Duncan said in a low voice.

The urge to throw herself into his arms was strong. It took every ounce of willpower she possessed to take one step back, then another.

"Excuse me, I need to find the bathroom." A lame excuse, maybe, but one that ensured Duncan wouldn't try to follow her.

She ducked into the bathroom, closing the door firmly behind her. Now that the point of losing Duncan forever was near, she could hardly bear it.

Tears threatened. She swiped at her eyes and took several deep breaths in an attempt to ward them off.

She splashed cold water on her face to hide the evidence of her distress, burying her face in a towel that smelled of laundry soap.

Enough. She'd be fine. She'd do this. God would show her the way.

Bolstered by the thought, she straightened her shoulders and opened the door. A dark shape caught the corner of her eye. Someone was in the bedroom!

"Duncan!" As his name left her lips, a man lunged at her, his strong hands digging into her flesh. She clawed at him, hoping and praying he didn't have a gun.

Duncan rushed forward first, followed by the two marshals. They quickly wrestled the guy off her, pinning him to the floor.

She eased backward, her heart hammering in her chest, her breathing uneven. Being grabbed like that had been more frightening than being shot at from a distance. She lifted a trembling hand to finger the fresh scratches on her face and neck.

If she hadn't caught a glimpse of him, he would have gotten to her before she could react. If he'd gotten her out of the cabin, where would they have gone?

She didn't want to imagine how that scenario might have played out.

"Who are you? Who sent you?" Duncan peppered the guy with questions as Slade tossed the guy's weapon aside and yanked his arms behind him to handcuff his wrists. Colt went into the bedroom where they guy had gotten in through a window, and quickly locked the door to prevent anyone else from getting inside.

The man sneered but didn't say a word.

"You'll want to cooperate with us," Slade said in a low voice. "Think about it for a moment. I'm sure that gun of yours will match ballistics of at least one unsolved crime, maybe more, which means you're going to be in federal prison for a long, long time."

The guy muttered something harsh and nasty under his breath.

"See, that's not going to help you," Slade drawled. "Let's try again. Who are you and who hired you to come after Chelsey?"

The captured guy didn't speak for a long moment. Finally he said, "I'm just a low man on the totem pole."

"Yeah, we already figured that out," Duncan said in a harsh tone. "After all, you failed to get Chelsey, didn't you? Once we put your mug shot out there for everyone to see, your boss will know you've failed him."

The guy's face turned beet red. "Fine, it was Wesley Strand who hired me to get the girl."

"To get the girl? Or to kill her?" Duncan asked.

The guy turned and looked directly at Chelsey. A

ripple of fear skittered down her spine at the sheer hatred in his eyes.

Never in her life had she been targeted by men who didn't hesitate to kill to get what they wanted.

But looking at this man, she knew he'd intended to kill her. And that he was only sorry about getting caught.

# TWELVE

"To get her, or kill her?" Duncan repeated. It wasn't easy to control his anger when he saw the marks this jerk had left on Chelsey's face and neck.

The assailant shrugged. "Doesn't matter."

It did matter to Duncan, very much. He stared at the guy, trying to mesh his face with that of the man who'd assaulted him on the side of the mountain. But he was certain they weren't the same.

"Your team failed several times now," Duncan said. "And we've always gotten the upper hand, right? I'm pretty sure Wesley Strand isn't going to be impressed at how your cohort failed to kill us."

Their perp looked away, and Duncan knew the guy didn't like being reminded of his shortcomings.

"You don't want to talk? That's fine," Slade drawled. "We can book you for one count of assault and battery against Chelsey. When we find the others, we'll add conspiracy to commit murder."

A flicker of concern shadowed the guy's gaze but then vanished. "Whatever."

"You're going to jail," Slade said. "You can either choose to cooperate or do the time, makes no difference to me." He jerked the guy to his feet. "Let's put him in the spare bedroom, the one he didn't breach, until we can hand him over to the authorities."

Duncan stepped back to give Slade room. Colt was still standing guard in the hallway between the two bedrooms, just in case someone else tried the same trick.

Duncan stood for a moment, willing his heart rate to return to normal. Then he approached Chelsey, lifting his palm to cup her cheek. "I'm sorry he hurt you."

"I'm fine." Chelsey's stricken expression contradicted her claim, so he gently pulled her into his arms. She melted against him, burying her face against his chest. He lightly stroked her soft curls. "This will never stop, will it?"

"It will stop if we find and arrest the people involved." Starting, he thought, with Wesley Strand and ultimately nailing Anthony Nettles.

Not to mention whatever role millionaire Travis Wolfe played in this. Too many suspects and not enough evidence.

Chelsey clung to him for a long time, then pulled herself together. She tipped her head back to gaze up at him. "Thanks, Duncan. For being my rock through this."

"I'm glad to be here for you." His voice was low and gravelly, and he cleared his throat to cover the emotional roller coaster he was experiencing. He cared about Chelsey, far more than he should.

Knowing they had so little time together didn't help.

She stepped back and drew a hand through her hair. "Before you ask, I've never heard Brett talk about anyone by the name of Wesley Strand."

He drew her into the kitchen, nudging her into a chair. "Let's see if we can find him online."

Slade and Colt returned to the kitchen wearing grim expressions. "We've secured the two bedrooms as best we can for now. We need to turn this guy over to the authorities, but we're not exactly sure who to trust," Slade said. "If there's a leak in the Jackson Police Department, I'm afraid this guy will slip away."

Duncan glanced up. "What about the park rangers? The attack on me was in the Grand Teton National Park, doesn't that give them some jurisdiction? We know this guy is working with the guy who attacked me."

"We can't prove he's part of the attack on the mountain, but the park rangers have a jail." Slade shrugged. "But they mostly hold criminals until the local law enforcement agency can take custody."

"Maybe we can convince Ranger Eric Connolly to hang on to him for a few days," Duncan suggested.

"It would be great if they'd hold him long enough to run his fingerprints through the database to get an ID," Slade said.

"He refuses to say anything else without his lawyer," Colt added. "I'm surprised he gave us Wesley Strand's name."

"Yeah, except he could very well be lying," Duncan said. "I'm trying to pull up information on Wesley Strand now."

The marshals crowded around him to see the screen, the only sound from the tapping of computer keys. Images bloomed on the screen, and he quickly narrowed his search to include Anthony Nettles and Travis Wolfe.

Bingo. A photo came up showing Anthony Nettles standing in front of a building with Travis Wolfe and Wolfe's chief of security, Wesley Strand.

"Got him." Duncan blew up the image on the screen

and turned the computer toward Chelsey. "Does this guy look familiar?"

She wrinkled her forehead. "No."

"Head of security for Travis Wolfe?" Slade echoed. "That's interesting."

"If it's true he really set up the hit," Duncan cautioned. "We can only trust the guy so far."

Colt let out a heavy sigh. "Okay, let's just say our perp is telling the truth. How does that fit in with the idea of organized crime? If Wolfe is already a multimillionaire, why does he need to get involved with Coyote Creek Construction?"

"Maybe crime is how he got to be so rich," Slade said thoughtfully. "We know that organized crime rings often have legitimate businesses intermingled with their illegal activities. It's the best way to launder money."

"But they also typically stay off the radar," Duncan pointed out. "Rather than flaunt their wealth."

The group fell silent, as they pondered the impact of what they'd learned.

Finally, Chelsey spoke up. "I still think we need to get to the Teton Valley Hotel to find Brett's folder."

Duncan glanced at her. "You have a point. The fact that this guy took a chance in slipping into the cabin in broad daylight reeks of desperation. The sooner we get out of Moose, Wyoming, the better."

Colt and Slade exchanged a glance. "It would be better to wait until dark," Colt pointed out. "But I agree, staying here doesn't seem to be a good plan."

"I'll call Ranger Connolly. Maybe he has an idea of where we can hide out for a while." Slade stepped away with his phone.

Duncan understood where the marshals were coming

from. Obviously, getting out of town would be best after dark, at least as far as making it difficult for anyone to follow them. But two attempts here in the cabin over the past couple of hours wasn't good, either.

Resting his hands on Chelsey's shoulders, he tried not to count down the hours that he had left with her. Less than twenty-four hours for sure. From his army experience he knew flying in small planes close to the mountains at night was extremely dangerous. The earliest Chelsey would be able to be flown out of Jackson was early tomorrow morning.

Eighteen hours. A wave of helplessness washed over him.

After attempting to keep an emotional distance from her, he was forced to admit eighteen hours wasn't nearly enough.

Not when he longed for so much more.

Chelsey sat at the kitchen table, listening as they made their plans for the next few hours. Duncan was unusually silent, and she wondered what he was thinking.

"Connolly and Davidson will be here shortly," Slade announced. "Davidson offered up his place for us to use."

"That's very nice of him," Chelsey said.

"I just hope his place is isolated from the others," Duncan said, breaking his silence. "I saw a long apartment building on our way in."

"I don't know where he lives," Slade said. "But at this point being surrounded by other rangers might not be so bad. At least they have law enforcement training and weapons."

She'd noticed Colt went back to keeping watch over

their captured assailant. She shivered, remembering the feel of his hands grasping at her, his hot breath on her face.

Maybe getting out of here was the best option. Why wait until darkness when the threats had been nonstop?

The two park rangers arrived a few minutes later. Duncan carefully checked the door before letting them inside.

"The man who assaulted Chelsey is in the spare bedroom. We have reason to believe he's part of the team who tried to shoot us in the mountains." He jerked a thumb over his shoulder. "US Marshal Colt Nelson is watching over him now."

"Okay," Eric said with a nod. "We'll lock your guy up first, then we'll relocate all of you to Davidson's place. He's the only one who has a home here. The rest of us use the apartment building on the other end of town."

"I want you both to know how much I appreciate what you're doing for me," Chelsey said. "This is above and beyond the call of duty."

Paul Davidson shrugged off her gratitude. "Not at all, it's our job. I don't like men shooting at civilians in my park."

The process took longer than Chelsey had imagined, but ninety minutes later, they were ready to leave. As before, Duncan and Slade shielded Chelsey with their bodies as they left the cabin, Slade disabling the alarm so they could tuck her safely in the back seat of the SUV. She was secretly glad when Duncan slid in beside her, leaving Slade and Colt up front.

Duncan took her hand, his fingers warmly curling around hers. She clung to him, hating knowing their time together would end soon.

"Hey, check out that van up ahead," Slade said from the front seat.

Chelsey craned her neck to see. Her jaw dropped when she realized the van was familiar, all white with tan lettering along the side, three capital letter *C*s, then in smaller lettering, the words *Coyote Creek Construction*.

"Let's follow it," Colt suggested.

"It might be better to grab the driver and question him," Duncan pointed out. "See how slow it's moving? He might be out here looking for the guy who we just hauled off to jail for attacking Chelsey."

"There's only one road, so it's not like I have any other option than to stay behind him," Slade pointed out.

"He's slowing down," Colt said, a hint of anticipation in his voice. "Maybe we should grab him."

"He could just be a construction worker for the company," Chelsey felt the need to point out.

"What's he doing in Moose?" Duncan asked. "I highly doubt there's any new construction going on here. This town is unincorporated, there isn't much to draw people to living here, unless they're working for the park service, the hotel or the restaurant."

She had to admit Duncan was right. But she also didn't like the idea of hassling an innocent man.

"He's turning into the gas station," Colt said. "Grabbing him while he's filling his tank is our best option."

"Let's do it," Slade agreed.

Chelsey tightened her grip on Duncan's hand, hoping he wouldn't volunteer. She could tell he wanted to but remained at her side.

Slade pulled in behind the van, then the two marshals

waited until the driver was pumping gas before getting out of the SUV and surrounding him.

There were no raised voices, but from the body language, it was clear the van driver was protesting his innocence. Duncan slid his window down a bit so they could hear.

"I don't know anything about Wesley Strand," the driver said. "Or about any plan to kill anyone."

"That's not your buddy's story," Slade said. "He's singing like a bird."

The driver flinched and tried to jump into the van, but the marshals had him surrounded. This time it was Colt who used his handcuffs while Slade came back to the SUV.

"Colt is going to take this guy to the rangers' jail, too," he informed them.

"But—he hasn't committed a crime, has he?" Chelsey asked.

"He's armed and has no driver's license on him and is refusing to give us his name," Slade said. "They can hold him for driving without a license until we can identify him but may also charge him with conspiracy to commit murder. From there, local law enforcement can take over."

She let out a frustrated sigh. "You mean the ones we don't trust."

Slade shrugged. "It gets him off the streets for a while, maybe even long enough for us to get you transferred safely out of Wyoming."

Out of Wyoming. A hard lump formed in her throat. She forced a nod, then sat back to watch as Colt pushed the handcuffed man into the Coyote Creek Construction van and finish filling the tank. Colt took the van, while Slade climbed into the SUV. Ranger Davidson was waiting for them in front of his house.

"It's nothing fancy," Paul said, opening the front door. "But it should be safe enough until nightfall. Oh, and I have these for you." He gestured to several dark vests hanging over the backs of his kitchen chairs.

"Bullet-resistant vests?" Duncan moved over to lift one up. "Nice, but I'm surprised the park rangers have them."

"They're several years old. We got them for an incident a while back when a group of poachers began shooting at us." Paul scowled. "Shot a friend of mine. He survived but can't work as a ranger anymore."

"I'm sorry to hear that," Chelsey murmured. "I had no idea being a park ranger could be so dangerous."

"Normally it's not that bad, but there are always times like this when things heat up." Paul reached out to pick up a vest. "This is the smallest one we have, so I thought it would be good for you, Chelsey."

Duncan reached over to take the vest. "Let me help you get this on."

The vest was black and heavier than she imagined. It was difficult to comprehend how she'd gone from being a bride at her wedding to hiding out from bad guys wearing a bulletproof vest in the span of two days.

It felt like a lifetime.

Duncan pulled his vest on, then turned toward Paul. "US Marshal Colt Nelson is taking the driver of the Coyote Creek Construction van to sit in your jail. We believe he's the assailant's partner."

"Two men down, then," Slade mused. "And how many more out there?"

Chelsey shivered, not really wanting to know.

Duncan fingered his vest for a moment, then turned toward Slade. "I have an idea. Maybe I can pretend to be one of them enough to draw others out of hiding."

"No way." Chelsey couldn't help her instinctive response. "That's a dangerous idea. Besides, why would they mistake you for one of them?"

"Why wouldn't they?" Duncan asked. "I can dress in black from head to toe, like they did, and keep my head down, maybe wear a bandanna around my neck. They wouldn't know the difference until they got close enough."

"And then what?" Twines of panic reached up to circle her throat. "They kill you?"

"I can hold my own," Duncan said.

Slade cleared his throat. "I don't think that's a good idea, Duncan. Let's keep our heads down for now, and work on a plan to get inside the Teton Valley Hotel." He looked at her. "I've changed my mind about you coming along. I think we'll need your help with the hotel layout, Chelsey. We need to know the best way to sneak in and out of the place."

Duncan didn't give up his idea so easily. "Don't you think getting rid of anyone else out there watching for Chelsey is our best way of getting to the hotel without being followed?"

Slade narrowed his gaze in frustration. "No, I don't think you risking your life is our best chance. I'm sure whoever is behind this already has men lined up to replace the two we've taken out of commission."

"Okay, fine. Chelsey, have a seat." Duncan guided her to the closest chair. "We'll work on a plan for getting Brett's folder, if it's still there."

"It will be," Chelsey said, striving to remain positive.

"Paul, we need paper and pencil to draw a map of the hotel," Slade said.

The ranger brought over the supplies. Chelsey thought about the hotel and began to draw a basic outline of the building.

"The main entrances are here, here and here." She drew squares to indicate the areas. "But we bring our supplies in through the loading dock which is located here." She indicated a spot in the back of the building. "And the employee entrance is back there, too, next to the area where the trucks pull up to unload." She drew a smaller door a short distance from the loading dock.

"All the employees go in that way?" Duncan asked.

"Not all, but the kitchen crew and the cleaning staff do. The restaurant servers and front desk staff come in through the main entrance. But going in through the loading dock makes it easy to get to my office located down the hall to the right."

"There must be other ways inside that guests might use," Slade said, gesturing to her rudimentary drawing.

"Yes, accessed with their room key cards." She quickly marked them, then glanced up. "But I hardly think anyone from Coyote Creek Construction would have a guest key."

"They would if they booked a room for the wedding." Duncan's tone was grim.

She nodded slowly. "I guess you're right about that. But Trish, my assistant manager, would make sure to deactivate those keys once they've checked out."

"If they've checked out." Duncan sighed. "I'm getting the feeling that sneaking into the building will be more difficult than I anticipated. After all, hotels are open 24/7 to their guests. We can try to sneak in, but who's to say others won't be wandering around as well?"

Her heart squeezed in her chest. The plan that had sounded so simple now took on a whole new level of complexity.

But she wasn't about to let that deter her from going along. If Brett's honeymoon folder was there, she wanted to see for herself what he might have as evidence.

Before the marshals whisked her away to start a new life under a new name in a place where she'd be surrounded by strangers.

# THIRTEEN

While waiting for darkness to fall, Duncan continued using Slade's computer in an attempt to investigate the murder that started all of this.

The killing of Roland Perry.

Duncan had tried to find something on Roland Perry before but had come up empty-handed. Now he tried again, using the Wyoming DMV access provided by Ranger Paul Davidson.

There. He finally got a match. Roland Perry had a Wyoming driver's license with an address listed in Cheyenne.

Excited to have a lead, he searched for the address. Then frowned at the screen when the building that popped up was an old abandoned store.

"What's wrong?" Chelsey asked.

"I found a guy named Roland Perry, but the address in Cheyenne is an old abandoned building." He turned the screen to show her the small and less than flattering DMV photo. According to the license, Roland Perry was five feet ten inches tall, weighed 175 pounds, had brown eyes and light brown hair. His date of birth was listed November 12 and he was thirty-six years old. "I don't suppose he looks familiar?"

Chelsey scooted her chair closer for a better look. She stared at the image for a long moment. "Maybe," she finally admitted. "I just can't remember where."

A spurt of adrenaline hit. "Was it possible he was in the hotel dining room with the rich guy, too?"

She grimaced. "No, I don't think so. I seem to remember him wearing dusty jeans, T-shirt and steel-toed boots, as if he was one of the construction workers."

"When would you have seen one of the construction workers?" Duncan asked.

Her expression cleared. "I remember now—he was one of the guys Brett brought over when we were discussing the plans for the hotel expansion." She pulled the drawing over. "See, we were thinking of adding a wing to the north, this way, with high-end suites. I don't remember this guy going by the name of Roland Perry, though. I think he was introduced to me as Ray."

Ray as a nickname to Roland? Maybe. "You think he actually worked boots on the ground for Coyote Creek Construction?"

She nodded. "Yes, but I have to say, he seemed to be more interested in the hotel itself, asking me about my parents and how long we owned it. He seemed interested in the fact that our hotel once belonged to my grandparents, and my great-grandparents before that. He also asked a lot of questions about Elroy Lansing's land." She frowned. "You really think this is the man who was murdered?"

Duncan didn't believe in coincidences, and this one was no exception. "According to his driver's license it appears that way. But I still don't exactly understand why he'd be viewed as a threat enough to murder him."

"Maybe Brett was wrong about who he saw that night," Chelsey said.

There was no denying Brett had lied to them more than once. But the local police had also claimed no one had seen the guy in a few days. And other than a fake address and a driver's license it seemed the guy didn't exist anywhere else online, certainly not on social media.

What did it all mean?

It still bothered him that the rich guy, Travis Wolfe, might be involved. He wished there was a way to bring Wesley Strand in for questioning. In his experience, loyalty to a boss went only so far when you were the one faced with doing jail time.

But he wasn't the cop in charge here. Just a concerned citizen trying to keep an innocent woman safe.

"Find something?" Slade asked, entering the kitchen.

Duncan quickly filled the marshal in on what he'd found about Roland or Ray Perry, including Chelsey's meeting with him and Brett at the hotel.

"You're right, it doesn't make any sense." Slade sighed. "Let me make more calls, going higher up the chain this time to find more about this guy's identity," Slade said. "The last time I checked, we were told the guy didn't exist, but that's clearly not the case if you found a driver's license for the guy. There's something fishy going on here, and I don't like it."

Duncan silently agreed. He thought for a moment about how he'd tried to go undercover, not taking a new identity, but pretending to be someone he wasn't in an effort to identify who had killed Max Callahan, the Milwaukee chief of police and patriarch of the Callahan family. It wasn't an easy task, that was for sure.

Could this Ray or Roland Perry have been doing something similar? There was no evidence that he was anything other than a construction worker, except for the fact that Brett claimed he was murdered.

And normal, average, everyday construction guys didn't get murdered for no good reason.

He really, really wanted to see what, if any, evidence Brett actually had in his honeymoon folder.

Slade was on the phone for a long time, listening without saying much. Duncan sensed that he was being sent higher up the chain and wondered what that meant.

"Duncan?" Chelsey's voice pulled him from his thoughts.

"What is it?" He leaned forward to take her hand in his. The ache in his chest intensified at the thought of not seeing her again after tomorrow. Even though they'd been reconnected for only a short time—days, really, since the moment Brett had been murdered—he felt as if he would be leaving a piece of his heart behind.

Not that Chelsey had asked for his heart. Or even indicated that she felt the same toward him. Despite having expressed her doubts about marrying Brett, he didn't think she was interested in jumping into another relationship, with anyone.

Including him.

And that had been okay, at first, but now? Despite his efforts he realized his feelings toward Chelsey had become…complicated.

"When we go to the hotel, we should look through Brett's room, in case I'm wrong about the honeymoon folder."

"I agree, although it seems to me that hiding the photos in plain sight, so to speak, would be a smart thing to do. How many bad guys would look there for evidence?"

"Do you think they killed Brett because of the evidence?" Her expression was grave. "I'm worried Trish is in danger just by being my assistant hotel manager."

"I don't know, Chelsey. At this point, we have to expect the worst, while hoping for the best."

"While praying for God to watch over us," she added.

He drew in a deep breath. "My sister, Shayla, and her husband, Mike Callahan, are believers." He offered a wry smile. "I've attended some church services with them, but I wish I had made more of an effort to understand their faith."

"Many people keep their faith private, but you need to know that leaning on God is the only thing keeping me going." She tightened her grip on his hand. "Maybe, once you go back home, you'll attend services, as a way to remember me."

"Chels," he whispered her name through a throat thick with emotion. "Of course I'll do that, but I won't ever forget you. That's a promise."

Her blue eyes glittered with tears, but then she swiped at her face and looked away. "It would be better for you to forget me, Duncan. We'll both have to find a way to move on when this is over."

No way. He'd never forget her, ever. For a moment he thought about joining her in WITSEC. Then he thought about his dad, and his sister, Shayla, and her two kids, Brodie and Breena. His heart squeezed painfully.

Give them up? His entire family? Never to see them again?

Yet leaving Chelsey was beginning to ache the same way as when he'd lost Amanda.

"I don't believe it," Slade said with frustration.

He pulled himself from his troublesome thoughts. Slade looked mad, which was unusual at least in the short time he'd come to know the guy. "What?"

"Roland Perry was an undercover cop." Slade shook his head with disgust. "He was assigned to infiltrate the construction company in an attempt to find evidence of criminal activity."

A cop? A chill snaked down his spine and suddenly it all made sense. "Okay, but why in the world didn't they tell you that when you learned Brett witnessed his murder?"

"Apparently Roland Perry's status was on a *need to know basis*, and my job as Brett's handler wasn't enough to put me in that group." There was no mistaking the bitterness in Slade's tone.

"Nettles killed an undercover cop." Duncan sighed. "We better hope Brett wasn't lying about that, and that he really did have evidence." He met Slade's gaze. "We can't let a cop killer walk."

"I know." Slade's voice held a note of resignation. "And I'd love nothing more than to prevent that from happening, but you have to understand my main job for the foreseeable future is to protect Chelsey."

Duncan knew that all too well. He wanted to be the one to protect her, but soon he'd be forced to hand her over to Slade Brooks permanently.

If Chelsey was right about God's plan, then maybe his role was to help solve the crime. After all, that was what cops like him did. Arrest the bad guys and toss them in jail.

If that was all he could do for Chelsey, then he wouldn't rest until he'd accomplished that task.

Chelsey forced herself to put some distance between her and Duncan. She had to stop leaning on him like this. The sooner she figured out how to manage on her own, the better.

Duncan couldn't assist with her transition into her new life. Apparently, that was Slade's job.

She tried to take solace that she wouldn't be alone, but knew it wouldn't be the same. Slade was a nice guy, handsome and dedicated, but he wasn't Duncan.

Her feelings toward Duncan were spiraling out of control. Worse than the way she'd fallen so quickly for Brett after her mother's death. She knew that these tender feelings she had for Duncan might not be real, but over the past two days, she'd learned he was far more honorable than Brett.

Which still didn't mean she was falling in love with him. Not like the tepid feelings she'd had for Brett, but for real.

The way her parents had loved each other for over thirty years.

"Colt is bringing pizza for dinner," Slade said. "With daylight savings time, I'd like to wait until ten o'clock before heading over to Jackson."

"At least we have a few clouds rolling in," Duncan pointed out. "The quarter moon shouldn't be too much of a problem."

"We'll drive without lights until we're out on the highway," Slade agreed. "From there we should be okay."

Chelsey tried not to worry too much about getting

out of Moose and to the Teton Valley Hotel. Of more concern was what they would, or wouldn't, find there.

Hearing that Nettles had killed an undercover cop was sobering. Had the murder been done because they'd uncovered his real identity? Or because they'd simply found him snooping around? Murder seemed a drastic punishment for snooping, but if organized crime was involved, she doubted they let little things like morals get in the way.

The evening hours went by slowly. The pizza was good, and the guys seemed relaxed as they sat around her at the table. It was almost as if they were just hanging out, rather than getting prepared for a dangerous expedition.

Exhaustion began to weigh her down at about nine o'clock. Duncan urged her to stretch out on the sofa for a while. She didn't argue. Better to get a little nap in now, in preparation for what could be a long night.

She didn't think she'd really get any rest, but she must have dozed because Duncan's hand on her shoulder gently shook her awake. "Chels? It's time."

Blinking away the remnants of sleep, she sat up, adjusted the bulky bullet-resistant vest and nodded. "Okay."

Slade, Colt and Duncan escorted her outside. There weren't streetlights in Moose, but lights were visible from various apartment windows. The mountains behind them were nothing but dark shadows, and she hoped that meant that anyone lurking there wouldn't be able to see them clearly, either.

"What if they have night vision goggles?" she whispered as they headed outside.

"We've got you covered, Chelsey," Duncan assured

her. "Besides, the assailant on the mountain didn't have them and neither did the guy who broke into the cabin. As much as they think they're professionals, they wouldn't have lasted long in Afghanistan."

Slade eyed him thoughtfully. "You served over there?"

Duncan nodded, but didn't elaborate.

She slid into the back seat of the SUV, followed by Duncan. The two marshals sat in front, and as planned, Slade drove out of the driveway without using his lights.

A tense silence reigned inside the vehicle, but after ten minutes and reaching the highway without a problem, the guys relaxed a bit.

Chelsey rested against Duncan. He kissed the top of her head, and she tried not to remember the heat of his kiss. Slade made exceptionally good time getting to Jackson. As they headed toward Teton Valley Hotel, Chelsey straightened and looked around.

She wasn't sure what she'd expected, maybe dozens of police vehicles still surrounding the place, but everything looked normal.

As if a groom being shot just before his wedding had never happened.

Slade hit the lights as they approached the hotel. Her map must have been pretty good, because Slade found the service drive leading to the loading dock without difficulty.

Tension returned as Slade, Duncan and Chelsey eased out of the SUV. Colt was designated to stay with the SUV and to watch the back door and the road. Large garbage dumpsters were located back there, too, and Chelsey wrinkled her nose at the ripe scent.

The guys didn't seem to notice. With Duncan in the

front, and Slade behind her, they made their way up toward the employee-only entrance. Chelsey punched in the key code and the door opened with a click.

No one spoke as they went inside. Duncan walked in front of her, so she gently pushed him in the direction of her office. The hour wasn't that late, going on eleven thirty at night, but there was no sound of activity coming from the area of the lobby.

Chelsey fought her instinct to go find out what was going on. Had the hotel lost business after the wedding fiasco? Had people cancelled their reservations because of the violence?

She reminded herself it didn't matter, because she wasn't going to be managing the hotel anymore. Upon reaching her office door, she tried the knob, belatedly realizing she didn't have a key.

What bride carried her keys down the aisle?

The door was locked. She looked up at Duncan in horror. He glanced at Slade and nodded. The US marshal nudged her aside then pulled some tools out of his pocket and went to work.

She'd never watched anyone pick a lock before and was impressed at how easy Slade made it look. A minute later, he pushed the office door open. Duncan went in first, with Chelsey directly behind him.

Not until Slade closed the door behind him did Duncan use the penlight Ranger Paul Davidson had given him. He made a wide arc with the light, verifying there was no one else in the office.

Eerily, the place looked as if she'd just left it. Maybe Trish was waiting for her to return. Chelsey instinctively moved to her desk and the stack of folders sitting off to the right. She lifted them, searching for the yellow honeymoon folder that she remembered Brett tucking under the pile.

It was gone.

"What's wrong?" Duncan whispered.

"The folder isn't where I expected it to be." Her stomach knotted painfully, and she quickly began to search the entire desktop.

The folder had to be here, it just had to be!

"Which room was Brett using?" Duncan asked. "I can check the place out while you keep searching here."

"Room 112, but I don't have a key and I don't think your lock picks will work on the room doors." She shifted another stack of papers aside. "I know the folder is here somewhere."

"Should I check the file drawers?" Slade offered.

She shook her head, trying to ignore the pounding of her heart. "Duncan? Shine your light here, please."

Duncan came up to stand behind her, so that she could see her desk. A glint of yellow caught her eye and she shoved the pad of paper aside and uncovered the folder. "Got it."

"Let's see what's inside." Slade came up to stand beside her. Duncan kept the narrow beam of the flashlight centered on the folder as she opened it up.

The photograph on top was an ad for an exclusive honeymoon resort. She shoved it aside without a second glance, riffling through the rest of the contents. It wasn't until the back of the folder that she found two photographs.

The picture was a little grainy, but not enough that she couldn't make out two men standing in a large building filled with boxes that appeared to be labeled with the Coyote Creek Construction logo. One man, a guy who looked vaguely like the picture of Anthony Nettles, held a gun and was clearly threatening the other man who she now recognized as Roland Perry. The second picture showed the man with the gun, and Perry lying on the ground in a dark pool of blood.

"That's it," Duncan said in a low, hoarse voice.

"I can't believe he kept this from us," Slade whispered harshly. "If he'd have turned this over to me right away, he'd still be alive."

"Take them." She stepped away from the desk. "I'm just glad we found them."

Slade picked up the folder when his cell phone buzzed. He glanced at the screen and quickly answered. "Colt? What's wrong?"

It was so quiet in the office it was easy to hear Colt's response. "We have company. Black truck just pulled in."

Chelsey froze and glanced at Duncan. "I know this hotel like the back of my hand. We'll find a way out."

"Colt? Stay out of sight. We'll be in touch." Slade disconnected from the call. "All right, Chelsey. Let's go."

Swallowing her fear, she gently turned the knob of her office door and cracked it open. For the first time since Brett's murder, she was responsible for the lives of these two men.

A heavy burden. *Please, Lord, show me the way!*

# FOURTEEN

Duncan put a hand on Chelsey's shoulder, preventing her from going out of the office. He lowered his mouth to her ear. "Me first. Tell me which way to go."

She shook her head. "Too difficult to navigate. Follow me."

He didn't like it, but arguing was a waste of time they didn't have. It seemed as if their planned late-night escape from Moose had only postponed being found by the bad guys, not circumvented it.

They should have gotten in and out of Chelsey's office as quickly as possible.

Over Chelsey's shoulder he could see the hallway was deserted and quiet. She moved out and headed in the opposite direction from which they'd come in. He tensed, hoping she wasn't planning to take them to the front door.

She didn't. Instead, she turned down another hallway, going past a couple of conference rooms that were thankfully empty. She turned right and led them down a narrow hallway with hotel room doors located on either side.

It was pretty quiet for a hotel, although thinking

back, he realized the wedding was on Saturday so that meant today was Monday. Not as much going on, apparently even in June.

"Colt? What's happening?" Slade asked softly. "We're heading toward the north end of the building."

"See you soon." In the quiet hallway Duncan could hear Colt's muffled response without the phone being on speaker.

Duncan glanced over his shoulder at Slade. "He didn't answer your question."

Slade gave a curt nod. "I know."

At the end of the hallway, there was a door leading outside to a flat parking lot.

Once again, he rested his hand on her shoulder to prevent her from going outside. "Wait for Colt."

She nodded and peered through the glass door. From what he could see of the parking lot, there was a scattering of cars on the left, all of them close to the door. For whatever reason, there weren't many cars parked on the right. Maybe they were parked closer to their rooms, overlooking the mountains.

The hotel was located in a valley—the mountains circled the property on all sides—which is why the loading dock was tucked away in the back of the building.

There was a niggling itch along the back of his neck, a sixth sense telling him something wasn't right. They'd gotten the evidence against Anthony Nettles but needed to stay alive long enough to use it.

A dark shape came around the corner from the right side of the building. Chelsey pushed against the door, but he held her back, waiting. Slade's phone vibrated.

"That you, Colt? Okay, we're coming," Slade said.

The SUV rolled to a stop right across from the door.

Duncan nudged Chelsey aside so he could go first. Less than a minute later, they were in the back seat of the SUV.

Colt drove slowly, going around the corner, then pulling up into a parking spot between two other cars. He shut down the engine, then turned to look at them. "I think we need to stay down for a while, long enough for the black truck to leave."

"Good idea," Slade said. "We'll stay low."

Duncan made sure Chelsey was crouched behind the passenger seat before doing the same.

They'd been settled in their hiding spots for only five minutes when bright headlights slowly swept past them. No one moved or spoke. Duncan had no doubt the vehicle would take a second pass, maybe even a third before leaving.

Unless…he swallowed hard. What if they decided to go from car to car searching for them? It wouldn't take long to uncover their hiding spot. He found himself praying they wouldn't. Praying didn't come naturally to him, but he bowed his head so his chin was resting on his chest.

*Please, Lord, guide us through this danger.*

Chelsey shifted, ever so slightly. He glanced over and whispered, "You okay?"

"Yes." A second later, the headlights washed over them again.

He didn't like it. "Colt? We may have to make a run for it. I'm worried they'll send someone to search each vehicle on foot. The alarm won't help if they have a gun."

"Already on it," Colt answered. "I timed their sweep.

In two minutes, I'm going to get us out of here. You and Chelsey need to stay down."

"Okay." Duncan flashed an encouraging look at Chelsey. "We can do this."

She nodded. "With God's help."

"Yes." There wasn't time to say anything more as Colt fired up the engine and backed out of the parking spot. From Duncan's position behind the driver's seat, he couldn't tell if Colt was using his headlights or not.

Colt didn't waste any time but headed straight out of the parking lot back out onto the highway. "Slade? Ideas on where to go from here? Take interstate 191 southeast or go off on the less traveled highway 20?"

"Stay on the main highway, more traffic that way."

Traffic? Duncan swallowed a protest. Wyoming didn't have traffic. Not like Chicago and other big cities did. "Don't forget you're flying Chelsey out of Jackson Hole Airport in the morning." He peered at his watch, his stomach clenching at the time. Midnight. "Which is only eight hours from now."

"Turn here," Slade said with urgency.

Colt cranked the wheel, taking a hard right. "Why?"

"Duncan's right, we need to stay in Jackson. I know there are a couple of hotels roughly seven to eight miles from the airport."

"Okay, but we'll need to find a place to hide the vehicle," Colt said. "If they start searching parking lots, they may recognize this one."

"Understood," Slade agreed.

Duncan's back and knees were starting to protest the uncomfortable position, but he ignored the aches and pains, more concerned with how Chelsey was doing. "How much longer, Colt?"

"Ten minutes," the marshal responded.

"Thanks." He stared at Chelsey. Eight hours to go before she'd be flown out of Wyoming, for good. The SUV slowed, then made a couple of turns before coming to a stop within the designated timeline.

"Stay down until I can get a couple of rooms," Slade instructed before easing out of the passenger seat.

It didn't take long for Slade to obtain two connecting rooms. Duncan stayed behind Chelsey as they headed inside, glad that their ground-floor rooms had easy access in and out.

"I'll park the SUV somewhere safe," Colt said. "Don't worry about how long I'm gone. It'll take me a while to hike back from the resort."

Duncan walked Chelsey through the connecting door to her room. For a long moment, neither of them said anything, even though there was so much he wanted to tell her.

"I'm tired but not sure I'll be able to sleep," Chelsey confided, dropping onto the edge of the bed. "It's all been so surreal. I don't know anything about where I'll be at this time tomorrow."

He sat in the only chair in the room, across from her. "I wish there was a way you could stay."

She let out a heavy sigh. "I think we both know that's impossible. The fact that they followed us to the hotel proves they won't stop until they get what they want."

He was very much afraid she was right. "I don't think they know about the evidence—maybe they believe we were there to get your personal things."

"Maybe." Chelsey looked down at the floor. "It's hard to accept the inability to take personal photographs with me."

"I can grab them for you," he offered. "That way if things change down the road you'll know that you'll be able to have them back some day."

"Really?" The offer caused her face to light up. "I'd love that, thanks."

"No problem." He hesitated, thinking back once again to his family back in Milwaukee. His dad, who might be marrying Maggie Callahan; his sister, Shayla, and her two kids. "I'll go with you, Chelsey."

"What?" She looked confused. "You mean to get me settled? That won't work, the location has to be secret to the point where Slade is the only one who will know where I am."

"No, I mean, we can go into WITSEC together. I care about you, Chelsey. You need a friend, and I don't want to lose you."

Her mouth dropped open, and hope flashed briefly in her eyes, before she shook her head. "No, Duncan, I can't ask that of you."

"You never asked, Chels. I'm offering." He knew doing this would bring his family pain, but his dad had Maggie, and Shayla had Mike and their kids. They would all go on with their lives.

"Oh, Duncan." Her eyes filled with tears. "That's the sweetest offer in the entire world, but I can't let you do this. I can't let you give up your family. Mine is gone, so the sacrifice isn't nearly as great. But your dad and your sister both need you."

"They'll be okay without me," he began, but she abruptly cut him off.

"No, Duncan. I'm not going to let you do this." She jumped up from her perch on the bed and moved away.

"I need to get cleaned up. I'll see you in the morning, okay?"

He stared at her for a long moment, trying to read between the lines. Was she refusing because she didn't care for him? Or because she didn't want him in her life?

Before he could try to clarify, she went into the tiny bathroom and closed the door behind her.

Leaving him little choice but to return to the room he was sharing with the guys, his gut filled with dread, his heart heavy.

All too soon, Chelsey would be leaving him forever. The same way Amanda had. Only Amanda had died, while Chelsey was making a conscious decision to go.

And there wasn't anything he could do to change that.

Chelsey collapsed on the edge of the closed lid of the toilet, her hands shaking as she hung her head.

That Duncan would make such a selfless offer was mind-boggling. And worse? She'd wanted nothing more than to throw herself into his arms and accept his sacrifice.

Refusing him had been one of the most difficult things she'd ever done. But she also knew it was the right thing to do.

Her feelings for Duncan were difficult to decipher. She might be falling in love with him but didn't trust her feelings. She'd made a hasty decision with Brett and look where that had landed her.

Right in the middle of this mess.

Yet spending time with Duncan prior to the wedding had shown her the truth about her feelings toward Brett. She'd been very attracted to Duncan. So much so, she'd realized how much she cared about Brett as a friend, not as a husband.

But Duncan had served in the army, and it was his nature to be a protector. And he'd done an admirable job guarding her.

She wouldn't be here if not for his expertise.

There was also the fact that if she hadn't agreed to marry Brett, she wouldn't have met Duncan again. He'd come to stand up as Brett's best man. Duncan hadn't come to Wyoming specifically to see her.

Foolish to think Duncan had fallen in love with his best man's bride. Duncan was too honorable for that.

No, the best thing she could do for Duncan was to let him go. Allow him to return home to his family, friends and career.

She loved him enough to give him the life he deserved.

What was left of the night dragged on forever. Chelsey woke up almost every hour and finally gave up trying to sleep at about six in the morning. The sky was beginning to lighten, several puffy white clouds floating across the sky, although a darker rain cloud hovered over the Grand Tetons.

She'd taken the bullet-resistant vest off last night and was doing her best to replace it over her dark blue cotton shirt when she heard a light rap on the connecting door.

"Come in." She turned in time to see Duncan step over the threshold. "Hey. I could use some help here."

He set a bag of food on the table, then came over to adjust the vest. "I brought breakfast from the fast food place across the street."

"How did you know I was awake?"

He shrugged, avoiding her gaze. "Heard you moving around, the walls are pretty thin."

She nodded and tugged on the edge of the vest to shift it into a more comfortable position. "What's the plan? What time are we heading to the airport?"

"Slade wants you to get there early, but it won't take long. They're hoping to leave here about seven thirty." Duncan finished securing the vest and stepped back, tucking his hands into his front pockets. "They want me to take the first flight back to Milwaukee."

"You should," she agreed. "Nothing more you can do here."

He scowled. "Other than help bring Anthony Nettles to justice for murdering an undercover cop and figure out what role Wesley Strand and Travis Wolfe play in all of this, if any."

"Surprised you haven't become a detective for the MPD," she said keeping her tone light and teasing.

"I'm scheduled to take the detective exam next month," he admitted. "But I'd give that up if it meant I could stay here to bring these guys to justice."

She wondered if he really understood how he'd be forced into giving up his career if she'd accepted his offer to come with her. Another reason for her to remain strong. "Well, you'll bring other bad guys to justice in Milwaukee, which will be good, too."

He glanced away. "Please come eat your breakfast before it gets cold."

"Is there coffee?" She moved past him to pick up the bag of food.

"I'll make some." Duncan busied himself with the small coffee maker available in their rooms.

She sensed he was upset with her but didn't want to

rehash the subject of his coming with her all over again. They had just over an hour together, and for the first time, she wasn't sure what to say.

Some things were better left unsaid.

"Were you serious about getting some of my personal items at the hotel?" she asked.

He brought over a cup of coffee, doctored with cream and sugar the way she liked it. "Yes. Tell me what you'd like me to have and I'll find a way."

"Not now, though, right? I mean, it's not safe to go back there yet."

He shrugged. "You're the one in danger, Chelsey, not me."

She took a bite of her breakfast sandwich, thinking back to the wedding. "Are you sure? I mean, it wouldn't be difficult for anyone to figure out you were the one helping me."

"So far the attempts have been specifically targeted at you," he pointed out. "And they can't kill all of us."

"Why not? From what I can tell, they haven't balked at killing anyone, not even an undercover cop."

He seemed to consider her point. "You may be right, and if that is the case, maybe I should be relocated with you."

She wanted very badly to agree, but forced herself to look him directly in the eye. "Is that what Slade and Colt say?"

"Not yet, but it may be the right thing to do, regardless."

There was no good response to that, so she remained silent. Slade poked his head into the room. "Chelsey? We'd like to be ready to go by seven thirty."

"I know. I'll be ready." She finished her breakfast

and coffee, then stood. "Give me a few minutes and I'll be set."

Duncan nodded. She took her time washing her face and brushing her teeth. She tucked two bobby pins in place to keep her hair out of her eyes. Looking at her reflection in the mirror, she found herself wondering what name she'd be given. Did she have a choice about that or had Slade already created new identification documents for her?

Did it really matter? Chelsey Robards would cease to exist and some new woman would be born in her place.

When she emerged from the bathroom, she heard voices from next door. Crossing over to the adjoining room, she could tell Duncan was pressing his case to be relocated with her.

They stopped arguing when she came in. "Ready to go?" Slade asked.

"Yes." She glanced around. "Where's Colt?"

"He left a while ago to retrieve the SUV." Slade pulled out his phone. "He'll text when he's here."

As if on cue the phone in Slade's hand chirped.

"Sounds like our ride is here," Duncan said. "Let's go."

They left the motel room, once again Duncan leading the way, Slade walking behind her. The SUV was parked a couple of spots down from where their rooms were located. As they approached the vehicle, they heard a high-pitched scream.

"What in the world?" Duncan spun toward the sound. Chelsey stopped in her tracks, trying to understand what was happening.

Then something hit her square in the chest, with enough force to send her reeling backward. She hit the ground, pain reverberating across her chest and along the back of her head.

She didn't move, couldn't breathe. For an instant she wondered if she was dead, but the overwhelming pain seemed to indicate she was alive.

"She's hit! She's hit!" The panic in Duncan's voice was the last thing she remembered before darkness claimed her.

# FIFTEEN

Duncan fell to his knees, throwing himself over Chelsey to protect her from the shooter even though he wasn't sure where the guy was hiding. He tensed, bracing for a second shot, even as he called, "Help me, she's been hit!"

Colt ran over from the SUV. "Check her pulse. Is she still with us?"

Duncan felt for a pulse, but his own heart was hammering so hard he couldn't be sure. "I don't know," he whispered hoarsely. "She's not moving."

"We need to get her back inside," Slade said in a low, urgent tone. "Colt, call an ambulance and then see if you can find the shooter."

Duncan barely heard what they were saying, his gaze focused on Chelsey. He was afraid to move her, but more terrified not to. He gathered her limp body into his arms, and rose to his feet, mentally kicking himself for falling for the oldest trick in the book.

The scream had been a diversion intended to separate him from Chelsey. And it had worked.

He set her down on the bed, gently placing a pillow beneath her head. The back of her hair was damp with blood and the room spun crazily for a moment before righting itself.

*Please, God, don't let Chelsey die!*

The wail of sirens could be heard in the distance, but he kept his gaze on Chelsey's still form. He felt again for a pulse, and this time was reassured when he identified the faint beat of her heart.

He bowed his head and silently thanked God for sparing her.

"Check her vest—see if the bullet is still imbedded there, or if it went through," Slade said.

He fingered the vest, easily finding the spot in the center of her chest where the bullet had penetrated the vest. Quickly removing the vest, he was doubly thankful to realize the bullet hadn't gone into her skin.

Although he knew the impact would leave a massive bruise, regardless. That she wasn't moving concerned him. "Chelsey? Can you hear me?"

Her eyelids fluttered open and she looked confused for a moment before her expression cleared. "Duncan? Wh-what happened?"

"You were shot." He held up the vest. "I'm sure your chest hurts, you may even have a few cracked ribs, but the vest saved your life."

"Yeah, hurts." Her eyelids drooped. "Head and chest…"

He glanced at Slade. "We'll need to get her to the local hospital."

"There's one not too far, but we might not want to go there," Slade said.

"Why? Just because you think the shooter will try to find her at the only hospital in this town?" Duncan felt his anger simmering to a boil. "I don't care. It's your job to get her the medical treatment she needs."

"Hear me out, Duncan," Slade said, holding up a hand. "What if we pretend she's dead?"

His anger quickly faded as he recognized the wisdom of that plan. "You mean, treat her as if she's dead, so that the shooter thinks he's finished the job?"

"Why not?" Slade shrugged. "Seems to me he must not have noticed the vest. Maybe because you were standing in front of her until the scream drew you out of the way. He only had a second to take the shot and she went down like a rock. He has no reason to believe he missed."

The reminder of how badly he'd failed to keep Chelsey safe burned, but he couldn't deny Slade's plan had merit. "I like it. But she still needs care."

"I'm okay." Chelsey's whisper had him turning toward her. "I'm okay with pretending to be dead if it helps keep the rest of you safe."

"Yeah, she has a point about that. The situation in general has been bothering me," Slade said. "I'm not sure why they haven't taken a shot at you, Colt and me. The shooter had plenty of time. He could have picked us off one by one without much effort."

"I had the same thought last night," Duncan admitted. "It didn't make sense that they kept going after Chelsey. If they thought Brett told her something in confidence, then they should assume she'd have shared that same information with the rest of us, right? So why keep going after her?"

Slade shook his head. "I'm not sure. But faking her death may help solve that problem." Slade turned toward Chelsey. "Who gets the Teton Valley Hotel after you're gone?"

Her brow furrowed. "It's a good question. The hotel has been in our family for generations, but I don't have any heirs or family left. If Brett was alive and we actually got married, there may have been a way for him to pass it along to his family, but I'm sure now it will simply go up for auction to the highest bidder."

"Travis Wolfe is a millionaire who has already bought up the adjoining ranch," Duncan said as the last piece of the puzzle fell into place. "The assailant at the cabin said that he was sent by Wesley Strand. Could it be because Wolfe wants the hotel, too?"

Slade nodded slowly. "Seems drastic, but maybe killing Brett first, followed by Chelsey, was a way for them to get rid of two problems at one time. Get rid of the witness and the hotel owner."

Duncan felt certain they were onto something. The photograph of Nettles killing the undercover cop was enough to open an investigation but having Brett's eyewitness testimony would have been necessary to prove Nettles took the shot. That only took care of Anthony Nettles, owner of Coyote Creek Construction. Yet there was nothing more than a business relationship between Nettles and Wolfe. There was no way to implicate the millionaire in the crime.

Was that how Wolfe had planned it all along? Was it possible Wolfe had paid someone off in the local police department and had learned about Brett's report of what he'd witnessed?

It was all starting to make sense, at least in theory. Proving any of it was another story.

The sirens were louder now, red lights flashing outside the hotel window. They were running out of time if they were going to pull off faking Chelsey's death.

He grabbed the blanket and pulled it up over Chelsey's head. Slade nodded and went to the door. He held up his credentials for the two EMTs.

"I'm sorry, but she's gone. We won't need your services," Slade told them.

The two EMTs glanced at each other and frowned. "We still gotta take her in for the doctors to pronounce her," the taller of the two said.

"I'm US Marshal Slade Brooks, and I'm not releasing her body into your custody. I'll notify the Jackson PD and take it from here."

It wasn't standard procedure, but Duncan could tell the EMTs were buying Slade's story. Federal agents often pulled rank over local law enforcement officials. They shrugged, turned away and headed back to their ambulance.

"The police will be here any minute," Duncan said in a low voice.

It wasn't even a minute before a squad car pulled in. Slade walked outside to chat with the female officer, leaving Duncan to sit beside Chelsey.

He pulled the chair close to the bed. "Stay as still as possible," he whispered.

She didn't answer, and he hoped that she hadn't lost consciousness again. Were they doing the right thing here? Faking her death to help save her life seemed reasonable, but lying didn't come naturally to him and he felt certain the same was true of Chelsey.

The minutes dragged by slowly, but Slade finally returned, bringing Colt with him. "Okay, we're good for now. I've convinced the locals that Chelsey was a federal witness and that we are going to take care of getting her body removed from the hotel."

Duncan stood and pulled the blanket off Chelsey. She blinked up at them. Shifted and winced. Duncan ran a washcloth under cold water and offered it to her. She placed it on the abrasion along the back of her head. "Okay, where are we going?"

"First we need a plan. I don't know that taking the private plane we arranged is the right thing to do, if we're faking Chelsey's death," Slade pointed out. He turned toward Colt. "Did you find anything on the shooter?"

"No, although there was a woman standing off to the side who seemed interested in what was going on. When I went over to talk to her, she took off. She was likely the screamer. I'm fairly certain the guy was set up on the top of the strip mall a few blocks from here." Colt's expression was grim. "They must have narrowed down the two possible locations as this place or the one across the street. The view from the strip mall encompasses both hotels."

"How did they know that?" Chelsey asked. When she tried to sit up, he slid his arm around her shoulders offering his support. She leaned against him just for a moment, and he fought the urge to kiss her.

"I don't know," Colt admitted. "They must have had someone up there watching since early this morning."

"No one is up there now?" Duncan asked.

Colt shook his head. "No, but that doesn't mean they aren't watching from somewhere close by."

"We need to get Chelsey out of here, then." Duncan didn't want to give these guys another chance to get to her. She eased away from him, so he rose to his feet. "Does the plane you arranged for have the ability to have Chelsey lying flat in the back?"

"No, but I can arrange a different plane." Slade pulled out his phone.

"Wait, where are you taking me?" Chelsey asked.

Slade glanced at Duncan. "I'm not sure yet, but I'll figure something out."

"I'm going with her," Duncan said in a firm voice.

"You can't," Chelsey protested weakly.

"She's right, it's too risky," Colt added.

He tamped down a flash of impatience. "First of all, it makes sense that I would go along with her body if she really was dead. Secondly, there's no risk since I'm willing to give up my old life to create a new one with Chelsey."

Colt and Slade exchanged a glance. Duncan was prepared for the argument, but it didn't come.

"Give me a minute to arrange new transportation," Slade said, turning away. "We'll have time to make a plan once I have that arranged."

Duncan let out a breath he hadn't realized he was holding. He smiled reassuringly at Chelsey. "Don't worry, it's going to be all right."

She gave a slight nod, then turned to lie down on the bed.

"Cold?" He drew the blanket up beneath her chin.

She shook her head and closed her eyes. Understanding she needed to rest, he left her alone.

Giving her time to recover from her injuries was one thing, but those moments he'd believed she'd been killed were too fresh in his mind.

No way was he letting her go.

She needed a chance to talk to Slade alone. Ignoring the throbbing pain in her head and chest was easy compared to the impact of Duncan's offer to give up his entire life for her.

She couldn't let him do it.

When Slade returned, she reached out to grasp his hand. In a low whisper she said, "Don't let Duncan give up his family for me."

Slade offered a wry smile. "I'll try, but he's pretty stubborn."

"Please, Slade. You need to find a way." She released his hand and dropped the subject when Duncan came into the room.

"The sooner we get out of here, the better," Duncan said.

"We need to carry Chelsey's body out of the hotel and place her in the back of the SUV," Slade said in agreement. "I recommend we cover her with a sheet, the way we would if she was dead."

"Maybe we use the blanket to carry her out in a sling," Duncan offered. "Use the sheet to cover her face."

It felt odd to hear them talking about how to move her out of the hotel. She hoped Slade and Colt were wrong about the shooter hanging around to keep a watch on the place.

If he were smart, he'd be long gone.

Keeping her body limp as the men lifted her in the blanket wasn't easy. She concentrated on not moving a single muscle.

Duncan and Colt gently set her in the back of the SUV. With part of the back seat lowered flat, she fit perfectly. Only after they closed the hatch did she take a deep breath.

So far, so good.

"Chelsey? The windows are tinted so no one is able to see in. Would you rather sit upright?" Duncan asked.

Her head still hurt, as did her ribs. "No, this is good."

The ride to the airport didn't take long, and she appreciated the way Slade drove with care, staying just under the speed limit.

From her position, she could see the airplanes taking off and landing as they approached the airport. She knew the Jackson Hole Airport was small with just six gates total. But that was for commercial flights. She didn't know where the private hangars were located.

Slade took a turn, then slowly brought the SUV to a stop. "This is it—the private plane we've arranged as transport is waiting inside. We're going to carry you in the blanket, the same way we did at the hotel."

Duncan reached out to lightly stroke her hair in a way that brought tears to her eyes, before pushing his door open. She swiped at her face and reminded herself to stay strong.

Duncan deserved to return to his family.

Once again, she made herself limp, not daring to breathe as she was removed from the SUV. Even when there was a slight bump against the back of her already sore head, she didn't react.

She was carried inside the hangar and placed in the back of a small cargo type of plane. There, she sat up and looked around. This was the first time she'd been in a small plane, and in a private hangar. The interior of the building was rather plain, but also vaguely familiar.

Maybe from something she'd seen on television?

The pilot came over to greet Slade. "I'm Jenkins, your pilot. I need to finish my preflight checklist and we'll be ready to go."

"Thanks. I'm Slade Brooks, and this is Chelsey. We appreciate you changing the plane at the last minute."

Jenkins shrugged. "It's no problem."

"Hey, isn't that building over there the hangar for Travis Wolfe?" Duncan asked.

She craned her neck to see what he meant. The building was larger than the one they were currently in, but the outside was labeled with a large sign that read Wolfe Industries.

Edging out of the back of the plane, she saw the three men staring in surprise. "We should have realized there would be a private hangar for Travis Wolfe," Duncan said in disgust. "What rich guy doesn't own his own plane?"

"Hey, it's a world outside my experience," Slade commented dryly.

"I need to take a look inside the place," Duncan said. "Could be something there to give us a clue if Travis Wolfe and his head of security, Wesley Strand, are working on the wrong side of the law with Nettles."

Her stomach clenched with worry. "I don't think that's a good idea. What if you get caught?"

"I just need a minute to check the place out." Duncan glanced at Slade. "Don't take off with Chelsey until I'm back, okay?"

It occurred to her that they could leave while Duncan was off peeking inside the Wolfe Industries hangar. It was the best way to ensure that he didn't try to relocate with her. But Chelsey couldn't do it. She wanted to hug Duncan one last time. She wanted to look into his deep brown eyes and tell him how much these past few days had meant to her.

She wanted to let him know how much she loved him. And would never forget him.

"Duncan, wait," Slade protested, but it was too late. Duncan had already edged out of the hangar, rounded the SUV and was walking purposefully toward the Wolfe Industries building.

"I'll go with him," Colt said. "Stay with Chelsey."

Slade sighed heavily and she knew he was annoyed with Duncan's determination to glimpse inside the building.

From her position in the back of the plane, she watched as Colt and Duncan made their way across the wide-open space that separated the two hangars.

The guys had just reached the edge of the building when a limo rolled into view. She hadn't seen any limos in Jackson and knew the passenger could only be the owner himself. "Slade? What if Travis Wolfe finds them snooping around?"

Slade's expression was grim as he picked up his phone. "Colt? You've got a limo driving up to the hangar."

She couldn't hear Colt's reply, but could only watch in horror as Duncan and Colt dropped down behind a couple of oil drums located right outside the hangar mere seconds before the limo rolled to a stop.

What was Duncan thinking? What if he and Colt were found? It was possible that Travis Wolfe wasn't involved in any criminal activity and would be upset only about the men snooping near his hangar, but she didn't really believe it.

*Please, Lord, keep Duncan and Colt safe in Your care!*

# SIXTEEN

Duncan made himself as small as possible behind the two oil drums located outside the Wolfe Industries hangar. Colt had unexpectedly joined him, and he was glad to have backup. Before taking cover, he'd gotten a glimpse of the interior of the hangar. The space was large, occupied by a plane, but there had also been a slew of boxes along one side of the building, several labeled with the Coyote Creek Construction logo.

As he hovered there behind the oil drum, Duncan slowly realized this was the same place he'd seen in Brett's two photographs of Nettles holding a gun—one photo the gun was pointed at Perry, the other with the undercover cop lying on the floor in a pool of blood.

The shooting of Roland Perry hadn't taken place in a company warehouse, as he'd originally assumed. It had happened right here in the Wolfe Industries airport hangar.

If only there was a way to prove it. The boxes alone wouldn't be enough. But maybe if luminol was used on the interior of the building, they'd find Roland Perry's blood had seeped into the concrete floor. Of course, they needed a warrant and probable cause to get that.

Was the photograph of Nettles and the dead cop standing near Coyote Creek Construction boxes enough? Probably not.

Male voices drifted toward them, and he strained to listen.

"You better hope she's dead," a deep, curt voice said. "I'm tired of paying for incompetence."

She who? Chelsey? Duncan risked a glance at Colt who was listening just as intently.

"Hey, it's not our fault she managed to get help," a higher whiney voice complained. "We've lost two of our own men in this."

"Shut up!" The deep voice struck with the force of whiplash. "Those men were stupid enough to get caught, so it's only right that they should suffer an *accident* while in jail."

Accident? Duncan's gut clenched. Like being silenced, permanently?

"Easy, Travis…" A third calm voice seemed to be taking the role of peacekeeper.

"No, I won't take it easy," the deep voice snapped. "Why would you guys use hunting rifles anyway? Why not high powered AK47s with silencers attached? This has been nothing but a debacle from the beginning. It's a wonder you were able to hit Thompson the way you did."

The reference to Brett's murder made Duncan's blood run cold. He peered around the edge of the oil drum just far enough to see four men standing there. He easily recognized three of them from the photos— Anthony Nettles, Wesley Strand and Travis Wolfe. The fourth man was standing apart from the other three, keeping his head down and shoulders slouched as if he were the low man on the totem pole in the group.

The guy with his head down turned so that Duncan could see his profile. *Wait a minute.* Duncan narrowed his gaze, wishing he had a pair of binoculars. The longer he looked, the more convinced he became that the fourth guy was the same one who'd attacked him on the side of the mountain. At least he was fairly certain. Even from a distance he could see the fresh wound along his temple. The spot where Chelsey had hit him with the log during their struggle with the knife.

He eased back behind the drum and glanced at Colt. "They're in it together," he said in a whisper. "The guy with the whiney voice and head down is the same one who attacked me on the mountain."

Colt nodded to indicate he understood.

"A hunting rifle doesn't raise suspicion. Every man in Wyoming has one," the whiney voice said. "But anyone catching a glimpse of a fancy AK47 would blab to the entire town."

"I told you to shut up!" Wolfe sounded as if he had reached his limit.

"Okay, Travis, you have a right to be upset. But the woman is dead and we'll get the property, which is what you wanted, right?"

"Right." Wolfe's tone had lost some of its edge. "I'm getting out of here until things cool off. The rest of you better keep your heads down and eyes open. Those guys who were helping the woman are law enforcement of some kind and might stick around to find out what happened to her."

"Not to worry, we have inside help, remember?" The

nasal voice must belong to Nettles, it was the first thing the guy had said since they'd arrived.

"Yes, inside help that I'm paying for," Wolfe responded harshly. "I'm funding all of this, so you guys better hold up your end of the deal."

Duncan realized this was exactly what they needed to nail these guys once and for all. Easing his phone out of his pocket, he held it along the edge of the oil drum, much the way Brett must have done a few weeks ago, and took pictures of the four men standing outside the hangar.

The only downside he could see was that he and Colt might be trespassing, although he felt certain the hangar itself might belong to the airport. Still, it was something that could get their testimony tossed out of a courtroom by a smart lawyer, one he assumed Wolfe had on speed dial.

He thought about the boxes inside the hangar and wondered what Coyote Creek Construction was shipping in or out of the state of Wyoming.

They needed something, anything to use as probable cause to search the place.

But what?

"What did you do with the hunting rifle, Stewart?" the calm voice asked.

"I—uh, still have it," whiney voice replied. "But I can get rid of it if you'd like."

"Why would you keep it?" Wolfe's tone was incredulous. "How incompetent are you?"

The sound of a fist striking skin followed by a muffled thud reached his ears. Duncan risked another glance around the drum to see someone lying on the concrete. Stewart, aka whiney voice.

One of the three men in charge had hit the underling hard enough to knock him unconscious.

And if he and Colt didn't do something, then there was nothing to stop them from killing him.

"Get rid of him," Wolfe said tersely. "I'm done here. Call me when you manage to get everything under control."

Duncan tensed. Wolfe was going to get on his personal plane and get out of Wyoming unless they found a way to keep him there.

But how?

There was a scuffle as Stewart was picked up off the ground and tossed in the back of the limo. Duncan risked another glance around the oil drum and couldn't see Travis Wolfe anywhere. He must have gone deeper into the hangar.

The other two men slid into the back of the limo as ordered. He eased back and glanced at Colt. "You take the limo, I'll try to delay the plane."

"How are you going to do that?"

Duncan shook his head because he didn't have an answer. All he knew was that if Wolfe took off, then their chances of getting him in custody dropped significantly.

Duncan took a deep breath and lunged from behind the oil drums. Without hesitation, he darted inside the hangar as the plane began to roll past.

Without thinking, he grabbed onto one of the wings, as if his weight would be enough to stop it.

But of course, it wasn't.

Someone from the limo must have noticed him dangling from the wing of the plane like a broken hood ornament because he heard someone yell out, "Hey! That's the guy who's been protecting the woman!"

He couldn't hear anything beyond the roar of the airplane engines as the plane gained speed. He mentally braced himself, expecting at any moment to feel the searing pain from a bullet.

Chelsey watched the drama unfold with disbelief. What was Duncan doing hanging from the plane?

In some part of her mind she heard Slade calling the police even though they had no idea who within the department they could trust. She jumped down from the back of the cargo plane, the jarring movement causing her head and ribs to protest with pain.

It wasn't easy to catch her breath, but she didn't care. She sprinted out of the hangar toward the limo that had come to an abrupt stop.

"What in the—she's alive?" someone shouted incredulously.

She'd blown her cover of pretending to be dead, but it didn't matter.

Not if Duncan died for real.

As if he'd heard her thoughts, he abruptly let go of the plane, falling and landing in a heap on the tarmac. Something whizzed past her head and after a few seconds it registered in a corner of her brain that one of the men from the limo was shooting at her.

*Again.*

"Get down," Slade roared, grabbing her from behind.

She fell forward onto her hands and knees as Slade placed himself in front of her. Slade fired at the limo, shattering one of the windows. From where she was, she could see several things happening at once.

Colt stood and took aim, firing at the plane. Smoke billowed out from behind the aircraft, and it lurched to one side. She watched in horror as the plane crookedly descended back down to the runway.

Duncan ran toward the limo with his gun in his hand. "Police! Drop your weapons, now!"

Slade leveled his weapon. "US Marshals Service! Toss your guns down or we will shoot."

When Colt turned, the men in the limo realized they were outnumbered. Even if they got a couple of shots off, one or more of them would die.

"Okay, okay!" Nettles caved first, tossing his gun down to the ground.

"Kick it away," Duncan demanded.

Nettles did as he was told. Wesley Strand followed suit, tossing his weapon down and kicking it aside as well.

"Slade, take over for me. I'm going after Wolfe." Duncan turned and headed back toward the plane that was now lopsided on the ground, like a wounded bird.

"Duncan, no! Come back!" She shouted as loud as possible, but he never hesitated, sprinting toward the plane.

"Where's the other guy?" Slade asked, ignoring her plea. "The one Wolfe hit in the head."

"Back there." Nettles jerked his thumb toward the inside of the limo.

"Cover them, Colt," Slade said. "I need to see if he's alive."

Chelsey pushed herself upright, her gaze following Duncan's form as he closed the distance to the plane. After seeing how callously Wolfe had struck one of the men, sending him crashing to the ground, she knew the millionaire wouldn't hesitate to do the same to Duncan.

Or worse.

* * *

Duncan held his gun in a two-handed grip as he approached the plane. No surprise that the bird sat there, without anyone coming out from the aircraft.

"Wolfe, I know you're in there," Duncan called, pressing his back against the plane. "We've got your cohorts in custody, so you may as well give yourself up."

No response from the plane occupants. Duncan knew this wouldn't be easy. The rich guy inside was accustomed to getting his way.

"Wolfe, the feds are putting you under arrest for assault and battery," Duncan continued. "Come out with your hands up where I can see them."

Still nothing. He wished he could hear what the conversation was inside the plane. Was Travis Wolfe trying to find a way to get out of here? There was plenty of wide-open space on the runway, but nothing could be done to fix the damaged plane.

Or did the millionaire know that Duncan didn't have jurisdiction here in Jackson, Wyoming? He wished he'd thought of asking the US Marshals to deputize him.

The door cracked open. "Don't shoot—I'm coming out." Wolfe's voice didn't sound as curt as it had before, but Duncan didn't think the guy was going to give up so easily.

One long leg came out, then the other. The guy jumped to the ground, then spun toward Duncan. In a nanosecond, Duncan saw the gun in his hand and pulled the trigger of his weapon.

The one that had once belonged to the guy Wolfe had struck to the ground.

Duncan ducked but there was no need as the bullet from Wolfe's gun went wide. Then a shout of rage erupted from Wolfe.

"You shot me!" Wolfe looked shocked that anyone had dared to do such a thing. But the gun he held in his right arm was pointing to the ground now as blood dripped from a wound in his upper right arm.

The arm holding the weapon.

"Put the gun down!" Duncan repeated. "Or I'll shoot again."

Wolfe dropped the weapon and then reached up to cover his wound. "I'll have your badge for this. You shot an innocent man!"

Duncan edged closer until he was able to put his foot on the gun and sweep it beneath the plane. Then he came closer still, looking Wolfe right in the eye.

"The feds are right here, and you're under arrest for assault and conspiracy to commit murder," Duncan said. "You have the right to remain silent. Anything you say can and will be used against you in a court of law." He was about to continue the Miranda warning when he caught movement from the corner of his eye from inside the plane.

Glancing over, he saw the pilot was holding a gun, the muzzle pointed directly at him. Duncan froze.

"Shoot him!" Wolfe screamed. "What are you waiting for? Shoot him!"

The pilot stared at him, and Duncan refused to look away. If the guy was going to shoot, he wanted to see it in his eyes.

But the pilot looked uncertain. Duncan suspected the guy had never shot at anyone before—and hoped and prayed that he wouldn't do so now.

Stalemate.

Long seconds ticked by, and he believed the pilot couldn't do it. Dragging his gaze back to Wolfe, Duncan shugged. "Guess that's not part of the plan, Wolfe."

"I pay you to do as I say!" Wolfe hissed at the pilot.

In response, the pilot dropped the gun and placed his hands in the air. "I'm not a part of this."

"Seems killing a man crosses the line." Duncan gestured at Wolfe with the gun. "Turn around and put your hands up against the plane."

"Duncan!" Chelsey's voice rang out from behind him, but he didn't dare take his gaze off Wolfe.

The millionaire's eyes widened comically. "What? She's alive?"

For the first time in what seemed like forever, Duncan smiled. "Yes, she is. And you're going away for a long time."

"I don't think so," Wolfe sneered. "My lawyers will get me out of this mess."

Duncan knew his threat wasn't an idle one. Money talked and the rich often found a way to get out of tight spots. Witnesses were paid off and recanted their stories, for starters.

But not this time. He wasn't going to recant his testimony and neither would Chelsey.

The US Marshals were witnesses, too.

Wolfe finally turned and put his hands up against the plane. Duncan didn't have a set of handcuffs on him, so he glanced at Chelsey.

"See if you can find something to tie him up with," he told her.

Her wide eyes locked on his before she nodded. Before she could head over to Colt and Slade, the pilot tossed out some rope.

"Use this," he said in a resigned tone. "I should have known this job was too good to be true. The guy pays well, but he's a massive jerk."

"Thanks." Duncan eyed the pilot carefully as he picked up the rope, just in case this was some sort of trick.

"Chelsey, hold the gun on him, will you? And if he moves, shoot."

Chelsey took the gun, holding it with both hands that indicated to him that this wasn't the first time.

The pilot jumped to the ground, and there was no sign of the gun. Duncan used the rope to tie Wolfe's wrists together.

"That hurts," Wolfe complained. "You shot me, remember?"

"Yeah, because you shot at me, first, remember?" Duncan shook his head in disgust. "Your pilot is a witness."

The pilot lifted his hands. "Hey, I didn't really see anything," he protested. "I'm hired to fly the plane where Mr. Wolfe wants me to, nothing more."

Great, just great. Wolfe's lawyers would surely find a way to turn this around on him, but he couldn't worry about that now.

"Duncan? Need help?" Colt jogged over. "We have the other two cuffed, and the guy in the back of the limo is still out cold."

"We should notify the local police," Duncan said.

"Already done. They'll be here any moment. Can't you hear the sirens?"

Duncan turned and saw that indeed two police cars were barreling toward them with lights flashing and sirens wailing. He knew Wolfe had an inside man, but it wasn't likely both sets of officers were involved in this.

It was over. He took a step toward Chelsey and she threw her arms around his neck, hanging on as if her life depended on it.

"I was so scared," she whispered.

"I know. Me, too." He clutched her close, then drew back enough to look into her blue eyes. Then, realizing it might be the last time he'd have the chance, he lowered his mouth and kissed her.

She melted against him, but he couldn't allow himself to read too much into her actions.

Gratitude and friendship weren't love.

And he couldn't allow his heart to be broken a second time.

# SEVENTEEN

Chelsey reveled in Duncan's sweet kiss, holding him tightly and unwilling to let him go. His kiss held a note of desperation that matched hers, and she knew they were both thinking along the same lines. That this was it.

The last time they'd see each other.

"Chelsey." Her name was a mere whisper as he lifted his head, and she ached with longing. In the moment she'd watched Duncan hanging from the plane, she'd realized just how much she loved him.

With a depth that wasn't a fraction of what she'd felt for Brett. But this wasn't the time to relive her previous mistakes.

"Duncan, I'm so glad you're safe." She blinked tears from her eyes, gazing up at him and memorizing the moment. It was all she'd have to remember him by once she was gone.

"You shouldn't have come out of hiding, Chelsey." His tone was gentle, but she saw the worry in his dark gaze. "Now these guys know you're still alive."

"Yes, but we have them all in custody anyway, right? So does it really matter? They'll all go to jail for this, won't they?"

He hesitated in a way that sent a frisson of alarm skittering through her. "You have to know that Wolfe is going to hire heavy hitter lawyers. If there's a way to get him off, they'll find it."

"But we have a lot of witnesses on our side." Chelsey didn't want to believe any of these men would get away with what they'd done. Killing Roland Perry, an undercover cop, then going on to murder Brett. Coming after her and Duncan, and finally shooting her outside the hotel.

Surely, they'd pay for their crimes.

God wouldn't let any of them, even Wolfe, simply walk away, would He?

Police sirens grew louder, and she noticed Duncan looking over her shoulder. Reluctantly releasing him, she turned to watch two police cars driving up to the Wolfe Industries hangar.

Duncan shifted so that he was standing in front of her. She frowned, then remembered they weren't entirely sure who to trust within the Jackson Police Department. Still, she didn't think it was likely a dirty cop would try something here with all these people around.

Including two federal marshals.

"Let's head back to the private hangar where the cargo plane is located," Duncan murmured in a low voice.

"I'm sure we're not going to be leaving anytime soon," she pointed out.

"Maybe not, but humor me anyway. It doesn't hurt to have a possible escape route in case things go sideways." Duncan moved toward the hangar.

Go sideways? She didn't like the sound of that. Still, she decided there was no reason to argue.

Four police officers had emerged from the two squad cars, coming over to talk to Colt and Slade. The three bound men had been shoved into the back of the limo. She frowned, wondering if the driver had remained behind the wheel.

As if hearing her thoughts, Colt opened the driver's side door and motioned with his gun for the driver to get out. She breathed a sigh of relief.

"Duncan, do you think that once we testify against these guys we can go back to our normal lives?"

He glanced at her, remaining silent until they'd reached the cargo plane. "Honestly, I don't know, Chelsey. If these guys are the main players, then maybe. But you have to understand the wheels of justice don't move fast. And with Wolfe's high-priced legal team, I wouldn't be surprised if this dragged on for years."

"Years?" The tiny flame of hope withered and died.

"Hey, we're going to be okay." Duncan smiled. "I'll be with you the entire time."

"Wait, what? You can't give up your family for me, Duncan. That's too great a sacrifice."

"After what I've witnessed here, I don't think there's any other option," he countered, his expression turning serious. "I heard them talk about how glad they were you were dead, Chelsey. And they mentioned Brett's murder, too. I'm just as much a part of this case as you are."

She stared at him for a long moment, knowing he was right, yet wishing he was wrong. "Even so, that doesn't mean we'd be relocated together. In fact, it would be more likely that the federal marshal program would insist we be separated."

His brow furrowed. "That's not happening. We're sticking together, Chelsey. You have my word."

"But... I don't want you to feel obligated to stay with me." It wasn't easy to put her feelings into words. "You have a family to return to when the trial is over."

Duncan's dark brown gaze bored into hers but before he could respond, Slade crossed over.

"The police want us to go to the station to provide statements about what transpired here." Slade glanced over his shoulder, then added, "I don't love the idea since we still don't know who to trust within the department."

"I know. Wolfe in particular mentioned how he was paying for the guy on the inside who might help them." Duncan gestured with his hand. "Colt heard it, too."

Slade gave a grim nod. "My plan is to have me and Colt go with the cops and the prisoners to the station together to make sure they don't escape. But that leaves you and Chelsey to get there on your own."

There was a moment of silence as Duncan considered Slade's offer.

"I feel safe with Duncan," she offered, in case there was any doubt.

"Okay, but we'll have to get a rental car. You guys should take the SUV," Duncan said.

"No, I think you and Chelsey need it more than we do," Slade protested. "We've requested a police transport van. The limo will remain here until it can be processed."

She glanced at the limo curiously. "You mean they'll look for evidence?"

Slade nodded. "Exactly."

"They need to look at the plane, too," Duncan said. "And they need to wash the inside of Wolfe's hangar with luminol. I'm convinced the murder of Roland Perry took place there. Brett's photos don't show enough of the building, but the photographs along with finding blood evidence should be enough to put Nettles away for a long time."

"Maybe he'll roll over on Travis Wolfe," Slade mused. "I'd think he'd be anxious to try to make a deal for a lighter sentence."

"A lighter sentence for murder?" Chelsey couldn't believe what she was hearing.

"Don't worry, he'll spend plenty of time in jail," Slade assured her.

"Looks like the police transport van is on its way," Duncan said, jutting his chin toward the road. "It should be here shortly."

"Take the SUV." Slade lightly tossed the key fob in the air. Duncan easily caught it. "We'll see you down at the station."

Chelsey watched as Slade made his way back to the group of law enforcement officers. The SUV wasn't far, and once the transport van arrived, Duncan cupped her elbow in his hand and nudged her forward.

"Let's go."

She nodded, glancing back at the cargo plane before sliding into the SUV's passenger seat. For a moment, she wanted more than anything to ask the pilot to whisk her and Duncan far away from there, but then a flash of shame followed.

She wouldn't be a coward, slinking away from this. If she needed to testify, she would.

Even if that meant losing everything—especially, and most importantly, Duncan.

Duncan kept an eye on the rearview mirror, watching the group of five men, the original four plus the pilot, being ushered into the police van. They grew distant as he pushed the accelerator to the floor.

In theory, the worst was over. They had the three main men in custody and felt certain they'd stay there, even if they had a cop on their payroll.

He had to physically unclench his fingers from the steering wheel in an attempt to relax his grip. For some reason, he couldn't relax. Couldn't find a way to believe the horror of Brett's murder and that of Roland Perry was over.

There was no reason to be paranoid, but he kept a keen gaze on the traffic behind them as they left the Jackson airport. He wanted to be ready to react, just in case.

So far, so good. He turned off the highway and headed through town to the local police station.

From what seemed like nowhere, a squad car pulled up behind them, red and blue lights flashing. The driver of the squad car also hit the siren, indicating Duncan should stop.

"Why is he pulling us over?" Chelsey asked, worry in her tone. "We didn't break any traffic laws, did we?"

"No." Duncan's gut instincts were screaming at him. Instead of pulling over, he wrenched the steering wheel to the left, and hit the gas. The SUV responded well, barely screeching as he took a hard left.

"What are you doing?" Chelsey gripped the armrest between them. "We can't outrun a cop!"

"Keep an eye on him," Duncan ordered, as he took more turns in an attempt to shake the squad car off his tail. Not as easy to do in downtown Jackson, a place he wasn't familiar with.

A city the cop behind him could navigate blind-folded.

Chelsey twisted in her seat. "I don't understand. Shouldn't we at least talk to him?"

"Not if he's the one being paid to help get rid of us." Duncan raked his gaze over the area, hoping, praying for some way to escape the cop sticking behind him like a pesky gnat.

Then another squad car materialized from the right, cutting directly in front of him. Duncan had little choice but to yank the SUV over and hit the brake hard, to avoid the inevitable collision.

"Be ready to run," he said in a low, urgent voice.

"No, I'm not leaving you," she whispered.

He didn't like it and reached for his gun, but a second too late. The officer was already at his driver's side window, his weapon pointed at Duncan.

"Put your hands in the air! Don't touch the gun!"

"I won't!" The last thing Duncan needed was for this guy to be trigger happy.

"Get out of the car with your hands up!"

"Don't shoot! I'm surrendering!" Duncan did as ordered while trying desperately to think of a way out of this mess. He didn't trust either of these guys, but the cop behind him less so than the younger officer holding him at gunpoint.

Holding his hands up high, he kicked the door open. The young officer had taken several steps back, so the abrupt opening of the door didn't come close to touching him. "My name is Duncan O'Hare and I'm a cop with the Milwaukee Police Department."

"Turn around very slowly and put your hands on the

top of the vehicle." The officer acted as if he didn't care that Duncan was a fellow cop.

"Thanks JT, I'll take it from here," a voice drawled from behind him.

"Are you sure, Lieutenant?" The officer's tone was respectful but held a distinct note of doubt. "I think it would be better to stay and back you up, just in case they try to make a run for it, again."

"Go ahead and cuff him and the woman," the lieutenant responded. "Then I'll take over."

Duncan shot a quick glance over his shoulder, eyeing the lieutenant. His name tag identified him as Goldberg. He was a big burly guy, with a gut that hung over his belt, and the coldness in his gaze made Duncan suspect this was the guy on Wolfe's payroll.

Not any low-ranking officer, but a lieutenant. He supposed it could be worse—at least the mole wasn't the chief of police.

Unless there were more than one of them on the inside. Not a happy thought.

"Don't leave us with Goldberg," Duncan said in a low, urgent voice, as the young officer slapped a silver bracelet around his right wrist and yanked it down behind his back. "He can't be trusted. If you leave us alone, he'll kill us."

His words fell on deaf ears. The officer brought his left wrist back and finished the job of securing his wrists together. "Hey, Lou, what's the story with these two? They rob a bank or what?"

"Something like that," the lieutenant drawled. "Thanks again for your quick response, JT. You go on, now, and I'll make sure to put a good word in for you."

"Thanks, Lou," the young man responded. Duncan

turned so that his cuffed wrists were up against the SUV. He wished Chelsey would have run away. The lieutenant probably wouldn't have been able to catch her, but instead she'd stayed and allowed young JT to place her in cuffs, too. She huddled next to him. He wanted nothing more than to pull her into his arms.

"You sure you don't need anything else?" JT asked. Duncan tried to catch the young officer's gaze—the guy had to realize this was not normal protocol.

Lieutenants rarely came out of their offices to make arrests on the street. Not even in a small town like Jackson, Wyoming, would something like that be a common occurrence.

"JT, you might want to mention this to the federal marshals at the police station," Duncan said quickly. "Slade Brooks and Colt Nelson."

"Marshals?" The young officer hesitated, glancing back at his lieutenant. "You know about that, Lou?"

"I do, and don't let these two innocent faces fool you," he drawled. "They're both wanted for murdering a cop."

"Cops killing cops," JT said in disgust. "Nothin' worse than that."

"You're right," Duncan agreed. "Just ask your lieutenant, after all his loyalty has been bought and paid for."

The lieutenant moved quickly, pulling his baton and whacking it hard against Duncan's midsection.

The force of the blow had him doubling over, pain shooting through him and the contents of his stomach threatening to erupt. Blackness hovered along the edge of his vision as he tried desperately not to lose consciousness.

"No! Stop it! Please, don't hurt him!" Chelsey's horrified tone helped keep him on his feet.

He would not fall to his knees in front of Lieutenant Goldberg.

"Hey, Lou?" There was an uncertainty to JT's voice that gave Duncan hope.

"I'll take it from here," Goldberg repeated. "Call a tow truck for their SUV, then get back to work." When JT hesitated, he added, "JT? That's a direct order, son."

For second Duncan thought the young cop might continue arguing, but he didn't. Instead, he turned and made his way back to his squad car. JT opened the driver's side door and slid in behind the wheel.

He backed up, then drove off without giving them a second glance.

Duncan tried to keep his breathing even, despite the throbbing pain. "So now what, Lou?" he asked, mimicking JT's nickname. "Where are you going to take us?"

"Start walking." The lieutenant looked irritated as he lightly tapped the baton against the palm of his hand. Duncan had a sneaking suspicion the man liked hurting others and feared that his next target might be Chelsey.

He couldn't let that happen.

"Okay, you've got us under your control," Duncan agreed. He glanced at Chelsey, using his gaze to indicate she should go ahead of him. "We're not going to cause you any trouble."

"You've already caused me a great deal of trouble," the lieutenant hissed. He moved forward, opened the back seat of his squad car and used the baton to point at the back seat. "Get in."

Duncan swept a glance over the area, hoping to catch the eye of someone, anyone nearby. But the bystanders stayed far back, as if in fear for their lives. Then another squad car sitting at a gas station caught his eye.

He stared hard, hoping the driver of the vehicle would take notice. But the car was too far away for him to make a connection.

Chelsey slid in first, moving awkwardly with her hands cuffed behind her back. He tried to give her a reassuring smile, but her pale features were a clear indication of her bone-deep fear.

He wasn't thrilled with the situation, either. But he felt certain the lieutenant would have to think this through. After all, JT knew about the two of them being in his custody. The lieutenant couldn't just shoot them and dump their bodies off in the forest somewhere.

Could he?

He slid in beside Chelsey, the interior of the vehicle stifling hot as the sun beat down through the windows. The lieutenant slammed the door and got in behind the wheel.

Goldberg didn't say anything as he eased into traffic, leaving their SUV behind.

Chelsey was squirming in her seat next to him. "You okay?" he whispered.

She nodded but didn't stop moving around. After a long moment she pulled one arm from around her back, gently brushing against his arm with her hand.

He didn't change his facial expression, even though he was secretly thrilled she'd managed to get one of her hands free of the cuffs. JT hadn't cuffed her hands as tightly as his, a rookie mistake.

Chelsey's being free didn't help much. Without a weapon, or his hands being free, their ability to escape the burly lieutenant unscathed was not looking good.

# EIGHTEEN

Chelsey kept her hands low, so that the big cop wouldn't notice she'd managed to get one wrist free.

Not that being uncuffed was much help. What could they do from the back of a squad car? Especially when the doors couldn't be opened from the inside.

"I told you to run," Duncan whispered.

She ignored him. Running and leaving him behind wasn't an option. If this was going to end—she swallowed hard—then so be it. She chose to believe in God's plan, and maybe being here with Duncan would make it easier for both of them.

Remembering the bobby pins in her hair, she lowered her head, and eased her left wrist up high enough to pull two from her curls. Was it possible they could use them to unlock Duncan's cuffs?

Without saying anything, she pressed the bobby pins against his hand so he'd know she had them. He didn't so much as glance at her, keeping his gaze on the cop behind the wheel, but he shifted just enough that she could access the cuffs.

Still, it was an impossible task considering she couldn't see what she was doing and needed to make it seem as if her wrists were still together. Thankfully, for whatever reason, the lieutenant didn't look at them, his attention focused on the road.

Was he right now trying to find a place to silence the two of them forever?

Chelsey swallowed hard and prayed that God would give her and Duncan the strength and courage they needed to get through this.

The squad car slowed and the lieutenant pulled off the main thoroughfare onto a winding dirt road. Chelsey tensed, sensing this was not good.

"Where are you taking us?" Duncan asked. "Shouldn't you be taking two people suspected for killing a cop to the precinct to be booked?"

"Shut up," Goldberg growled.

Duncan shifted again, giving her better access to his cuffed wrists. She realized his conversation was a diversion from her attempt to free him.

"I wasn't kidding about the federal marshals," Duncan said. "When we end up missing and/or dead, they're going to know someone within the police department was involved. Even the not-so-bright JT will put two and two together to come up with four."

The lieutenant didn't respond. The squad car jostled side to side as the road grew more uneven. Chelsey bumped against Duncan, still working the bobby pin in the keyhole of the handcuffs.

Somehow, the rocking motion of the squad car along with her efforts caused the lock to spring open. She wanted to smile and shout with joy when Duncan's wrists came apart but managed to keep her expression impassive.

A minor victory, because they weren't out of this mess, not by a mile. The cop was armed and they weren't.

"Travis Wolfe is going to throw you under the bus," Duncan said as he gently took the bobby pin from her fingers. "You know very well he'll do whatever is necessary to save his own skin. Millionaires are not cut out for prison. Killing us isn't going to stop the avalanche of evidence the feds have against him. In fact, if you were smart, you'd take the money you've squirreled away and get out of town before anyone else realizes you've been working for him."

"I said shut up!" The sudden shout from the lieutenant startled her so badly, she was glad she didn't have the bobby pins, or she'd have dropped them. Risking a glance down to his hands, she could see that Duncan still had the two bobby pins, straightened into thin spears.

Hardly a lethal weapon, but better than nothing.

"Okay, fine, have it your way." Duncan glanced over with a grim expression. She could tell there was a lot he wanted to say but couldn't.

She felt the same way.

The squad car jerked to an abrupt halt. She tensed, then quickly followed Duncan's lead by placing her hands behind her back in an effort to hide the fact she was free.

The large man climbed out of the squad car and opened Duncan's door. "Get out."

Duncan turned in his seat, swinging his legs out of the car. As he braced himself to stand, she heard the sound of a car engine.

From there, things happened fast. The lieutenant glanced over to see who was driving on the road as Duncan launched himself from the squad car, shoving at the cop with his unbound wrists, the bobby pin stabbing near the lieutenant's eye.

The big cop screamed in pain and the sound of a gunshot made her ears ring. She scrambled out of the vehicle after Duncan, frantically looking for something she could use as a weapon against the cop. There was a rock near the edge of the vehicle and she quickly bent down and scooped it up.

Duncan and the cop were struggling for the gun, the blunt end pointed upward. It was reminiscent of the struggle Duncan had with the assailant on the mountain that first night.

The engine noise grew louder. Chelsey wasn't going to wait. Darting around the two men, she brought the rock down on the back of the lieutenant's head.

Again, the big man howled in pain and it proved to be enough of a distraction for Duncan to wrench the gun free. But somehow, the gun went off during the struggle. It took her a minute to verify Duncan hadn't been hit.

With a blood-curdling scream, the man went down, clutching his wounded arm. "I'll kill you for this!"

"Chelsey? We have to go." The words barely left his mouth when another Jackson PD squad car pulled up, a female officer swiftly jumping from the vehicle, her gun pointed at them.

"Put your hands in the air where I can see them!" she shouted.

The lieutenant managed to stop his screaming long enough to register what was happening. "Kimball, shoot them! They're trying to escape!"

"You know that's not true," Duncan responded in a low, even tone. "You saw him take custody of us back in downtown Jackson, didn't you? You were in the squad car parked in the gas station."

Officer Kimball didn't answer and stayed where she was, her weapon trained on them.

"You have to ask yourself why your boss would bring us here rather than down to the police station," Duncan continued. "It's because he intended to kill us to prevent us from telling everyone the truth about the bribe money he's taken over the years from Travis Wolfe."

Officer Kimball's gaze flickered to the lieutenant then returned to Duncan. "Put the gun down."

"I can't do that, not until your boss is neutralized." Duncan held his hands up so the weapon in his hand wasn't a threat. "He won't hesitate to kill you, too."

Chelsey stepped forward, her gaze pleading with the female cop, who was roughly her own age, to believe them. "I'm Chelsey Robards, the owner of the Teton Valley Hotel, and I've been on the run since my fiancé was shot at our wedding. I know you'll find this difficult to believe, but your boss really did intend to kill us. Because we know the truth."

Kimball hesitated, then gave a short jerk of her head. "Okay, back away from the lieutenant and keep the gun where I can see it. If you make a move toward me, I will shoot first and ask questions later."

"You…believe us?" Chelsey asked as she and Duncan took several steps far away from the lieutenant.

"I was under the impression you were dead, Chelsey. At least, that's what the federal marshals told me at the hotel." Officer Kimball's tone was wry. "I'd rather get everyone down to the police station to sort this out."

"Can't you see these two shot me?" the lieutenant raged. "I'll have your badge for taking their word over mine."

"I don't think so, Lou." Kimball's tone held a bit of

snark that Chelsey appreciated. "I followed you here, remember? And I can't think of a good reason for you to have brought two suspects to this remote location unless it was to get rid of them. Now shut up while I call for backup. Preferably anyone other than JT."

A wave of relief washed over her. Chelsey leaned against Duncan, her knees weak.

Officer Kimball believed them.

It was over.


Duncan didn't like being separated from Chelsey. As a cop he knew the importance of interviewing key witnesses separately, but he didn't like not having her close.

He loved her. As much as he'd tried not to, he'd fallen deeply in love with Chelsey. And when this was over, he wanted to be with her. No matter where, or what names they'd have or what they'd be doing for work.

His life wasn't worth living without Chelsey.

Yet he wasn't entirely sure she felt the same way about him, considering she'd refused his offer to go into WITSEC with her more than once.

He decided to try to put his worry into God's hands, knowing He had a plan for them. Hopefully, a plan that included the two of them being together.

He'd told the story of Lieutenant Goldberg taking him and Chelsey away at gunpoint and driving them to the dirt road and abandoned building several times now. He admitted the gun had gone off in the struggle, injuring the lieutenant. Yet he knew the drill. Any cop being shot in the line of duty was a big deal and this was no exception.

He imagined Chelsey had told the same story several times as well. Hopefully they'd let her go by now, since he was the one who'd accidentally used the lieutenant's gun against him.

And where were the feds? Did Slade and Colt have Wolfe, Nettles and Strand locked up in the same cell or had they been separated, too?

How many jail cells did Jackson have anyway?

The door to his interview room opened and Slade Brooks walked in. Duncan managed a weary grin. "About time you showed up."

"It took longer than it should to get the police chief to believe Goldberg was really a dirty cop," Slade admitted, dropping into the chair across from him. "Colt managed to dig deep enough to find recent phone calls between Strand and Goldberg, so that helped. Once we find the money Goldberg has stashed away, we'll have everything we need."

"Officer Kimball tell you what happened?" Duncan asked.

Slade nodded. "Yes, Officer Kimball told me exactly what she'd witnessed both in Jackson and again out on the dirt road." Slade shrugged. "It helped that I'd spoken to her after we decided to fake Chelsey's death. She remembered me and Colt and was smart enough to figure out the rest."

"If she hadn't arrived when she did, we'd be dead," Duncan said. "All I had to defend myself was a couple of bobby pins Chelsey used to unlock the cuffs."

"I don't know. I think you'd have found a way," Slade drawled.

The backhanded compliment drew a reluctant grin. "Thanks for the vote of confidence."

Slade glanced at the door. "The cops picked up Kenny Martin as he arrived at the airport hangar, and he's already talking about cutting a deal. And I think once Stewart regains consciousness, he'll add his two cents."

"Good. Sounds like you'll have everything tied up in a nice bow."

"That's the plan." Slade hesitated, then added, "They're letting you go for now, but both the federal marshals and the local police will need you to testify against Nettles, Wolfe and Strand."

"I know." Duncan cleared his throat. "What about Chelsey?"

Slade considered him for a moment. "Fact is, Chelsey doesn't really have as much evidence to provide compared to you, Duncan. We have Brett's photographs, and both you and Colt heard Wolfe, Nettles and Strand talk about killing Brett and attempting to kill Chelsey. She doesn't have anything additional to offer, other than to corroborate what we already know."

Duncan straightened in his seat. "What are you saying, Slade? I'm the one that needs to go into WITSEC instead of Chelsey?"

Slade spread his hands wide. "The main reason we offered WITSEC to Brett Thompson was because he was a witness to a murder and we believed the death was related to organized crime. Now it's looking more like Wolfe is the brains behind everything. He got greedy, the boxes in the airport hanger contain drugs, which is what Kenny Martin had come to pick up, and of course we know Wolfe wanted the land. But other than that, we haven't found any true organized crime ring. With Wolfe and the others in custody, I'm not sure WITSEC is really necessary for either of you."

"Not necessary?" Duncan frowned. "I'd rather Chelsey be safe."

Slade shrugged. "We can certainly provide new identities for you both, if that's what you'd prefer."

Once again, Duncan thought about his dad, Ian O'Hare, his sister, Shayla Callahan, his brother-in-law, Mike Callahan, and the other Callahans.

Plus his nephew, Brodie, and niece, Breena.

He would miss his family very much. But there was no way on earth he could live without Chelsey. "I want Chelsey to be safe," he repeated. "Whatever it takes. And her staying here in Wyoming doesn't seem reasonable."

"Okay, we'll put some things in motion." Slade stood and crossed over to the door. Then he paused and glanced back over his shoulder. "I did a little research on you, Duncan. Not only are you a cop, your dad is a retired cop, and your sister married into a family full of law enforcement types. If you ask me, there isn't a safer place for you and Chelsey than with them. After all, Milwaukee is pretty far from Jackson, Wyoming." Slade opened the door and left.

Leaving Duncan to absorb the impact of his words.

Was Slade right? If there weren't any true organized crime members to come after them, was it really necessary for him and Chelsey to disappear forever?

Or was this nothing more than wishful thinking on his part?

The door opened again and this time, Chelsey stepped in. He rose to meet her halfway, stunned when she launched herself into his arms.

"Oh, Duncan, that took forever. I couldn't wait to see you."

He nestled her close, lowering his cheek to her hair. "I'm okay, Chels. How are you?"

"Fine now," was her muffled reply. She wound her arms around his waist and hung on as if she'd never let go.

He didn't mind. If he had his way, he'd never let her go, either.

"I love you, Chelsey." He'd promised himself if they got away from Goldberg alive, he'd tell her how he felt. "I know you probably don't feel the same way, and I know you don't want to mistake friendship for love, but it's important to me that you know the truth."

"Duncan." Her voice was so low he could barely hear it. She hesitated, then lifted her face to his. Tears shimmered in her eyes. "I love you, too, and I realized my feelings for Brett weren't the real thing because I was attracted to you from the start. I've fallen in love with you, but I can't ask you to give up your family for me."

"Really?" He searched her gaze, afraid to hope. "Slade told me that I'm the one who is more at risk as far as needing to testify against these guys, Chelsey. So if anything it would be me needing the protection of being in WITSEC, not you."

Her brow furrowed. "Slade said that?"

The tiny flicker of hope in his heart went out. "Yes, but even so, Chelsey, I don't think staying in Wyoming is in your best interest. I thought it might be better for you to relocate to Milwaukee, the place where you once lived with your parents. My family will look after you for me."

"And where will you be, Duncan?"

He longed to kiss her, but forced himself to do what was best for her. "I plan to trust God's plan for us. And if that means me disappearing, while you stay safe with my family, then I'll gladly take that. Anything is possible as long as I know you're safe."

Her blue eyes softened. "And what if I want to be with you?"

His heart stuttered in his chest. "I'd like nothing more, but I need you to be sure, Chelsey. This is a big step with some level of risk involved."

There was a series of shouts and cries from outside the interview room. Duncan reacted by spinning Chelsey away from the door and placing himself in front of her, ready to fight if necessary.

The minutes ticked by slowly, then Slade poked his head inside. "You both okay?"

Duncan gave a curt nod. "What happened?"

"Fight broke out in the jail cell. Wolfe lost his temper and attacked Strand." Slade sighed. "Strand won that fight, but Wolfe has died of his injuries. Looks like the only one you have to testify against is Strand, who doesn't have nearly the same high-powered attorneys Wolfe had access to." The marshal grinned wryly. "Our job just got a whole lot easier."

The news swirled in his head. "You really think it's safe enough for me to return to Milwaukee with Chelsey?"

"I do." Slade didn't hesitate. "I wouldn't lie to you, Duncan. Not after all this." Slade reached up to rub the back of his neck. "I have to go. Thanks to that fight, there's more paperwork to complete. The locals have to report to their boss, while I have to report up to mine."

Duncan turned to face Chelsey. She stepped into his arms, wound her arms around his neck and drew him down for a kiss.

He loved kissing her and didn't want to stop, but they still needed to talk. "Chels?" he managed when he could breathe.

"Hmm?" She rested her head in the hollow of his shoulder.

"I love you and I want you to be safe."

She lifted her head, smiling at him. "I love you and want you to be safe, too. Sounds like the best option is for us to live in Milwaukee."

"Are you sure about that? About leaving the hotel behind?" He forced himself to ask the question, mentally bracing himself for her response.

"Yes, I'm sure that I want to be with you, Duncan. Even though Travis Wolfe wanted to buy the hotel, I happen to know the federal government will also be interested in taking it over, as the land is part of the Grand Teton National Park. They offered before, when my grandparents had the place."

He was humbled by how she was willing to give up her parents' home for him. "I'd like to plant a couple of trees in your parents' memory."

Her smile widened. "I'd love that."

"Chelsey, will you please marry me? I don't have a ring, but I want you to know that I love you with all my heart. I'd be honored if you'd agree to be my wife."

"Yes, Duncan, I'll marry you. I only have one request."

*Anything*, he thought. "Like?"

"No big fancy ceremony, just your immediate family and a few close friends. And I'd really like to be married in a church."

It was very different from what she'd planned with Brett, but he wasn't complaining. "Done. You'll like the church Shayla and Mike have taken me to. It's perfect for a small, intimate wedding ceremony."

"Good." She tugged his head down toward hers. "Please kiss me again, Duncan. Because this is the happiest day of my life."

He was more than willing to oblige her request. Because it was the happiest day of his life, too.

# EPILOGUE

*Four months later...*

October in Wisconsin was beautiful. The blue skies were clear and the leaves on the trees were a burst of yellow, orange and red. Chelsey knew she and Duncan were blessed to have such a wonderful wedding day.

She stood in the back of the small church she'd grown to love, in a simple dress that didn't have a long train or a veil. As the organ music swelled she looked up the aisle and saw Duncan standing in a dark suit, no tux, waiting for her.

She smiled. There wasn't a single doubt in her mind or her heart about marrying Duncan O'Hare. Thankfully, their testimony against Wesley Strand had resulted in a guilty verdict. Nettles, Martin and Goldberg all agreed to plea deals. The nightmare in Wyoming was over, but the move to Milwaukee had been the right decision. She'd lived there for the first fifteen years of her life, so it was a bit like coming back home.

And there was Duncan. The most wonderful, kind, caring and compassionate man she'd ever met. He'd do anything to protect her and always followed through on his promises.

There wasn't anyone in the world like him, and she was blessed and humbled that he'd chosen her to be his wife.

The church was filled with people, more than she'd expected. But not only was the Callahan family huge and growing by the minute, there were Duncan's close friends: Hawk Jacobson, his wife Jillian, and their two kids; along with Ryker Tillman, his wife Olivia, and their two kids.

She liked how Duncan had surrounded himself with family men. Well, except for Slade and Colt, who hung back as if afraid to be bitten by the love bug.

"Ready, Chelsey?" Per her request, Duncan's father, Ian O'Hare, was the one giving her away. Maggie Callahan O'Hare, Ian's new wife, also treated Chelsey like a daughter. She felt it was fitting for both of them to be an intricate part of their wedding and she already loved them both, very much.

Her parents would have adored them, too.

"Yes." She slid her arm through the crook of Ian's elbow and together they began their walk down the aisle toward the front of the church. At one point she must have picked up the pace because Ian whispered, "Slow down, lass, I promise he'll wait."

That made her smile. And when she caught Duncan's gaze, the love shining there was enough to bring tears to her eyes.

As Ian handed her over to Duncan, she gave her soon-to-be father-in-law a quick hug, then clasped both Duncan's hands in hers. "I love you," she whispered.

"I love you, too," he whispered back.

Feeling secure with Duncan's and God's love surrounding them, they turned to face the pastor.

It was time to begin their new life, together.

\* \* \* \* \*

# Get 4 FREE REWARDS!

## We'll send you 2 FREE Books plus 2 FREE Mystery Gifts.

**FREE**
Value Over
**$20**

Both the **Love Inspired®** and **Love Inspired® Suspense** series feature compelling novels filled with inspirational romance, faith, forgiveness, and hope.

# HARLEQUIN
## PLUS

Announcing a **BRAND-NEW**
multimedia subscription service
for romance fans like you!

---

## Read, Watch and Play.

Experience the easiest way to get
the romance content you crave.

Start your **FREE 7 DAY TRIAL** at
<u>www.harlequinplus.com/freetrial</u>.

# LOVE INSPIRED

*Stories to uplift and inspire*

Fall in love with Love Inspired—
inspirational and uplifting stories of faith
and hope. Find strength and comfort in
the bonds of friendship and community.
Revel in the warmth of possibility and the
promise of new beginnings.

Sign up for the Love Inspired newsletter
at **LoveInspired.com** to be the first
to find out about upcoming titles,
special promotions and exclusive content.

## CONNECT WITH US AT:

**f** Facebook.com/LoveInspiredBooks

**𝕏** Twitter.com/LoveInspiredBks

LISOCIAL2021

SPECIAL EXCERPT FROM

# LOVE INSPIRED SUSPENSE
### INSPIRATIONAL ROMANCE

*An FBI agent who is undercover as a bank robber
must risk his cover to keep a teller alive.*

*Read on for a sneak preview of*
Christmas Hostage *by Sharon Dunn,
available October 2022 from Love Inspired Suspense!*

Even before the shouting and the woman's scream, Laura Devin sensed that something was wrong in the lobby of First Federal Bank. The bright morning conversation between bank employees stopped abruptly, but it was what she saw on her computer screen that told her they were in the middle of a bank robbery. All the alarms and cameras had been disabled, just like with the other small-town banks that had been robbed in the last two years.

Her back was to the open door in the room next to the lobby, where she was working at a computer. When she whirled her chair around, she could only see the back of one of the tellers. Then she saw a flash of movement on the other side of the counter.

"This is a bank robbery! Do as I say, and no one will die here today!"

Even if one of the tellers had time to push the silent alarm, it had been disabled. The police would not show up.

Laura's gaze jolted to her purse across the room, where her phone was. The door was open. If she went for it, they might see her. Closing the door would alert the robbers to her presence that much faster. But she had no choice.

She sprinted across the carpet and grabbed her phone, pressing 911.

"Hey, there's somebody in that room! Get her!"

The operator came on the line. "What is your emergency?"

"Bank robbery—"

A hand went over her mouth. She dropped the phone before the thief could grab it from her. He must have seen that she was making a call, or at least heard the phone when it landed on the carpet. And yet, he didn't tell her to pick it up. Maybe it was still on and the operator could hear what was happening.

He whispered in her ear, the fabric of the ski mask he wore brushing over her cheek. "It's going to be okay. Just do what they say."

*Don't miss*
Christmas Hostage *by Sharon Dunn.*
*Available wherever Love Inspired Suspense books
and ebooks are sold.*

LoveInspired.com